BITTER SWEET RETALIATION

MADDISON KINGS UNIVERSITY

LEON & MACIE DUET

USA TODAY & WALL STREET JOURNAL BESTSELLING AUTHOR

TRACY LORRAINE

THE DEVASTATION YOU REAP

MADDISON KINGS UNIVERSITY #6

1

MACIE

"What the——" I start as the guy my roommate was with storms from the room, slamming the door in his wake.

If I had any idea she was in here with a guy I never would have barged in. But I was convinced her screams were in fear not out of pleasure.

"Oh, pfft," Charlie scoffs as she scrambles naked from her bed and grabs her robe to cover up. "Get that judgmental look off your face, Mace."

"This?" I ask, pointing at what I can only assume is my pale face. "This isn't judgment. This is shock," I state, recalling the image I walked in on.

No one ever needs to see their roommate on all fours getting spanked by... by...

"Who even was that?"

"Leon Dunn," she says, like all of this is no big deal.

I know his name, of course I do, but in my quest to stay as far away as possible from the football team, I hadn't really studied the faces of our beloved kings.

"I didn't think you were interested in a football player," I say. Up until now, it's one of the things we've bonded over since starting at MKU last year and finding ourselves as roommates.

"I know but he was there and clearly up for it so I thought, why not find out what all the fuss is about. You know?"

No, I don't know. But I don't tell her that.

My need to stay as far away as possible from them means that I've never even considered breaking my one fundamental rule about who I spend time with.

"It wasn't worth it," she says, walking into her adjoining bathroom. "Pretty sure he couldn't even get it up."

My stomach turns over at her words as I vividly remember him not having that issue when he pressed his body against mine and not so subtly suggested I join the party.

My knees give out and I fall down onto Charlie's bed. That is until I glance at the crumpled sheets and I jump up as if it's on fire as I think about what—or what didn't—go down right there only moments ago.

I'm still staring at her bed when Charlie emerges, laughing at me.

"You're such a prude, Mace. You should have taken him up on the offer. It might have helped dirty you up a little."

"I'm not a prude." I cross my arms as I turn to her, immediately irritated by the raised brow she gives me. "What? I'm not."

"Sure, sure. I forgot you kissed someone the summer before senior year."

My cheeks burn with embarrassment as I regret ever admitting my lack of experience with boys. It's not entirely my fault. Up until my time at college, I've only attended all-girls schools. That means the majority of my time was spent with said girls, and the only boys I've ever really been around were football players who I wouldn't touch with a barge pole.

"I'm waiting for the right guy. There's nothing wrong with that."

"I agree. There's not. But you need to loosen up a little. Kiss a few frogs before you find your prince."

I stare at her as she brushes her hair. She probably still smells like that douchebag and isn't even bothering to wash him off.

"If the frogs are like him, I'll pass, thanks."

"Your loss. He was kinky as hell."

"Yeah, I heard," I mutter, backing up to the door.

"You know," she mutters, holding my eyes in her mirror. "The quiet ones are always the dirtiest. I bet there's a kinky little freak under those cardigans you wear all the time, Mace."

"Whatever, I'm going back to bed."

Closing her door behind me, I make my way back to my room next door, wishing—and not for the first time—that I was on the other side of the dorm with two bathrooms between our rooms like Nathan and Jace have.

"She still alive?" Nathan calls from his room as I pass his door.

Looking up, I find him lounging on his bed in only a pair of shorts reading a book.

When I first started here in our co-ed dorm, the sight of a male chest used to make me blush like a nun in a sex shop. But after a few months, I've almost become desensitized by both Nathan and Jace. Almost.

Seeing them shirtless and having *him* pressed against me only minutes ago are two completely different things.

A wave of heat rushes through me as I remember just how harsh his grip on my throat was, and how every inch of his solid body felt pressed up against me.

"You okay?" he asks, lowering his book to his chest.

"Huh, what?"

It's not until his eyes drop to my neck that I realize that my fingers are lightly brushing the skin where he touched me.

"Y-yeah, sorry. I just..." I look behind me at Charlie's door, my head spinning, the blood that's pumping through my veins suddenly feels too hot.

"Jesus, what did you see?"

"Oh... um... n-nothing."

"Sure, well... if you wanna talk about it—"

"You mean gossip?" I correct him.

Leon would've had to storm past Nathan's room to get out so I can only assume that he already knows who was behind the blood-curdling screams of our roommate that dragged me out of my own bed.

"Me?" he asks, pulling the best innocent face that he can muster. "Never."

"Riiight. I'm going to bed."

"Sure, see you in the morning."

I nod, but my body doesn't actually move straight away, my head is still firmly back in Charlie's room and hella confused by everything.

"You sure you're okay?" Nathan asks again.

When I look up again, I find he's now sitting on his bed, concern etched onto his face.

"Yeah, really. I'm just tired. Night," I say, forcing my legs to move so I don't stand there looking any weirder than I've already been.

I know I'm the odd one out amongst my roommates. That was abundantly clear the first day I moved in. I knew I'd lived a sheltered life, it's one of the reasons I decided to live on campus instead of getting myself a place to hide in. I wanted to experience this. I wanted to have friends, to party, to just be... normal.

It's the first time in my life where I'm not being controlled by someone else and I want to embrace it. Even if it does make me feel like a fish out of water most days.

The drinking, the partying, the easy sex.

Maybe Charlie is right, maybe I am just a prude.

But I don't think I am because... I want it all.

I want to experience all the things she does. I want to know how it feels. I just... don't want to do it with some random guy I'm probably never going to see again. Or worse, a member of the football team who'll leave here and brag to the rest of his guys about how he broke the innocent prep school virgin.

I close my door behind me and lean back, my head tipping to the ceiling, my eyes squeezing closed as I remember how he felt. How his tall, hard body felt pressed up against mine. How his wicked words rocked me to my core and made me feel things I never have before.

I tell myself that it was the shock, the fear of the evil glint in his eyes as he stared at me. But... I don't think it was that.

Pushing from the door, I force myself to put the whole situation out of my head. I shouldn't have gotten involved in the first place. I know that all of this is my fault because I panicked that Charlie was actually in trouble. In hindsight, the fact that Nathan and Jace hadn't bothered to do anything about it should have told me that nothing was really wrong. But I've never been one to sit back and think when I decide something isn't right.

I learned that from my past. From my regrets.

I lie in bed, staring at the shadows on my ceiling and force my mind away from memories of other times in my life where I've done something similar and regretted it almost instantly.

As mortifying as tonight has been, what I've been through in the past was a million times worse. I'd take walking in on Charlie any day of the week over that.

———

I wake with a start and immediately kick the sheets off my burning body. My skin is covered in a layer of sweat and my heart is racing from the dream I was in the middle of. A dream that had no right being inside my head. *He* has no right being in my head.

I lie there with my eyes squeezed tight, willing the lingering image of him standing before me, one hand around my throat as the other one slipped down my body.

My skin erupts in goose bumps as a shiver of fear races down my spine.

I gasp, sitting up, my eyes scanning my room as if someone's here. As if I'm being watched.

But it's empty.

I fall back on an exhale and laugh at myself.

Stop being paranoid, Macie.

With a groan, I put everything behind me and head for a shower, needing to forget everything about the night before and get focused on a new week of classes.

"Good morning," I sing, finding both Nathan and Jace in our kitchen when I emerge.

"Morning," Nathan says with a smile while Jace nods in my direction looking a little worse for wear. "Didn't think you were meant to party during the season."

"Shut up," he grumbles, rubbing at his temples.

"Suck it up, man," Nathan says. "Coach will be waiting for us."

"Can't you just tell him I'm sick?"

Nathan stares at Jace, his eyes twinkling with amusement. "No. I can't. I told you not to do those shots."

"Ugh," he complains, looking between the two of us. "You prep school kids are a pain in my ass," he grumbles, dumping his coffee mug in the sink and disappearing toward his room.

"I didn't even hear him come in last night," I say to Nathan as I head for the coffee maker.

"That's because he's only just appeared."

"Jesus."

"We're not in Kansas anymore, Mace," he jokes.

We might have gone to very different prep schools, but the things we've experienced, the loneliness, the abandonment, they're one in the same. After only a few days of living here together we discovered that we had more in common than we first thought. Much like Charlie and Jace with their need to spend every day battling with a hangover.

"Right, let's go, asshole," Jace states, marching through the kitchen still looking like death.

"Later, Mace." Nathan winks before swiping his bag from the door and disappearing.

I'm almost done with my breakfast and ready to head to the library before my first class of the day when Charlie finally emerges from her room.

"Ugh," she moans the second she looks at me dressed and ready for the day.

I've always been a morning person, whereas Charlie is the ultimate night owl.

She shuffles toward me, her dyed red hair resembling a bird's nest on her head despite the fact she was brushing it when I left her last night, her makeup is smeared all over her face and I can smell the stench of alcohol permeating from her skin from all the way over here.

"What the hell happened to you?"

"I went back out."

My head rears back in shock.

"What?" she asks, plodding toward the coffee maker and slamming her hand down on it until it starts working. "You ruined all my fun last night. I had to go and find some more."

"Oh, yeah. Of course. Sorry about that."

"Nah," she says, waving me off. "Best thing that could have happened. Leon Dunn can go fuck himself. I found a much better playmate who could get the job properly done."

"Great. I'm glad," I deadpan as I rinse my plate off. "I'm heading out."

"Already, it's like..."

"Eight."

"Exactly."

"You've got class in an hour."

"I know, I know." She holds her hands up in defense. "I'll be there, *Mom*."

"Good. But shower first. No one's gonna wanna sit next to you smelling like that."

"Bitch," she squeals as I make my way down to my room to grab my books.

She's still in the kitchen hugging a mug of coffee when I return.

"You coming out for drinks tonight?"

I stare at her, wondering why she's even bothering to ask me.

"Oh come on, Mace. It's freshman year, you seriously can't be boring the whole time. You need to let your hair down at some point."

"I do. Just not on a Monday night. You know I volunteer tonight."

"Yeah, until like nine. Come after."

"Not happening."

"Fine. Be like that. But you'll never lose those V plates hanging out with kids at the community center."

"Who says I want to?" I shoot over my shoulder as I leave our dorm.

"Prude."

"Slut."

I'm still laughing as I jog down the stairs.

Charlie and I might be the most unlikely of friends, but somehow she's wiggled her way into my life. She might spend most of her time giving me shit about my life choices, much like I do hers. But all of it is lighthearted, and I'm pretty sure I'd miss it—miss her—now if anything was to happen.

She's the type of girl I stayed the hell away from in high school. She was the popular one. The cheerleader. The ones who hated me equally as much as I hated them. But opposites attract and now I can't imagine my life without her, even if she causes more drama than I probably need in my life.

I spend a little over thirty minutes in the library finding all the books I need for my next assignment before heading to class.

I breathe in the scent of the clean auditorium as I step inside. I find my seat at the front along with a few other keen students before pulling everything out that I need and rereading my notes from our last class so I'm ready for today's lecture. And finally, thoughts of last night, my dream this morning, completely disappear in favor of focusing on my future.

2

———

LEON

I don't get even a second of sleep. I stare at the shadows moving across my ceiling all night as I replay the events of the evening over and over in my head.

I found her.

After all these fucking years, she's been right here. Right under my nose.

I wished for it time and time again. Prayed that one day I'd just walk headfirst into her.

I wanted to believe in fate. In karma. I wanted to believe that the universe would give me a chance to make things right somehow. I was willing to be patient, I was willing to wait until the right time, but after everything that happened with our da—with Brett, my patience has been vanishing faster than ever.

And something tells me I was right to believe, because look what the universe just handed me on a silver platter.

Not only do I have that monster exactly where I want him, but I've just crashed into Macie's life and she has no idea what's about to hit her.

A smile curls at my lips as I reach for my cock, wrapping my fingers around the steel length.

I've been hard since the second my eyes landed on her shocked ones last night.

Throwing the covers back, I move my hand slowly, letting my mind drift off to that dark place within me that I've spent most of my life trying not to drown in.

My mouth waters as I remember how she smelled like coconuts. How her shocked gasps filled my ears as my free hand grasps as if I'm holding her throat again.

Fuck she looked good like that.

I jerk myself faster, harder.

The feeling of having her racing pulse right beneath my fingertips, her life in my hands means my balls draw up all too soon . I groan out her name as I spurt hot jets of cum on my stomach.

Sitting on the edge of the bed, I look around my room.

Everything is in place, everything is tidy and finally, for the first time in over ten years, my life might soon feel the same.

I might feel like me again. I might be able to rid myself of the beast that lives inside me, that fuels my need for revenge, my need to destroy and ruin the lives of those who tried to break me.

Yeah, karma exists. And the universe has just handed a fuck load to me on a platter.

Now all I need to do is decide how I'm going to handle it.

A loud female cry of pleasure comes from the room beside me and I shake my head, standing from the bed and padding naked toward the shower.

I'm happy for Luc. I am. But listening to them every fucking night —or morning—is getting to be difficult to endure.

I stand under the hot spray of the shower. The list of things I need to do running through my mind, my need to find the answers I've craved for so long making my muscles tighten once more.

It's less than ten minutes later when I pull my bedroom door open, dressed and ready to head out of the house.

I take two steps when the door in front of me opens. Luca steps out with an easy, satisfied smile playing on his lips.

"You can wipe that look off your face," I mutter, my eyes jumping between each of the bright red hickeys on his neck.

"You're one to talk. It's not like you haven't been fucking your way around the redheads of MKU recently," he quips. "I'm amazed there's anyone left. Or are you now forced to go for round two with all of them?"

"Fuck off," I mutter, hating that he knows me so well. "There are plenty of freshmen," I deadpan as we both continue toward the stairs.

He barks out a laugh. "I'm surprised there isn't a support group who's already warned them about you. Ow," he complains when I slap him upside the head.

"I don't like you being this happy."

"Well, you're gonna have to get used to it, you miserable fuck, because this is it now. Got my girl back. Brett is gone. Things are good, man."

I glance up at him. Although his eyes are lighter, and his shoulders are more relaxed now than they've been in a long time, I can still see his concern. The anger that's lingering in the depths of his green orbs that look so much like my own.

"Yeah, I agree. Things are good."

His brows pull together. He knows I'm hiding shit. I never expected him to believe the crap I fed him the night I got back from dealing with our father after he attacked Luc's girl, but it was all he was going to get.

Luca got his punches in and he no longer has to deal with our father's overbearing presence in his life.

What happens next to Brett, it's mine to decide.

The pain, the suffering, all of it is mine.

"You know you can—"

"Don't say it, Luc," I cut him off before he tries to offer me a sympathetic ear and a shoulder to cry on once again.

"Fine," he says, holding his hands up in defeat as he walks to the coffee maker. "I only want to help, you know. Peyton does too."

"I know, and I appreciate it. But I'm good. For real."

"You're a shit liar, Lee," he says, turning his back on me.

"Whatever. Believe whatever you want." I grab an energy drink from the refrigerator and swing the door closed. "I'm out."

"Where you going? You don't have class this morning."

"Careful, Luc. I'll start to think you've turned your stalker tendencies on me.

Look, I'm going out. Meeting some friends."

I'm at the doorway ready to get the fuck away from my inquisitive brother when he calls my name and my body stops without instruction from my brain.

"I will find out, you know that, right?"

I shrug.

"And whatever it is, it'll be better coming from you."

"Nothing to tell, man."

I take off before he gets a chance to call me out on my blatant lie.

Jumping into my car, I start the engine and take a deep breath.

I hate lying to Luc, but it's how everything has been for a long time now. It almost comes naturally.

With every day that passes, the time when we were tight, when we knew literally everything about each other, becomes a little more distant.

I remember those two fun-loving, happy little boys. Kids who were too young to understand what a cunt our father was. How much pressure we were already under compared to other kids our age. And most importantly, we were totally unaware of the pain that comes with life and growing up as Brett Dunn's kids.

I've never figured out which one of us had it worse. From as early as I can remember, I knew that Luca was his favorite. The second Luc picked up a football, it was obvious that his future was going to be following in our father's footsteps. Being a quarterback comes as naturally to him as breathing. I remember Dad's eyes lighting up as he realized what was happening and he pulled Luc into his arms and called him his boy.

His boy.

From that moment on, Brett seemed to forget that he actually had two other boys. Every day after that one, Shane and I lived in the shadows as he pushed Luca harder and harder to be the best.

I got it, Luca was his little protégé, but that didn't mean that Shane and I weren't—aren't—kick-ass players who deserved the recognition and praise from him too. Hell, to this day, I'm Luca's right-hand man, his wide receiver, his fucking offense. Part of our success has been how well we can work together, our silent communication, our ability to know what the other is thinking. Yet I was cast aside in favor of him.

But I know that being singled out as Brett's favorite hasn't been easy for Luca. Just like being the forgotten one hasn't been easy for me. At least I've lived most of my life without our father breathing down my neck.

Movement catches my eye and when I look up, I find Luca standing in the living room window watching me, his face tight with concern.

He probably has every right to be worried, but I can't help feeling that it's too little too late. His concern isn't going to help me now.

I crack my knuckles before putting my car into drive and flooring the gas pedal.

There's only one thing that will help me now, getting to cause the pain I've been craving for years.

I've got two of those who wronged me in touching distance, all I need is the third and I can deliver the same kind of devastation on their lives that they did on mine.

———

The house is in silence when I pull up, but all their cars are here so I have no doubt that the people I need are inside.

"Yeah, all-fucking-right," a deep voice booms from inside after I knocked solidly for a good five minutes. "What the fu— Oh, it's you," Devin says when he pulls the front door open as he takes a good look at me with eyes barely open.

"Morning."

"Fuck off," he grunts, running his hand through his unruly hair.

"Who is it, baby?" a fake blonde asks as she runs down the stairs.

Devin straightens a little.

"What the fuck's it got to do with you?" he barks, causing her chin to drop. "You might have choked on my cock last night, sweetheart, but I'm not your fucking baby. Get out." He pulls the door back open and gestures for her to walk through it, but to her irritation.

"You can't be serious." She stands with her hands on her hips, her collagen-filled lips twisted in frustration.

"Deadly, *baby.* You can give me my shirt back too." His eyes drop to what I assume is the only thing she's wearing.

"But I'm not—"

"Shirt," he demands, holding his hand out.

She flicks a glance over her shoulder at me, but she's barking up the wrong tree if she thinks I'm gonna stand up for her.

She's Devin's problem and he's more than welcome to her.

"And if you're a good girl, I might let you go and get your shit."

She huffs and with very little concern, peels his shirt up her body, leaving her standing there as naked as the day she was born.

Devin whistles in appreciation.

"What do you think, bro?"

Devin glances at me with a wicked glint in his eye.

"Uh..."

"I'm sure she'd be up for a bit of fun if you are. Suck good cock, don't you, baby?"

I'm too enthralled watching the two of them to respond to his question. He steps up to her, takes her tits in his hands and slams his lips down on hers.

She moans like a whore before pulling back and slapping him so hard across the face that I feel the hit from the other side of the room.

"Oh, baby. You know how hard that gets me."

"You're a fucking pig, Devin Harris."

"I know. And you love it, Mia."

"It's Maya, you dick," she sasses, turning around to face me, a wide, calculated smile playing on her lips.

"O-oh no. I am not getting involved," I say, holding my hands up in defense.

Tits out or not, they're fake and she's not my type.

"Get out of here, Mia. You know where the door is."

Devin blows her a kiss, his cheek still glowing bright red as he points over my shoulder.

"Go on."

"Uh... s-sure. She a regular of yours?"

"Nah, she came for Ez but he never came home last night so..." He shrugs. "Oh come on, don't tell me that you and golden balls have never shared."

I can't help but laugh. "More than I care to admit."

"Yes, bro." He holds his fist up for me to bump and I just stare at him.

"There's something fucking wrong with you, man."

"Funny, you're not the first to say that. Coffee?" he asks, walking over to the appliance as if the previous few minutes didn't just happen.

"Y-yeah, that would be great, thanks."

"So..." he asks, sliding the mug toward me. "What the fuck drags you here in the middle of the night?"

I glance at the clock on the wall above his head.

"Classes have started, Dev."

"Huh." He glances around as if he's looking for something. "Who knew?"

"Clearly not you."

"So you need some help moving another body or something?"

"Nah, not this time. I need to find someone. Thought you might know someone I could get to do that."

"Hell yes, I do."

Pulling his cell from his pocket, he taps on the screen before lifting it to his ear.

"Bro, where you at?"

Whoever is on the other end says something before footsteps thunder down the stairs.

"And he's closer than you think."

"Lee, meet my little brother, Ellis. He will find you anything you could possibly need... for a price."

Ellis and I nod at each other. We've met before, but not officially, and he wasn't one of the Harrises who jumped at the chance to help us deal with Brett and his little bitch Julian last week. Devin and Ellis's twin, Ezra, and their older brother Reid were more than up for the challenge when Kane put in the call for backup.

"You kids have fun. I'm going to wash this chick off my cock."

Ellis looks at his older brother like he's some alien creature. I get it, Devin is... unique.

We're both silent as he takes his coffee and disappears.

"Is he always so..."

"Weird? Yeah. I would say that you'll get used to him but I'm not sure it's possible."

"Right."

"So what do you need?"

3

MACIE

I love Monday nights. It's my favorite part of my week getting to spend time with a group of kids who more than deserve a little one-on-one attention and someone who'll listen to whatever they've got to say. I always leave with a massive smile on my face knowing that I made even the tiniest bit of difference to a young person's life.

And on top of that, I get to stop in the sandwich shop that I found down the street which has the best meatball sub and homemade cookies in the entire state.

My stomach is growling long before I even approach the shop just knowing what's going to be waiting for me.

"Macie," Paulo says the second I step into the shop. "You're late tonight, darling."

"I know, I had to let one of the boys beat me at pool."

He smiles at me and shakes his head.

I don't have any grandparents. I met the ones on my dad's side as a baby apparently but I was too young to remember. Hell, I barely even remember having parents. But I like to think that my Monday night visits to Paulo, no matter how short, is something akin to spending time with a grandfather.

"You're a good girl, Macie," he says, reaching for a pair of gloves so he can prepare my sandwich for me. "The usual?"

"Of course."

"One of these days, you're going to come in here and demand something else."

"Never," I say with a laugh as I watch him make my order without having to ask me a single question about my preferences. It's a certain sign that I eat too many of Paulo's meatball subs, but I really don't care. We're all allowed a couple of vices in life, right?

Charlie's is sex. Jace's is vodka. Nathan's is basketball, and mine is... sandwiches.

Maybe Charlie has a point about my boring life.

"Well, would you look at that," Paulo says, dragging me from the depressing thoughts. "I've got two cookies left tonight."

"Ah, must be my lucky day," I joke as he places them into a bag for me.

After tapping my cell to pay for my dinner, I wish Paulo a good night before spinning on my heels. I head for the door, only I don't get that far because before I look where I'm going, I slam into what feels like a brick wall.

Warm hands land on my upper arms sending warmth surging through my body as his manly scent fills my nose.

I know that smell. I remember it from... I lift my head and lock onto a familiar set of eyes.

Holy shit.

I swallow nervously as the green twinkles with amusement.

"Hi," I squeak, feeling like a tiny mouse right in the fox's path.

My heart thunders in my chest as the skin of my neck burns, remembering his fingers wrapped around it last night.

Oh God.

But then something unexpected happens.

His lips twitch at one side of his mouth before it curls into a smile. It's not just any smile, but one that would knock most women on their asses with how beautiful it is.

My stomach somersaults and my chest burns red hot.

"I-I-I'm s-sorry," I stutter like an imbecile. "I-I wasn't l-look—"

"It's okay, Red." His eyes drop from mine momentarily in favor of my lips and I suck in a shocked, sharp breath. "Entirely my fault. I wasn't paying attention."

"Uh..."

He stands there staring down at me, blocking my exit, waiting for me to do... I've got no idea.

"C-can I buy you a sandwich to apologize?" I ask, knowing that it's entirely unnecessary because we both know it was an accident. But the awkward, polite girl inside me screams to do something to make this better.

"I can buy my own. How about you eat it with me though," he suggests, making my stomach damn near drop into my feet.

"Y-you want to eat your sandwich... w-with me?"

"Yeah," he confirms, staring at me like I'm some magical creature he can't figure out.

"Why?"

He shrugs. "I feel like it."

"But you're a football player."

"Ah, someone's been doing their homework. I'm glad I made an impression on you last night."

"N-no, I didn't—"

"Turkey sub, please," he says, interrupting me and turning to look at Paulo who I now discover is watching this weird exchange with an amused smile on his face.

"Of course. Sorry about your last season. Must have been tough."

"Yeah, well. Can't win them all, eh?"

"Better luck next season. I see that Jake Thorn is joining the team. Your brother is going to have his work cut out for him."

I stand there watching them chat about football with alarm bells ringing in my head.

I shouldn't have agreed to eat with him. I know it's only a sandwich, but still. He's a football player and I should run as fast as I can in the opposite direction. Not to mention that I saw his ass last night before he almost screwed Charlie.

Hoping that they're distracted by the topic of the upcoming season and the new players who will be joining the Panthers, I take a step around Leon. Doing so in the hope of bolting from the shop and hiding in the park around the corner.

But just as I'm about to pass him, his arm shoots out, stopping my progress.

"No running, Red," he growls so quietly that Paulo won't have heard it.

Leon's eyes hold mine, the emerald green darkening the longer our connection holds.

"Here you go, superstar," Paulo says, but even still, Leon doesn't look away from me.

I can't help feeling like he's trying to tell me something, but I have no clue what it might be.

"Thank you." He shifts, I assume to pay until Paulo assures him that it's on the house. "I appreciate that, sir. Thank you very much."

"Anytime. Good luck with practice and all that."

Finally, Leon rips his eyes from mine and smiles at Paulo.

"Have a great night."

"Good night, Macie," Paulo says. "Don't do anything I wouldn't do." He winks at me before shooting Leon a look. My cheeks once again heat up as I pray that the ground will open up and swallow me whole.

"You don't need to worry about me, Paulo. Football player's charms don't work on me." I smile at him, ignoring Leon's amused stare that's burning into the top of my head and march from the shop.

"You're quite the opposite of your roommate, huh?" he mutters, catching up with me in a second with his long-ass legs.

"If by that you mean I didn't immediately roll on my back and spread my legs for you, then yes, we're polar opposites."

"Ah, well. If I remember correctly, she wasn't actually on her back."

"Oh my God," I mutter, embarrassment blooming within me as he drags the memory up I don't want in my head once more.

I continue walking, hoping that at some point he might realize that I'm not the kind of girl he's interested in and disappear.

"What is it you wanted?" I snap when we come to the park entrance.

"I just want to eat." He admits, a knee-weakening smile pulling at his lips once more.

Damn him, he really is a little bit too pretty for a dude.

"And that involves me, how exactly?" I cringe the second the words are out of my mouth. This is why I should never talk to guys.

"Well, as good as I'm sure you'd taste," he says, blatantly running his eyes down the length of my body. My skin tingles with every inch he looks at me, making me wish I was wearing more than my jersey dress, leggings and denim jacket. "I was thinking about just sitting on a bench and eating this. But if you have another suggestion, I'm all ears."

"I'm sure you are." I can't help but roll my eyes at him. "A bench is fine."

Spinning on my heels, I march toward the one I usually sit at and drop down at the farthest end in the hope of keeping some distance between us.

I love it here. We're up on a hill that showcases all of Maddison County beyond.

Until I came to look around the campus the summer before my senior year, I'd never been here before. But the second I arrived, I just knew it was the right choice.

I came here because of Mom's legacy, but I never expected to immediately feel like it was my home. Where I belonged. All I knew up until that point was that Miami with my uncle was not my home and the school he shipped me off to, that place was almost as hellish.

Maddison County was my first experience of belonging, of that comfort that wraps around you when you're in a place you feel safe. I was too young to remember a time when I might have felt that before.

The sun has long set, leaving us with the silvery light from the moon and the glow from the lights before us where life continues like normal. I sit here with my head spinning and Leon's manly scent filling my nose, mixing with that from the sandwiches. I tell myself that it's the latter that makes my stomach growl and my mouth water, but I fear a part of that might just be a lie.

He lowers himself down beside me. He's entirely too close, seeing as I left him almost all of the bench to sit on. And yet, when he rests back, I can feel his burning heat down the entire right side of my body.

I've no idea what game he's playing, but it needs to stop. And not just because I fear it might be working.

We sit in silence and I can't help but stare as he lifts his sandwich and unwraps it.

His hands are huge, I guess that's necessary when you spend your life throwing and catching a ball. But it's not so much the size that catches my eye as the healing skin on his knuckles. Apparently, Leon Dunn doesn't just use his hands for football. I can't imagine his coach would be too thrilled if he knew.

A thought hits me and it immediately sends a shiver of fear down my spine. My eyes fly up to his and I study him, mindlessly.

"What?" he asks, a cocky smirk curling at his lips.

Damn him. He knows he's good-looking, and hell if he doesn't know how to use it.

"Your coach know you've been beating the crap out of someone?" I ask exactly what I was thinking with little thought.

His eyes narrow on mine for a beat before he cockily says, "Who says it was a someone?"

"Because hitting a wall makes it so much better," I deadpan with a roll of my eyes.

His eyes hold mine as his smirk gets wider.

"It's nice that you're concerned, Red. I'll remember that."

"N-no, I'm not... I was just..." I let out a frustrated sigh and lean back against the bench.

He chuckles but doesn't say anymore as I rip my sandwich open and take a massive bite. I usually try to savor it, but my need to shut myself up means I take the biggest bite I'm capable of.

I might be seen as the quiet one, the shy one, but when I'm nervous, all sorts of crap can fall from my mouth. It even got me in trouble a time or two in school, and the last thing I need to do while with Leon Dunn is to let my thoughts fall out of my mouth. He really doesn't need to hear that I think he's hot. An asshole, but hot all the same.

As if he heard me, his eyes turn toward me, making my cheeks burn.

"Just eat," I demand around a mouthful of food.

To my surprise, he does what I say and takes another huge bite of his turkey sub.

Closing my eyes, I force myself to take a breath and will the butterflies that are fluttering in my belly to abate.

So what if he's hot, and apparently wants to sit here with me. He's also a football player.

"What's your name?"

I have to give him a double-take but I guess it was stupid to assume that just because everyone on campus knows who he is that he'd have any clue about me.

"Macie S-Smith."

He studies me, his eyes taking in every inch of my face as my heart pounds so fast my head starts to swim as I wait for him to call me out on my lie.

He doesn't know who you are, Macie. No one knows who you are.

"Huh," he finally says after what feels like the longest silence of my life. "It suits you."

"Um... th-thanks, I think."

"So what are you doing out here on a Monday night then, Macie Smith?"

"Just some volunteer work. What about you?" I ask quickly, needing to turn the conversation away from me.

"Nothing much."

Crumpling up the paper that was around his sandwich, he turns his whole attention to me.

My skin pricks with goose bumps and my blood heats.

"I make that shot, and you've got to go out with me again."

He looks away from me and nods toward the trash can on the other side of the path.

"N-no, I'm not—" My words falter as the ball of paper bounces on the edge before it falls right in.

Looking back at him, I find a shit-eating grin splitting his face.

"I'm not going out with you."

Wrapping my barely eaten sandwich, I shove it back in the bag along with the cookies.

"You lost, Red."

"To a bet I didn't agree to," I argue.

"Still a bet though." The skin around his eyes crinkles with his amusement as if he already knows he's won.

To be fair, he probably has. I'm not naïve enough to think that Leon Dunn doesn't always get what he wants.

"I don't date football players."

He laughs, shaking his head as if it's an excuse he's heard a million times.

Resting his arm along the back of the bench, he slides a little closer. His already unignorable scent only getting stronger as the heat of his thigh burns mine.

"Oh yeah, and why's that?"

"Because you're all arrogant, conceited assholes."

"Whoa, Macie Smith, tell me how you really feel," he says, faking his hurt as he covers his heart with his palm.

"You all think you're God's gift to the world and expect everyone to do exactly as you say."

"Huh." He nods as if he's thinking about my words. "So how about you go out with me again and I'll prove you wrong."

"Why? Why do you want to go out with me? I'm the one who stopped you from getting laid last night. You should hate me for cockblocking you."

Something flashes in the green depths but it's gone too quickly to be able to decipher it.

"I think you did me a favor actually," he admits, his hand lifting toward my back.

Leaning as far forward as I can, I glower at him.

"See," I say, glancing at his still outstretched hand. "You think you can do exactly what you want and can get away with it."

His eyes hold mine, the intensity in them rendering me useless and allowing him to continue with what he wanted to do.

Sweeping a lock of hair off my cheek, he tucks it gently behind my ear before letting his knuckles lightly brush down my neck.

I gasp at the sensation that races through my body at his simple touch and his eyes flash with heat.

"As I was saying, I think you did me a favor. Your roommate wasn't really my type."

"Easy isn't your type?" I blurt out, instantly kicking myself for the comment.

"Good friends, huh?"

"W-we're just very different people."

"I'm starting to see that," he murmurs, sucking his bottom lip into his mouth as his eyes flick down to mine.

Uncomfortable with the feelings he's causing within me, I hop up and take a huge step away from the bench.

Not willing to let me go though, he stands and runs his hand through his dark hair, pushing the loose strands back from his brow as his eyes run down the length of my body.

"I-I don't think this is a good idea. I need to leave."

"Because I'm a football player?"

"And because I caught you in bed with my roommate last night. I'm not that kind of girl, Leon."

"I know. That's why I'm here right now and not with your roommate. It's the reason why I walked away from your roommate."

"Ah I see, I thought that was because you couldn't get it up." My eyes widen as I hear the words fall from my lips.

Holy crap, you did not just say that.

Much to my surprise, his only reaction is to laugh. Surely any other guy would be offended that I just accused his manhood of not working.

"Like I said, Red," he says, once again closing the space between us. "She wasn't my type. But I think we both know that I didn't have any issues in that department, don't we?"

He steps so close to me that I've no choice but to look up to keep eye contact with him.

The air around us crackles with electricity.

Time seems to stop as we stand there in the moonlight lost in each other.

I startle when his hand lifts and he once again tucks some hair behind my ear.

My breath catches when he leans in a little, the move is so slight that it's probably not even intentional but I see it and it makes my heart jump into my throat.

"Let me walk you to your car, Red."

"I— uh..." I swallow, licking my dry lips as I try to remember how to talk once more. "I don't have a c-car."

"Okay, then I'll drive you back to your dorm."

Thankfully, he takes a step back and I'm able to drag in a lungful of air and try to regain some kind of control of myself.

"N-no it's okay, I like to walk."

"It's dark. I'm not letting you walk back alone."

"I do it every other week. No one's attacked me yet," I say, wincing the second the words are out.

"Maybe not, but if tonight was the night then I'd never forgive myself."

"Huh..." I bite down on my bottom lip as I stare at him, wondering for the first time if I'm just a judgmental asshole when it comes to football players.

"Come on, I promise to show you a good time."

Aaand there it is.

Nope. He's just like every other football player I've ever met.

Full of big promises and even bigger egos.

"That's not what Charlie said."

"I'm never going to live that down, am I?"

I glance over at him as we fall into step, side by side to make our way out of the park.

"It wasn't your finest moment. But don't worry, I'm sure you've got a whole harem of girls willing to take her place."

"What if I don't want a harem?"

I shrug. "None of my business who's ass you're slapping next."

My cheeks burn so hot that I swear they must glow like a freaking beacon.

"That's funny because something tells me that you want it to be very much your business," he mutters, almost as if I'm not meant to hear, which is exactly what I pretend to do.

We walk side by side in silence. The atmosphere still so thick with tension between us that it's hard to breathe. But I figure all I've got to do is suffer the journey home and then someone will inevitably distract him from whatever this is and we can go on about our lives as if this weird little non-date in the park never happened.

"This is me," he says when we approach a sleek black BMW.

"Wow, no wonder you're not a fan of walking places."

4

———

LEON

Her judgmental comment rubs me the wrong way as she looks at my car with her lip curled. She seems to think she knows me and I'm sure that this image right now doesn't help, but she knows fuck all.

Well, that's not entirely true. She knows more about me than almost anyone on the planet but she doesn't seem to remember that right now, which is perfectly fine with me. It actually works in my favor because if she knew who I really was then I'm sure she'd never willingly give me the information I need. This way though, despite the fact she wants nothing to do with me right now, is perfect.

She might think she can stand up to me, stick by her little rule of no football players. It might have worked for her so far, but her little run of staying away from the likes of me is firmly over because she's not getting away now that I've found her.

"Got a problem with my car, Red?" I ask, caging her against it, leaning in enough to get another hit of her coconut-laced scent.

"W-what are you doing?"

Her eyes are wide, her face pale as I lean in closer.

"You smell like coconuts," I tell her, my hand lifting to her hair once again. I can't help it, it calls to me every time it falls across her face as if she's using it to try to hide behind.

"I-it's my sh-shower gel," she stutters.

"Do I make you nervous, Red?"

"You terrify me," she blurts out, and I can't help but smile at her knee-jerk response.

I've spent no more than thirty minutes with her tonight but I've already learned so much about her. The most important being that if I want her to speak her mind then I need to push her out of her comfort zone, make her uncomfortable.

"I know that feeling," I confess, holding her eyes so she knows that I'm serious.

Reaching for the door handle, I lean in closer, my chest brushing against her breasts. She sucks in a sharp breath and it tells me everything I need to know.

"You know," I whisper in her ear. "I spent all night regretting walking away from you."

"You're a liar," she breathes.

"Is that right?"

I stand back to full height, keeping my forearms on the roof and her tiny body caged between me and the car.

"You were horrible to me last night."

"You interrupted and messed with my head," I admit, hoping that giving her a few of my truths will help her to trust me. "I wasn't really into it with Charlie."

"Funny, because she sounded very invested."

"Trust me, Red. If I really wanted her, I'd have had her long before you barged in on us. But one look at you, and she lost what little appeal she had."

Her chest heaves as she continues to stare up at me. The small crease between her brows is cute as hell as she tries to convince herself that what I'm saying is true.

"You were right, I was struggling to... get it up, as you put it. Until I saw you."

"Oh God," she whimpers, her tiny palms pressing against my chest as if she stands any kind of chance of pushing me away as I crush her against the car. "L-Leon."

"Just proving a point, Red."

"Y-you've got nothing to prove to me. I don't care about whether you can or can't perform."

"You mean... fuck?" I growl.

Her eyes darken momentarily before her anger takes over and her lips purse.

"Whatever. Can you get off me now?"

I smile down at her, seeing right through her little innocent look. I know for a fact that she's about as ready for more as I am. But I'll play along, for now.

I'm more than happy to continue this little game to get what I need because I fully intend on getting some serious benefits out of it before we're done. And I can guarantee that that little innocent twinkle in Macie's eyes is going to be obliterated by the time I'm finished with her.

"Sure. Whatever you want."

Pushing from the car, I open my passenger door and gesture for her to get in.

I can tell from the hard set of her shoulders that she's not happy about getting inside, but I think she's aware that she has little choice. She either gets in willingly or I'll put her in there myself.

She lowers her head, keeping her gaze on her feet as she decides against arguing and making this harder than it needs to be and drops into the seat.

"See, it's not that hard to let me be a nice guy, is it?"

"Jury is still out on how nice you are."

With a smile, I jog around the hood of the car and climb in with her.

I realize the second I close the door behind me that I've possibly made a mistake because the only thing I can smell is her.

My fingers wrap around the wheel, my knuckles turning white with my need to get exactly what I need out of this woman.

Focusing on keeping my breathing steady, I reach out and press the ignition letting my baby rumble to life beneath us.

"Oh my God," Macie squeals as I tear from my parking space next to the sidewalk and shoot off down the road.

"I promised you a wild ride, Red. I suggest you hold on."

"I didn't think this through," she whispers as she white-knuckles the seat.

"You walk this regularly?"

"E-every week," she admits.

"Don't you have a car?" I ask, already knowing the answer.

She might be covering up who she really is, but I know for a fact that she's got more than enough money to own a car.

"Yes. I just prefer to walk."

"Right."

"Is wanting to do my part to help the environment so bad?" she snaps, her sudden frustration coming from nowhere.

"Whoa, did I say there was?"

Releasing the seat, she folds her arms over her chest. "No. Sorry. I'm used to people judging me."

"Ironic seeing as you've spent all night doing that to me."

She glances over at me, her lips parting to argue but she hasn't got a leg to stand on and she knows it.

All too soon, I'm pulling into the parking lot for her dorm building. It's full of cars but there's a brand new baby blue Mini at the other end of the lot that I already know is hers.

"That yours?" I ask, parking in the space beside it.

"Uh..." Her brows pull together in confusion.

"It is, isn't it?"

"Yeah, how'd you know that?"

I shrug. "Dunno. Just looks like the sort of car you'd drive. Brand new, top of the line. You a secret millionaire or something?"

"It was a gift," she lies.

"Aw, Mommy and Daddy send you off to college in her?"

"Something like that," she mutters, undoing her seat belt and reaching for the door handle.

"So I'll pick you up tomorrow night for our date?"

She lets out a long breath as if she'll magically find some strength from somewhere. Not that it matters if she does, she's not going to get out of spending more time with me.

"I'm not going out with you, Leon. Whatever this is," she says gesturing between us, a look of disgust on her face at the fact we're merely sharing the same air. "It ends the second I walk away from you."

"I guess I should take you home with me then."

Her breath catches, her eyes flying to mine. Disbelief fills her stare and it's almost enough to throw my car into reverse and do exactly what I said.

"Yeah, that's not happening. We're done, Leon."

She pushes the door open and climbs out.

"I'll see you tomorrow then. Make sure you wear something cute."

"Are you always this... this... insufferable?"

"I dunno. I guess you'll be able to tell me soon enough."

"Argh," she complains but movement outside her dorm building cuts her groan of frustration short. "Goddammit," she mutters, slamming the door closed, finally cutting off our conversation. She marches toward the guy who's standing by the main door watching us with his brow furrowed in concern.

He points at me as she gets closer, clearly asking what she was doing with me. She waves her hand around, dismissing me as if I'm nothing and disappearing into the building without so much as a glance back in my direction.

"Motherfucker," I bark, slamming my hand down on the wheel as anger surges through me.

Why is it that the one girl I need to get information out of, the one girl I've waited for years to get my hands on, is the only one on the fucking campus who can turn her back on me, turn me down, without a second thought?

I should have known this wasn't going to be easy.

But then I guess nothing that's worth it ever is.

They do say that the fun is in the chase. So I guess I've just got to enjoy the ride before the inevitable devastation at the end.

The guy is still watching me when I finally throw my car into reverse and back out of the space.

It only takes me a few minutes to get to our side of campus and to pull up outside the house beside Luca's car.

Peyton gives me a double-take when I join her, Colt and Evan in the kitchen.

"Whoa, you remembered where you live then," she sasses.

"Funny. Nice to see he's let you out of his bed."

Peyton sticks her tongue out at me while the guys look between the two of us.

"Beer?" Colt asks, throwing a bottle over before I even get a chance to say anything.

"Cheers."

"We're hanging out in the den if you're down."

I nod at them before they both disappear each with a six-pack in hand.

"How's it going?" I ask, hopping up on the stool beside where Peyton is.

"It's okay. It was nice to get away this weekend after everything."

A piece of jewelry on her wrist catches my eye.

"He gave it to you then?" I ask, remembering going shopping with Luca when we were kids to pick it out for her sixteenth birthday only for him to never have the chance to give it to her.

"Yeah. He set up a picnic at our place at the end of the beach, it was so sweet."

"What a pussy," I mutter jokingly.

"What happened to you?"

"Met up with some friends, got a little carried away. You know how it goes. I did see Mom before I left so don't bother getting on my case."

Peyton holds her hands up in defense. "I'm not saying anything."

"How's Libby?" I ask, knowing that she'd have gone straight to see her sister in the hospital the second she got back into town yesterday.

"She's good. Tests and everything seems promising. She's got a little weakness in her left arm, but all things considered, she's been damn lucky."

"That's really good. They gonna be moving her to rehab soon?"

"Probably next week. They're still monitoring her closely."

"I'm happy for you, you know that, right? With Luc, and your sister being okay. I'm glad things are working out for you."

"Thanks, Lee," she says with a soft smile. "What about you though? I mean, you're home so at least you're giving the redheads a rest tonight."

I stare at her in disbelief. "You've been spending too much time with my brother."

"We're worried about you. All that crap with your—with Brett, and—"

"I'm fine, Peyton. You don't need to worry about me."

She scoffs. "Yeah okay. It might help if you talked to us, told us what happened."

"There's nothing to tell." She pins me with a look that makes me feel about two feet tall. She knows I'm lying. Luca knows I'm lying, but for some fucked up reason, they're not pushing me for information.

I'm fucking glad though, because if they knew the truth... if they knew what we'd done to Brett, where he is. Well, they'd probably have me fucking committed.

But they don't understand. Even if I did tell them everything, every dark and twisted truth that I hold inside me, they still wouldn't understand my need to do what I'm doing.

"It'll all come out eventually, you know that, right? You can only lie to everyone around you for so long."

She's right. Of course she is. But the thought of that happening sends a chill racing down my spine.

Just imagining the way they'll look at me. The disgust, the pity, the attempt at compassion when really, they have no fucking clue what it was like. How each day is a struggle to put the nightmares behind me and live my life as if I'm fucking normal.

My grip on the bottle in my hand tightens. My need to walk straight back out of the house so I can go and feed the beast living inside me with some of the revenge it craves becomes almost too much to bear.

"Whatever," I mutter, pushing my stool back and standing. But I'm not quick enough in my escape and Peyton's hot hand lands on my forearm, halting my movement.

"I'm here, Lee. Luc too. Letty. Aunt Fee if you want someone impartial. We just want to help."

A lump forms in my throat as I stare down at her delicate hand on my tan arm, unable to look up and meet her eyes for fear of what she'll see in mine.

"I know, and I appreciate it."

Without another word, I rip my arm free and march out of the room.

"Everything okay?" Luca asks, turning toward the kitchen as I make my escape.

His eyes hold mine for a beat before he looks over his shoulder at Peyton.

"Yeah, everything's great."

His eyes narrow in warning, but it's not necessary. He should know I wouldn't try anything with Peyton no matter how shit life gets. He still doesn't trust me after the whole Letty thing. I get it. But everything is different now. I'm on the cusp of getting everything I've been craving for years, and there's nothing that's going to fuck that up for me now.

Forgetting about heading for the stairs, I turn back toward the front door and barge past my brother.

"What the fuck is your problem?" he barks, having no choice but to move aside.

I flip him off over my shoulder before storming through the front door and toward my car.

I wasn't going to go tonight. I was going to fight it. But fuck it. A quick visit to see my new pet won't hurt.

5

———

NATHAN

"Uh... Macie?" Nathan calls from the bottom of the stairwell as I race toward our floor in the hope of avoiding his inquisition. I know it's wishful thinking, I just got out of Leon Dunn's car. He's going to have a million questions.

I keep running, my heart pounding in my chest but it's pointless. Nathan is six foot four of pure muscle and legs that are almost longer than my entire body.

"Nice try," he says when he catches up with me at the door of our dorm room. He barely looks like he made any effort whereas I'm a panting, sweaty mess from the exertion I'm not used to.

"There's nothing to tell," I say, pushing through into our living area and praying the others aren't here to also witness this.

"Oh really. So it's a normal thing for you to catch rides with the football team, is it? You hate those guys."

"I know, Nate. I know," I say, irritation flowing through me at his big brother act. I yank the refrigerator door open and pull out a bottle of water. "I'm aware of how I feel about guys like Leon Dunn. Trust me, you don't have to remind me."

"Shit, Mace," he says, lifting his hand to the back of his neck. "I didn't mean—"

"It's okay. I'm sorry, it's just... it's been a crazy night."

"Wanna talk about it?"

I shrug. Is there anything to really talk about?

"I just ran into him at Paulo's. He demanded we eat together in the park. I dunno, it was weird."

"He wanted to eat with you after you ruined his hook up last night?" Nathan asks, his brow quirked.

"Yeah, see... weird. Then he insisted on driving me home and—" I slam my lips shut before I blurt out about his demand for a date tomorrow night. There's no point telling anyone about that because it's blatantly a joke... right?

There's no way a guy like Leon Dunn would ever want to go out with a girl like me. I'm the epitome of the opposite of his type.

Shy, quiet, book nerds aren't usually the girls the football team— hell, any sports teams—pick out. They all want the loud ones, the party girls, the ones who'll show them a good time. Maybe that's one of the reasons I am the way I am. My need to keep as much distance from any football players as possible has turned me into a girl they'd never look twice at.

I'm okay looking, sure. But most people won't ever spot me to even notice when I'm too busy trying to hide in the shadows. The only thing that makes me stand out is my hair, but now we're at college, no one really cares about teasing the ginger girl anymore so I really can just disappear.

"And what?" Nathan asks, not missing my slip up.

"N-nothing. It's nothing."

With my purse still over my shoulder and my unopened bottle in hand, I start toward my room.

"I've got an assignment that I really need to work on."

He doesn't say anything as I walk down the hall but I know he's hot on my heels and I know he's worried.

Nathan is like the brother I never had. Even though I really, really appreciate our easy relationship—the first of any kind I've had with a guy—I really don't need him being totally overbearing. I can handle Leon Dunn. Although I seriously suspect I won't even have to try because the second he drove away tonight, he probably forgot all about me.

I drop onto my bed and look at where I know he's loitering in my doorway.

"Everything's fine, Nate. It was just a lift. He's probably forgotten my name already and gone off hunting jersey chasers."

He narrows his eyes on me as if he knows something I don't.

"Okay, well, I'm gonna..." He thumbs over his shoulder and starts backing away.

"Have a good night," I call out just before he disappears from my sight.

"You too."

I work on my assignment until long after midnight—long after the time I should have stopped—but I was making good progress. When the end was in sight, I knew that I'd regret having to pick it up again the next day to finish, so I kept going.

I might not regret finishing the next morning, but when my eyes refuse to open as my second alarm starts blaring, I already know I regret the late night.

I never usually hear my alarms, they're usually totally unnecessary because I'm always awake before them, but not today.

I groan rolling over and hitting the button to silence the irritating thing.

There's movement outside my door, probably the guys getting ready to go to practice.

As I lay there, trying to find the energy to get out of bed knowing that I've got back to back classes all day, I can't help but think back to yesterday, or last night, to be specific.

Why did Leon want to eat his sandwich with me?

The whole thing was just bizarre.

Nate was right, he should have been pissed at me for ruining his hook up. But he was... weirdly sweet.

My body heats as I remember the way he pinned me to his car. How he so blatantly proved that he has no issues with what he's packing in his manhood department like I had suggested.

I should have been appalled that he wanted to make his point so clear. But with his scent in my nose and the heat of his body burning my skin, I couldn't find it in me to feel that way.

And I hate myself for it.

Throwing the sheets off, I jump from my bed and push thoughts of him and his hot body from my mind. I've got other things that deserve to take up space in my thoughts. Leon Dunn certainly isn't one of them.

The guys are gone by the time I emerge after I've showered and got ready for the day.

"Morning," Charlie sings, looking much more put together than she did yesterday when she finally joins me for coffee. "Your hair looks nice."

Lifting my hand up, I twirl a curl around my finger.

"Uh... just wanted a change."

"You got a hot date or something, you don't usually make that kind of effort?"

"N-no, of course not. I dunno, just needed to feel good about myself today so..." I trail off, feeling utterly ridiculous now.

Did I spend extra time on my hair because of the possibility of seeing him again?

No, I absolutely did not.

Liar.

"You should let me do your makeup too. Maybe that way you'll end the day with the possibility of a date."

"I don't need makeup to get a date," I sulk.

"You don't need to do your hair either yet here we are."

My lips part to argue but when Charlie cocks her hip and places her hand on her waist, I know there's zero point in trying to come up with any comeback.

"Okay fine," I say, knowing that now she's suggested it, that I'm not going to get out of it. "But I need to leave here in no more than ten minutes without looking like a clown."

"You think I'd do that?" she asks, faux hurt on her face at my words.

"Just keep it light... natural."

"You got it, babe. Come on, we'll knock him on his ass with your beauty, whoever he is."

"There isn't a guy."

"Honey, there's always a guy."

His green twinkling eyes pop in my head as I remember him looking down at me last night with the moonlight reflecting off them.

Damn him.

To give Charlie some credit, the makeover takes not a second more than eight minutes. When she allows me to turn around and look in the mirror, I'm pleasantly surprised because I don't find bright red lipstick or dark smoky eyes that would make me look like some kind of drag queen. Instead I see a subtle makeup job that only accentuates my blue eyes and high cheekbones. The foundation she's applied is even light enough that it doesn't cover my freckles.

To put it simply, I just looked like a better, less tired version of myself.

"Whoa."

"You had no faith in me at all, did you?"

"Um..."

"Come on, let's get your sexy ass to class. See if you can catch the attention of a fellow nerd."

"Who says I want a nerd?" I ask following her out of her room, grabbing my purse that I left on the table.

"Honey, we both know that the only type of balls the guys you date can manhandle are their own... ergo... nerd."

"Ergo? That Latin class you took last semester to get into Dwayne's pants sure paid off."

"Wha— Girl, I've no idea what you're talking about," she says with a wink as we leave our dorm and head out for the day.

————

"Hey, is this seat taken?" a guy asks standing beside the table I'm sitting at alone in the library.

The professor from my last class of the day is sick. So unlike almost everyone who smiled in delight and took off to spend the afternoon doing anything but work, I decided to head here to complete both the classwork and the assignment that were both posted on the university portal for us.

"U-uh... no. Go for it," I say, looking up to find a dark-haired guy with glasses looking down at me with a shy smile playing on his lips.

He's cute.

"Th-thank you. I'm Micah, by the way."

"Macie."

"Huh," he says. "We'd make great twins," he deadpans before clearly thinking better of it. "Shit," he mutters to himself.

"Yeah, they'd be great twin names," I agree because as goofy as the comment might be, he's right.

"What are you working on?"

"Oh, a law paper. You?"

"Computer hacking."

"As in you're doing the hacking or you're writing a paper about it?" I ask with a smile.

He looks up at me with a wide smile of his own that displays the most perfect set of white teeth. "Definitely the paper. Although," he leans in so he can whisper. "For the right price, I could probably find you whatever you wanted." He winks before barking out a laugh at the shocked look on my face.

"You're joking? You are joking," I say, answering my own question.

"Sure. Of course I am."

I stare at him for a beat, trying to work out if he is actually joking or not but all he does is smile coyly at me.

"Right, well. I should probably..." I point to my computer.

"Of course. Don't let me distract you."

But despite saying that, I can still feel his attention on me as I look down at my Word document and force myself to focus on what I need to do though.

I manage a few pages before I'm unable to ignore it, I look back up again and catch him red-handed.

He smiles nervously before finally looking down.

This is more like it, I think to myself. A guy who's as nervous as I am. Not one who thinks it's appropriate to press his manhood against my stomach three seconds after almost putting said appendage into my roommate.

"Are you okay?" he asks, and it's not until his deep voice rumbles through me that I realize I was mindlessly staring at him.

Reaching out, I slam my laptop down.

"Yep. I think I'm done," I force out as my cheeks burn.

"O-oh okay. Could I... uh... buy you a coffee or something?"

"Uh... I was just going to walk back to my dorm but I—"

"I can walk with you."

I smile, appreciating his offer and more than willing to get to know him a little better. He's definitely much more my type, and the kind of guy I should be having coffee with, that's for sure.

"Yeah, that sounds good."

He packs everything back up and stands. He's not as tall as Nathan or Leon, but he's still over a head taller than me.

"After you then, Macie."

"Thank you," I murmur, taking a step forward as he falls into step beside me.

We fall into easy conversation about classes and college life as we make our way to the coffee shop. Micah insists on buying me a hot chocolate with all the extras and all too soon we're walking toward my building.

"Thank you for this, it was nice."

"Oooh," he says with a wince. As our time has gone on both of us have relaxed a little and lost our initial shyness.

"What?"

I don't hear anyone approach but I sure as hell feel him when he wraps his arm around my waist and drags me into his body.

"Thanks for walking my girl home, Micah. Appreciate it."

"What the hell?" I gasp, attempting to pull myself away from Leon's side but failing miserably against his strong grip.

"We've got a date, remember, Red."

"Oh n-no we don't. He's talking bullshit, he's not—"

"You really should go and drop your bags off. Maybe pick up an overnight one."

"What?" I screech, finally removing myself from his body. "Micah, no. Please don't listen to him."

Micah looks between the two of us but it's clear that he and Leon know each other.

"Have a great night," he says, finally ripping his eyes from Leon's to mine. He gives me a sad smile before taking off. "See you around, Macie."

He's gone before I get to say anything.

"What the hell?" I snap, irritated that he's not only turning up when I don't want him to but ruining a potential date that I might actually want.

"You dropping your bags off and getting changed or are you coming like that?"

"I'm not going anywhere with you."

"But our date. I've planned it and everything." His green eyes twinkle with excitement and I will the butterflies that want to take flight in my belly away. Where the hell were they when I was talking to Micah anyway?

"Then go and find a jersey chaser to impress and leave me alone."

He takes a step forward and I take a huge one back.

"I don't need to impress jersey chasers, Macie. And they're not really interested in dates outside of the bedroom."

"Really?" I deadpan.

"Humor me. Just one night."

"You already had one. I'm still far from impressed."

"You're really gonna make me work for it, huh?" He tries to close the space between us once more.

"Nothing to work for. Nothing is happening here."

Before I know what's happening, my back collides with the wall beside the door to our building.

"Oh yeah, is that what you really think?"

His scent fills my nose, the exact one that I've been remembering all day as his forearms lift, caging me in.

"I don't just think it. I know it. Now can you please leave me alone. I'm not interested."

"Yeah, see... I think you're lying."

I fight to keep my breathing steady so I don't give him anything to prove that he's right.

"I'm not."

I gasp when his hot hand cups my cheek.

"Your pupils are dilated. You keep biting your bottom lip." In case I don't know where my bottom lip is, he drags his thumb across it. "And your chest is heaving."

My eyes narrow on his but before I manage to come up with a witty response, he leans forward. His breath tickling my ear that sends a shiver racing down my spine.

"And I'd put money on the fact your nipples are hard right now behind that padded bra."

The breath I didn't know I was holding comes racing out of me in a rush.

No one has ever spoken to me like this before and it makes my head spin with confusion.

"Want me to prove it to you?"

"What? No," I gasp, folding my arms in front of my chest.

"One night, Macie. Then if you don't want to spend more time with me, I'll leave you alone."

I study him, searching for any hint that he might be lying.

Why I'm even considering his terms I've no freaking clue but something just feels wrong about turning him down.

He's playing you, a little voice screams in my head. And while I might totally agree with that voice, I'm also intrigued to find out what game he's actually playing.

"Is this some kind of bet or something?"

"What? No. What kind of guy do you think I am?"

"You really want me to answer that?" I ask, raising a brow.

"Yeah, I do. But not right now."

His hand slips around the back of my neck and my body freezes in panic but all he does is pull me from the wall and twist me toward the door.

"Do you mind not manhandling me?"

"Not really. You're too small and cute not to." He steps right up behind me, his crotch pressing against my ass. "I like knowing that I can make you move in any way I want."

"I'm not weak, Leon. I won't bend to your needs."

"Trust me, Red. You're making it harder than most."

"Good. Something tells me that the challenge will do you good."

"I'm a sucker for a challenge," he confesses as we climb the stairs. "But do you know what else?"

"I'm afraid to ask."

His arm wraps around my waist, pulling me firmly back against him, his lips brushing the shell of my ear.

"I never lose."

"Oh God," I moan, as heat floods my veins.

"Nah, Red. Just Leon is fine."

"You really are something, you know that?"

"Sure do. Lead the way, Red. I can't wait to see your room."

"Oh no, you're not—"

"We'll see." I don't need to turn around to know that he's got the cockiest smirk on his face right now.

6

———

LEON

The second she steps inside the dorm, Macie looks around as if there's going to be someone here to help. She's soon going to realize that she's about to be disappointed because I saw Charlie and the two guys she lives with leave not so long ago.

It's just the two of us all alone with no one to help her out.

If I were a less patient man, I could probably drag the information I need out of her tonight. It's tempting, but that would mean missing out on the fun we're going to have together. And despite the fact she thinks she's going to be able to resist me, I already know that she won't. I'll make sure of it.

One way or another Macie Fletcher—not Smith—is going to drop her guard and open herself up to me before I play my final hand and introduce her to the man who she's willingly handed herself over to.

"Looks like we're alone," I murmur, following her deeper into her dorm. "It's a shame we've got plans or we could have made the most of it."

She spins toward me, her eyes holding mine. She tries to look like she's strong and in control. But I can see all the cracks in her armor, her fear, and all they do is feed the darkness inside me that I'm willing to stay away, if only for a few hours.

"I don't know who you think I am, but that isn't going to be happening. I'm not that kind of girl."

"So you've said."

"I don't understand why you're even bothering. You're not going to get what you want from me." Her determination to do the right thing, to appear unfazed by me is amusing. It's going to be even better when I prove her wrong and show her how really, deep down, she's just like all the others.

"Who says I want anything?" I say, resting against that counter and crossing one leg over the other in an attempt to look casual. She doesn't need to know that I've waited years for this opportunity, that I'm more excited than I've been in a very long time at the prospect of shattering her guard and taking exactly what I need.

"Guys always want something."

"Like Micah?" I ask, battling with the jealousy that swept through me like a tsunami when I saw them together as they approached the building.

"Micah didn't want anything, we were just chatting."

"He walked you home, Macie. Dude wanted something."

"Not all guys are like that," she huffs.

Pushing from the counter, I walk toward her, blatantly running my eyes down the length of her body. She's wearing a blazer over a white shirt and dark pair of skinny jeans. She looks hot. Innocent. Just asking to be dirtied up if you ask me.

"Trust me, Red. He was more than thinking of it. Probably wondering exactly what kind of lingerie you're wearing beneath your clothes." Her lips purse in frustration. "Want to know what I think?"

"No."

I continue anyway. "I think that you try to play it all innocent, that you give off the vibe that you're wearing white cotton panties, but really, I think you're a lace girl. That this layer of modesty hides your inner vixen."

"Interesting theory, Dunn. It's also one you'll never discover the answer to."

"You wanna bet?"

"No." She once again crosses her arms, pushing her tits up and giving me just a flash of the cleavage that's hiding.

"Probably the right call, you lost the last one, after all."

A growl rips up her throat as we stare at each other. Both of us willing the other to stand down but clearly, we're almost as stubborn as each other.

"So did you want to get changed?"

"I'm not going to some fancy restaurant so you can flash your wealth and celebrity status around to try to impress me."

"It's a good thing that I haven't planned something like that then."

She looks at me and for the first time actually pays attention to what I'm wearing.

I'm not dressed all that dissimilar to her wearing a dark pair of jeans and a black fitted shirt with the sleeves rolled up to the elbows and open at the neck. It should be enough to tell her that what I just said was true. There is no table in any expensive restaurant waiting for us.

"Fine," she says, throwing her arms up. "But only because I'm intrigued to know what you think is an appropriate date that doesn't involve flashing the cash."

"I already told you, Red. I'm not the guy you think I am."

"Pfft, whatever." She marches toward the bedrooms and I take off behind her, catching her door when she tries to swing it closed.

"What are you—"

"Waiting," I say, dropping onto the chair in front of her desk. "Nice room you've got here. Brand new car, one of the biggest rooms I've been in. Your parents must really love you."

Her jaw pops at my mention of her parents and her eyes shoot over to a photo frame on her nightstand.

"Can you wait out in the living area?"

I sit forward, resting my elbows on my knees as I check out her space. It's pretty much as I expected. Clean, tidy, and full of books. There is no sign that she does anything other than study. It makes me even more determined to show her a different side of life.

"No. Can you hurry? Unless you want me to cancel my plans and we just hang out in here all night."

Her cheeks heat, her eyes shooting toward the bed momentarily letting me know that her mind went straight into the gutter.

"I'm sure we could have plenty of fun. Especially with no one here to hear you scream—"

"We're going out," she says in a rush, spinning on her heels and pulling open her drawers, rummaging through it to find something to change into.

"D-don't move or touch anything," she says, pinning me with a warning glare before disappearing into the bathroom.

"And here I was thinking I was about to find out if I was right about your panties."

"My panties are none of your concern, Dunn," she snaps before the door closes behind her.

I'm still laughing when I push up from the chair and walk straight over to her nightstand.

The photograph of her parents is old, no surprise there really, but despite the fact I was young when her dad played football, I still recognize him. I think most players would. He was pretty prolific before his life imploded on him.

Walking around her bed, I come to a stop in front of her drawers, my eyes tracking over every item sitting on the top. But none of it gives me any information, it's all just random girly shit and a few pieces of jewelry.

I've got my fingers wrapped around the handle of the top drawer when the bathroom door opens again and she steps into the room.

My chin drops as I take in her outfit of choice while her face reddens in anger when she realizes that not only have I moved, but I'm most definitely touching something.

"What the hell—" we both say simultaneously.

I take a step back from her dresser, too shocked by her outfit of choice to continue on my mission to find her underwear drawer.

"You're not fucking serious?" I spit, although I can't wipe the smile off my face as I stare at her. I'm almost proud, I think.

Macie might make out that she's all shy and meek, but I'm pretty sure it's an act because this girl clearly has balls.

"What? You didn't tell me what not to wear."

"A fucking basketball jersey?"

She shrugs. "What? You didn't expect me to own a football one, did you?"

My lips part to respond but I don't have any words. Instead, I stand there mute as she flips her hair over her shoulder and drops herself into the chair at her desk I recently vacated.

She makes quick work of running a brush through her hair and then applies a layer of gloss to her lips as if I'm not watching her every move, my fists curling at my sides and my cock tenting my pants.

This girl.

This fucking girl.

"Okay, I'm ready." She turns to me and holds her arms out to the sides, allowing me to check her out.

She's still wearing the same jeans, but she's teamed it with a long-sleeved white shirt beneath her purple Panthers basketball jersey.

"You look beautiful, but for the love of God, don't tell me that has some guy's name on the back."

A wicked smile curls at her lips, giving me all the answer I need before she spins and lets me see for myself.

"Motherfucker."

Before she knows what's happening, her back is against the wall and my hand is back at home around her throat.

It's not a move I was planning on using against her anytime soon. I still remember the fear that was in her eyes on Sunday night when I pinned her to the wall. The last thing I need right now is to scare her off, but the knowledge that she's trying to fire me up on purpose makes all my well thought out plans fly right out the fucking window.

But this time, I don't see fear in her light blue eyes, instead, I see defiance and fuck if it doesn't make my cock ache for her.

"You're not going to win this game, Macie. You may as well give up now."

"Is that right?" she sasses, her pulse thundering beneath my fingertips.

"You've got no idea who your opponent is."

"There's something you should know, Dunn." I continue to stare at her, fighting like hell to keep my eyes on hers and not let them drop to her lips. "I never lose, either."

Long seconds pass as we both stand there staring at each other, our chests heaving and our breaths mingling.

The last thing I want to do is take her out on the date she forced me to plan, but that's exactly what needs to happen.

Shifting my grip on her, I grip the back of her neck and push her toward the door.

"Let's go before you find yourself in a position you can't get out of."

"Wait, I need my purse."

I allow her to grab it before leading her from the dorm, regretting it with every step that we take.

Her coconut scent fills my nose as we make our way down to my car, and it only gets stronger, more tempting the second we're shut in the enclosed space.

"You got me on this non-date. So what happens next? What line and plays does Leon Dunn use to get what he wants."

"I have no lines."

"Oh, so you rely on your personality and wit to woo a woman?"

"Firstly," I say, starting the engine and backing out of the space beside her Mini. "I don't woo anyone. It's no longer the nineteen-twenties if you hadn't noticed. And secondly, you're implying that neither of those are good enough to get a woman when really, I don't need either. Everything I need to convince them to spend time with me is right here," I say, cupping my junk.

"I don't know who I feel more sorry for, you and your big head, or the delusional women who fall for your crap."

Looking over at her, I can't help but laugh at the disgusted look on her face.

"You know, for someone who's trying to prove he's not the person I think he is, you're doing a really stellar job."

"I think you love it. Plus, I know I've got you as curious about what I'm rocking under my clothes as much as I am you."

"I couldn't care less. But experience tells me that if you need to make such a big deal about it, then you're probably just trying to compensate."

"Got a lot of experience, huh?"

"Less than you, I'm sure."

7

MACIE

He neither confirms nor denies my comment. I can't help but smile as his grip on the wheel tightens as he continues down Main Street heading toward the other side of town.

Silence falls between us, but weirdly, it's not uncomfortable.

I think back over what's happened since he steamrolled Micah and I can't help but wonder who this sassy woman is, who stood up to him.

Pulling the stunt with Nathan's basketball jersey isn't something I ever thought I'd do. But the second the idea popped into my head, I knew it had to happen.

In the space of forty-eight hours, I've gone from being a blundering idiot pinned between him and the wall as he growled at me, to the girl who's getting more joy than I ever thought I would trying to play him at his own game.

I just wish I knew what the endgame was.

I glance over at him, wondering if he's lying about this not being a bet. It has to be. There's no way that Leon Dunn would willingly put this much effort into chasing anyone if there wasn't some fucked up football team dare at the end of it.

His hair is perfectly styled, almost too perfect. His green eyes are focused straight ahead but there are creases at the sides as if he's trying not to laugh at me. I'm not sure if that amuses or annoys me. His nose is perfectly straight and his lips... they're so full. I wonder what they'd feel— *No.*

I slam the doors on my thoughts and rip my eyes from him, wrapping my arms around myself as if they'll protect me from... from whatever this is.

"What are you thinking about, Red?" he asks, clearly sensing my attention.

"Still trying to figure out the game."

"Why does there have to be a game? Why can't I just want a date with you?"

"Because boys like you don't date girls like me."

"Says who? There are no rules."

"If there were, I suspect you'd break them all anyway."

"You already know me so well, Red."

"Where are we going?" I ask, realizing that we've passed all the restaurants, the movie theater, and the arcade. I'm not sure where else he could take me.

"You'll just have to wait and see. Pretty sure you're going to like it."

"Verdict's still out as to whether I'm regretting getting in this car again."

"I thought I'd been pretty polite."

"Hmm..."

"So why MKU then, Red?" he asks, making my heart jump into my throat. I really, really don't want to have to talk about me or my past.

"My mom studied here. I always wanted to follow in her footsteps."

"Nice."

"What about you?"

"Obvious, isn't it?"

"Football," I mutter.

"My twin brother, Luca, and I have pretty much had our entire lives mapped out for us by our father."

"That sounds... restrictive."

"Like you wouldn't believe."

"You enjoy it though?"

"The game? Yeah. It's all I know. My entire life has been about football and making the NFL. If I didn't have it, I'd have no idea what I'd do, who I'd be."

"It's nice to have something you care about so much," I mutter, feeling sad that I've never really had that. My biggest focus has always been just surviving.

"You have any hobbies?"

"Er... reading, I guess. I've never really been the type to enjoy organized activities."

"Well, you sure make them sound like fun, putting it like that."

"I'm not really a team player. I've always been better at doing things alone."

He glances over at me, an understanding I wasn't expecting flashing in his eyes.

"That's a damn shame, Red. There's a lot of fun to be had with others."

"I'm sure. Seriously, where are we going?" I ask when he suddenly takes a right down a dark dirt road that's enclosed on either side by low-hanging trees.

"Worried you're about to meet your untimely death?" he asks with a smirk.

My heart rate increases until I can feel it in every inch of my body.

"I wasn't but I am now. What the hell, Leon?"

"Just wait. I think you're going to like it."

He continues forward, his pristine BMW bouncing into all the muddy potholes, branches scraping down the sides as the road gets narrower.

"This is really creepy," I whisper as it gets darker and darker with the tree coverage above us hiding the light from the moon.

"Trust me."

"Pfft, yeah, that's gonna happen."

He slams his foot on the brake and turns to look at me.

"What the hell?"

He studies me for a beat making my brows pull together as I try to figure out what he's trying to read on my face.

"You can trust me, Red. Nothing bad is going to happen."

I swallow nervously.

"O-okay," I agree, but I think we both know I'm lying.

"I'm not the bad guy here, Macie."

I nod, wishing he'd just get on with whatever he's doing.

He stares at me for another two seconds, allowing me to see just a hint of some vulnerability in his eyes before he pulls on his usually cocky mask and turns back to the wheel.

We only drive a few more feet before the trees that were in front of us open up and reveal a vast mass of water. The top ripples in the moonlight.

"Oh, it's so beautiful," I breathe, leaning forward to get a better look.

"Just wait for it."

Leon turns the car and I gasp in shock at the sight before me.

"Y-you did all this? F-for me?"

He shrugs and when I finally rip my eyes from the romance fest before us I find a shy smile playing on his lips.

"Yeah. You like it?"

I look back at the twinkling fairy lights that are wrapped around some kind of gazebo looking out over the lake.

"I-it's... not very football player-like of you."

"I told you, Red. You've got me all wrong."

I look between the most romantic picnic spot I've ever seen to the enigma that is Leon Dunn sitting beside me.

Who the hell is this guy, really?

"You want to get out and enjoy it, or are we gonna sit in here all night?"

I'm still too stunned to move.

"Okay, well... I'm hungry so I'm gonna..." Leon pushes the door open and climbs out.

The second his door slams closed, I scramble to join him.

By the time I start walking over, he's already standing under the canopy with the lights twinkling around him. It's really quite a sight.

Lifting his hand, he runs his fingers through his hair. His usual confidence and cockiness is gone and in their place... nerves, maybe.

"Did you really do this for me?" I ask as I step up to him.

"I really did," he confirms.

"B-but why? You don't even know me."

He shrugs. "But I want to, and I figured you'd like something like this."

"I do, I love it. It's just so..."

"So?"

"Unexpected."

"I told you," he says, closing the space between us, forcing me to look up at him.

His hand lifts and he reaches out, tucking my hair behind my ear.

"I'm not the person you think I am."

His words and his featherlight touch do weird things to me. My stomach damn near explodes with a million butterflies and my skin tingles, my need for him to keep touching me almost strong enough to force me to reach for him myself.

"You look beautiful, Red." His smile that follows those words is so damn endearing he almost makes me forget everything. Almost.

Instead, I force a little reality back into our situation and will my body to get a hold of itself.

It doesn't matter how much he might prove to me that he's different. That he's the opposite of all the football players I've been let down by in my past. I refuse to believe it, to accept that he won't just hurt me like them. Disappoint me like them.

"No one's ever called me beautiful before," I confess.

"Then you've been spending time with the wrong people."

A humorless laugh almost bubbles up my throat. Ain't that the freaking truth.

"What did you bring to eat?" I ask before he starts digging into the people, or lack thereof, in my life.

It takes him a second but my question eventually registers in his head and he takes a step back.

"I didn't know what you liked—aside from meatball subs—so I just got a little of everything."

"Sounds perfect."

I follow his lead and lower myself to the blanket on the ground and wait for him to pull out everything from the basket.

The entire situation is like a dream as I watch him lay out the food between us, stealing bites here and there as he goes, I can't quite believe it's actually happening.

My head wars with itself as I try to hold on to the person he was when I interrupted him with Charlie. The angry, vicious way he held me, the wicked promise he left me with.

It's at total odds with this version of Leon in front of me right now.

So which one is real?

"You're meant to be enjoying yourself, Red. You looked stressed."

"You confuse me," I blurt out.

"Well, relax and let me help to unconfuse you."

"But—"

He picks up a carrot stick and scoops up a dollop of hummus, holding it out toward me. "Here."

"I-I... uh..." He moves it closer until the hummus touches my lips.

"Open up, Red."

Unable to do anything but follow orders, my mouth opens and he pushes the carrot inside.

I take a bite of it, then he throws the other end of the stick into his mouth and chews.

And damn him because even while chewing he looks hot.

He finishes getting everything out and then lays down beside the plates and starts picking at the food, encouraging me to do the same.

We eat in silence, my gaze alternating between Leon, the food and the insane view.

This date is literally the thing of romance novels. It is the kind of romance that every woman dreams of. So why do I feel like the blanket is going to be pulled from beneath me any minute now?

"You still looked stressed," Leon muses.

"I'm sorry. I keep getting stuck in my own head. Did you bring something for us to drink?"

"Shit, yeah. Sorry."

He sits up and rummages around in a bag that's hidden behind the basket.

"Champagne, really?" I ask, lifting a brow.

"Cliché, I know. But what else could I get to go with this."

"Fair point. A bottle of Bud wouldn't really go."

He passes me two glasses before getting to work on popping the cork.

"I... uh... don't really drink."

He pauses and looks at me, although he must have me figured out better than I do him because a soft smile plays on his lips. "Why am I not surprised? You're too good, Red."

"Nothing wrong with that," I snap, like I always do whenever someone criticizes my life choices.

"It's not a bad thing. It just really makes me want to turn you a little bit bad."

"I'm already breaking all my rules by being here. One thing at a time."

"Just a little one?" he asks, already pouring the bubbles into the glass.

"Sure. As long as you promise that if I get drunk, you'll make sure I get back in one piece."

"Huh."

"What?"

"I just thought you were going to warn me about taking advantage of you if you get drunk. Maybe you are starting to get to know me."

"Thank you," I say, lifting my glass to my lips when he takes his and ignoring his comment about taking advantage, mainly because there is no way in hell that I'm letting him get me drunk. I need to be on full alert when it comes to Leon Dunn.

I take the smallest sip before placing the glass in the grass behind me.

"So, tell me something else about you aside from football," I demand, popping an olive into my mouth and licking the oil from my fingertip.

His eyes zero in on my lips and the tingles I tried to banish earlier return full force.

"U-uh..." he stutters, dragging his eyes back up to mine. Although when I look into them, I find they're significantly darker than they were before. The sight makes my heart beat that little bit faster. "What do you want to know?"

"I don't know." I shrug regretting the question. I can't ask about family and those normal kinds of things because I know it'll invite questions into my own life and I refuse to go down that path tonight when we're meant to be enjoying ourselves. "Where do you live? Friends. Parties. Classes. Anything, really."

He studies me for a beat and I can't help but wonder if he noticed my lack of questions about his life outside MKU.

I tell myself I'm just being paranoid and continue eating as he starts talking.

"I live in a house with my brother and a few of the guys from the team over by the frat houses. Parties? Every weekend. Classes? I go occasionally," he jokes... I think. "There's not really much to tell. During the season I'm either training or sleeping and in the off-season, I just try to enjoy myself as much as possible."

"Which leads us to my next question..." His eyes widen knowing what's coming next. "Charlie?"

"What about her?"

"That night... The way you were..." I sit up and look at the lake, feeling overwhelmed by his intense stare. "You were different."

He's silent as he moves some of the food aside and comes to sit beside me, the heat of his body warming mine.

We might be having unusually warm weather for this time of year, but we're still sitting outside at night in winter.

A shiver rips through me and before I know what's happening, he's pulling a hoodie from the bag and wrapping it around my shoulders.

"Th-thank you," I whisper, pulling it around me and breathing in his scent.

"Charlie was..." He blows out a long breath as he tries to find the right words. "My life hasn't been all that great recently. I went to a bar, had a little too much to drink and I just needed to forget for a bit, you know?"

I nod, understanding that concept more than I'm sure he appreciates. Although I've never used drinking and sex to make it happen. But I do get it.

"But she wasn't what I needed, not really."

"Because she's not your type."

"Partly. I thought I was looking for something meaningless to just take the edge off but I don't think that's what I needed."

I wince slightly at his ability to use sex and another person like that but I fight to keep my reaction inside because I really don't think he needs me judging him right now. And let's face it, I've already done plenty of that where he's concerned.

"I know you think I have it all. That I'm some pigheaded football player who thinks he's God's gift to the game and women. I probably act like that more than I should. But it's not who I really am. Meaningless nights with faceless jersey chasers isn't all it's cracked up to be."

"No? I thought it was what you all lived for," I deadpan.

"As high school kids, yeah. But things aren't always as incredible as they're made out to be."

"So what do you want?" I ask, pulling my knees up to my chest and wrapping my arms around them.

"Something more." I suck in a sharp breath when his fingers touch my ear once more. "I want more than one night, Red. I want more than just sex.

"My brother, my best friend. They've found it. I'm surrounded by these couples and I want it. I want to look at my person and to have her know exactly what I'm thinking just from my eyes. I want to fall asleep with her in my arms and wake up the same way the next morning knowing that she's mine."

My breathing becomes labored the more he speaks.

"It sounds perfect," I whisper, trying to imagine what it must be like to have that kind of connection with someone. Especially since I've spent the better part of eighteen years believing it only exists in the movies.

"I want it."

His fingers touch my jaw, giving me no choice but to turn my head to look at him.

My lips part the second I look into his eyes.

"Do you?" he whispers and I nod despite the fact I've no freaking clue what I'm agreeing to.

I blame the half a glass of champagne I've consumed.

His hand wraps around the side of my neck. His touch is at odds with how he held me Sunday night, and even earlier when he pinned me against the wall. But despite the lightness to it, it ignites something within me, something intense, something that I've never felt before.

His eyes hold mine as he leans in toward me.

Time stands still.

I stop breathing.

Until it all comes out in a rush when his lips brush mine.

"Tell me no, Red," he breathes. His lips gently caressing mine with each word.

"I-I can't," I whisper so quietly I don't think he's heard it.

But then a second passes and I realize that he did because his grip on my neck tightens and his lips press against mine with much less hesitancy.

Oh God.

He keeps it innocent for long seconds, kissing me gently, nipping at my bottom lip until he finally loses his fight with his restraint because his tongue sneaks out and teases my bottom lip before slipping into my mouth the second I open for him.

"Macie," he moans, tilting my head exactly as he wants it and plunges his tongue into my mouth, searching for mine which is more than willing to join in.

Our kiss goes on and on, and I totally lose myself to the feel of it, to the sparks that shoot off around my body from his simple hold on my neck and the brush of his tongue against mine alone.

A tight ball of desire forms in my lower belly making me want things I never really thought about before. Images of this going further pop into my mind, and it takes me a while to realize that it doesn't freak me out. Part of me wants him to push, just to see how I'd react. He might have been right earlier about making me a little bad. Because right now, I feel wild and I know it's all because of him.

When he brings the kiss to an end, it's entirely too soon.

Dragging his lips away, he rests his brow against mine, and after a few seconds, he opens his eyes.

The green is so dark, cloaked with desire and need and it makes everything south of my stomach clench.

I did that.

I caused that.

"I should get you back."

"B-back?"

"Yeah, it's getting late."

He pulls back and the space allows a little reality to slip back in.

"Y-yeah, I guess it is."

My cheeks burn as he watches me ensuring that all the things I was thinking about while he kissed me never really leave my head.

"What are you thinking about, Red?" he asks.

Mindlessly, I lift my fingers to my lips.

"You."

The smile that curls at the sides of his lips makes me want to crawl onto his lap and allow him to make me as bad as he wants. But I swallow my inner wild child down knowing that nothing good will come from her rearing her head.

He pushes up from the ground and holds his hand out to pull me up.

I slide my much tinier one into his giant paw and he hauls me up and directly into his body.

Wrapping his arm and mine behind my back he holds me in place.

"Thank you for tonight," he whispers.

"Shouldn't I be the one saying that? You did all the work."

"But you made it perfect."

I can't help it, I swoon hard. Too hard.

"Come on, you need your beauty sleep for class tomorrow."

He releases me, although he looks reluctant to do it and together we tidy everything up before heading to his car.

"What about the rest of it?" I ask, the fairy lights still shining bright.

"I'll come back. Don't worry."

I smile at him across the trunk of his car. "Okay."

The second he's put the car into drive, he reaches over and takes my hand, lacing his fingers through mine, holding it tightly. I find it way more comforting than I know I should.

"Where'd you grow up?"

"Pittsburgh," I lie, my stomach twisting painfully that I still feel the need to do so. It's not an all-out lie. Pittsburgh is where I lived with my parents before they died. I just haven't been back there since then. "You?"

"Rosewood. It's the next town over. You miss it?" he asks.

"Nah. This place feels more like home than anywhere else I've lived."

He nods, accepting my words as the truth.

Guilt sits heavy in my stomach but it's the way it has to be. He might have somehow managed to break down a few of my barriers tonight, as well as shatter my clearly mistaken assumptions about him, but he's not getting anything else out of me. I've told no one the truth about my life. My roommates know more than most, but even that is the least I could get away with so they can feel like they actually know me.

"What about when you're done here? Any plans for where you want to play next?"

"I've got a wish list sure, but I'm not putting all my hopes on one team. I'm happy to go with the flow."

"That probably makes it easier."

"I can only hope."

We chat about other nonsensical things as we make our way back across town once more, and all too soon, we're pulling up outside my dorm building.

He undoes his seat belt like he's about to walk me up and I panic.

"It's okay, you don't need to."

Looking over, he studies me for a beat.

"You ashamed of me, Red?"

"What? No."

"So you're not hiding this from your roommates."

"I don't know what this is, Leon. I don't want them sticking their noses in my business."

"You think they won't approve?"

"I don't know. They don't know you. I don't know you. And you're a football player and I—"

My words are cut off when he pulls me over the center console and claims my lips like he now owns them.

He kisses me long and hard until I damn near forget my own name, let alone what we were just talking about.

"It's okay," he says when he pulls back, rubbing his thumb over my bottom lip. "I get it."

I nod, believing that he does.

This thing, whatever it is that's crackling between us, if it's as confusing to him as much as it is to me then I can't imagine he wants one hundred and one questions about it either.

"Some friends of mine are having a party on Friday night. You wanna come with me?"

"Uh..." His face drops a little that I might be about to say no. "I'm not really a partier," I confess.

"How about we just show our faces for a bit then we can go do something else?"

"Okay, sure. So I'll see you Friday then?"

"Not sure I'll be able to wait that long."

"Stop," I beg, not believing it.

"You need to go before I change my mind and take you home."

"Okay, I'm going."

He drops one more chaste kiss to my lips before he releases me and I'm able to climb from the car.

8

LEON

My fists curl as I watch Macie disappear into her dorm building after giving me a girly wave. My short nails dig into my palms giving me just a hint of the pain I need.

She's... not what I was expecting.

I'd made her out in my head over the years to be this confident, evil, gives zero fucks redhead. And yet meeting her I discover that she's this shy, slightly sarcastic yet totally endearing young woman.

Stretching my legs out, I pull on my pants, giving my semi some fucking breathing space.

Kissing her. Fuck. It's addictive.

It shows me just how innocent she is and fuck if that doesn't make me hard as fucking nails.

For years I've imagined how I would get revenge for what she did to me. I've come up with a million and one creative ways to make her pay. Never did I even contemplate that it would actually be this easy.

I mean, a few fairy lights and a picnic by a lake and her well built up walls are already beginning to crumble around her feet.

I'd be naïve to think it's going to be that easy though.

I haven't missed the way she dodges any kind of conversation about her past, her family, or the blatant lies she told me about her life before MKU. It's going to take more than half a glass of champagne and a romantic date to get the information I need out of her. I also know that I'm not giving her until Friday to realize that she made a massive mistake by letting me get close tonight.

Macie has no idea, but I'm not letting her forget about me for even a second because one way or another, everything I've dreamed about since I was eleven years old, is going to happen.

My mouth waters. The devastation I need to reap is almost in touching distance, and I can't fucking wait.

Running my hand through my hair, I shift in my seat once more. I throw the car into drive to head back across town because my night so far has been way too sweet and romantic for my taste. I need to remember just who I am and what my MO is here.

Pain, and vengeance.

I repeat the journey back through town until I cross the border out of Maddison County toward Harrow Creek.

The warehouse where the Harris brothers took Brett is in the middle of nowhere. I never would have known it existed if they didn't take me there, and I'm sure the rest of the locals have no idea it exists either. It's perfect for the Hawks to do their business though.

I find myself on a second dirt road for the day as I head around the back and park under the cover of the trees just like Reid and Devin instructed. I grab the key from the glove box along with a pair of gloves.

My blood burns hot through my veins with my need to hurt someone. I might be okay with a little delayed gratification but now that I have Macie in my grasp, my patience is waning.

The rattle of the metal door echoes through the silent space as I unhook the padlock and throw it to the ground, letting myself into the cold and damp warehouse.

I have no clue what's behind the other doors in the vast building. Other prisoners? Guns? Drugs?

I figured the first time I was here with the Harrises that it was probably for the best I don't even ask. I can't help being curious though as I pass each door and head toward our beloved father.

"H-hello?" he rasps the second I step inside and slam the door behind me.

The room smells like piss, I guess that should come as no surprise really seeing as he's shut in one tiny room with absolutely zero facilities.

Reid and Devin promised me that they'd... keep him alive for me. I want to say I'm grateful, but I'm not entirely sure that I am.

"S-son?" Brett asks, looking up at me from the other side of the room when I locate the switch and illuminated the space with a harsh electric light.

The room itself is all gray, concrete and incredibly cold.

Brett is huddled in the corner with a dirty blanket over his shivering body, a chain attached to both his legs to stop him from moving more than a few feet.

The sight of him settles something inside me. That dark monster that began to grow the second he sent me to hell all those years ago.

"I'm not your son," I spit, lowering myself into the chair that's well out of his reach. Leaning forward, I rest my elbows on my knees and keep my eyes on his.

This is the first time I've been here and he's been awake.

I have no idea what they gave him Friday night to knock him out, but it was good stuff. Last night when I came, he was still out cold.

As far as I know, this is his first sign that his own flesh and blood has anything to do with his current situation.

"P-please. Get me out of here. I have no idea who they are but... but they're savage."

A laugh bubbles up my throat at his words.

"Why do you think you're here? Do you think they give two shits about you?"

"I-I don't—"

"If it were up to them, you'd already be dead and in the ground, you sick fuck."

"W-wha—"

"Don't," I boom, my voice echoing off the walls around me. "Don't try and play the innocent card with me. I know the monster you are. I know the evil that flows through your veins. Do you know how?"

He swallows, holding my eyes but he never responds.

"Because it runs through mine too. Your need to ruin everyone's lives? Yeah, I seem to have inherited it. And do you know who I'm starting with?"

I'd imagine that if he weren't already pale as fuck, that the blood might have just drained from his face, but as it is, I just have to imagine that reaction.

"The sick cunt who thought it would be a good idea to go after a minor in order to ruin the best thing in his son's life. The monster who got that minor pregnant. Drove her to a life of addiction which meant she couldn't be a mother. And the same woman who just OD'd because she can't cope with her reality. A reality that a certain fucking joke of a man caused."

"W-what are you talking—"

"I said don't," I seethe, pissed off beyond belief that even now, when he's utterly helpless, that he just can't admit the truth. "We know everything, *Dad*," I spit. "I've even met my little brother."

"No," he cries, pushing to sit upright but not having the strength in his arms to do it.

Seeing him so weak, so useless fills me with so much fucking joy after all the years of control and bullshit.

"Yes."

"And do you know what else?" I ask, although I don't wait for a response. "I found... *her.*"

His brows pull together as he tries to keep up with me.

"Her?" he whispers, his voice hoarse from lack of liquid.

"Macie Fletcher. You remember her, right? You remember what I told you she saw?"

He shakes his head.

"She's going to lead me right to him."

"Leon, please—"

"No," I shout, standing abruptly, sending the chair crashing to the ground behind me.

"Too late, old man. The time has long passed for you to tell me that it's okay. That it's normal. That I just need to be a fucking man. He might have been the one to hurt me, but you let it happen. I told you. I fucking told you," I seethe, marching over to him, spittle flying from my mouth. "I told you everything and you brushed it under the carpet just like you always do because the only fucking thing that matters to you is our success so that you look good. Who gives a fuck if your sons are falling apart beneath it, huh?"

Before I know what I'm doing, my shoe connects with his ribs and a painful crack fills the room before he screams in pain.

With a satisfied smile playing on my lips, I bend down to my haunches.

"All you did, old man, is create a monster who's as sick and twisted as you. And while you've tried to ruin our lives, you've failed because I'll be the one to put an end to all of it.

"You," I spit. "Macie. *Him.* And I'm going to enjoy every fucking second of it."

"Leon, no. Please," he cries as I march from the room, knowing that if I stay any longer, that I'll end up killing him.

If I wanted that to happen, I'd have let Reid and Devin do it on Friday night.

No, death is too easy. Too fast. He's made us suffer for twenty-one fucking years. This isn't going to be quick.

The slam of the door echoes around the space for long seconds as I talk myself down from going back in there.

"Fuck. FUCK," I shout, slamming my palms down on the wall in front of me when I realize that the only thing that distracts me from walking straight back in there is her.

Her and her innocent eyes and sweet smile.

"FUCK," I boom. My fists clench and my muscles tighten to throw a punch, but I know I can't. Busted knuckles will invite questions I can't give her the answers to.

I force myself to think back to that day. The day she looked into my eyes, saw what was happening, turned her back and left me there. Left me in the hands of a monster.

She could have saved me. But she didn't.

So now, I need to remember that I have no reason to save her.

———

"Where have you been?" Peyton asks the second I get to the top floor of the house.

"Out, obviously."

She rolls her eyes at me but doesn't get to respond because the door opens and Luca appears.

"Ah, you remember where you live."

"Fuck off."

"Come on, baby," he whispers to Peyton, nuzzling her neck.

The move sends a wave of jealousy through me. What I said to Macie earlier was true. I want what Luca and Peyton, and Letty and Kane have. Although I'm aware that I'll probably never have it. If I let anyone too close, they'll run a mile. If by some miracle they don't, then I have no doubt that I'll fuck it up one way or another. Self-sabotage is my specialty. So the second things are looking like they might just go well, I'll do something stupid and ruin it all in the process.

"Just give me a minute," she says, dropping a kiss on his cheek and pressing a hand to his chest to make him go back inside.

"I don't need the speech, Peyton," I say, predicting the words that are about to fall from her lips.

"Who's the girl?"

My brows draw together.

"The girl you went out with tonight."

"H-how do you... No one."

"That's bullshit and you know it. She's the reason you were asking me about my picnic date with Luca on the weekend, wasn't she?"

"I don't know what you're talking about," I lie.

"Leon," she breathes, sounding exasperated. "Letty knows too."

"Fucking Micah," I mumble.

"You can't blame him, he was pissed. He wanted to ask her out."

"He's a little bitch. She can do better."

Peyton rears back in shock.

"Oh? I thought she was no one."

"She is. Fuck. I..."

"Talk to me, Lee."

"She is no one. A redhead I want to roll around in the sack with."

I take a step back toward my room—my escape.

"You're lying."

"And? Stay out of my business, Peyton."

"We will find out what you're hiding, Lee."

"Whatever." I slip into my room and lock my door behind me.

They're not going to find out because not only do none of them deserve to be tangled up in this mess with Brett, but learning the truth would kill them. And I refuse to do it to them when they've already been through so much because of that cunt.

Falling down onto my bed, I blow out a long breath. I push my hand into my pocket, pulling out Macie's cell.

Ignoring the guilt that threatens knowing that I stole it from her jacket pocket before she got out of my car. I wake it up and stare at the quote that covers her home screen.

Don't tell people your dreams. Show them.

I think over her words for the longest time, wondering what her dreams are. Wondering who she really is.

Unsurprisingly, when I eventually try to unlock the cell, the passcode pops up.

I tap my finger against the side as I attempt to predict what she might use.

Something tells me that it won't be random. Her room was nothing if not organized, everything in its rightful place.

I try a few combinations but eventually get locked out.

"Dammit."

Placing it on my nightstand, I head for the shower, combinations of numbers running through my head.

Thanks to Ellis, I've got all of Macie's MKU enrollment details. If I can't find something in there to get me into her cell then I guess, I'll be visiting the Harrises again to get him to hack into it.

9

___

MACIE

"**Y**ou gonna tell me where you were last night, yet?" a familiar voice says from behind me before Charlie steps up beside me as I walk across campus after my last class of the day ready to head home.

"I... uh..."

"Don't say you were at the library, we know you weren't."

I blow out a frustrated breath.

"Why does it matter? I was out."

"Hmm..." she mumbles, her eyes focused on the side of my face. "Your cell broken or something? I messaged you to meet for lunch," she says, thankfully diverting from interrogating me about last night. She already tried before class this morning. I thought she'd get the message that there wasn't anything to talk about.

"No, I think I left it in my room," I lie. I know it's not in my room, although I don't actually know where it is. But the last place I remember having it was sitting on that blanket with Leon last night. Thoughts of it falling out and lost in the grass somewhere fill my head.

Even if I found my way back there, it rained all morning so it's probably ruined now anyway.

It's no big deal. There's nothing on it, and I can count the people I talk to on it on one hand.

"Well, you got a million messages from me."

"Great, I'll look forward to them," I deadpan, already knowing that I'll have a stream of totally inappropriate memes if I ever do find it again.

"Yo, Charlie," a guy calls the second he emerges from the building in front of us. He smiles as he blatantly checks her out and she squeals in excitement.

"Hate to love you and leave you but..."

"Go. Go. Just maybe don't bring this one home."

"Aw, you know you love it."

"Oh yeah, the highlight of my week listening to you scream for God." I roll my eyes at her as she bounces off toward whoever the guy is.

It makes my mind wander to last night. To him.

Even after what could possibly be described as the most romantic date ever, I'm still completely confused by the whole situation.

The naïve little girl inside me who wants to be liked wants to believe that maybe he did just want to spend the night with me, get to know me. But the rational, more sensible side of me knows that there's no way it can all be real.

Boys like Leon Dunn just aren't interested in introvert nerds like me. Not in a million years.

My life isn't like the movies. And I'm under no illusion that I'm about to buck the trend and be that shy geek who gets the popular boy in the end. That is not real life.

I trudge up to our dorm, knowing that I'm going to have to go back out and get a new cell and see if I can get the number switched over in case of emergencies.

The place is empty with Charlie distracted with her latest bed buddy and the guys are at training. So after grabbing a giant bag of chips and a can of soda from the kitchen, I make my way to my room ready to get to work while I've got some peace and quiet.

Juggling my snack and bags, I manage to get the door open without dropping anything, and I'm just about to turn and dump everything on my desk when a figure in my room scares the crap out of me.

"What the hell are you doing?" I squeal as everything clatters to the floor around my feet.

"Surprise," Leon says, a wide smile curls at his lips.

"Jesus, you could have warned me," I say, covering my racing heart with my hand.

"Sorry," he says, pushing up from my bed and coming over to help me.

Well, that's what I expect him to do, but when he gets to me, he ignores the disaster around me, takes my face in his hands and instead just stares down into my eyes.

"Hey," I squeak.

"Hey, Red." His lips are on mine before I even have time to think about what I might say next.

His kiss is brief, almost innocent but I can feel his need to make it more. Hell, my own need is almost too hard to ignore. I remember all too well how good it felt making out with him last night.

"So... uh... how'd you get in here?" I ask when he pulls back and eventually helps me pick everything up.

"Now that would be telling," he says with a wink. "But I do have something that belongs to you."

He places my bags on my chair and turns to me, pulling my cell from his pocket.

"You left it in my car."

"Ah, thank you."

I light it up to see if I've missed anything, but exactly as I was expecting the only message alerts are from Charlie.

"Popular as always, I see."

Ignoring her messages, knowing they'll be pointless, I place it on my nightstand.

"So you just broke in to return my cell?"

"And to see you."

I stand in the middle of my room, staring down at him sitting on the edge of my bed like he belongs, and wonder what the hell happened to my quiet, reclusive life.

"Shouldn't you be training or something?"

"Trying to get rid of me, Red?"

"N-no, I-I just... I wasn't expecting this."

"What did you have planned for the night?"

My lips part but I hesitate because my plans make me sound like the most boring person on campus.

"Party for one with my chips and law assignment."

"You really know how to party," he says with a smile. "When's it due?"

"Th-the assignment?"

"Yeah."

"Umm... in four weeks."

"And you're doing it tonight?"

"Well, it was assigned today and—"

I cut my words off when his smile only gets wider.

"You're cute."

"I'm not. I'm focused. I've got plans, and I want to stay ahead."

"I noticed." He nods toward my cell, or more importantly, the quote I'm sure he read that's my screensaver.

I know that most people usually have a photo of friends or family on theirs, but seeing as I'm mostly lacking both, I went with a reminder of what I'm trying to achieve.

"I know you think I'm boring. But I—"

"I don't," he says, reaching for my hand and pulling me onto the bed with him.

My heart jumps into my throat as he sits me across his lap and places his giant hands on my denim-clad thighs.

"I don't think you're boring, Red. I think you're dedicated and passionate. I like that."

His hands slide up to my waist, slipping under the fabric of my shirt and burning my bare skin.

"Leon," his name rips from my lips as a moan. A plea, maybe.

"Don't apologize for being you, Red."

His fingers tighten against me with his words and I melt.

Sitting forward, he brushes his lips against mine.

"I need to study too," he confesses, "but I was planning something much more... hands on than a law textbook."

His tongue delves past my lips as I suck in a shocked gasp and I'm powerless but to respond despite the fact my body is damn near trembling with nerves.

I don't do this. I don't have boys in my room.

I don't—

"Oh God,' I sigh when he kisses down my neck and sucks on this spot that makes my entire body erupt in goose bumps.

"L-Leon," I stutter, fighting like hell to keep my head and not let my body take over this situation.

Pressing my hands to his chest, I push lightly and he pulls back.

His eyes are so dark they're almost black when he stares into mine, his lips swollen from our kiss.

"Wanna go and get dinner?" he asks, clearly sensing my need to slow this down a little.

"D-dinner?"

"Yeah, you know, food that people eat in the evening."

"I know what dinner is, you fool." I swat at his chest. "I just... you want to go and get dinner with me?"

"Why are you finding all of this so hard to believe, Red?" He reaches up and cups my cheek. "You're beautiful, smart, funny. Why wouldn't I want to go to dinner with you?"

All my insecurities come rushing forward but I force them down because he really doesn't need to see that side of me. He knows I'm confused by all of this, I really don't need to keep bringing it up.

"O-okay. Dinner." I smile at him, part of me regrets agreeing because it means we'll no longer be alone and I can't deny that there's something a little thrilling about being in a room with just the two of us.

"You're going to need to get off me then," he says with a wink.

"Crap, yeah. Sorry."

"Red." The dominance in his tone makes me stop my escape immediately. "Never apologize for wanting to get on top."

"Oh my God," I mutter, my cheeks burning with the image he plants in my head. Heat surges through my body, my lower half clenching with need. "I'll just be a few..." I trail off as I head for my bathroom but when I'm at the door, something makes me turn and look over my shoulder.

My eyes almost pop out of my head when I find him rearranging himself. Rearranging himself because of me.

I'm not stupid, I know I don't have the appeal of Charlie or any of the girls I grew up around, but knowing I've affected him in that way causes a wave of pride to wash over me.

Maybe I am more than the shy geeky girl I've always tried so hard to be.

As if he senses my attention he glances up through his lashes at me.

He looks too damn beautiful. It should annoy me that he knows it too, but I can't find it in myself to care.

"What?" He smiles at me, not having a care in the world that I just caught him.

"W-we could order in," I offer.

His smile widens more, a dimple appearing on one side and I realize that I could have just made a mistake.

It's clear what he wants from me. But after two days of knowing him, that is not going to happen, no matter how much he looks at me like I'm the only woman in the world.

Leon Dunn might make my head spin, but it's going to take more than a wicked smile and a few hot kisses to get anything else out of me.

I haven't waited this long to just give it all away on a whim. And certainly not to a football player.

"I'm easy."

I can't help it, I snort out a laugh.

"Yeah, most of campus is aware of that, Dunn."

His lips part as faux hurt covers his face.

"Oh please, don't even try to look offended. I might not go to all the parties and see you in action but I know your rep just as much as anyone else."

"I didn't come here to hook up, Red. I came to hang out, to get to know you better."

"I thought you came to bring my cell back."

"Yeah, that was the perfect excuse."

"Ah, so you stole my cell so you had a reason to see me again."

He holds his hands up in surrender, with a playful smile on his lips. "Guilty."

"You're a goofball."

"Your call, Red. Takeout, or go out?"

I hold his eyes for a beat, while my head and body is at war with my decision.

"Out. Give me five."

I slip into the bathroom, close the door behind me and lean back against it.

My heart is still racing from when I first found him here and my whole body is burning up, just two of the reasons why the decision I made is the right one.

The less time we spend locked in a room and on a bed is probably for the better. At least until I do figure out what this is.

I use the toilet and refresh my hair and makeup before sucking in a steeling breath and stepping back into my room.

I find Leon exactly where I left him, sitting on the end of my bed only now he has his cell in his hand, scrolling through something

"What, no basketball jersey?" he deadpans.

"Not tonight. Ready?"

"Sure."

He follows me out through our still empty dorm and in only a couple of minutes, I'm in his car once again.

"Where to tonight then?" I ask, completely confused as to how sitting in Leon Dunn's passenger seat now almost feels normal.

"Burgers?"

"Sure. I'm easy."

He glances over at me, amusement sparkling in his green orbs.

"I thought that was me."

"When there's food involved, it's a different story."

"Good to know, Red. Good to know."

He puts the radio on and we drive through town chatting about nonsense until I realize that we've once again passed almost everything.

"Where are we going?"

"To the most insane burger place in the state."

"Oh? And here I was thinking you were taking me somewhere we wouldn't be recognized," I confess, allowing a little of my insecurity out. I can't help it, I'm too intrigued to know his reasons for coming this far out of town.

"Never. I just want to make sure you're satisfied."

"I'm sure you've more than got that covered, Dunn."

He laughs as he pulls into a parking lot behind a diner and kills the engine.

"You're still coming to the party Friday night, right?"

"Um..."

"Now who's the one who's hiding?" he raises a brow but I know he's only teasing.

"If I thought you wanted it, I'd tell the world, but something tells me that's the last thing you'd ask me to do."

"You're right. I like my life in the shadows," I confess.

"Well, you're going to have to get used to coming out a little."

Before I can respond, he's out of the car and I've got no choice but to follow.

10

MACIE

Leon wasn't wrong. The burger was probably one of the best I've ever had in my life. But it's not the food that has a smile on my face the whole way back toward campus, because he's the reason.

The whole evening has just been perfect, much like the previous one and I'm finding it harder and harder to remember that this can't be real.

Everything about it is just too... right. He's too sweet, too thoughtful. Too... perfect.

He's making my head spin and I'm slowly losing grip on the armor I've built up around myself. No one else I've ever met has managed to get through. It's the reason I've never had any kind of meaningful relationships, whether that be friendships or more. From a very early age, I learned not to trust people—even those who claim to love you—so I force everyone out.

I told myself I didn't need people. I've been my own cheerleader, voice of reason and sounding board for years. It's the way I always told myself it needed to be.

Yet three days with Leon. Just three days and I'm already starting to question just how lonely my previous life was.

Sure, I've always had people around me. But none of them have ever known me, even got inside my head... my heart.

Nathan is the closest friend I've ever had, and yet, he's still very much on the periphery of my life. I told myself that it's because he's an athlete, and I know that I need to stay well and clear of them. But since spending time with Leon, I know it's not that. Nathan and I are just friends.

But the football player I've always fiercely told myself I'd never go near. Yeah... he's making all kinds of crazy thoughts whip around my head, causing unfamiliar feelings to shoot through my body.

It's all wrong because even before meeting him, I knew I couldn't trust him. Yet here I am, having had my what... third date with him in as many days. And wondering if I should invite him back up to my dorm room consequences be damned just because something about this, about the connection that's always crackling away between us, just feels so right.

"What are you thinking about, Red?" he asks. It seems to be his favorite question. "I hope it's me again."

I nod, unable to deny that it is, but I swallow down the questions that want to blurt from my mouth. My need to know what he thinks this is, where he thinks it could go.

We met on Sunday under circumstances I mostly would rather never think of again. Somehow he's caught me up in this whirlwind that I'm not sure I want to escape from if I'm being really honest with myself.

"Thank you for tonight. You really are quite good at this dating thing, but then I guess that's what happens when you've had so many."

His fingers tighten on the wheel and he glances over at me.

"Last night..." he starts, lifting his hand to his hair and pushing it back from his brow almost as if he's nervous. "That was the first time I planned any kind of date for a girl."

"Shut up," I argue, not wanting to accept that it could possibly be true.

"It was. The girls I've hung out with before... I've only..."

"Screwed them," I finish for him.

Pulling into the lot behind my dorm once more, he kills the engine and turns to look at me.

"Yeah. I've got a rep for a reason and I'm not going to pretend I don't. Although, I can tell you that it's not actually as bad as people make it out to be."

"Sure."

"Seriously, compared to some of the other guys, I'm a saint."

"Saint Leon... good to know."

"None of them meant anything, Red."

"And I do?" *Shit.* I mentally kick myself for letting that question slip out.

"Yeah," he breathes, his eyes holding mine for a beat before they drop to my lips. "Let me walk you up tonight."

"U-uh... okay. J-just to the door though," I blurt out, knowing that I can't trust myself, let alone him if I allow him back into my room.

He nods before pushing from the car and coming around to meet me when I join him.

The second I'm at full height, he pulls me into his body and wraps his arm around my waist.

His warmth, his scent, his touch, all of it makes me feel too safe, too comfortable. It's dangerous because all the while my blood is boiling having him so close and as much as it excites me, it terrifies me in equal measures.

For the first time in my life, I'm scared I'm going to throw caution to the wind and jump in with both feet when I really should keep a levelhead.

But isn't life all about taking a few risks when it feels right? A little voice pipes up as we make our way to the building.

There are other students milling about but no one pays us any attention as we make our way inside and up the stairs to my floor.

The seconds we're at the main door to our dorm, Leon pushes me back against the wall and cages me in.

My heart thunders in my chest as I stare into his dark, heated eyes.

I know what he wants, I can read it on every inch of his face. But he's trying to be a gentleman and I can't help but appreciate the fact he's trying. Since I know full well that a kiss goodnight with a girl isn't his usual MO.

"Thank you for tonight," he murmurs.

"Thanks for bringing my cell back."

"The pleasure's all mine, Red."

His hand moves the side of my neck as his lips descend on mine.

My stomach tingles with butterflies before my muscles pull tight when he plunges his tongue into my mouth and twists it against mine.

A low growl rumbles up his throat and it causes a wave of heat to wash through my body.

"Oh God," I moan when his hand wraps around the back of my thigh and he lifts it around his waist.

"Can't get enough," he groans in my ear, lightly nipping at it, sending a bolt of pleasure right between my legs.

"Leon," I moan as he kisses down my throat, licking and nipping at the skin as he goes.

His lips hit the neckline of my shirt as he replaces them with his hand, pinning me back against the wall like he did that very first night.

I gasp when his dangerous eyes bore into mine.

If I'd ever thought about being in this position before, then I'd have thought I'd be terrified. But that is the opposite of what I feel as I stand pinned to the wall with his hard body pressed against me and his hand around my throat.

"You've got no idea, do you?"

My brows pinch together as I stare at him, wondering what he's talking about.

"No fucking idea just how badly I want you. Need you."

His fingers tighten for a beat before his lips slam back down on mine.

He consumes me, utterly freaking consumes every single thought and feeling in my body as his tongue caresses mine. His hips roll, allowing me to feel exactly what I do to him.

"Fucking hell, Char— whoa," Nathan barks the second he realizes that it's me.

Pushing against Leon's chest, I eventually get him to back up as

Nathan looks between the two of us with a bemused expression on his face.

Wrapping a hand around Leon's wrist I pull his hand from my throat, immediately missing the pressure of it.

"I'm sorry, I'll just..." Nathan steps toward the door to give us some privacy.

"Nate," I call out to him before he disappears.

He looks back, concern for me written all over his face.

"P-please, don't—"

"I hope you know what you're doing, Mace."

He's gone before I get to tell him that I have no freaking clue.

"Jesus," I breathe, resting my forehead against Leon's heaving chest.

"Hey, you okay?" he asks, tucking his fingers under my chin and forcing me to look up at him.

"Y-yeah. I just..." My head spins as I look at him. I'm still vividly remembering exactly how he felt only seconds ago pressed against me, his length rubbing against my core.

My cheeks heat at the memory, at the way my body burned for more.

"You should probably go."

I expect him to refuse. To demand that I let him come in with me and continue what we've started. But much to my surprise, he nods and takes a step back, putting some space between us and taking his heat with him.

"Yeah, I really should."

My fingers curl with my need to reach out to him, to feel him against me once more.

"Friday night, yeah?"

I nod.

"Okay. Friday night."

With his eyes still locked on mine, he backs away.

The air between us crackles but both of us fight it.

With one final nod, he turns away from me and sets off down the stairs.

Jesus Christ.

Lifting my hand to my chest, I rest back against the wall. I close my eyes for a beat as I try to get myself under control.

If Nathan didn't interrupt us I have no idea where we would have ended up. I want to say I'd have stopped him but... part of me wonders if I would have.

Lifting my hand, I run my fingertips over my lips and then down my neck to where he held me.

You shouldn't like that, a little voice says in my head.

But I did. I loved it.

Damn you, Leon Dunn. You're messing with my head.

Once I've got my heart rate somewhat back to normal, I pull my key out of my purse and let myself inside. The place is empty so I head straight to Nathan's room.

I notice that his door is slightly ajar, I knock on it lightly and hesitantly push it open. I've got no idea what he's going to say to me about what he witnessed. If he's going to be pissed that the first person he's seen me with is the exact person I said I'd never go out with. Well, not Leon specifically, but a football player. I'm not exactly quiet with my hatred of them so I can only imagine his reaction to this.

"Hey," I say, finding him sitting at his desk staring at his laptop.

"You came up for air then?"

"Christ," I mutter, threading my fingers through my hair and pulling it all back from my face.

"You know who he is right?"

"Of course. He's Leon freaking Dunn. The Panther's wide receiver. Number fourteen. A freaking football player." He cocks his brow at my excessive amount of detail. "I-I— crap." Throwing my hands up in frustration, I invite myself into his room and drop onto the end of his bed.

"You've seriously got no idea what you're doing, do you?"

Falling back, I stare at his ceiling.

"No," I confess.

"I knew something was up when I saw you getting out of his car the other night."

"Monday night was a coincidence."

"But I'm assuming tonight wasn't."

"Well, actually it kind of was but only because of our date last night."

"You went on a date with Leon Dunn?" he asks, sounding astounded.

"Yeah, why?" I ask pushing up to my elbows so I can look at him.

"He doesn't date girls."

"No, he just... he just does that in hallways." Nathan's brow lifts as if to say 'and then some.' "Yeah, I know. I know, I just..."

"Mace," he says softly, dropping down beside me. "I don't know him that well, but... you need to be careful."

"You think I don't know that? This wasn't meant to happen, Nate. I wasn't meant to fal—" He looks at me with sympathy in his eyes. I thought there might be some judgment in there too, but thankfully, all I see is just concern.

"I just don't want to see you hurt."

"Me either. I know he's not a happily ever after kinda guy, but when I'm with him... I don't know... I'm... less boring, I guess. He brings something out in me."

"You're not boring, Mace."

I hold Nathan's eyes for a beat.

"I love you, Nate, but I think we both know that's a lie. The only thing I do that doesn't involve classes or studying is volunteering."

"That doesn't mean you're boring. There's nothing wrong with being focused on the future and knowing what you want."

"Even if that means I don't experience the present?"

"No one says college has to mean parties and hangovers."

"Or kissing hot guys in the hallway," I add, but regret it the second I think back and the tingles reemerge.

"Or that. It can be whatever you want it to be."

"He's invited me to a party Friday night," I blurt out. I know that he probably won't be impressed because he's been inviting me to weekly parties just as much as Charlie has.

"You going?"

"Um..."

"It's okay if you are."

"I told him I would."

"Do you know which party?"

I shake my head, feeling silly for not even asking.

"Charlie is going to be pissed. She's been desperate to corrupt you since the beginning of the year. I don't think she ever thought she'd lose the chance, especially to a football player. A football player she was seconds away from fucking Sunday night, I might add."

"Don't. Trust me, I'm not likely to forget about that."

"Imagine if you didn't walk in. You might not have met him."

Despite the fact I hate that I first came across him while he was otherwise engaged with Charlie, I can't deny that the thought of us not colliding into each other doesn't sit right with me.

"You really like him, don't you?"

"I don't really know him. I think it's too early to—"

His expression cuts my words off.

"Sometimes, I think you just know."

"Like we both know that it's going to end in disaster," I say with a wince.

"You don't know that."

"Don't I?"

He opens his mouth to respond but I continue before he gets a chance.

"I'm just going to enjoy the ride. See where it takes me. I might even learn a thing or two about myself along the way." *Like the fact I'm not totally boring and maybe people do actually see me in the shadows.*

11

LEON

"**A**nd here I was thinking you were going to make this hard for me," Letty says with a knowing smirk when I walk into the coffee shop she works in twenty minutes after leaving Macie.

"Thought I'd save you from chasing after me."

"I'm finishing in five. Grab a seat, I'll make you a drink."

The place is dead with only one other customer as I lower myself to the booth in the back of the small seating area.

I watch Letty as she moves around, cleaning up as she goes and chatting with the other lady who's working tonight.

After a couple of minutes, the other customer leaves and I watch as Letty locks the door behind her and flips the sign to closed before letting out a sigh.

"Long shift?" I ask when she heads over with my coffee in a takeout cup in hand.

"Long day," she says, smiling at her colleague who looks like she's about to disappear out the back before dropping onto the bench opposite me.

"Regretting it yet?" I ask as she pulls her cell out and taps away at the screen, probably messaging Kane.

"Never," she says with a wide smile. "I'd work all the hours if it meant Kane and I got the life we have together."

I can't help but smile at the happiness that radiates from her.

There was a time not so long ago that I'd have done anything to protect her from Kane, but it turns out that the only person she needs to protect her is him. It just goes to prove that things really aren't always simple and straightforward.

"He's coming to pick me up, I've just told him to wait for a bit so we can talk."

"Great," I mutter.

"Well, that's what you're here for, isn't it?"

I shrug, sliding down in the seat a little more. I reach for my coffee and take a sip, regretting it instantly when it damn near takes a layer of skin off my top lip.

"I guess."

Coming here and seeing her seemed like a good idea as I walked away from Macie. She's my voice of reason and I know that she'd never judge me if I ever found the courage to confess all my sins to her. And now that I'm sitting opposite her, staring into her dark eyes, I'm wondering if it was a mistake.

I should have just gone home and locked myself in my room. But I guess it's too late for regrets because I'm here now and she's looking at me like I'm about to bleed my secrets all over the table between us.

"So who is she?"

"You are aware that you're all a bunch of gossips, right?"

"Meh," she says with a laugh. "You totally rained on Micah's parade there, you know?"

"He isn't right for her," I say without thinking, which only serves to make Letty even more interested in what I've got to say.

Leaning forward, she rests her elbows on the table and waits.

"Her name is Macie. She's... different."

"So I heard. Micah said that she's shy, quiet. Not exactly the usual jersey chaser you hook up with." She raises a brow as she waits for me to argue.

"Maybe that's the appeal. I don't know," I say, scrubbing my hand down my face.

"You know, I've never seen you ever interested in a girl. It looks good on you. You look... I don't know, more relaxed."

I can't help but laugh. "Trust me, I really shouldn't be after what I just walked away from."

A smile curls at Letty's mouth. "She making you work for it?"

I can't help but smile to myself as I think about Macie's innocence. I tell myself that it's just because I'm already a little too invested and excited about ruining it, but I know that's mostly a lie. While I might want to ruin her, punish her. There's also a part of me that wants to claim her. Make her mine.

"Yeah. She's driving me crazy."

"Good. It's about time someone made you put a little effort in."

"I can do effort, I've already taken her on a date."

"Shut up, you haven't," Letty gasps, her eyes widening in shock.

"Yeah and it was all romantic as shit. I've got moves, Cupcake."

"I'm sure you have, Lee."

Silence settles between us as I drink my coffee. I keep my eyes on Letty, relieved to see that she's buying this little catch-up session because I can see her concern for me beginning to leave her.

I hate how everyone's been looking at me recently, like I'm a ticking time bomb. They're right of course, that's exactly what I am. What they're unaware of though, is that now that I've found Macie and got Brett exactly where I want him, that fuse is shorter than ever.

Years of patience, of waiting for vengeance on those who have wronged me, who hurt me, who used me are finally going to come to an end. And I can't fucking wait.

"I'm taking her out again on Friday," I confess.

"Wow, who are you and what have you done with Leon Dunn?"

"You know more than anyone that the right girl can change a guy."

"Hell yeah, I do."

And right on cue, there's a soft knock at the front door and when I look up, I find Kane standing there already smiling at Letty.

She rushes over and lets him in.

He immediately pulls her into his arms and shoves his tongue down her throat.

I'm instantly taken right back to the hallway with Macie and my cock swells once more. Fuck if I didn't want her to invite me in, even though I knew it would never happen.

She's not that girl, and despite the fact I'm not in this for the reasons she thinks I am. I like that she's different. I like the challenge. After all these years, I think I'd have been disappointed if I got to fuck her over right away.

Clearing my throat makes fuck all of a difference, both of them totally ignore me.

"Feel free to go at it if you want, you know I'll enjoy the show but I'm not sure the diners in the restaurant across the street want that kind of entertainment with their meals.

"Fuck you, Dunn," Kane mutters, flipping me off over Letty's shoulder. "You've had your time with my girl."

"Hell yeah, I have," I say with a wide smile and a wink, knowing that it'll wind him the fuck up.

"Did you want anything specific, Dunn?"

"He came to tell me about his girl," Letty interrupts our banter.

"A girl? She must be brave."

"I don't know about brave but she sounds like a sweet one."

"Then she must be stupid if she hasn't run a mile already."

"You're funny," I say, sliding from the bench and stealing Letty from Kane's side. "Thanks for the coffee, Cupcake."

Kane growls like a wild animal when I drop the quickest kiss to Letty's lips.

"Watch it, Dunn. I know some of your secrets, remember?"

I hold his eyes knowing that I can trust him with what he knows. There might have been a time when I wouldn't have trusted him with anything. But I love Letty like a sister, and I trust her, so that now extends to Kane. Plus, he did me a solid by hooking me up with the Harris brothers to help out with my little issue with my father.

"Should I be worried about whatever this is?" Letty asks, looking between the two of us.

"Nah, the only thing you should be worrying about is the fact Leon's found a girl."

"Right, on that note, I'm out," I say, moving toward the door.

"You know where I am if you need anything," Letty says softly.

"Sure do. See you later." With a smile at Letty and a nod at Kane, I slip out of the coffee shop knowing I achieved what I set out to achieve.

Letty's going to tell Peyton everything. I'm not all that happy about them digging into things with Macie, I just really need them to stop looking at me with sympathy and concern in their eyes.

I don't want it and I sure as hell don't need it.

I'm happy that things are moving in the right direction. When I get back to the house and find the others shooting the shit in the den with an old game playing on the flat screen on the wall, I join them for the first time in weeks.

If I really want everyone to believe that shit is getting back to normal then it's time to rejoin my old life.

Colt nods at me as I drop onto the other end of the couch.

"Good to see you, man," he says, throwing me a bottle.

None of us have ever been the kind of guys to talk about feelings and shit, but I can see in his eyes that it's his way of asking if I'm genuinely okay.

I smile at him as Evan continues telling everyone who's willing to listen about a chick and her two friends that he hooked up with over the weekend. Utter bullshit, he's got no idea what to do with one pussy, let alone three but everyone humors him while losing themselves in their own imaginations. I, however, only have one girl on my mind, and I can't help but wonder if she locked herself in her room and finished off what we started.

Pulling my cell from my pocket, I open my messages and find her contact.

If she thought I didn't get into her cell, then she's about to learn that that isn't exactly true.

12

MACIE

I'm almost asleep when my cell buzzes on my nightstand.

I'm tempted to ignore it knowing it'll be some spam message but something forces me to pull my arm from the warmth of my sheets and reach for it.

My eyes almost pop out of my head the second I get a look at the screen and see the name of the sender.

Your King.

I can't help the laugh that erupts from me as I read those two words.

I don't need to put any thought into who it is as I unlock my cell and open the message.

> Your King: Can't get you out of my head, Red.

My teeth sink into my bottom lip and heat races through my body once more as I read those words over and over.

He can obviously see that I've read the message because he starts typing.

> Your King: What are you thinking about?

Butterflies erupt in my belly knowing that he's on the other end waiting for my response.

> Macie: You.

My hands tremble as I hit send knowing that I'm about to embark on a conversation I'm not entirely sure I'm ready for with that response.

> Your King: I wish I was still there with you.

> Macie: Not sure you'd fit.

> Your King: Trust me, Red, I'll fit. We can make anything work.

"Oh God," I breathe but unable to wipe the smile from my face.

> Macie: I'm looking forward to Friday.

> Your King: Red… are you changing the subject?

> Macie: Maybe.

> Macie: What are you doing?

> Your King: Hanging out with the guys. You?

My hands tremble once more as I look down at my sheet-covered body. I should lie, I know I should.

> Macie: In bed. About to go to sleep.

> Your King: What are you wearing?

I almost change the subject again until a thought pops into my head.

> Macie: White cotton panties.

My laugh echoes around my silent room as I imagine his eyes widening at my comment.

> Your King: RED!! Fuck. The images in my head right now…

Truth is, I'm wearing a pair of pajamas that are covered in doughnuts, but he doesn't need to know that.

> Macie: Have a good night, Leon.

> Your King: You can't say things like that and then leave me hanging.

> Macie: Sorry, Dunn. I'm going to have to leave you with your imagination.

> Your King: Do you have any idea how badly I want to come back to see you right now?

Everything south of my waist pulls tight as I imagine him driving over and barging his way into my room to continue from where we left off earlier.

> Macie: Have fun with the guys. I'll see you Friday.

> Your King: Tease.

> Macie: Player.

I send it as a joke but then instantly regret it thinking that I might have offended him when he doesn't respond right away like all the previous messages.

I breathe a sigh of relief when the dots start bouncing once more.

> Your King: Only with you, Red. I like our games. ;-)

> Macie: Night, Leon. x

I hesitate over sending the kiss symbol, which is ridiculous seeing as I was all over him like a bad rash only a few hours ago. But still, it feels like a big deal when I see it in black and white on the screen.

In the end, I think screw it, and I hit send.

> Your King: Sweet dreams... of me. x

With a laugh, I place my cell back on the nightstand and curl back up. But sleep doesn't come for the longest time because I'm restless after that brief conversation. As well as the memories of his lips on mine and his hands on my body, of his... excitement against me.

I toss and turn for hours, most of my body out of the sheets because it's burning up with the thoughts. It's long past my usual bedtime when I finally do fall asleep.

—————

The first thing I do the next morning is reach for my cell. I immediately chastise myself for it, but equally, I can't help it.

I also can't help my stomach sinking in disappointment when I don't find anything from Leon.

I don't know what I was expecting, he's probably not even awake yet but still...

Unable to stop myself, I open our chat from last night and scroll back through our messages. As I read each one, I wonder again who this girl is he's turning me into.

I barely message anyone, let alone flirt with them.

I shake my head at myself and throw the covers off to get ready for the day.

I can't allow him to consume all my thoughts. He might be changing me in ways I never thought possible, but I refuse to lose myself to him or any guy.

I am not that kind of girl.

I make quick work of getting ready. I grab everything I'm going to need for a day of classes and my study session in the library tonight.

I battle with myself the whole time as to whether I should message and wish him a good morning. In the end, I manage to stop myself.

I don't want him to think I'm too eager, mainly because I shouldn't be this eager.

He's a football player, Macie I remind myself.

You shouldn't want him.

It doesn't matter what the little voice in my head says. My body seems to be getting more and more insistent because it knows exactly what it wants... more of last night.

"Morning, Mace," Nathan says when I make my way to the kitchen.

"Hey." I can't help the embarrassment that still floods me knowing what he saw last night.

"You okay?"

"Y-yeah. You?"

"Yeah."

He stares at me, his brow creased in concern. I know he probably wants to say a million and one things to me about the situation but he knows as well as I do that it'll be a waste of energy. I already know them all and I'm doing the total opposite.

"I'm ready, I'm ready," Jace says, running down the hallway still getting dressed.

"Jesus," Nathan mutters. "Have a good day, Mace. You know where I am if you need me."

"Thank you." I smile at him and watch the pair of them leave before making myself a coffee and following their footsteps not long after.

The morning drags as I sit in class waiting for my cell to buzz. But I get nothing until just before I head out for lunch.

Your King: I wish it was Friday already.

Macie: You should be in class.

Your King: I am. It's boring. Would rather be in yours.

Macie: I'm a dedicated student with serious classes. I hope you're not insinuating you'd be doing anything but working hard.

Your King: Of course not. I'd be studying real hard...

My fingers hover over the screen as I battle with myself not to tell him that I'm heading for lunch and asking if he can meet me.

Since we ran into each other at Paulo's four days ago, I've seen him every single day. Even now all I can think about is the next time I'm going to see him.

I'm not sure I like this new version of myself.

Never before have I cared where anyone else is, what class they're sitting in, or what they're doing afterward. I usually spend my time actively forgetting anyone else exists and avoiding as many people as possible.

Cutting my thoughts off, I shove my cell into the depths of my bag. I push through into the coffee shop to grab some lunch and read over some notes for this afternoon.

———

I can barely keep my eyes open as I sit around our usual table in the library for our weekly study group. My lack of sleep the night before has long caught up with me.

I know I should be paying attention to the debate everyone is having around me, but I don't remember the topic let alone what they're actually arguing about right now.

"Macie, you usually have something interesting to add," Wyatt says, turning his stare toward me, and in turn the rest of the table's.

"I... um... I'm sorry, I spaced out."

A mixture of disappointment and concern covers the five faces staring back at me.

"I'm just going to go and get some air."

Without waiting for them to respond, I push my chair out and race away from the table, embarrassed that I'd lost focus and had no choice but to admit it.

I can see the stairwell in the distance that will lead me outside when I collide with a body.

"Whoa... this is a nice surprise," a very familiar deep voice rumbles from above me.

I blink a couple of times, his Panthers jersey that's spread across his wide chest appearing before me.

"Are you stalking me?" I blurt out.

He laughs. "No, Red. Stalkers stay hidden in the shadows. I have every intention of you seeing me."

My lips part but I don't have any words to respond with, my head is still half zoned out.

"What's got you running so fast?" His brows pinch together in concern as he looks behind me to see if I was actually running from something specific.

"N-nothing. I'm in a study session but—"

"Must be good if it's got you running in the opposite direction."

"I... uh... couldn't focus," I confess.

"Oh?" A cocky smirk appears on his lips. "Something got you all distracted, Red?" He takes a step closer and reaches up to tuck a lock of my hair behind my ear.

"U-uh."

"Wanna get out of here?"

"I-I can't. I need to—" I look back over my shoulder.

"Really? You're running away. You can't tell me that you'd rather be there than wherever I can take you."

"And where would that be exactly?"

He leans in, his breath tickling over my ear and down my neck. "Paradise, baby."

All the air rushes out of my lungs in shock. "You did not just say that," I mutter, although something tells me it's true. He's had enough experience after all.

"Go and get your stuff. I'll wait by the entrance."

"Aren't you in the middle of something?" I ask, assuming he's actually here for a reason.

"Nothing that can't wait."

I look back again knowing that my study group is going to expect me to come back and participate. Even if I turn down Leon's offer, I know I'm not going to be able to focus.

"On one condition."

"Name it and it's yours," he says with a smile.

"I want pizza and ice cream."

"Done. Go and get your stuff."

"Okay." I take off with renewed excitement for what the rest of the day might hold.

"Are you feeling better?" Wyatt asks the second I approach the group.

"Um... no. I think it's actually better if I call it a night."

"But we're about to move onto this week's assignment planning next," Sasha says from beside him. She looks completely perplexed as to why I'd turn down wanting to discuss that. Clearly, she doesn't have someone like Leon to entertain her.

Christ, I'm turning into one of those girls.

"It's okay. I already know what I'm doing." It's a big fat lie, but for possibly the first time ever, I don't actually care.

They all watch me as I gather up my things

"Okay, well... I'll see you guys later," I say, turning on my heel and leaving them to it. A rush of adrenaline surges through me at my rebellious behavior. Okay, so blowing off a study session isn't all that wild in the grand scheme of things, but for me, it's kinda crazy.

Even more so knowing I'm blowing it off for something I really shouldn't be this excited about. Another date with a football player.

Butterflies riot in my belly by the time I get back to where Leon is waiting for me.

He's leaning back against the wall by the staircase with one foot propped up and his hands deep in his pockets.

His jersey fits him like a second skin, showing off the sculpted body I'm sure he's rocking beneath. I run my eyes over his torso, wondering just what he might look like without the jersey on.

"I can read your thoughts, Red," he says, when I get close enough to hear, making my cheeks burn red hot. "And I have to say I approve."

"Oh my God."

"Fuck," he growls, taking my chin in his hand and tilting my face so I have no choice but to look at him. "I love it when you blush." His thumb brushes over my cheek before he ducks down for a quick kiss. "Let's get out of here. I'm ready to get you alone," he whispers against my lips.

"Okay," I breathe, completely on board with his plan.

"Come on." He takes my stack of books from my arm and I can't help but swoon hard. "What?" he asks when I don't immediately fall into line beside him.

"N-nothing."

He continues to look at me until I spill.

"I think you might have been right," I confess.

"Oh?"

"You're nothing like I was expecting."

"A douchebag?" he laughs. "That's good to know."

"I'm sorry I judged you. I just... I've had bad experiences with football players in the past."

He studies me for a beat.

"You've seen nothing yet, Red."

Reaching out with his free hand, he catches mine. He twists our fingers together to finally pull me out of the library.

———

Leon follows behind me carrying a huge pizza box as I walk through to the kitchen in our dorm.

Nathan, Jace, and Charlie, along with a couple of Charlie's friends, are all sitting at the table. Each of them looks between Leon and me as if we've both sprouted an extra head.

I guess Nate didn't tell anyone about what's been going on then.

"Uh... hey, Lee." Charlie bats her eyelashes at him while the other girls smooth down their hair and smile at him as if he's just hung the moon.

"Hey. You put that in the freezer, I'll meet you in your room," he says, completely dismissing any of the girl's attempts to get his attention.

He takes off and I watch with amusement as all sets of female eyes follow his ass down the hallway.

"What the hell, Macie?" Charlie hisses the second he disappears into my room.

"What?" I ask, as if hanging out with someone like Leon is an everyday occurrence for me. The truth of the matter is that the only males who've been inside my dorm room are Nate and Jace. And that's only because they live here.

"You and Leon Dunn? Are you serious?" I'm not sure from the look on her face if she's horrified or impressed.

"Leave her alone, Char. She's just enjoying herself, ain't that right, Mace?" Jace adds with a wink, making me wonder if Nate had kept my secret after all.

"I'm just surprised. Sunday night when he was in my room, he wasn't exactly friendly."

"Ever think that was more to do with you than it was him?" I ask, mentally patting myself on the back for standing up for myself.

"Oh my God," Jace blurts out, as Nate sprays all three girls with the mouthful of soda he was attempting to drink.

"Ew," they squeal, jumping up from the table.

"I'll leave all of you with that," I say after putting my ice cream in our small freezer and following Leon down to my room.

Jace and Nate's laughter follows me until I close the door and shut them out.

"What the hell was that?" Leon asks, sitting on my bed and surprisingly, waiting for me with a still closed pizza box.

"I think I gave them the shock of their lives turning up with you in tow."

"You were right, you know?" he says, watching my every move. I pull my boots off and place my jacket over the back of my chair before climbing onto my small bed with him.

"Oh yeah, right about what?" I ask. I flip the box open, letting the scent of rich tomato and melted cheese flood the room.

"I'm not like everyone expects me to be."

I reach out for a slice to silence my growling stomach. When I glance up at him, I can see the honesty in his expression.

"I know. I'm glad you've had the chance to prove me wrong." I know it's only been a few days, but he's surprised me at every turn. Proving to me that my previous opinions about football players may have been a little jaded by my past.

I always knew it wasn't fair of me to tar them all with the same brush. But it was easier to deal with by putting them on my no-go list. Well, it was until this one forced his way through.

"And this sure beats a dull study session," he says, stuffing almost half a slice into his mouth in one go.

"Hey, how do you know it was boring?"

"Red, if it were interesting, you wouldn't have run into me."

"You should have seen their faces when I told them I was leaving. You'd have thought I'd just told them I'd killed their puppy."

"Well, they're the ones missing out. Their loss is my gain."

"You're cute," I blurt out, my cheeks burning again.

"Not sure anyone has called me cute before, Red. I like it." He winks and I can't help but laugh.

"So why were you in the library?"

"I was with the guys."

"And you just left them?"

"Yeah, they'll figure out I've had a better offer at some point."

We fall into easy conversation as we eat. As usual, it's just the basics like college stuff and with every minute that passes, I relax more in his company. Everything just feels right sitting here with him. It's as unnerving as it is exciting.

"What? Have I got pizza on my face?" Leon asks when he catches me staring at him.

"N-no. I-I... I feel like I've known you forever." His eyes widen a little in shock. "I've just never felt quite so comfortable in someone else's company before," I confess.

"That can't be true, you must have had tons of friends."

I shake my head, dropping the last bit of pizza crust back into the box. "I went to an all-girls prep school. I never connected with any of them. They were all about money and showing off and who their parents were. I didn't care about any of that. Nathan is the best friend I think I've ever had."

His brows lift.

"I'm sorry," he whispers. I hate the pity I see in his eyes.

"Don't be. It's not your fault my childhood sucked."

Dropping the box to the floor, he reaches for my hand and pulls me so I'm sitting beside him.

"You wanna talk about it?"

I shake my head, a humorless laugh falling from my lips. I never want to talk about it. I've mostly dealt with my past by shoving it deep into the back of my mind. It's easier to forget about it because dealing with it, talking about it, is just too painful.

"Okay. I do have one question though..."

I risk a look up at him, my brow creasing as I try to predict what he's going to ask.

My heart jumps into my throat as he reaches for the photo on my nightstand. I kick myself for not putting it away knowing that there was a chance he'd get himself back in here.

"I'm sorry," he says sincerely. "I can't imagine how hard it must have been to lose them like you did."

I shrug, not wanting to dive into the details of my parent's deaths.

"I guess your hatred of football players is a little understandable. Why Smith, though? Why not embrace who you are?"

I blow out a breath as I try to formulate my words. "Smith was my mom's maiden name. It meant that I could hide. Most people would never connect me and my father just by my surname, but the risk was great enough to stop me."

"But why does it matter if you're connected to him? He was one hell of a player," he says, proving that he does know exactly who my father was. "And from what I've read over the years, a pretty great guy."

Leon lowers the frame to the nightstand once more and turns to me.

"He was, until he became a coward. I just didn't want to be that person. It's hard to explain. I wanted to start fresh in the hope some of my past might be erased."

His eyes bounce between mine as if he's trying to read what I'm hiding within them. Whatever he does see thankfully stops him from asking any more questions.

"I get it, you know. Wanting to forget who you are, who you're related to."

Silence settles around us as we both get lost in our own heads for a few minutes.

I want to ask him what he means. Of course I do, but I understand the pain and I'm more than happy to leave it buried.

"You want your ice cream?"

I shake my head. "I'm too full."

"Okay so—" His words are cut off as I lean forward and brush my lips against his. "Mmm... I can get on board with this kind of dessert.

Sliding down the bed, he pulls me with him, skimming his hand down my thigh until it slips under my skirt as he wraps my leg around his body while he kisses me so deeply I feel it in my toes. His hand curls around my waist, the heat of his skin burning into me.

"I'm getting a little addicted to you, Red."

His words send desire rushing through me.

"Hmm..." I mumble. "You're making me break all my rules."

"Feels good, doesn't it?"

"Mm-hmm."

13

LEON

Her moan rumbles through me, turning my blood to lava and making my cock ache with need.

But my need isn't just for her because with each sweep of my tongue against hers, the monster inside me begs to be released.

My fingers curl in her shirt as I try to keep myself in check.

If she were any other girl it wouldn't matter if I went a little wild. But I already know that I need to tread carefully. Push too hard and I'm going to lose this opportunity.

And fuck if I'm not going to get exactly what I've come here for.

I will get all of her truths out of her and I will find out the location of the final person who needs to experience my wrath.

She might not talk today, tomorrow or even next week. But she will. And then one by one, I'll tear down every single part of all their lives because they need to learn a very important lesson. No one, I don't care who they are, how famous they are, how innocent, no one messes with me and gets away with it.

Ripping my lips from hers, I kiss down her neck. I suck her sensitive skin into my mouth and letting her taste explode on my tongue.

Her hands run down my back, her nails scratching lightly. A move that I'm not even sure she's aware of.

Sliding my hand from her waist, I cup her breast and squeeze lightly.

Her eyes fly open as her back arches and lips part on a moan.

"Let me make you feel good, Red," I damn near growl.

She hesitates, a war raging behind her eyes. Her body is fully on board, but her head is another matter. It just goes to prove I've got a little more work to do yet to get her to trust me.

"L-Leon, I don't—"

I move her so she's on her back and wrap her legs around my waist. I resist the urge to see if she's wearing her white cotton panties, but only just.

"Shh," I say, leaning over her and caging her head in with my forearms. "I won't do anything you don't want, Red. You want me to stop, all you gotta do is say the word."

She holds my eyes for a beat before nodding slightly.

Dropping lower, I let my lips brush her ear.

"Has anyone ever made you come before, Red?" I whisper. Her fingers twist in my shirt as she registers my words.

After a second, she shakes her head.

"Good. You're always going to remember this then."

"Oh God," she whimpers when I kiss across her jaw and down her neck.

When I sit up, I find her blue eyes are darker than I've ever seen them.

"So fucking sexy," I mutter, trailing my fingers down her neck and between her breasts.

She bites down on her bottom lip, her desire and nerves colliding makes her tremble beneath me.

Her eyes drop from mine to my chest momentarily and I'm reminded of the way she mentally undressed me in the library earlier. I make it easier on her by reaching behind my head and pulling my jersey off in one smooth move so she can see me in the flesh.

"Oh God," she gasps. Her eyes taking in every inch of me as her cheeks burn redder and her chest heaves more violently.

"That good?" I ask, a cocky smirk playing on my lips.

"I think you already know the answer to that."

"It doesn't matter what I think. Right now, I only care what you think."

"I think... I think you should still be kissing me."

"Hell yeah, I should."

Leaning back over her, I capture her lips with mine, plunging my tongue into her mouth. I wrap my hand around the back of her neck to tilt her to the perfect angle.

I drop to the side to give me better access to her. I lower my hand, touching every inch of her I can get to.

"Leon," she moans when I squeeze her breast again. She arches into my hand, her body desperate for more.

Flipping us over, I place her on top of me. I wrap my fingers around the bottom of her shirt and quickly pull it up her body, dragging it over her head before she knows what's going on.

"Perfect," I groan, sitting so we're chest to chest, just the light pink lace of her bra between us as I find her lips again.

"You feel that?" I ask, gripping her hips and holding her against me, swallowing down the moan of pleasure that wants to rip from my throat at the move. "You do that to me."

"Leon," she moans, her head falling back as I continue to grind against her.

Latching onto the exposed skin of her throat, I suck hard until I know it'll hurt. I'm unable to ignore my need to cause her pain, to mark her as she loses herself on me.

Ripping one of her bra straps from her shoulder, I expose her and pinch on her hard nipple.

"Oh God," she cries. Her hips beginning to move against me as she completely loses herself to what's going on.

Unhooking her bra, I pull it from her body and take both of her swollen breasts in my hands.

Her skin is like porcelain, her light pink nipples just begging to be sucked on, bitten.

Every muscle in my body pulls tight as she grinds down on my hard length beneath my pants.

It would be so easy to take more from her right now. And while there's a huge part of me demanding I take it, I force it down. Something tells me that I'm going to get plenty of chances in the upcoming days and weeks to really enjoy this little game she has no idea she's playing.

"Leon. Oh God. Shit."

Threading my fingers in her hair. I twist until it hurts and she has no choice but to look into my eyes.

"Let go, Red. Show me how good it feels."

I pinch her nipple hard and her movements get erratic against me as she chases her release.

"That's it, baby. Use me. Use me to make you feel good."

I thrust my hips up against her and with another pull of her hair and pinch of her nipple she cries out. Her eyes slamming closed and her chin falling as she lets the pleasure crash through her.

The blush burning up her cheeks spreads down her neck and chest. Her tits bouncing as she moves, forgetting about everything but this moment.

The burn of pain from where her nails pierce the skin of my shoulders eases the beast begging to get out and I focus on it as she rides out her orgasm.

"Holy shit," she gasps, falling into me the second she's done. "Oh my God," she mutters into the nape of my neck as she fights to catch her breath.

"Good, baby?" I whisper. I tuck her hair behind her ear and suck it into my mouth, nibbling on the shell.

She doesn't move for the longest time.

"Red, you okay?" I ask, lightly pressing against her shoulder to move her from her hiding spot.

The second her body leaves mine, she wraps her arms around her bare chest and looks to the corner of the room.

"I shouldn't have let you do that," she whispers.

"Hey," I say, cupping her cheek and encouraging her to look at me. "It's okay."

After a few seconds, she finally gives in and looks into my eyes. The sight of her blinking back tears does something to me that I don't want to acknowledge, let alone even consider accepting.

"You should go."

"Fuck that, Macie. That was fucking hot, and I'm not leaving here with you feeling like... like whatever you're feeling right now."

"I-I just..." She trails off, looking away from me once again.

"What, baby? Talk to me."

"I-I've never... you know... and I always said I wouldn't—"

"Life's too short for regrets, Macie. If something feels good, you should allow yourself to have it. There's no shame or embarrassment in what just happened."

"But you're a football player," she finally says.

"Yeah, but that's not all I am. I'm also not your dad, Mace." Her body relaxes at my words. "I'm not like any of the ones you've experienced before."

I'm worse.

I hate that a little bit of guilt trickles through me, but I never expected to actually like this woman. Like this, right now, it's easy to forget about who she is and what she did to me. It's too easy to get swept away in her innocence, her purity.

Reaching for my jersey that's hanging over the side of her bed, I hold it up for her. She slips it over her head, allowing her to cover up.

'Thank you,' she mouths.

"If you really want me to leave, I will. Or, we could put Netflix on and just hang out."

"But..." She looks down at where she's still sitting across my lap.

"I told you, I wanted to make you feel good. And, I'm pretty sure I did."

A shy smile curls at her lips confirming what I already know.

"I don't expect anything in return other than your company. I'm happy to go at your pace with this."

She studies me, her eyes bouncing between mine and then dropping to my lips. She brushes her fingertip against my bottom one.

"Who are you, Leon Dunn?"

"Just a guy who's enjoying spending time with you."

She smiles, lowering her head so she's able to hide behind her hair.

Tucking it all behind her ears, I duck down so she has no choice but to look at me again.

"You're beautiful, Macie. You don't ever have to hide from me."

Finding her lips once again, I kiss her until she relaxes and I lay us both back on the bed.

The suggestion of putting the TV on is long forgotten as we continue making out. Her earlier regret seems to vanish as her hands trail over me As if she's familiarizing herself with all the lines and muscles of my body.

I let her take the lead and neither of us push to take it any further.

I have no idea how much time has passed when she finally pushes up onto her elbow and stares down at me. Her teeth sink into her bottom lip and I know instantly that she's trying to drum up the courage to ask me something.

"What is it, Red?" I ask, cupping her cheek and running my thumb over her swollen bottom lip.

"Do... do you have to leave?"

"No, baby. I don't have to do anything."

She nods shyly. "O-okay. W-would you... would you stay? With me?"

"I don't want to be anywhere else."

"Yeah?"

"Yeah. Well... I could do with using your bathroom."

She presses her hand against my chest and sits up.

"Go," she says with a laugh, pointing toward the door.

Her eyes follow me as I pad across the room. My cock trying to burst out of my pants with every step I take making me wonder briefly if I just made a colossal mistake in agreeing to this.

I probably would have been better off going home and jerking off a few times to the image of her grinding down on me in the hope of taking the edge off.

Stopping at the doorway, I turn back and look at her sitting in the middle of her small bed. Her hair is a mess, her makeup smeared, her lips swollen from my kiss and her body covered in my jersey.

Fucking perfect. All of it.

"Get ready for bed, baby."

She smiles at me, lifting her hand to push her hair back from her face. While my heart tumbles in my chest.

Fuck.

I'm fucked.

Royally fucking fucked.

Closing the door behind me, I force my head to take me back ten years. To that fateful day that changed my entire life and turned me into the dark, angry version of myself that I struggle to control on my worst days.

My fists curl as I remember that one moment which sealed her fate as far as I'm concerned. It might have taken me ten years to get here, and she might be nothing like I was expecting. But that's not going to stop me.

No fucking chance.

14

———

MACIE

I expected him to get up and leave the second I fell asleep. So when I wake the next morning, my cheek stuck to his hot chest and his arm still locked around my waist possessively, I couldn't be more shocked.

I didn't really think he'd agree to stay. Especially after the way I freaked out because it was obvious that he wasn't going to get anything else out of me.

But he floored me when he didn't even bat an eyelid about it.

Guilt knots my stomach for the way I reacted after… *that* yesterday. I know it's not how it should have been. The second the pleasure ebbed away my panic rushed in and I was hit upside the head with the fact I'd just done what I'd told myself I'd never do.

Okay, so we didn't go all the way. Hell, we were barely even undressed—which makes it all the more mortifying—but I did it with a football player.

"I know you're awake," a deep, husky voice whispers, sending a shiver down my spine.

I give myself a second before dragging my eyes open and looking up at him.

My breath catches in my throat at the dark green orbs that stare back at me. And hell if he's not beautiful every other second of the day, but first thing in the morning with his messy hair, he's downright devastating.

"H-hey," I squeak. "You're still here." I cringe the second the words pass my lips because they didn't really need saying.

"Where else would I be?"

Ripping my eyes away from his, I open myself up and say the words that are on the tip of my tongue.

"I thought you'd leave in the middle of the night."

"Macie," he sighs, reaching out to tip my face back to his. "I told you, I'm not that person."

I nod as much as his fingers under my chin allows.

"I-I know, I just... I've always convinced myself that I'd be let down, you know?"

"I do." I sense there's more he wants to say but instead of letting the words out, he leans down to capture my lips.

"Morning breath," I mutter, trying not to open my mouth with him so close.

"You're cute," he chuckles, threading his fingers through my hair at the back of my head and crushing his mouth against mine. His tongue teasing the seam of my lips until I give in and open up for him.

He kisses me so deeply I forget all about my morning breath and cling onto him as I lose myself in everything he makes me feel.

"As much as I'd love to spend the day here with you, I need to go meet the guys."

I hold onto him tighter, loving the feeling of his hot and hard body beneath me.

A smile curls at his lips when he realizes that I'm holding on tighter.

"You're making it really hard to leave."

"Pun intended?"

He throws his head back and laughs. "Oh, Red. You've got no idea."

My stomach somersaults as wild thoughts begin to flash through my mind.

"Stop it," he growls, rolling me onto my back and staring down at me.

"I didn't do anything," I say innocently.

"I can read your thoughts, and they're wicked."

I gasp when his hand slips under his shirt that I'm wearing and finds my bare breast.

"Oh God."

He lowers his lips to my ear.

"Later," he whispers.

"Is that a promise?"

"Damn right it is. I want to watch you come, over and over."

My thighs squeeze together at the prospect.

"And, I really want to taste you."

My breath catches at his words.

"You want that, Red? You want to see my head between your thighs as I enjoy just how sweet I already know you're going to be."

"Leon." His name was meant to be a warning but it comes out sounding anything but.

"You're going to get me in trouble, Red." His lips find mine again before I press my palms against his chest and push him back, albeit lightly.

"Go. You should go."

Reluctantly, he stands and takes two huge steps back from the bed. Almost all of his body is on display and what little fabric he does have covering him really doesn't do all that much to conceal him.

My temperature soars as I stare at the bulge.

"You're not making it easier," he mutters, reaching for his pants and tugging them up his legs. Once they're on, he stands before me as if he's waiting for something.

"W-what?" I stutter, dragging my eyes up to his smug face.

"You're wearing my shirt."

I look down at myself. "Oh."

"I mean, I can go like this if—" he offers, reaching out as if he's going to leave right now.

"N-no, it's okay."

"I'm gonna use your bathroom."

I sit there staring at where he was long after he's closed the door behind him. I'm trying to convince myself that convincing him to stay and blowing off any commitments we both have today is a really bad idea.

When the sound of the faucet running hits my ears, I remember that I'm meant to be doing something. I jump from the bed, reluctantly dragging his shirt from my body as I walk toward my dresser.

I pull on a tank before lifting his shirt to my nose for one last sniff. Unfortunately, that's exactly how Leon finds me when he walks back into my room.

"Damn, Red," he mutters with a wide smile on my face.

"I'm sorry. Here," I say handing his shirt over.

"Never be sorry for looking like that."

His eyes leisurely run over my body as if I'm standing naked, not in a tank and panties.

"I'll pick you up at seven, okay?"

"S-seven?" I ask, thinking it's a little early for any kind of college party.

"Yeah. We're going for dinner first."

"Another date?"

"Yeah, Red. Another date," he says reaching for my hand once he's pulled his shirt on and drags me into his body. "That okay?"

"More than okay. I can't wait."

His hand slides up my throat before stopping once it's cupping my jaw.

"Good. I'll see you later then."

He drops a chaste kiss to my lips before slipping out of my room.

I suck in a deep breath and drop down onto the end of my bed. I lift my fingers to my lips as I remember everything that happened in here over the past few hours.

It only takes two minutes tops for someone to knock on my door. Rushing over to my chair, I wrap an oversized cardigan around my body. Calling out for them to come in as I sit back on my bed.

The door swings open and I find Nathan leaning against the frame with a smug smirk playing on his lips.

"Don't even say it," I mutter.

He holds his hands up in defense as his smile gets wider.

"I wasn't going to say anything, Mace."

I quirk a brow at him.

"You okay?" he asks, his face turning serious.

"Yeah, I'm good. Possibly making the biggest mistake of my life, but for once, I could care less."

"That's... good, I think."

"Yeah, maybe it's about time I embrace college life, huh?"

"As long as it makes you happy."

"Right now, he is," I say, feeling sappy even admitting it.

"That's good, I'm happy for you. Charlie, however..."

"Oh yeah, I bet she's thrilled. He couldn't even get it up for her."

Nathan's eyes damn near pop out of his head.

"Who are you and what have you done with my friend?"

"Don't you have training to get to?" I say before I blurt out anything else I probably shouldn't.

"Yeah, I just wanted to make sure you were good before I left."

"I am, thank you."

With a nod and a smile that would melt most other panties, he leaves me to it.

I don't have any classes today and usually, I'd spend the day in the library working. But seeing as I've got a date and my first college party tonight, I decide to do something that I would never usually do.

I head for the mall.

———

Charlie was still in her room when I left, and despite the fact I knew she had classes today, I almost invited her to join me. I don't have a freaking clue about what sort of thing I should wear tonight, whereas she'd be able to pick the perfect outfit. But the thought of having her grilling me about Leon all day stops me. Or the possibility of having her look at me wondering what the hell he sees in me that he didn't with her.

I'm already having enough of my own thoughts along those lines, I don't need anyone else feeding into my insecurities.

For a girl who hates shopping, I spend an obscene amount of time at the mall. I wander in and out of the shops trying to find the perfect outfit for tonight.

Sadly, that perfect dress doesn't seem to exist because when I leave a few hours later I'm still not one hundred percent sure with my purchase.

Knowing that time is closing in on Leon coming to pick me up, means my nerves about tonight are starting to multiply.

Will I look good enough?

Will everyone look at me with Leon and wonder how he's managed to get stuck with me?

Will everyone think it's some kind of bet?

Is it a bet?

I feel physically sick by the time I get back to the dorms.

I was hoping that someone would be here. Mainly Nathan so he could talk me down from my panicking but the whole place is deserted.

Needing something, anything, to take the edge off my anxiety, I pull open the kitchen cupboard, pulling out a bag of chips, despite the fact Leon's taking me out for dinner in a few short hours. When I get to the refrigerator, I can't stop myself from reaching in and grabbing one of Charlie's pre-mixed cocktail drinks.

I stand there arguing with myself. I'd normally never steal any of her stuff, let alone alcohol, so I know I must be desperate to even consider it.

I grab the bottle and a glass and without putting any more thought into it. I take it all, along with my bags to my room.

Putting some music on, I pour myself a glass of Charlie's cocktail and hesitantly take a sip. The coconut and pineapple taste explodes on my tongue. I barely even notice that it's alcoholic, which is kinda dangerous because seeing as I'm the world's biggest lightweight, who knows what will happen if I keep drinking.

Forcing myself to put it down, I grab a handful of chips and head through to the bathroom to shower.

I scrub and shave every inch of my body, exfoliate my face and apply my favorite moisturizer. By the time I step back into my room, the piña colada has begun to take effect and I'm feeling good. Excited.

I take off the tags of the new underwear I bought. Pulling them on before stepping into the dress I finally settled on and stand in front of the mirror.

I have no idea what I should be wearing. My experience with real dates followed by college parties are lacking to say the least. I wanted something... classy but cute, sexy maybe, if I can even pull that off.

Blowing out a long breath, I run my hands over the soft black fabric of the flared skirt that stops just above my knee.

Yeah, maybe it's too cute.

I twist and turn not really knowing what I think about everything when a knock on my door cuts through the sound of the music.

"Come in."

"Hey, how are you— That's cute," Charlie says, running her eyes over the dress.

"Yeah. That's what I was afraid of."

"Want some help?" she asks, slipping into the room and closing the door behind her.

The image of her and her friend's shocked faces when I turned up last night with Leon in tow fills my mind and I narrow my eyes at her suspiciously.

"Nate said you've got a date then a party."

"Y-yeah," I stutter as she walks toward me, assessing my outfit.

"This is cute, but I think we can do better. Really blow his socks off, you know?"

"Y-you want to help me get ready?"

Charlie and I might be friends, albeit the most unlikely ones, but I can't help questioning her intentions right now.

"Yeah."

"Why?" I regret the question the second it falls from my lips and her brow crinkles.

"I know this is weird, and yes, I can't deny that I'm shocked about the two of you but I still want you to enjoy yourself, look your best. You deserve to have some fun. You always work so hard."

I hold her eyes, trying to decipher if she's being honest. Seeing nothing other than her wanting to help me, I find myself agreeing.

"Okay."

"Awesome. Wait right here."

Before I know what's happening she's gone once more, leaving me standing in the middle of my room even more confused.

"Okay," she says. A couple of minutes later reappearing with a dress hanging over her arm and her giant makeup box in her hand. "This is perfect for you."

"Uh..." I watch her, dread settling in my stomach because I know the kinds of dresses she wears on a regular night out. They're typically not the kind of things I want anywhere near me.

"Trust me." She throws the fabric at me. "Go try it on."

"O-okay." I take it from her and disappear into my bathroom.

I strip out of my dress and pull her much more fitted one up my body.

It is more revealing but to my surprise, it's not slutty or overly tiny. It just hugs my body in a way the one I chose didn't. I can't deny that when I look in the mirror, a little thrill races through me because I actually look good. Really good.

The black bodycon dress isn't one I ever would have picked out for myself. But I'm starting to question why not because I look... hot.

Gathering up my other dress, I step out into my room.

"Yes," Charlie cries. "Yes. Yes. Yes. Tell me you love it."

I stand in front of my full-length mirror twisting this way and that. Running my eyes over my curves and wondering where they've been hiding all this time.

"I... I love it."

"Yesss," she hisses. "I've never worn it. It just didn't feel right when I tried it on and I never got a chance to take it back. It's yours if you want it."

I look back at my other dress briefly and Charlie notices.

"You're gonna bring him to his knees in this dress, girl. And trust me, you want him on his knees."

My cheeks burn as the image of exactly that pops into my head.

"I'll take it from your reaction that you've not done the dirty yet."

"What do you think?" I mutter, dropping into my chair and grabbing my hairbrush.

"I think you're making him work for it, and I think he loves you for it."

"Do you... do you think he actually wants me?" I ask. I hate the fact I feel like I'm ripping myself wide open saying the words out loud.

"I don't know," she says honestly. "You don't need me to tell you that you're not his usual type. That he doesn't chase, or even date, women. But there's always one who breaks the rules for even the biggest of players. Who says that can't be you?"

I study her for a beat. "Are you a bit of a romantic at heart, Charlie?"

"I think most women are deep down, Mace. The biggest question here is whether you're willing to find out the answer to that question yourself. But then again, the fact you've even agreed to hang out with him this week tells me you've already made a decision about that."

"He breaks all my rules."

"You know what I say about rules, Mace. They're always made for breaking." She winks, coming over with her giant box and placing it on my desk ready to get to work.

"You're not mad at me?" I ask with a wince, needing to address the elephant in the room.

"Honestly," she says, pulling out some brushes. "I was pissed to start with. But clearly, me and him weren't a match. It was fun while it lasted. Sorry," she laughs when she notices the look on my face.

LEON

"Whoa, Leon is pulling out all the stops tonight," Colt booms as I descend the stairs at the house. "It's not like you to put in this much effort to getting some pussy, Dunn."

A couple of the others appear from the den to get a look before Luca and Peyton emerge from the kitchen.

Of fucking course I wasn't lucky enough to get out of here without getting spotted.

I hold his amused stare as I hit the ground floor.

"Jealous because no woman wants to actually spend time with you, Colt?"

"Oh, they all want to spend time with me." He rolls his hips.

"Sure they do," I mutter. I shove past him and reluctantly head for my brother.

"You look nice," Peyton says with a smile although I can see the curiosity in her eyes. There's no doubt in my mind that she's spoken to Letty already and got at least some of the details about Macie.

"Thanks." I slip past them and into the kitchen.

"I'm gonna head out," Peyton says to Luca.

"Okay, say hey to Libby for me."

I glance over my shoulder as Luca pulls her in for a kiss. Just like always my chest aches at how easy it is for them when they're together.

It makes me wonder what people will see tonight when they look at Macie and I together. Will they think we're like that, or will they be able to see what Macie is failing to... that I'm using her.

Guilt begins to flood me but I quickly shut it down. It doesn't matter how sweet she is, how easy it would be to fall into something regular with her. That's not the reason I embarked on all of this and I refuse to let my heart get involved and fuck everything up for me.

I've had a plan for damn near ten years and nothing is going to stop me from ripping apart the people's lives who destroyed mine.

"How's Libby doing?" I ask when Luca joins me.

"Yeah, she's doing really good, all things considered."

I nod, genuinely happy that Peyton's sister might just be able to find a way past the hell that our father put her through when she was only a kid.

"I've been meaning to go and see her," I say hoping that keeping the conversation away from me and my night will be enough to stop him digging into my life.

"Oh yeah?"

"Figured she needs as many people in her corner as she can get right now," I mutter honestly. Well, somewhat honestly. I don't mention the fact that we share a special kind of mutual hate for Brett Dunn.

"True that. Hopefully, she's going to be discharged in a few days and we'll be able to check her into the facility I've booked for her."

"She's up for rehab?"

"Yeah, she seems to be. I just hope it works out for Peyton and Kayden's sake."

"We still going for breakfast in the morning?" I ask, thinking about our morning breakfast with our half-brother last week.

"Yeah, and you'd better be there or you'll ruin that little kid's life."

I chuckle to myself as I think about his excitement last weekend. He really is pretty awesome despite the shit that life has handed him. I guess being Brett's offspring means having to have some kind of built-in resilience to survive our father let alone the rest of this fucked up world.

"I'll be there, man. Wouldn't miss it for anything."

He nods, accepting that I'm telling the truth. "So this girl..."

"Do we have to?"

"Certainly fucking do, Bro. Letty seems to think she might be important."

Oh yeah, she's real fucking important.

"I don't know, we're just taking it one step at a time."

He stares at me like I've just sprouted a second head.

"Wow, my little brother is finally growing up."

"Fuck you, man. I'm not about to put a fucking ring on it like someone else I know."

"I'm not proposing to Peyton," he argues.

"Maybe not today but you know it's fucking coming. You would've nailed her ass down when you were both kids if you had a chance."

"I should have fucking done it too. Might have stopped all the bullshit we've been through."

"Not sure anything could stop the force that is our cunt of a father."

I realize my mistake the second I say the word and Luca's features harden.

I know that I should probably let him at Brett. If I'd caught him on the verge of raping my girl I'd want his fucking blood too. But Luca doesn't need to know Brett's whereabouts. He also doesn't need to revisit that dark side of himself.

He's got Peyton back now, they're happy, she's safe. That's how it should stay.

"Where is he, Lee?"

"Exactly where he should be. Out of our lives."

"But—"

"It's not happening, Luc. Beg me as much as you like."

"I want to fucking kill him."

"Exactly why I'm not giving you the answers that you want. Things are good now. You've got your girl, a future. Just focus on that."

"And you?" he asks, his brow lifting in curiosity.

"I'm doing what needs to be done."

"What did he do to you, Lee?"

"Me?" I ask with a laugh. Our father's neglect of me for his favorite flickering through my mind like a fucking movie. "He didn't care enough."

Luca's lips part to respond but I beat him to it.

"I gotta head out. I don't want to keep her waiting."

"I hate this, Lee," he confesses, running his hand through his hair. "I hate being in the dark, forced to feel like I don't even know you anymore. It never used to be like this."

Yes, it did, I think to myself. I was just better at covering it up.

"It's life, Luc. We're not seven-year-old naïve little boys with zero responsibilities. We've both got lives now. You've got Peyton and—"

"And you?" he asks, his eyes widening with his need to know about Macie.

"It's early days. It might be nothing."

"Or it might be everything."

"Yeah, maybe," I lie. "I gotta go."

"Sure." The sadness in his tone makes my chest ache but it's the way it's got to be. Once I've laid all my ghosts to rest, maybe things will change. But for right now, I need him at arm's length because if he gets too close, I already know he's not going to like what he finds.

With a heavy heart, I turn to leave.

Dropping into my car, I feel like the shittiest brother in the world, but I know it's the way it's got to be. If he knew the truth, he'd want to raise hell on my behalf. I refuse to allow him to go down that road.

I'm the one who's owed the revenge. He's dealt with his shit now and got his girl back. It's time for him to begin his future while I try to lay my past to rest in the hope I have a future to enjoy.

My head is a mess as I head for Macie's dorm.

Part of me wants to blow her off to go and take my frustration out on our dad. Only the knowledge that doing so will fuck everything up keeps me moving forward.

And fuck am I glad I do when she opens her door and I get my first look at her.

"Fuck, Red. You look..." My words trail off because. Wow.

Her hair has been pulled up with just a few curled strands hanging around her face. Her makeup is heavier than usual, the smoky gray around her eyes making the light blue of her eyes pop. Her lips are red and full, making my mouth water for a taste of her. And the dress... fuck me, the dress.

"Leon?" she whispers, making me realize that I've been standing here silently for a few seconds too long.

"Shit, I—" Reaching up I rub the back of my neck feeling all kinds of things I know I shouldn't be right now. "You look... wow."

"Yeah?" A shy smile pulls at her lips as she reaches up to fiddle with a loose lock of her hair.

"Yeah." My heart pounds in my chest, my cock hard and ready from just one look at her. "Maybe we shouldn't go out," I say, taking a step toward her and sucking in a deep breath filled with her coconut scent.

"Oh?" A little disappointment slips into her tone.

"Yeah, I'm not sure I want any other men looking at you like that. Not when you're mine."

"Y-yours?" she stutters.

"Yeah, Red," I say, lacing my arm around her back. I pull her into my body, allowing her to feel exactly what she does to me.

She gasps as I hold her tight and drop my lips to her ears.

"Mine," I breathe, making her shudder in my hold. "You look breathtaking," I confess, dropping my lips to her neck and nibbling on the soft skin making her tremble with desire.

"Th-thank you," she breathes.

My breath catches in my throat when I pull back and look into her darkening eyes.

Movement over her shoulder catches my attention. I look up to find Charlie leaning back against the kitchen counter watching us curiously.

I nod in greeting, wondering what the hell I was thinking coming back here last weekend. She really, really isn't my type.

"Have fun kids," she says with a genuine smile. "I won't wait up." She winks before pushing from the side and disappearing down toward her room.

"So where are we going?"

"Just a little place I know."

"What about the party? Is it a team one or..."

"It's just some friends."

"Okay," she says without a second thought. She laces her fingers through mine when I reach for her.

Macie chats away about her day at the mall. Then she tells me about Charlie helping to get her ready and her confusion over the fact she was willing to do so knowing that she was going on a date with me.

I soak up every word, noting her vulnerability and lack of confidence in her friend. I mean, I get it. Macie and Charlie are like polar opposites, and Macie and I met when I was seconds away from sinking balls deep into Charlie so I understand why it would be weird, but equally, I'm glad she's got the support. Something tells me that in a few weeks she's probably going to need it.

"We're eating here?" Macie asks as I lead her to a small Italian restaurant that sits on a quiet street on the other side of town.

"Yeah, you like Italian right?"

"Of course, who doesn't? It's so cute."

"I thought you'd like it." I hate that those words are true. This was the first place I thought of when I mentioned dinner. I could just picture her sitting in this small family restaurant enjoying Antonio's homemade pasta.

"I love it. The food smells incredible."

"It is. Best Italian in the state."

"Oh, I don't know about that," Gianna, Antonio's wife says, coming over to greet us. "We haven't seen you for a while." Her soft smile is infectious.

"Things have been a little crazy but I knew I couldn't take my girl anywhere else."

Gianna's eyes flick to Macie, her smile only widening at the sight of her.

I've never been here with a girl before, unless it's a friend's girl, and Gianna clearly knows it.

"Well, it's a good thing I've got the best table in the place free then, isn't it?"

"Lead the way," I say, gesturing for her to do so.

She takes us to a table right at the back of the restaurant that's hidden in the shadows to give us some privacy. She leaves us to look at the menu, not that it's necessary, I already know my order.

"This is on the house," Gianna says when she returns a few moments later with a bottle of wine, and a bowl of olives for us.

"Thank you so much," Macie says softly as Gianna pours her a glass.

Macie turns to me the second Gianna leaves us again. The sparkle in her eyes and the smile on her lips makes my breath catch in my throat.

She's so pure, so beautiful, so innocent. I almost feel bad for how this is all going to end. Almost.

I watch her as she tentatively sips the wine, focusing on her lips as they press against the glass. I can't help imagining what they might look like wrapped around my cock instead.

Shifting in my seat to make space for my hardening dick, I reach for her thigh under the table.

"What are your plans for the weekend?"

She shrugs, placing her glass down. "Same as every other one, assignments. You?"

"Not much. I've got a breakfast date in the morning with my little brother."

"Aw, how old?"

"Five."

She studies me for a beat as if she wants to ask more but she swallows down the questions and looks at the table.

I know why. She thinks that by asking me about my family that it'll encourage me to do the same about hers. She's not wrong. It's the reason why I'm here. Well, my reason aside from showing her just how much pain she caused me all those years ago. I'm just hoping I can get a two-for-one deal. Her and her cunt of an uncle who seems to have vanished into hiding somewhere.

Not wanting to let her change the conversation, I dive into a place I know will make her uncomfortable.

"Do you have any siblings?"

"No," she states matter of factly. "My parents died when I was young, as you know, there wasn't really a chance."

"What about after? Who did you live with when they passed?"

Her lips part as something dark passes through her eyes but she shuts it down before I get a chance to read what it is.

"I stayed with my uncle for a while, but he shipped me off to prep school and the staff there pretty much raised me after that."

I know she's only partly telling the truth. Richard Fletcher might have sent her to some fancy prep school but she also spent time at his estate in Miami. I know because I saw her there. She saw me, she just doesn't remember, it seems.

"That sucks."

"Meh, being there alone was better than being with him. Do you have any others or just Luca and the little one?" she asks, spinning it back on me.

I give her the basics about only discovering Kayden's existence recently. I don't dive into any details of who his mother is or what a cheating, disgusting piece of shit our father is. Before moving onto Shane, Chelsea and their baby, Nadine.

Macie sips away at her wine as I talk. I can't help but wonder if she realizes just how much she's drank.

I know from the other night that she's a lightweight but feeling awkward with the family topic of conversation keeps her drinking it nonetheless.

By the time we finish our desserts almost two hours later, she's managed to drink over half the bottle and is more than a little tipsy.

"Are you ready to party?" I ask, leading her from the restaurant after paying our bill and promising Gianna that we'll come back soon.

"Yes. I've never been to a college party. I'm excited," she says animatedly. Her eyes are sparkling with excitement as she bounces on her feet beside me.

I open my car door for her, swallowing down my warning that the party we're heading to isn't your standard college party because I don't want to ruin her high.

I'm sure there are a million parties tonight that I could take her to. That's if I wanted to introduce her into my life, to Luca, Peyton, Letty and all the others who I know will be more than interested to meet her.

But I can't. It's bad enough that they know she exists. The last thing I need is for them to fall in love with her and then be forced to watch as I rip her life to pieces.

The less they know about all that shit, the better.

Excitement tingles through my veins as I pull up in a space a little down the way from the house where tonight's party is already raging.

Thoughts of what might be happening inside, and Macie's reaction to it, makes my cock swell once more.

Getting her out of her comfort zone shouldn't get me going this much. It's wrong, I know it is but I can't stop myself.

"Out you go then, Red. It's time to party."

16

MACIE

I look around as Leon leads me to the front door to the house where tonight's party is. It's a little more out of town than I was expecting, and it's certainly not a frat house.

A mixture of excitement and anticipation churns in my stomach as my head spins from the wine.

I knew I needed to stop, but the way he was looking at me as he dug into my family, talked about my uncle. I needed it. I needed the distraction or at least a way to numb the memories that he threatened to drag up from the depths I've buried them in.

Sure, people have asked about my family in the past. Usually they don't really care about the answer, let alone look at me the way Leon did. It looked as if he was invested in what I had to say and what my life was like before I started here.

No one needs to know the truth about my life. I spend most of my time wishing I didn't even know.

The bass of the music hits my ears long before we get to the front door which is already open, people spilling out with drinks in their hand.

My grip on Leon tightens as he leads me into the house. Past all the people, and into the living area.

I try to school my reaction but I don't think I do a very good job as the scene before us emerges.

"What's that smell?" I shout when the unusual bitter scent hits my nose.

Leon chuckles beside me.

"Weed, Red."

"Oh."

I scan the room finding a group of dangerous-looking guys lounging on the couch with what I assume are joints in their hands. While a group of three girls dance on the coffee table in the middle of them. Well, when I say dance, what I really mean is paw at each other as they grind their hips.

"What the hell?" I hiss, my eyes flicking at everything around us as my skin heats at the inappropriateness of it all.

"They're just letting go and having fun, Red." Leon pulls me into his body and turns me so the only thing I have to look at is him. "Just like you last night," he growls in my ear.

My cheeks burn as I remember rubbing myself up against him and just how good it felt.

I press myself against his body, resting my arms over his shoulders.

He lowers his head to mine and stares into my eyes.

"Let go, Red. Everyone just wants to enjoy themselves."

His lips brush mine, once, twice, and the third time, I kiss him back. My alcohol fueled body allowing me to forget our surroundings momentarily as his tongue slides against mine.

For a few seconds, maybe even a minute, it's just the two of us in my room like last night. His hands slide up from my hips, over the curve of my waist until his thumbs brush over my nipples.

I gasp in shock and pull away from his lips, ready to chastise him for being so... so wicked in public. But the second I look into his eyes, I forget everything I was about to say.

Lifting my hand, I run my fingertips over his lips, wiping my lipstick from him.

"Maybe this party was a bad idea. The only place I want to be right now is alone with you in your room."

My heart races as every muscle below my waist clenches in desire.

The thought of having his hands on me again, of feeling that rush he gave me yesterday. Damn, I want it.

"Maybe we should—"

"Leon," a deep booming voice says from behind me, cutting off the suggestion I was about to make.

Leon twists me away and tucks me into his side allowing me to see the man who wants him.

I look up, and up, as he approaches before all the air rushes from my lungs.

Holy crap. He's scary.

Sure he's hot. But just looking at him terrifies me.

"Hey. Wasn't expecting you to be here."

"Just checking on the kids," he winks, shooting a glance over at the guys on the couch.

"Have you been to—"

"Yeah. Just came from there. All's good, man. The rat is going strong."

I narrow my eyes at the guy before looking back at Leon suspiciously.

"You met JD?" the guy asks as another steps up beside him.

The guy nods in greeting.

"This is Macie," Leon adds, clearly remembering that I'm standing here.

"Nice to meet you. Reid," the scary guy says, holding his hand out.

Hesitantly, I reach mine out and watch in horror as his engulfs it.

"Nice to meet you. Now if you don't mind. I've got business to attend to."

They both disappear as fast as they arrived leaving me wondering just what kind of party this really is.

"Who was that?" I ask turning to look at Leon once more.

"You heard of the Hawks?"

I narrow my eyes at him, assuming he means a football team but the only others I know of who are close aren't Hawks.

"Err... no."

"Good. That's good. Stay the hell away from them."

"Easier said than done seeing as we seem to be at their party."

"You're with me. You're safe."

He drops a kiss to my temple and I can't help feeling exactly as he just said. He makes me feel safe, and that's a scary prospect. No, actually, it's terrifying.

I've spent almost all my life looking after myself. So having someone else make me feel comforted and secure standing by my side is unusual, to say the least.

"Leon, what are we—"

"Leon, my man!" Someone booms out across the room before he bounces up to us.

The guy is clearly drunk as he wraps his arm around Leon and pulls him in for a man hug.

"Didn't think you were coming, bro."

"Wouldn't miss it."

"Why the fuck would you want to? You know we throw the best parties around here."

"I've heard some rumors," Leon jokes.

"I can guarantee they're all true." He winks before his eyes shift over to me.

"Who's your girl?"

"Macie," I say, summoning up as much confidence as I can.

Something tells me I'll get eaten alive if I act like myself right now and try to shy away into the shadows.

Thankfully, the effects of the wine from the restaurant gives me the boost I need.

"Devin. Nice to meet you. This is my house, just in case you need to know after Leon screws this up."

"Fuck you, man," Leon laughs. "Get your fucking eyes off my girl."

My girl.

His words echo around in my head, warming me from the inside.

"She's all yours, man. For now." Ripping his eyes from his perusal of my body, he looks back at Leon. "Come hang with us. I've got something you need to try."

We follow Devin over to the couches, and after he's dismissed a few of the guys who were sitting around, I drop down onto Leon's lap.

The girls who were keeping them entertained are shooed away, much to their disappointment.

I discover that Devin is actually Reid's little brother before I'm introduced to two more, twins, Ezra and Ellis.

They all shoot the shit as they take pulls on their beers and drags on their joints.

"Ellis," Devin barks. "Go get Leon's girl a drink."

"Oh n-no, I'm—"

"I'm not your fucking slave, Bro," Ellis sulks, although he does push to stand. "What would you like, doll?" he asks much more softly when he looks down at me.

"Oh, I'm really okay. You don't need to—"

"I'll make it a surprise then," he says with a wink. He spins away from us and disappears toward what I assume is the kitchen.

"You okay?" Leon whispers in my ear. As he wraps his hand possessively around my hip.

"Err..."

"We don't have to stay long, I just said that I'd show my face. They guys are solid, I owe them."

I think back to what Reid said about the rat, whatever the hell that was about, and I can't help but wonder why Leon could possibly owe them. I already know that's not a good position to be in and I barely know them.

"I-it's okay."

He studies me, no doubt trying to work out if I'm lying or not.

Honestly, I'm not sure if I am or not.

Yes, these guys terrify me, but I fully believe Leon when he said I'm safe with him. I can't deny that there's a part of me who wants to just embrace everything in front of me. That's still the main thought in my mind when Ellis reappears and holds a glass out for me.

"What is it?"

"My own special cocktail." He winks.

"But be careful because it's strong as hell, no doubt," a soft female voice says. It's a relief to hear, but Leon seems to have the opposite reaction to it because his entire body tenses beneath me.

"Thank you," I say to Ellis, taking the glass, before he moves and reveals the person behind the voice.

She's gorgeous. Her golden skin is flawless and her thick dark hair falls over her shoulders like a waterfall. And when I look at the guy standing beside her with his arm thrown around her shoulder, my breath catches in my throat. They really are quite a couple.

"Lee, what are you doing here?" she chastises, her brows pulling together as she fixes him with a hard stare.

"I was invited."

Her eyes flick to me, a softness creeping into them that wasn't there when she stared at Leon.

"Are you going to introduce us?"

Leon blows out a long breath. His grip on me tightening as the tension crackles around us.

I want to say that we've just come across his ex, but I don't think that's what's going on here.

Unable to bear the atmosphere, I put my glass to my lips and take a sip.

The sweet fruit juice hits my tongue a beat before the strong alcohol assaults my throat. I start coughing as it burns all the way down.

"What on Earth is that?" I splutter, watching as Ellis disappears to get the two of them drinks as well.

"Don't say I didn't warn you."

Another of the guys gets up allowing the woman to drop onto the couch opposite us while her guy moves over to talk to Devin.

"So?" She leans forward on her knees, holding Leon's eyes once more.

She's pissed, that much is obvious. But I have no idea why.

Ellis hands her a drink and she happily takes a sip without reacting like me.

"Macie, this is Letty, one of my oldest friends. Her guy is Kane. He's friends with the Harrises. Letty, meet Macie."

"See, now that wasn't so hard, was it?" she deadpans.

"It's nice to meet you, Macie. This one has been tight-lipped about you."

My chin drops to say something but I quickly find I have no response.

"Didn't you have anywhere better to take her on a Friday night than a Harris party?" she asks, turning her attention back to Leon.

"We've actually been to Antonio's for dinner. I just promised Devin that I'd stop in."

A smile twitches at her lips as Leon mentions the Italian restaurant he took me to. She almost looks impressed.

"That makes it a little better," she mutters before Kane drops down beside her and pulls her in for a kiss.

Leon's lips brush my ear now his friend is distracted.

"Letty is the nicest person you'll ever meet. Trust me, her mood is entirely my fault."

A shudder rips through me as his breath tickles down my neck.

"Why?" I breathe.

"Because I haven't told her as much about you as she'd like."

His lips brush down my neck making my already heated body burn from the inside out.

"We can leave if you like."

My agreement is right on the tip of my tongue, but I can't help feeling like I'd be running and hiding if I did.

I glance around once more at everyone enjoying themselves. At the friends laughing, the couples dancing.

This is college life. Surely I should have at least one night like this.

"No, I want to enjoy myself."

"I'm sure we could do that alone," he growls in my ear.

Making a snap decision, I take a huge mouthful of my drink. I try to ignore the burn down my throat before I turn to him and look right into his eyes.

"Dance with me."

"Yeah?"

"Yeah. Show me how this party thing is done."

He drains his beer, giving me a chance to drink a little more. Then he lifts me on my feet and guides me to where the others are dancing on the other side of the open-plan room.

Leon walks me over with his hand at the small of my back until he turns on me and steps up into my body, pressing his entire length against me.

"Hey," I squeak, suddenly feeling unsure about this decision.

Now we're in the middle of all the grinding bodies, I realize that I'm totally out of my comfort zone.

I've never danced in my life. Well, unless I'm alone in my room. I've certainly never done it with anyone watching or with someone else.

"Relax," Leon whispers in my ear. "Just do what feels natural."

Running feels natural, but I don't tell him that.

Instead, I rest my arms over his shoulders and press myself harder against him as his lips find mine.

He kisses me as if we're the only two people in the room.

I guess it's a tactic to get me to relax, and damn if it doesn't work. I forget about where we are, about who could be watching us, and the scary faces of the Harris brothers on the other side of the room.

The beat of the music flows through me. His touch burns as his hands run up and down my back until they drop lower, grabbing onto my ass as he rolls his hips against mine.

"Oh God," I moan feeling his hardness pressing against my stomach.

Desire rolls through me, mixing with the alcohol filling my veins and lowering my inhibitions.

Before meeting Leon, I'd never even kissed anyone, not properly, anyway. Yet here I am now with desire coiling around me in the middle of a houseful of people.

Ripping his lips from mine, he kisses across my jaw and down my neck, sucking on the sensitive skin.

"Leon," I moan. It's so quiet that he can't possibly hear me, but he must be able to feel the vibration of my voice because his grip on me tightens.

He finds my lips once more, kissing me as if he needs it like he does his next breath.

Each song blurs into the next until I completely lose track of time. Although, with the way my head is spinning from whatever Ellis gave me, I'm not even sure if I could read a clock right now.

A shadow falls over us, and Leon releases my lips in favor of looking at whoever it is that's joined us.

Letty studies me with a soft smile playing on her lips as she steps into Kane's body and moves against him.

"Bro, you gotta try this," a voice says from the other side of us, ripping my eyes from the loved-up couple.

I find Devin standing before us with a joint between his fingers, holding it out for Leon. I tense, not knowing what to even do with it if he offers it to me.

Not expecting him to take it, seeing as he's on the team. But my eyes damn near pop out of my head when Leon takes it, moving it to his lips.

"You shouldn't do that," I blurt out. "Football."

I watch enthralled as Leon's lips purse around the end of the joint, taking a hit.

I find myself mimicking the move, not really knowing how I feel about it but knowing that he looks hot as hell right now. He looks downright wicked with that naughty glint in his eyes.

"It's fine," he says, smoke billowing from his mouth with each word. "It's a one-off. And we're celebrating."

"We are?" I ask, my voice slow and slurred.

"Yeah, we are."

He holds the joint out to me. I panic, shaking my head and making the room spin around me.

A wicked smile curls up at Leon's lips as he takes another hit. But instead of letting it out this time, he holds it in, threads his fingers through the hair at the back of my neck and crashes his lips to mine, releasing the smoke into my mouth.

I gasp, realizing what he's doing. I can't deny that a wave of desire races through me.

"Fuck, I need you," he moans into our kiss as my head spins.

Once again he totally consumes me. I don't even realize that Devin has vanished with his joint for the longest time.

"Wanna get out of here?" Leon asks me, his eyes dark with lust and need.

The sight makes everything south of my waist clench.

"Y-yeah, but I need to pee."

"Okay." He presses his hand into the small of my back and moves me through the room. I assume toward a bathroom.

"Come on," a soft voice says from behind me. "We'll use Kane's old room."

Looking over my shoulder, I find Letty and Kane following us out.

Letty smiles at me, and despite how she was earlier, I can't help but warm up to her. I understand she must be frustrated with Leon if he's kept secrets from her. I've spent almost all my life living with females. I understand how most of their minds work.

Just before I turn back to look at where I'm going, I spot something pass between Kane and Leon but I'm too drunk and possibly high to even attempt to decipher it.

With his hands on my hips, Leon guides me through the hallway that's full of couples getting a little too friendly in public and up the stairs, allowing Kane and Letty to overtake us and lead the way.

His lips trail down my neck. The move ensures that the desire he kick-started downstairs continues to flow through my veins, making my skin tingle with need.

We walk through into an unused bedroom. The mattress is bare and there are no personal possessions in sight.

Letty points to another door on the other side of the room. I slip inside, reluctantly leaving Leon behind to do what I need to do.

Staring at myself in the mirror, I take in my wide sparkling eyes. I look alive in a way I'm not sure I ever have before. My cheeks are rosy, my lips were swollen from Leon's kisses and my body is still wrapped in Charlie's figure-hugging dress.

I feel good. Sexy even. It's weird after being the boring girl who's spent her life hiding in the shadows.

After washing my hands, I pull the door open and step out, the image before me makes my steps falter a little.

The bed is no longer empty in the middle of the room, instead, Kane has Letty pinned to it with her arms above her head. Her wrists in one of his large hands as he kisses her like he might die without it.

My chest heaves as I shamelessly watch their bodies move against each other for a few seconds.

Their chemistry, connection, unfiltered need is palpable.

I don't even register what I'm doing, that I'm standing here watching something I'm sure they'd rather I'd not. That is until Leon steps up behind me, his hand snaking up my stomach, over my breasts until it comes to a stop holding my throat loosely.

"You like watching them, Red?"

"I... uh..." I swallow nervously.

Letty moans as Kane sucks on her neck.

"You look so beautiful tonight, baby," he growls, stepping around me and capturing my attention.

I forget all about the other couple in the room as I drown in his hungry green depths.

"You have no idea how hard it's been to keep my hands off you."

You haven't. The words are on the tip of my tongue. Even if I wanted to say them, I couldn't as his fingers around my throat squeeze a little before I'm pushed backward.

As I collide with the wall, all the air rushes from my lungs. He takes advantage of the situation and plunges his tongue past my lips, searching out my own.

His free hand wraps around my waist before dropping down to my thigh. He lifts my leg around his waist allowing him to grind his length against me.

An embarrassingly loud moan rips from my throat as we connect.

"Macie," he moans into our kiss.

Our tongues duel, our teeth clash as we devour each other. My hands grasp at his shirt, desperate to pull it from his body so I can feel his skin against mine.

Another moan rips through the air, reminding me that we're not alone in this small room.

Heat explodes within me as I imagine what might be happening on the bed only a few feet away.

Kissing across my jaw, Leon's lips linger at my ear.

"Do you trust me?" he whispers. His voice is so low and rough it sends a shiver down my spine.

"Y-yes."

"Good. I'm gonna make you feel so good, baby."

Before I know what he's doing, his fingers tuck under the lace of my panties, pulling them aside and exposing my most intimate part.

"Le—" I gasp as his fingertips brush against my sensitive skin. "Oh God."

The sensation is so intense that I have no idea if I want to hold him there for more or push him away.

It seems that he makes the decision for me though when he moves his hand lower. Pushing one of his fingers gently inside me.

"Oh God, oh God," I chant as he teases me. My body clenching around his digit in its need to drag him in further.

"Good?"

I thrash my head from side to side, unable to answer his question as I drown in what he's doing to me.

"Kane," Letty cries. Reality crashes into me and my body tenses.

"Ignore them," he says, pushing his finger deeper inside me as he kisses the corner of my mouth.

"They've long forgotten we're even here. Just enjoy, baby."

He does something, touching a part of me that makes every muscle in my body sag.

He holds me up but doesn't let up his assault on my body. His thumb presses against my clit as his finger continues to rub that spot.

"Leon," I moan. His name ripping from my throat without instruction from my brain.

"Fuck, Red. You've seriously got no idea how hot you are, do you?"

"Lee, please. Please." I have no idea what I'm begging for, all I know is that I need it. I need it so freaking badly.

He ups the speed, his thumb circles my clit and my entire body explodes like a box of fireworks.

Wave after wave of indescribable pleasure races through me.

My knees go weak, my heart thunders and my skin heats until I swear I'm about to combust.

"We need to leave before I do something I'll regret," he says, taking a step back and pushing his hand into his pants to rearrange the more than obvious tent he's sporting. "Come on." He holds his hand out for me and the second I place mine in it, he pulls me from the wall and tucks me into his side.

We keep our backs to the couple on the bed, but right before I step through the door, I thoughtlessly look over my shoulder.

All the air rushes from my lungs at the sight of Kane's ass as he thrusts into his girl.

My grip on Leon's hand tightens, forcing him to see what's caught my attention.

"Hot, right?"

"I... um..." I stutter, but my cheeks are burning brighter than I'm sure they ever have in my life.

"That was only the beginning, baby."

He leads me through the party, which seems to have gotten significantly more wild since we left. I see more things in those two minutes than I have in my entire life.

Leon goes out the back of the house via the kitchen. He swipes a bottle of something off the counter as we leave, and without a backward glance, rush toward his car.

17

LEON

I breathe a sigh of relief as I push Macie through her dorm and find it empty. The last thing I need right now is an interrogation from any of her roommates.

When we came back here last night, Charlie was clearly pissed about us spending time together. Yet the guys looked about ready to rip me to pieces if I so much as hurt a hair on her head.

I get their need to protect her and I can't deny that when our time is done, they'll have every right to kick my ass. But until that time comes, I'm going to play the perfect boyfriend because it's not just Macie that I need to convince with all this, it's everyone around her.

She might not think that she relies on others opinions or their advice but I know that with her innocence that she needs them. If they so much as think there's something up here, then they'll plant doubts in her head, and I know she's already got enough of her own.

My fingers flex against her lower back as I guide her toward her room, my other hand holding the bottle I lifted from the Harrises' kitchen, my mouth watering for a taste of both.

Those few minutes with her in Kane's old bedroom were nowhere near enough after the way she was dancing against me. She probably thought it was innocent enough, but the images playing out in my head every time her hips rolled were anything but.

All the ways I could ruin her, make my mark on her, ensure she'd never, ever forget me were the only things I could think about.

Part of me expected her to take me up on the offer of leaving the party only minutes after we arrived. I knew it wasn't her kind of thing. But a part of me wanted to test her, see if she really did trust me like she's beginning to say she does.

And she must because not only did we stay, but she got drunk, took a hit and let me get her off in front of two other people. Okay, so Letty and Kane were more than distracted. Neither probably had any idea that we were in the room let alone that anything was going on, but Macie didn't know that.

The second we're inside her room, I kick her door shut behind me. I push her back against it, my hand resting gently around her throat. A move that I never thought she'd allow, but it seems my innocent little redhead likes to surprise me at every turn.

"Leon," she breathes, her blue eyes darkening as her chest begins to heave once more.

"You look sinful tonight, you know that?"

She shakes her head, a coy smile playing on her lips telling me that she's more than aware that she looks good.

"I've spent all night wondering what you're hiding beneath that dress. Picturing what you might look like as I drag it down your body and let it pool at your feet. Imagining just how you taste."

Her pulse pounds harder with every word that comes out of my mouth.

Taking a step toward her, I press the length of my body against hers.

"You looked so hot coming on my fingers earlier, Red."

Her eyes shutter as she remembers.

"Did it feel good?"

She nods so slightly I would've missed it if I weren't so in-tune to her movements.

"I didn't hear you, Red."

"Y-yes. It felt good."

"You want another?"

Her cheeks heat giving me her answer, but I'm not going to let her get away with that.

Lifting the bottle that's still in my hand, I release her and twist the top off before tilting it to my lips.

The vodka burns but fuck if it doesn't feel good as it slides down my throat.

"Want some?"

It's a rhetorical question because before she even has a chance to respond, I'm lifting the bottle to her lips.

I pour knowing that most of it is going to miss. I watch as it drips from her chin and down onto her chest, running down the valley of her breasts.

"Look at that, Red. You're all dirty."

Tucking my fingers over the top of her dress, I tug exposing her cleavage. Dipping my head down, I lick up the skin, lapping at the river of vodka.

"Fuck, you taste good."

Blindly reaching out to place the bottle on the dresser beside us. I lick around the swell of her breasts, sucking the soft skin into my mouth while she mewls above me.

Her back arches, offering herself up to me and I make the most of the offer.

Wrapping my fingers around the straps of her dress and bra, I tug them down her shoulders until I expose her breasts to me.

"Perfect," I whisper. I dive forward, sucking one of her peaked nipples into my mouth.

"Leon," she cries as I tug hard on her before biting down until I know it'll sting in the most delicious way. "Oh God, y-you bit me."

"Yeah, and you loved it. You're soaked for me right now, aren't you, Red?"

Her head slams back against the wall as I move to the other side and repeat my previous action.

"Answer me, Red. Or I'll stop." It's a lie, one that I'm pretty sure we both hear loud and clear but it works.

"Yes."

Her chest heaves, her nipples glistening from my mouth, stiff and begging for more.

"And what do you want me to do about it?"

I stand back to full height.

"I-I..." She stutters as I stare her dead in the eyes. "I-I want... I want you to do that to me again."

"That?" I ask, quirking my brow.

"M-make me c-come."

"Oh baby, all you have to do is ask."

Lifting her from the floor, I wrap her legs around my waist and pull her from the door.

"Oh God," she cries, clinging to my shoulders as I spin her around. Her head no doubt spinning from whatever drink Ellis made for her earlier.

Threading my fingers into her now very messy updo, I slam her lips against mine, kissing her like she's the air I need to survive. I lower her down onto her bed and crawl over her.

"Ready to discover heaven, baby?"

"Such a player," she mutters as I kiss down her neck and toward her breasts once more.

"I'm about to show you just how seriously I take the game too."

Teasing her nipples with my tongue, I reach behind her and unhook her bra, throwing it to the floor. I wrap my hands around her dress that's pooled around her waist and pull it down, exposing her pretty lace panties.

"Damn, where's the white cotton? I was looking forward to ruining them."

She laughs briefly before I brush my lips across her belly and dip my tongue into her navel once the fabric passes it.

"Oh God."

I stand back up, pulling her dress off fully and dropping her shoes to the floor. Leaving her in just her panties.

The second I look up at her, her arms move in an attempt to cover herself up.

"Don't," I bark. "Never hide from me, Macie. You're beautiful. Sexy. Gorgeous. I could look at you forever."

A smile plays on her lips at my words.

I shed my shirt, and grab the bottle from the side, lifting it to my lips. I down a few shots as I run my eyes over her squirming on the bed.

Dark, wicked thoughts fill my mind at the sight of her waiting for me. It would be so easy to play my hand right now. To lay all my cards on the table and demand the answers I know she's got for me.

My fingers curl into fists. I could do that. Or I could prolong it, make it hurt more in the long run.

And that's exactly what the twisted monster inside me does.

Lifting the bottle to my lips once more, I try to drown out my need to cause pain, to push her right to the edge and get a hold of myself.

Make her trust you.

Make her fall.

Only then do you show her who you really are.

Stepping up to her, I meet her wide, hungry eyes. A smile curls at my lips knowing that this whole thing is playing out exactly as I hoped it would.

"Tell me if you need me to stop," I say, knowing it's what she wants to hear right now.

I crawl to the bottom of the bed by her feet, shedding my pants. I reach up and wrap my fingers around her final piece of clothing, dragging them down her thighs.

Throwing it over my shoulder, I wrap my hands around her ankles and force her legs wide despite her attempt to keep herself hidden.

My eyes lock on her slick pussy. So fucking pretty, and just desperate to be ruined.

Trailing my fingers down her thigh, I smile as her entire body trembles.

"Scared, Red?"

"N-no. I j-just... I don't know what to expect," she admits. The alcohol in her system is making her mouth run away with her even more than normal.

My fingertips hit the small patch of hair between her thighs before I drop one lower, dipping into the wetness covering her.

"Oh God," she gasps, trying to move away from me.

"I'm going to fucking ruin you, Red," I promise.

Her eyes widen with desire. Her chest heaving even more violently as she reads my statement differently to how I mean it.

Plunging two fingers inside her tight channel, I hold onto her hip as she tries to move away from me.

"Leon," she moans, squirming as she tries to get used to the alien feeling of having something, someone inside her.

Fuck, could she be any more perfect?

"This is mine, Macie." An uncontrollable wave of possession washes through me. "No matter what I do, know that all I want is for you to feel good. Trust me, yeah?"

She nods, watching my every move, trying to figure out what I'm going to do.

She looks apprehensive. No. Scared. And it makes my cock rock fucking solid.

Dragging my fingers from inside her, I lift them to my lips, sucking them into my mouth.

Horror and embarrassment colours her cheeks and down onto her chest. But there's more than that because her eyes are almost black with desire.

"Fuck," I bark, my need for her almost getting the better of me.

Pressing my palms to the inside of her thighs, I open her up wide for me.

"Beautiful," I mutter before dropping to my front and licking her ass to clit.

Her fingers find my hair and twist until it burns. I relish in the pain, I need it as a reminder for what I'm doing here.

She might taste like fucking heaven. Feel like an angel. But I'm the motherfucking devil ready to rip her of the purity she likes to try to convince everyone she has.

I know what she's witnessed in the past, I know she's not as innocent as she makes herself out to be. She knows the world is a harsh and cruel place, and that the money that has bought her freedom comes at a cost.

"Leon, oh God. That's... fuck," she cries when I graze her clit with my teeth, smiling at the same time at her language.

My good little Macie.

How the mighty fall.

"Want me to keep going, baby?" I ask, letting the vibrations of my deep voice flow through her.

"Yes. No. I don't— shit," she gasps as I plunge two fingers back inside her. Bending them until I find her G-spot.

Her back arches, her fingers twist until I swear she's going to rip my hair clean from my scalp, but I don't let up. Not until she's crying out my name as her pussy clamps down so hard on my fingers. I damn near come in my boxers from imagining just how it'll feel on my cock in the near future.

"Oh God. Oh God," she chants, her entire body going limp. I pull away from her and wipe my hand across my mouth.

"That good, huh?" I ask with a smirk as I crawl up her body.

"I just... I don't... I... fuck," she laughs at herself before covering her face with her hands to hide her embarrassment.

"Never," I spit, wrapping my fingers around her wrists. "Hide." I pull her hands away and stare down into her eyes. "From me."

She stills for a beat when I slam my lips down on hers. Plunging my tongue into her mouth, I assume from being able to taste herself on me.

"You taste so sweet," I whisper in our kiss. "I could eat you all day and still be desperate for more."

I don't give her a chance to react, instead, I pin her wrists to the bed above her head. I deepen the kiss once more, all the while rubbing myself against her swollen pussy.

My need for friction gets to be too much to bear. I release one of her hands and shove my boxers down over my ass, letting my cock spring free. I take her hand and wrap her delicate fingers around it.

"Oh God," she moans, squeezing it so tight my eyes cross.

"Feel how hard I am for you, baby. That's how badly I need you."

I move my hand with hers, showing her what to do. I don't fight the moan of pleasure that rumbles up my throat.

Getting jerked off shouldn't feel so good. Not unless you're twelve.

Shit.

Once her movements are a little more confident, I release her hand and leave her to it.

"Don't let go," I demand. I shift our position until I'm sitting across her body, my cock right above her tits.

Her eyes lock on her fingers wrapped around me as she works me to the release I'm so desperate for.

"Feels so good, baby," I groan, feeling my balls beginning to tighten.

An accomplished smile twitches at her lips at my words.

"You're going to make me come, Red. And I'm going to do it all over your sexy tits." Reaching forward, I take one in my hand, plucking her nipple until she whimpers.

"You want that? Want to see the evidence of what you do to me all over your skin?"

Her lips part but she doesn't say anything. I'm not surprised. I can't imagine anyone has ever said such things to her before.

"Answer me."

"Yes. Yes, I want it."

Good.

With one more jerk of her hand, my head falls back as pleasure races through me.

My cock twitches violently in her grasp as I do exactly what I said I was going to do and come all over her perfect breasts.

"Fuck, Macie," I groan, looking down at the mess I've made on her. "You look so fucking perfect right now."

Her eyes flick between me and my jizz that covers her, a bemused expression on her face.

"That was fucking incredible, but next time," I say dipping my finger in my seed. "I want your mouth." I trail my wet finger over her bottom lip. Her eyes widen in shock but it doesn't stop her tongue from sneaking out and getting a taste of me.

My cock threatens to go full mast again at the sight.

"Do you have any idea how badly I want to fuck you?"

She bites down on her bottom lip as her nerves slam into her.

"Not tonight, baby. When I fuck you there won't have been any alcohol past your lips. When it happens, I want to ensure you remember every second of it."

She nods, still attacking her lip.

"Let's get you cleaned up." I wink, jumping from the bed, shedding my boxers as I move toward her bathroom.

After grabbing a washcloth, I clean her up and crawl into bed beside her.

There's a huge part of me that demands I leave, but I can't. As I pull her lax body into my arms and breathe in her scent, I know I made the right decision.

That being said though, the second I wake up the next morning. I know that slipping from beneath her and disappearing before she wakes is the only thing I can do.

It would be too easy to get swept away by her. And despite my resistance, I can already feel it happening.

18

MACIE

I wake up hot. Really freaking hot. My skin is slick with sweat and my heart pounds so hard in my chest that I can feel it all the way down to my toes. But nowhere seems to beat quite as strongly as that place between my legs.

Realization of what I was just dreaming about comes back to me.

Leon's head between my thighs. His fingers inside me. My back arching as pleasure like I've never experienced before consumes me and makes me want to do it again and again and again.

Moving my hand to the side, I expect to connect with another reason for my temperature issue, but I don't find him.

Dragging my eyes open, I push up on my elbow and look around for any evidence that he was actually here. But the second my head leaves the pillow, I forget all about my dream and the desire coursing through me because my head spins and my stomach turns over.

Oh God.

With my hand clamped over my mouth, I throw the covers off and run full speed to my bathroom.

Dropping to my knees, I puke up what's left of last night's alcohol. My body trembles as I heave and for the first time since I realized he'd got up and left in the middle of the night, I'm relieved he did. No one needs to see this, hell I don't even want to experience it.

This is why I don't drink. And what the two of us got up to last night both at the party and back here is exactly why I hate losing control.

Slumping back against the wall, I drop my head to my knees as it begins to pound like there's a marching band up there.

So this is what a hangover feels like.

Gulping in long breaths, I will my stomach to settle before tentatively standing and risking a look at myself in the mirror.

Jesus, no wonder Leon ran in the middle of the night. I look horrendous.

Filling my hands with cold water, I throw it over my face. It does little for the eye makeup that's smeared all over my skin or the lipstick that's stained everything red. How Leon didn't kiss all that off, God only knows.

I brush my teeth, hoping that might make me feel a little more alive. The reality is that it just makes me want to puke again.

Stumbling back into my room, I manage to grab myself a clean pair of pajamas before diving head first back into bed.

I press my nose into the pillow, breathing in his scent before chastising myself for being so pathetic. For wishing he was still here so I could cuddle into his side and feel his strong arms holding me, keeping me safe.

All the things I said I never wanted to feel with a man, let alone a football player.

I pass out once more, faster than I thought necessary. It's hours later when I wake again to the sound of voices and people crashing around outside my door.

When I sit up this time, everything feels a little more normal. My throat still burns from throwing up and my head still pounds, but none of it is as bad as earlier. And when I make my way to the bathroom again, I don't feel the need to use the furniture or walls for support.

Stripping out of my pajamas I step into the shower, letting the cool water wake me up. I pour a generous amount of shower gel onto my sponge and get to work washing last night off me.

It's not until I run the sponge over my inner thighs that I think about the details of the night before. I look down, only to find multiple obvious fingerprints bruised into my skin.

"Oh my God," I breathe, staring at the dark marks.

Heat floods my body as I recall exactly how it felt while his fingers were digging into my skin. I didn't even realize that he was being rough with me.

I forgot everything. My lack of experience, my reasons for not wanting to get involved with anyone, knowing Leon's reputation, and all the reasons that falling into this thing with him is a bad idea. I already know that I'm the one who's going to end up hurting at the end of it. Guy's like Leon don't get their hearts broken. But girls like me have theirs obliterated by guys like them.

With a frustrated sigh, I turn the water off and step out. I guess it's better late than never to start my day.

"Whoa, here she is," Nate says with a wide smile as I emerge to find him Jace and Charlie nursing coffees at the table. To be fair, they all look about as bad as I feel, but at least they'd already emerged from their rooms. From the look of the kitchen, I'd say they've been up a while too.

"Good night?" Charlie asks, a knowing glint in her eye.

"Um..." I look around at the three of them. "Any of you have painkillers?"

Charlie chuckles but gets up and disappears to her room.

"Are we witnessing good little Macie Smith's first hangover?" Jace asks with a smile.

"Leave me alone."

"Did you have a good night?" Nate asks a little more sincerely.

"Yeah, from what I remember of it," I mutter. I head for the kitchen to make myself the biggest coffee I can manage.

"Most of the team were at the same party as us. We were expecting to see you."

"Oh... Um... We didn't go to a college party."

"So where did you go?" Jace pipes up.

"Some of Leon's friends off campus."

They both watch my every move, clearly sensing that something is up. The football team usually party as a unit so for Leon to be missing and with other friends is unusual.

"Who were they?" Charlie asks, passing me a bottle of pills. She returns to her seat, clearly eavesdropping on our conversation from her room.

"Who were who?" I ask innocently.

"Leon's friends."

"Oh..." I rack my brain for something to tell them when a thought, or more a realization slams into me. "We were with Kane Legend and his girlfriend." I don't know why I didn't put two and two together last night. *Probably the cocktail of pure alcohol Ellis Harris gave you,* a little voice says.

"At an off campus party?" Charlie asks, her eyes narrowed in suspicion.

"Yeah, problem?"

"N-no not at all. Just... Be careful, yeah?"

"Jeez, I'm a freaking adult. I can look after myself," I snap, really not in the mood to be babied by my roommates. Yeah, okay, so I'm the innocent one who doesn't usually do this stuff but that doesn't mean I'm an idiot who'll willingly put herself in danger.

The image of the first guy I was introduced to last night pops into my head.

Reid Harris.

A shiver rips down my spine as I remember his cold, hard eyes.

Yeah, something tells me that being anywhere near him is dangerous.

"We don't mean anything bad by it, but rumor has it that Kane is connected to some... interesting people," Nate says, concern written all over his face.

"It was one party," I say dismissively. As I grab my mug from the coffee maker, disappearing back to my room.

If all they're going to do is judge me for having the night out—one that they've been trying to get me to go on since the beginning of the year—then they can screw off.

I'm suffering enough as it is. I don't need their opinions on my life.

They must get the message because none of them try to follow me. The only time I see them for the rest of the day is when I emerge from my room for food and drink.

"I'm sorry about earlier," Nathan says, joining me in the kitchen when I'm making what must be my sixth coffee of the day.

"Yeah, whatever," I wave him off, not wanting to make a big deal out of it.

"No, Mace," he says, placing his hand on my forearm. He gives me little choice but to turn toward him.

He studies me for a beat. His eyes dropping to my neck where he no doubt noticed the hickeys darkening the skin.

"We just want to make sure you're happy," he murmurs, looking back up into my eyes.

"I know what I'm doing." He quirks a brow at me, knowing that I'm lying. "Okay fine, I'm just... Going with the flow. Enjoying myself."

"How's the first hangover going?" he asks, thankfully changing the subject.

"It's hell. Why do people do this to themselves willingly every weekend?"

"Was last night fun?"

I think back, my cheeks heating as images of everything we did flicker through my mind.

"Yeah," I whisper. "More than I've had in... a while."

"That's why." I nod my head as he continues with his reasoning.

"Sometimes letting go of control and dropping your barriers is exactly what we need."

"Yeah, I think you're right," I muse.

"Maybe next time you can do it with us. I kinda want to see you letting your hair down for once."

"You trying to say I'm uptight?" I place my hands on my hips, staring him down.

"Oh, never, Mace. Never," he jokes. "Come here." He pulls me into a hug. We might be fairly close but it's not the kind of thing we usually do. "I'll kick his ass if he hurts you," he growls in my ear, his voice low and rough.

"It won't be necessary," I say. Hoping like hell it's the truth because the last thing I want is Nathan getting hurt because of me.

"I've got your back, Mace."

"Thank you."

He releases me so that I can grab my coffee and retreat back to my room to the assignment I'm meant to be working on. If I'm being honest with myself, I spent most of the last hour writing, deleting and rewriting messages to Leon. None of which I've been brave enough to send.

I knew he was busy with family stuff this morning, but I kinda hoped he'd reach out after.

My heart sinks as I begin to wonder if last night wasn't as big a deal to him as it was to me.

Of course it wasn't. You're just another notch on his bedpost, a little voice laughs. *He's probably already forgotten all about it.*

Forcing my doubts away, I open my laptop to get to work. With the hope that a few hours will pass of worrying whether I did something wrong or if I just wasn't good enough.

———

By the time the sun rises on Sunday morning, I've pretty much come to the conclusion that anything there might have been between Leon and me has been obliterated. All night I kept my cell close, thinking that he'd send something. But it remained silent.

And this morning... Still nothing.

With a frustrated sigh, I head for the bathroom knowing that I've still got all the work to do that I failed to complete yesterday. I better get to it if I want to get a head start on my week.

I'm standing at my mirror moisturizing my face when my cell finally pings. The bottle in my hand clatters into the sink as I run into my bedroom. Tossing the covers off my bed until I find it.

My heart thunders in my chest, anticipation pulsing through me for what he might have to say.

But that all comes crashing down when I see it's just an alert from the security company who monitors my uncle's estate in his absence.

Dropping down onto my bed with my cell in my hands, tears burn my eyes.

I hate myself for it, but I can't stop the rejection washing through me.

I really want to believe there's a reason he bailed without a word. But my insecurities are at an all time high after what I allowed to happen between us.

Sucking in a few deep breaths, I finally lift my head and swipe my screen.

The alert tells me that the security alarm was tripped but assures me that everything is okay.

Great.

I hate that place, and I wouldn't bat an eyelid should I get an alert to tell me that someone has burned it to the ground.

There's only one reason I continue any kind of relationship with my uncle. His money. People might judge me for it, but I don't care. Out of all the bad, I want to do something good. And if it means that I have to make things a little harder on myself than necessary, to keep certain promises to the monster who's ruined so many lives, including mine, then I'll do it. All with the purpose of knowing that in the future, I'm going to be able to give back to kids like me. Boys like the ones who put their trust and futures in the hands of a man who was meant to only want the best for them.

Movement outside my door catches my attention. But any hope I have of Leon storming through and sweeping me up in his arms have long vanished.

Placing my cell on my nightstand, I walk over to my dresser to pull out a pair of leggings and an oversized shirt to hibernate in for the day.

I damn near jump out of my skin when a knock rattles my door.

"Mace," Nathan calls. "You've got a visitor."

My eyes widen as I suck in a sharp breath.

"Oh my God." I reach for my hairbrush and quickly attempt to tame my red mane. "I'll be right there."

My hands tremble as I try to make myself look presentable. I walk toward the door on weak knees, my stomach doing somersaults as my trembling hand reaches for the handle.

I suck in a huge breath, hoping some confidence will come with it and pull the door open.

My eyes find Nate first before I look over his shoulder, desperate to find Leon's green eyes staring back at me.

Only, it's not him I find standing confidently behind Nate, but instead Letty.

"Oh... Um... Hey," I say nervously as an image of the last time I saw her, or more so her fiancé, slam into me.

"Hey," she says, stepping around Nate and coming to stand in front of me. "I was hoping we could talk."

"Uh... yeah. Sure. Come in."

I nod at Nate who disappears down the hall and step aside to allow Letty into my room.

"Is everything okay?" I ask, terrified that something from my overactive imagination might have happened to Leon to stop him from getting in touch.

"Yeah, everything is good." She looks around my room, taking everything in. "I just thought I should introduce myself properly. Friday night probably wasn't the best time for it."

"Are their parties always like that?" I ask.

"Honestly, that one was pretty tame."

Lifting my hand to my hair, I tuck it behind my ears, swallowing nervously as I consider how much wilder things could get. Drink, drugs, sex. What more is there?

"Oh... right. I'm not really a party girl," I confess.

"Yeah, I suspected as much. You mind?" she asks, pointing to my chair.

"Of course not," I say, backing toward my bed and dropping down on the edge.

She studies me for a few seconds as if it's the first time she's seeing me.

"I wanted to apologize for Friday night. I can't imagine you left with all that great of an impression of me."

"I-it's okay."

"I was pissed at Leon. That wasn't meant to rub off onto you. I'm sorry."

"Honestly, it's fine."

"He came to see me the other night to tell me about you."

"He did?" My eyebrow almost hit my hairline at her confession.

"Yep. It seems you've managed to get well under his skin."

A humorless laugh falls from my lips. "I'm not so sure about that. I've not heard from him since Friday night."

"He's a guy, Macie. That's the kind of shit they do. I wouldn't read too much into it if I were you."

"I'm totally out of my depth here," I admit, resting back on my palms and looking at the corner of the room to avoid her stare.

I don't know her, but there's something about the way she looks at me that makes me think she gets me. It's unnerving.

She's Leon's friend, not mine. Yet I feel drawn to her in a way I'm not to most people.

"So is he."

Those three words force my eyes back to hers as my chin drops.

"I've known Leon for years, Macie. And not once have I ever known him to see a girl twice, let alone for a—"

"A week," I muse, finishing her sentence for her.

"Yeah, that's unheard of," she mutters almost to herself.

"Is that what you've come here to tell me? That he's behaving weird."

"Well, no. Mostly I came in the hope I could correct your first impressions of me but I don't feel like I'm doing a very good job with that. I also wanted to just meet you. See what it is that's got Leon twisted in knots."

"There's nothing much to see. I think I'm probably Leon's opposite in every single way. He's also everything I always said I never wanted. Match made in hell if you ask me."

Her response to my comment is to burst out laughing which confuses the hell out of me.

"Um..."

"I'm sorry, it's just I have some experience with relationships like that."

"Oh?"

"Kane and me... I'm pretty sure we were matched in hell too."

"But you look so... Together. So happy."

A soft smile plays on her lips as she thinks of him. "We are now. Things weren't always so smooth."

"Oh wow. I never would have guessed."

She shrugs. "Things aren't always as they seem."

"That's what I'm worried about," I blurt out, instantly regretting it.

"Why do you say that?"

"He's got to be playing me, right? I mean Leon freaking Dunn has been here spending time with me, taking me to his wild parties and giving me romantic dates. Me," I say, pointing to myself in case she didn't get it the first time. "He could be spending time with any girl on campus, why me?"

"Because he wants to. Leon's been..."

"A dog?" I supply for her.

"Yeah, you're right. But he's never, ever let anyone close to him. Even me, Luca, the rest of the team. He keeps us all at arm's length."

"Why?"

She shrugs. "No idea. It's just the way he is. But when he spoke about you the other night, I saw something different in him. He seemed... happy. Relaxed. At peace. I didn't realize just how bad he was before I saw that shift."

"I did that?"

"I believe so, yeah."

"Wow," I breathe, not really knowing how to deal with all this.

"He's going to fuck this up, Macie. I mean, he already is if the look on your face when you saw me instead of him in the hall is anything to go by. He's going to need you to let him do this at his own pace."

"I get that. It's just so weird going from one-hundred miles an hour to nothing all of a sudden. I can't help wondering if I did something wrong. I don't exactly have experience with guys, and Leon... Well... we all know his reputation."

"He's got some shit going on with family right now. He—"

"His new brother?"

She smiles again. "He told you that?"

"Yeah. He told me they were all going for breakfast yesterday morning. That's why I wasn't too concerned when I woke up and he was gone. But it's been radio silent since then."

"Have you reached out to him?" She quirks a brow at me.

"Err…"

"Maybe you should message him. He might be sitting at home thinking that he's done something wrong," she suggests.

"Yeah, maybe," I whisper, wondering if me and all my insecurities will be the thing to screw this up, not Leon.

I'm still lost in my own thoughts when she asks me the dreaded question.

"So… Tell me about you. Leon was pretty tight-lipped."

"Oh, not much to tell really. I went to an all-girls school in Tallahassee then I came here. My mom studied here and I wanted to follow in her footsteps."

"Fair enough. I'm from Harrow Creek originally but I moved to Rosewood where Leon and Luca lived then Luca and I became close friends. Leon kinda got stuck with me because of that," she jokes.

"Harrow Creek?" I ask, thinking the name of the place sounds familiar.

"Yeah, you've probably heard it mentioned on the news. The place is the pits of hell."

"Oh. So you were lucky to get out then?"

"You have no idea. Sounds like our previous lives couldn't be more different if you were at a prep school. We were just lucky no one burned down our school," she deadpans.

"It wasn't all it was cracked up to be."

"Oh, I'm sure places like that have their own issues."

I think of the girls, the drugs that were snuck in and all the things rumored to have gone on inside the expensive walls.

"So what classes are you taking this semester?"

We fall into easy conversation about school and other nonsense. I realize that my first impressions earlier were right—she really is my kind of person.

"Can I ask you something?" I ask when our previous conversation trails off.

"Sure. Hit me with it."

"Those guys at the party. Who are they? They all looked... Well, dangerous."

She laughs, an amused twinkle in her eyes. "That would be because they are. I have no idea why Leon thought it was a good idea to take you there last night. I don't even know why he was there to be honest, I didn't realize he was friends with any of them."

"So who are they?"

"Harrow Creek Hawks." A shudder runs down my spine from the three words alone.

Leon had called them Hawks, but the fact Letty has just tagged on the name of the awful place where she grew up doesn't make me feel any better about them.

"A... a gang?"

"Yeah. A pretty dangerous one. If I were you, I'd stay as far away as possible."

"You're friends with them?"

She nods. "Yeah. They're actually decent guys when you get to know them and are able to see beneath what they do for a living."

"Which is?"

"Stuff you don't want to know about."

"Fair enough."

My cell dings again and I rush over to grab it hoping once again that it might be him. But just like earlier, it's just the security company telling me that the alarm tripped again.

"Ugh."

"Not him then, I assume."

"What gave me away?" I joke.

"The disappointment that was written all over your face was a clue."

"He's messing with my head, Letty. I said I've never let a man do that to me. Ever."

"Don't we all. Unfortunately, sometimes they just get on up in there and refuse to get the hell out."

"Great."

"I need to head off, I've got work later, but I'd love to hang out again, if you'd like to, of course. I could let you in on a few of Leon's secrets." She winks but despite her words, I already suspect she's loyal to the core and would never tell me anything that was actually a secret.

"I'd love to," I say with a wide smile. I've never had many friends, but something tells me that there could be something here.

"I've got a couple of friends who I think you'll really get along with."

"Don't they get out much either?" I deadpan but she doesn't laugh like I was expecting.

"There's nothing wrong with taking college at a slower pace, Macie. You just do you. Whatever that is."

'Thank you,' I mouth, a lump of emotion clogging my throat and stopping me from saying the words aloud.

"Let me give you my number." She holds her hand out for my cell, and after unlocking it, I pass it over and she taps her digits in. Hers rings in her purse two seconds later. "I'll be in touch. And when that boy gets in touch, give him hell, yeah? Let him know you're not a doormat who'll let him get away with acting like a douchebag."

"I'll do my best, but mostly he turns me into a stuttering idiot."

"It's the eyes. I get it," she jokes. "Just don't look at him as you do it."

"Thanks for this. I really appreciate it."

"Anytime. We'll all need each other once the season starts and our men spend all their time playing with balls." She winks.

"Don't they do that all year round," I deadpan.

She bursts out laughing. "I like you, Macie. And I think you're going to be really good for Lee. He's been going through some shit, and I think you might just be the light he needs."

"We'll see."

"We will. I'll see myself out."

She slips from my room and I fall back onto my bed with a smile on my face.

It feels good after the frown I've been walking around with since yesterday morning. I can't help wondering what I did wrong.

19

LEON

"Hey." I say, slipping into the sterile hospital room and closing the door behind me. I hoped she'd be alone seeing as Peyton was still at the house with Luca when I left.

Libby's eyes narrow on me as I step further inside the room. I didn't expect her to remember me. It's been years since I saw her last. Although I can confidently say that I don't look as different as she does. It's clear from her face alone that she's been to hell and back recently.

"Leon," I say. "Luca's twin brother."

"Y-yeah," she stutters. "I know."

She sits herself up in the hospital chair that looks out over the trees and forest in the distance. Right now she's not taking in the peaceful vista, instead her eyes are tracking my every movement across the room.

Dropping down into one of the chairs on the other side of the room. I leave the bed between us, sensing she needs the space, as I turn toward her.

"How are you doing?" I ask, genuinely interested in her progress.

"Things could be worse. Rumor has it I might be getting out of here in a few days."

"That's great news. Are you heading to the facility Luca organized?"

"Yeah." Lifting her hand, she scratches at her forearm. Something tells me that she's not even aware she's doing it as her eyes hold mine. "Let's hope it works, hey?"

"Well, you've got a pretty incredible little boy hoping that it does."

All the air rushes from her lungs as I mention her son, my half-brother. "You've met him?"

"I have. He's incredible."

"Against all the odds, hey?"

"Don't be so hard on yourself, Libby. None of this is your fault."

She scoffs, clearly a long way from being able to lay all the blame for this whole fucking nightmare at the person who deserves it.

"I was a stupid, naïve little girl who fell for every trick in the book. I was almost eighteen, I should have seen it a mile off."

"He had a game plan, Libby. I doubt he'd have failed. That's not on you. It's on him. Manipulative cunt that he is."

She stares at me, a million questions swimming in the depths of her eyes.

"I hated him long before I found out about all of this," I confess, answering one of those questions. "You're not the only one who's bore the brunt of his manipulation."

"What did he do to you?" she asks, her brows pinching.

"He never laid a hand on me, if that's what you mean. It's what he allowed to happen. What he turned a blind eye to and brushed under the carpet."

Her eyes widen as she hears my unspoken words.

"I see." She falls silent as a nurse knocks on the door. She does a couple of checks before taking away the leftovers from Libby's dinner.

It's not until we're alone once more that she speaks again.

"Why are you really here, Leon? I'm sure it's not to swap stories about how your father has wronged us both."

I can't help but laugh despite the situation being anything but amusing. "No, that's certainly not why I'm here. Although, I have no doubt that we understand each other in ways others can't." She nods, telling me what I already know. "But I wanted you to hear from me, that he's not going to get away with it anymore."

"What have you done?"

"Nothing I can give you details about. But I wanted you to know that when you get out of here, you're not going to bump into him. He's not going to turn up wanting to see your son or demanding anything of you."

"That's good to know."

"I'm also going to ensure you get everything you deserve after what he put you and your family through."

"I appreciate that, Leon. But I don't want anything from him. I could never regret having Kayden despite what a shitty mother I've been. But he is certainly all I ever want from that cunt."

"I understand that. Trust me, I do. And if you don't want it, then I won't force it on you. But know that it will be sitting somewhere safe for Kayden's future. Prep school, college, traveling... Just about anything he could want, he'll be able to have it."

Tears fill Libby's eyes and she quickly lifts her hand to swipe away the one that falls.

"That little boy deserves so much more than I can give him."

"You're wrong, Libby," I say, walking around the bed and lowering down in front of her. Hesitantly, I reach for her hand and squeeze it in support. "All he needs is love. From you, Peyton, your aunt Fee. His brothers. He's got a huge family around him who only wants the best for him. He's one lucky little boy. None of us will allow him to be treated as we've been in the past. He's got the world at his feet. He's the luckiest boy in the world."

"Oh God," she sobs, lifting her free hand to dry her cheeks once more.

"I'm sorry. I just... I thought you might need to hear it."

She nods, sniffling as her tears continue to fall.

"Thank you," she finally says.

"Anything you need, Libby. We're here for both of you... For all of you."

She nods, starting to get herself together.

And that's exactly how Peyton finds us, with me on my knees and Libby with tears streaked down her face.

"What the hell is going on?"

"Shit," I breathe, releasing Libby and jumping to my feet.

"Nothing. We were just having a heart to heart."

"So I see. Is there something I need to know?" Peyton looks between the two of us, her brow wrinkled with confusion.

"No," we both say in unison, sounding guilty as fuck I'm sure.

With a small smile and nod at Libby, I move across the room until I'm in front of Peyton.

"There's nothing you need to worry about, we were just... Airing some grievances, shall we say."

"What does that even mean, Lee?"

"It doesn't matter." She studies me for a beat before saying something that makes my world momentarily fall out from beneath me.

"That's good because I don't think Macie would be overly impressed with you being here holding my sister's hand and wiping her tears."

All the air rushes from my lungs.

"How do you—"

"Letty spent the afternoon with your girl."

"Fucking hell," I moan, running my fingers through my hair and pulling it back from my face.

"Did you know you're in the doghouse? You've barely even made her yours and you've fucked it up."

"Don't beat around the bush, Peyton."

"Why should I? I'm on Macie's side here."

"H-how... You don't even know her."

"Maybe not. But Letty does. And let's just say that girl code is a real thing."

"You know, there's a very good reason why I haven't told any of you about her yet."

"Oh we know. But unfortunately for you, we can play the game too."

"Game? What are you talking about?"

She takes a step toward me, her eyes hard and holding a warning. "If you're fucking her around, then you need to walk away now."

"Who said I'm fucking around?"

"No one but we all know you better than you think we do, and something is going on with you. Your past that everyone pussyfoots around, Brett—" A shudder rips through me at just hearing his name on her lips. "Now Macie? You don't do serious, Leon, so what's going on?"

"What do you know about what I do and don't do? You haven't been here for almost six years. You don't get to stand there and judge me," I hiss, aware that Libby is watching and listening to everything.

"Judging? Are you being serious? I'm worried, Leon. We're all worried."

"Yeah well, you don't need to be. I know what I'm doing."

"I hope for everyone's sake that you do because if you hurt anyone I care about—like the innocent girl who believes you're something you're not—then that family you were just talking to Libby about, may no longer exist for you."

A bitter laugh rips from my throat.

"You have no idea what you're talking about."

"I really hope you're right, Leon. I really do."

She steps aside so I can pass. After a brief look back at a very confused Libby, I take a step forward to leave, but Peyton's tiny hand wraps around my bare forearm.

I pause beside her but keep my eyes locked on the door.

"I'm sorry, Lee," she whispers. "I..." She sucks in a breath, giving herself a moment to gather her thoughts. "You're my family, my brother. I love you and I'm worried about you. I know something is going on and it's killing me that you won't open up to any of us."

My chest aches as her words flow through me.

I have no idea how it's happened, but I lived for years with no one knowing there was anything up with me. Even Mom never really questioned me, she probably just believed I was a grumpy teenager. But the last few weeks something has changed. I've got no idea if I let my mask slip or what, but people are starting to see my cracks and I fucking hate it.

My fists curl at the thought of those I love learning the truth about my life. About what I've hidden from all of them all these years.

"I love you too, Peyton. I'm so glad you're back in our lives. But please, I beg you. Stop digging."

Without another word, I pull my arm from her grip and storm from the room. My heart pounding in my chest. And my muscles straining to do something, to hit someone, to cause some pain.

And right now, there's only one place I need to go for that.

20

MACIE

I'm already curled up in bed with the tub of ice cream we didn't eat the other night. Drowning in my sorrows when the guys come storming through the dorm.

All three of them went out this afternoon after Letty's visit, leaving me with some much needed peace and quiet.

I managed to get some work done, but not as much as I wanted. My head was still spinning with the conversation I had with Letty.

I picked up and put down my cell more times than I could count. I even opened up our chat a couple of times and typed a message. But I bailed before I hit send.

Would he think I was being needy because I couldn't go a few hours without contact? Is he just busy? Do I need to just be patient?

With each thought, my irritation level at myself grows.

I don't want to be that girl. The one who second guesses herself because of a guy. But here I am freaking the hell out, when deep down, I know I've done nothing wrong.

I'm better than this. I'm stronger than this.

I'm Macie freaking Fletcher for Christ's sake.

My life has taught me to deal with things better than this.

He. Is. Just. A. Boy.

I tell myself this over and over in the hope that at some point, it'll begin to come true. But there's something deep down that knows it's not.

Leon isn't just a boy. He's someone I was meant to meet.

For whatever reason I've yet to figure out why our paths were meant to cross. I just wish I knew why because right now, he's giving me more stress than I need.

I'm still lying there lost in my own irritating head when there's a loud bang in the distance. It doesn't sound like it's in our dorm, so I ignore it assuming it's some drunken students trying to make their way back. But what I hear next has me sitting bolt upright.

"Macie."

It's muffled, but I know it's my name.

Scrambling out of bed, I race through the dorm to our main door. The guys must have locked it on their way out, knowing that I needed some peace.

Flipping the lock, I pull the door open an inch. What I find has me flinging it open as my heart tumbles in my chest.

"W-what happened?" I cry, reaching for him.

But instead of moving toward me when I wrap my hand around his forearm, he rips it from my grip and takes a step back.

"I shouldn't be here," he mutters. "Fuck, I shouldn't—" He lifts his bloody hands to his face as he stumbles back into the wall and bends over as if he's in physical pain.

"It's okay," I soothe, walking over to him and gently pulling his hands from his face.

He looks... He looks so broken.

The sight makes my chest split in two.

This strong, ballsy, independent man is shattering right in front of me.

"Come on. I'll clean you up."

When I take his hands and pull him forward, this time he doesn't fight as I lead him inside, closing and locking the door behind us. Something tells me he doesn't want the entire building witnessing this.

I don't stop again until we're in the safety of my room.

"Sit," I instruct, gently pushing him down on the edge of my bed. "I'll go get the first aid kit."

I have no idea where all the blood has come from, but he doesn't seem to be injured. Despite the fact his knuckles are wrecked, it doesn't look like anyone has hit him. His face, aside from his expression, is as perfect as ever. There are just a few splashes of blood that seem to be covering every inch of him.

I run a small bowl of warm water, and grab a cloth. I make my way back, dropping to my knees in front of him.

His eyes track my every move as I take one of his hands and begin cleaning him up.

The skin is split open across all his knuckles. Whoever or whatever he hit must have really hurt. But despite that, he barely even flinches as I carefully wipe the blood away.

"What happened, Leon?" I ask, looking up at him. Only to find him staring down at me with an intensity that makes my breath catch in my throat.

After a few seconds, he must register that I asked a question because he shakes his head.

"Should I be worried about the person who was at the other end of these?" I ask lifting his knuckles and squeeze his fingers.

A bitter laugh falls from his lips.

"No."

"Okay," I say, trusting that he's telling me the truth.

"Talk to me, Leon. Please."

He shakes his head once more. "You don't want to know. It would change the way you look at me. The way you feel about me."

I want to tell him that I'm sure it won't, but I swallow down the words.

"Did this have something to do with the guys from Friday night? I know they're in a gang."

"No, this is my shit."

I sit back on my heels and look up at him, willing him to open up and tell me what's got him in such a state. But while his eyes are dark and tormented, I can see the walls building back up in front of them from when he first arrived.

"I shouldn't have come here," he says again.

"So why did you?" I ask without thinking.

"Because all I could think about was you."

All the air rushes from my lungs at his confession.

"Is this... Whatever this is, the reason you vanished this weekend?"

"Partly. I was busy yesterday with family shit. But mostly I was freaking out," he admits, making my brows pull together as I try to read between the lines. "This," he says, gesturing between the two of us. "I've never... I've never done this, felt this. It's—"

"Unnerving?" I finish for him.

"Y-yeah."

"I don't know what I'm doing here either, Leon. If that wasn't already abundantly obvious. I don't do this—" I repeat his move from earlier gesturing between us. "I've never let anyone this close to me. Ever."

His eyes flick to the door, thinking of my roommates I'm sure.

"Not even them. Nate is the closest thing I have to a true friend. We've both lived a similar life with our prep school background. But he doesn't know who I really am."

He blows out a long breath as if what I just said has utterly floored him.

"I don't deserve to be the person who knows you, Macie."

"This isn't about what either of us deserve, Leon. Do you believe in fate?"

He shrugs. "I've experienced too much shit to believe that it all happens for a reason. You?"

"Until last week, no. But then I met you and..." I hesitate, feeling crazy for even thinking it, let alone saying the words out loud. "And I can't help but wonder if there's a reason that I crashed into your life."

"Not just to cockblock me with your roommate?" he deadpans.

"Well, yeah. That too. You think I'd have gone near you if you'd been inside Charlie first?" I slam my lips shut, not believing I just said those words. "You drive me crazy," I blurt out. "I've never had such an issue with my filter."

Flipping his hand over so he's the one holding me, a small smile twitches at the corner of his lips.

"I like it. I like that you can't help but tell me what you're thinking, how you really feel."

My lips part to respond but I find no words.

"I shouldn't have come here toni—"

"I already told you it's okay."

"Shush," he soothes, pressing two fingers to my lips to stop me. "But I'm not sorry I did."

I stare into his eyes, which thankfully have lightened since I found him, chemistry crackling between us as the seconds pass.

"W-what do you need?" I whisper, needing to know what I can do to make this better.

He presses my palms to his jean covered thighs and slides them up.

My eyes drop from his to his crotch, finding his hard length obviously pressing against the fabric.

My mouth goes dry as I remember what he said to me about the next time I get him off.

'But next time, I want your mouth.'

Swallowing down my nerves, I rip my eyes from his bulge and back up to his eyes.

He must see my hesitation because his expression softens. He reaches out, tucking a lock of hair behind my ear and cups my cheeks in his hand.

"As much as I like what you're thinking. What I really need is a shower."

My lips part as my chin drops.

He's turning me down?

Hurt coils around me like a snake.

I mean, I know that I'll probably be a disappointment but that doesn't mean I wouldn't have given it my best shot.

"Oh, okay," I whisper, pushing from the floor. I step away from him before he can see the dejection in my eyes.

But I don't get very far because he catches my hand and pulls me back between his legs.

His eyes lock on my tank covered breasts for a beat. Making my nipples pebble beneath the thin fabric before he lifts them to meet my stare.

"I didn't mean alone, Red."

Standing, his chest brushes against mine. The sensation sends a wave of heat through me that pools between my legs.

He wraps his hand around the side of my face, staring down into my eyes.

"You're a fucking angel, you know that?"

I shake my head, refusing to accept his words.

His head lowers toward mine and I lick my lips ready to accept his kiss, only, he never makes it. Instead, he reaches behind him and drags his blood splattered shirt over his head.

He should probably terrify me right now. He clearly went out tonight and seriously hurt someone. But I can't find it in me to care when he's standing right before me with wicked promises filling his eyes.

I did that. I helped banish whatever demons he was battling with when he arrived and I put that look there instead.

Me.

My head spins with the knowledge. I feel more powerful right now than I have in my entire life.

"As sexy as this tank is," he murmurs, wrapping his fingers around the bottom. "I much prefer just seeing what's underneath."

In a heartbeat he has it off my body and on the floor with his.

"Now that's what I need," he mutters, staring shamelessly down at my bare chest.

My fingers twitch to cover up. I haven't been naked in front of anyone since... Well, since I was a kid, so it feels weird standing here like this.

"Fuck, I need to feel you against me so bad," he says in a rush. He rips open his fly and shoves both his pants and boxers down his legs. I take a step back so he has space to toe off his shoes and abandon it all on the floor.

Just like I already knew, his cock is hard and standing proud from his body. The tip glistening, making my mouth water as I wonder what he might taste like.

Since the thought hit me when I was sitting on the floor, sucking him into my mouth is now the only thing I can think about.

"Fuck, you're sexy" he whispers, stepping up to me he pushes his thumbs into my shorts and panties. "I love it when you look at me like that."

"L-like what?" I ask, needing to know what he sees when I look at him.

"Like you can't get enough. Like you want to taste me. Like you never want to let go."

My chest heaves with each observation he makes.

I don't say a word in response. How can I? He's right.

He pushes my remaining clothes to my ankles before he presses the length of his hot and hard body against mine. He leans down to grip the backs of my thighs, lifting me into him.

My legs wrap around his waist, my arms around his shoulders as he continues to stare at me.

"I-I want to," I confess, my cheeks flaming red.

"You want to what, Red?"

Leaning forward, I brush his ear with my lips, unable to believe what I'm about to admit.

"I want to taste you."

"Motherfucker," he groans as if he's in pain. He eats up the room with his long legs and pushes through into my bathroom.

I gasp when my back connects with the cold tiles of my shower stall.

"Leon," his name rips from my throat without instruction from my brain. He palms my ass, digging his fingertips into my flesh until it begins to burn.

"Need you, Red. I fucking need you."

His lips find mine, his tongue pushing inside.

I return his brutal kiss move for move. My tongue slides against his, twisting, turning and fighting for dominance. Our teeth clash, our hands roam, grabbing, scratching, not knowing where we want to touch first.

At some point he must release me because freezing cold water rains down on both of us.

"Oh my God," I squeal against his lips.

"Hmm..." he groans, placing his hand back on my ass and lifting me a little higher.

His hard length brushes against my core and my entire body tenses in panic.

"Relax, baby. I'm not going to do anything you don't want. Just enjoying your heat."

To prove his point, he thrusts his hips slowly dragging the head of his cock against my clit.

This time when I still it's not because of fear, but pleasure.

"So wet for me," he murmurs, his lips dropping to my neck as he sucks on the skin.

My head falls back against the wall as a familiar sensation begins to build in my lower stomach.

Surely he can't make me climax from this alone. He's barely touching me.

"I need you, Red," he groans.

His desperation from when he first arrives deepens his voice. I'm reminded of the broken man I answered the door to, as well as what I told him I wanted to do.

I wasn't lying. But I would be if I were to say that I wasn't scared.

Releasing my legs from his waist, he allows me to stand although he doesn't move away from me.

"I'm addicted, Macie," he confesses quietly. "You're the only thing I can think about. And if you knew the shit going on in my life then you'd understand just how big that is."

Honesty pours from his dark green depths. I have to bite back the demand for him to tell me exactly what he's dealing with right now.

My need to help consumes me. All I want to do is make things better for him.

But I already know that he won't tell me. Leon might be opening up about how he's feeling but he's a long way from trusting me with his secrets.

I get it.

Hell, I more than get it because there's a chance I'll go to my grave with mine.

He holds my eyes for a few seconds longer, a silent plea for me to make it all better. And without putting too much thought into it, I slide down the wall.

Only, I don't get very far because his hand catches me around the throat and I've no choice but to look up at him.

"You can't do this wrong, Red. Stop worrying."

I nod once before he releases me and allows me to drop to my knees.

Sucking in a deep breath, I stare at his solid length before me.

Granted, I've not exactly seen many before but damn if Leon's cock isn't as perfect as the rest of him.

Feeling his stare burning into the top of my head, I look up.

His eyes are like fire as he watches me before him.

"Fuck, you look hot."

His fingers run through my wet hair as he waits to see if I'm going to follow through with this.

"Suck me, baby."

My breath catches in my throat as his dirty words send a wave of heat to my pussy.

Oh God.

Reaching out, I wrap my hand around his length, unable to fight my smile as it twitches violently at my touch.

"Macie," he groans, almost sounding like he's in pain.

Taking in every line and muscle on his torso, I finally make it up to his eyes again.

I gasp as we connect. The fire in his depths spurring me on.

Leaning forward, I poke my tongue out and lick the tip of him hesitantly.

"Fuck," he barks, his eyes closing for a beat. "Macie," he begs.

A feeling of power I've never experienced before washes through me.

Parting my lips, I wrap them around the head of his cock, letting his taste fill my mouth. He twists his fingers in my hair, sending a bite of pain down my neck.

Feeling brave knowing that he's enjoying it, I take him deeper.

"Yess," he hisses above me, encouraging me and ensuring I know he's loving what I'm doing to him. "Deeper, baby."

So I do, I take him back until he hits the back of my throat as I gasp in shock.

"You look so fucking beautiful on your knees for me, baby."

I smile up at him, for the first time in my life, feeling sexy, in control, and wanted.

Feeling a little more confident, I suck him into my mouth again. I take him all the way back before slowly pulling off once more.

His moans and groans tells me how good it is. So I keep going and taking a little more of him every time.

"Macie," he moans, his fingers tightening even more in my hair. "Red, I'm gonna come if you don't want—"

I suck him deeper, knowing that I need to see this through.

"Fuck. Fuck," he barks. His cock swelling in my mouth before it jerks and his cum hits the back of my throat.

I fight the need to pull away but I swallow it all down. Pride swelling in my chest for what I just did.

The second he's finished, he reaches down, tucking his hands under my arms and hauls me from the floor like I weigh nothing.

"Fuck, you're amazing," he says before slamming his lips against mine. He's clearly not bothered that I probably taste like him and presses me against the wall.

He kisses me like a man possessed and I drown in it as his hands roam around my body, pinching, squeezing, driving me crazy. That is until he dips them between my legs and I gasp, ending our kiss as the sensation rushes through me.

"So wet for me, Red," he murmurs against my neck. His fingers move to my entrance, teasing me.

"Leon."

"Did you enjoy sucking me, baby?"

"Y-yes."

"I can feel it."

"Oh God," I moan when his fingers push deeper.

"So tight, Red. I can't wait to feel your pussy wrapped around my cock. You're going to make me come so fucking hard."

Heat surges to my core at his words.

"Oh you want that, don't you, baby? You just got so wet thinking about it."

"Leon," I moan again. My mind full of the image of him doing what he just described while I wonder just how much it'll hurt.

"One day soon, Red. It'll happen one day soon. All you gotta do is say the words."

My chest aches knowing that he's waiting for me. He could so easily push it right now and I'm sure I'd give in. But he's not even trying and I love that about him. Despite what everyone thinks, what his reputation says; he's sweet, caring, totally unselfish.

He bends his fingers until they hit a spot inside me that makes lights flash behind my eyes.

"Fuck, I need to taste you, Red."

Dragging his fingers out of me, I lift my head from the wall and stare at him. He parts his lips and pushes his digits inside, sucking them clean.

My eyes widen as more heat hits my pussy.

Christ, that's hot.

"So sweet," he mutters around his fingers. "But not nearly enough."

My breath catches when he drops to his knees before me. He throws one of my legs over his shoulders and pushes his head between my thighs.

"Oh shit," I gasp when his tongue connects with my clit.

"Fucking love this," he growls, lapping at me like a starved man.

"Oh God," I squeal when he wraps his hand around the back of my other leg. He lifts me from the floor, holding my weight as he pushes his tongue inside me.

"Fuck, Leon," I cry, my filter obliterated by what he's doing to me.

My fingers twist in his wet hair as the water pounds down on me only adding to the sensations he's causing.

"Come all over my face, Red," he demands against me. The vibration of his deep voice making my release surge forward.

"Yes, yes, yes," I chant as I start to fall.

"Come, Red. Now."

"Leon," I scream. My body locking up in pleasure as my pussy squeezes his tongue that's deep inside me again.

Wave after wave washes through me. He doesn't let up, teasing me until my entire body sags in his hold.

Somehow—I have no idea how—he manages to get me to my feet without me tumbling to the floor. The second my feet connect with the tiles, he wraps his hand around the back of my neck and slams our lips together.

"Taste how sweet you are, Red." His tongue surges inside my mouth much like it did moments ago between my legs.

He kisses me long and deep, his once again hard cock pressing against my stomach. When he pulls away, he doesn't press for anything further, instead, he reaches for my shampoo, demanding I turn around.

In hindsight, I probably shouldn't have gone to see Libby. I hadn't expected just what looking into her broken eyes would do to me. I didn't anticipate the anger that would surge through me. The need to hurt the man who turned her into the junkie she's become.

It's not fair. Any of it.

She didn't deserve it.

Yes, she was a bit of a wild child, and maybe she'd have found hard drugs without my father's involvement. But he certainly helped to speed up the process no matter what.

He ruined her life. Of that I'm sure.

Add Peyton's meddling into the mix and there was only one place I needed to go after Libby's hospital room. And that was to inflict just a little bit of the pain that cunt has caused to others.

He was asleep when I arrived in his dark cell but he soon was aware of my presence when I woke him with a swift kick from my sneaker right into his gut.

He didn't even try to fight back. Part of me was disappointed, the other part was relieved that maybe he's figuring out that he's in the wrong. That he's messed with too many lives. That he's had this coming for a long, long time.

As I stand with Macie, my fingers massaging her scalp as I wash her hair, I can barely even remember what happened after that. I'm not even sure if I left him breathing or not.

The person I was in that room wasn't someone I ever want to meet again. The anger, the need for vengeance, the thirst for his blood was terrifying.

I don't even remember the journey here. I was too lost to the past, memories and pain that felt too real.

It wasn't until she opened the door and I looked into her eyes that I realized I probably fucked up.

She looked terrified.

I understood why, I was covered in my father's blood. I looked like a crazed psycho, of that I'm sure.

She should have slammed the door in my face. It was what I more than fully deserved.

But instead, I'm now standing here with her naked before me and her taste still on my tongue.

Leaning forward, I press a kiss to her shoulder as I continue to massage her head.

"So good," she moans, pressing back against me.

Sliding one hand out of her hair, I trail my fingers down her neck and over her chest. She gasps when I pinch her nipple. Her ass grinding back against my hard cock.

Cupping the other one, I pinch the nipple between my fingers.

"Leon," she moans as I slip my hand down her stomach. Parting her lips, I press two fingers against her clit.

"I want to hear you come again," I confess in her ear. Knowing that I could listen to her cries and mewls all fucking night.

She's still soaked. Her pussy slick from her last orgasm, sliding two fingers inside her.

"Shit," she moans.

"Good, baby?"

"So good," she sighs as I press my thumb to her clit.

It only takes minutes for her to shatter once more. Turning her head with my hand still in her hair, I swallow down her moans of pleasure by kissing her.

"Turn around," I whisper, releasing her so she can do just that.

Tilting her head back, I rinse out the shampoo before grabbing her bottle of conditioner. I pour some into my hands, running it through her long red locks.

Her eyes hold mine the entire time. Concern and her lingering desire darkens their usual bright blue.

"I'm okay," I breathe in an attempt to rid her of the concern.

She nods, but I don't think for a second that she believes me.

I rinse her hair once more before grabbing her coconut shower gel, squeezing it onto a sponge, I begin to wash her body.

It's not until I've scrubbed every inch of her that I hand it over, allowing her to do the same to me.

Her scent surrounds me. Her gentle touch rubs all over my skin and I can't help but sigh in contentment.

I'm pretty sure I've never felt this relaxed in my life. But while I allow myself to drown in it for a few minutes, I know it's not a feeling I can get used to.

I'm not here to carve out a future for the two of us. I'm here to get information so that I can finally put an end to the events of my childhood that have darkened every single one of my days since.

The second she's finished, I turn the water off and step out. I wrap her in a towel, tucking another around my waist.

"Are you hungry?" she asks as we pad into her bedroom.

"Yeah." *Although not for food,* I think as I watch her walk over to her dresser and pull out some clothes.

"Okay, I'll order pizza."

"You don't have to, I can leave," I offer. But I honestly can't think of anything worse than being alone right now.

"Leon, don't do that."

"What? You were in bed, weren't you?"

"Yes. But if you need me, I'm right here."

Her words make my chest ache.

Everything I wanted to achieve from the moment she barged in on me with Charlie last weekend is happening.

I'm breaking down her walls, making her trust me.

Only, what I wasn't anticipating was just how bad it would make me feel.

I was expecting to hate her. That my memory of her from the past would be enough to keep me from liking her.

But then I discovered who she really is and when we're together, the past just melts away.

I nod at her, unable to speak through the lump in my throat. Dropping the towel, I grab my boxers, dragging them up my legs before falling down on her bed.

I watch her every move as she pulls on a pair of panties followed by a tank and sleep shorts.

It's a damn shame to cover up that banging body, but still, she looks unbelievably hot. And she has to know I think so because once again, my cock is trying to break free of my boxers.

Grabbing her cell, she taps away on the screen before announcing. "It'll be here in thirty."

"Perfect. Come here," I say, holding my hand out, more than ready for her to join me.

"Okay." She locks her cell, but before she places it down, it pings in her hand.

Pulling it back in front of her, she looks down at the screen and lets out a sigh.

"Everything okay?"

Walking over, she drops down beside me, allowing me to see the screen.

"What's that?" I ask, not understanding the notification on the screen.

"It... It's the security system at my uncle's house. There's something wrong with it."

"Why doesn't he deal with it?" I ask innocently.

"He's... um... out of town." She looks over at me, guilt written all over her face. I didn't need to see it to know she's lying to me.

I know he's not there. I've been there looking for him.

But the issue is, I also can't find him.

Hence, why I'm here.

Dark excitement flutters in my belly at the thought of getting the information out of her.

"It's been sending me alerts all weekend. They assured me the house is secure but it keeps going off."

"Maybe you should go and check it out."

"I know but it's on the other side of the state and I've got classes." Her excuses are valid. I can't help feeling like they're a cover up for deeper reasons for not wanting to go there. "It's not important," she says, placing her cell on the side and pressing herself into my body.

"Um... not right now, no."

Rolling her over so she's lying right on top of me, I capture her lips and kiss her until the buzzer rings telling us the pizza is here.

Her cell goes off with the same alert three more times before she finally turns it off.

"Maybe you should go. It could be serious."

"I know," she mutters sadly.

"Don't the two of you get along or something?" I think back to our previous conversation. When she changed the subject about him at the first possible opportunity and wonder what the story is there. I can't imagine him being a doting uncle, but the thought of him treating her the way he did the boys sends a shiver of fear down my spine.

Could we have more in common than I ever thought?

No. No, that can't be true.

My stomach turns, my pizza threatening to come back up from the thought alone.

"It's... complicated. I don't think he ever wanted kids, then he found himself stuck with me."

"But he was a coach, wasn't he?" I ask, risking the subject.

"Yeah, but I'm pretty sure he hates kids."

"What makes you say that?"

"You're in the game, you must have heard what a hard ass he was with his boys. They breathed at the wrong time and he came down on them like a ton of bricks."

"I heard rumors," I lie.

"You're lucky," she whispers. "You're lucky you don't have firsthand experience"

My entire body tenses at her words and it doesn't go unnoticed.

She lifts her head from my chest, looking at me with those concerned eyes again.

"You okay?"

"Yeah, baby. You're in my arms, I'm more than okay."

"A-about earlier," she stutters. "Did you want to talk about it?"

I stare at her, the confession of what I did—what I've done—right on the tip of my tongue. I've never felt compelled to tell anyone any of my secrets before. But Macie, there's something about her that makes me want to spill all the darkness inside me. Let her dance in its bottomless depths with me, if she's brave enough.

"One day," I finally say, pushing the need to confess all down.

She snuggles back against me and I relax.

No matter how much I might want to tell her, I know I can't. Not until I've got what I need. Not until she understands who I really am. Then I can lay all my truths out on the table. We'll see if she's so willing to stick around then.

———

"I was thinking," Macie says, the next morning as she gets ready for class. I'm also getting dressed. I can hardly walk into college wearing clothes stained with my father's blood so I'm going to have to swing by my house first and attempt to sneak in without getting caught.

Luca and Peyton are already concerned enough. I'm sure finding me like this would only make things worse.

The time is coming where I'm going to have to either do something drastic or confess. The thought of having to do the latter makes me want to run. Run as far away from this place and the truth as possible.

I've spent all these years protecting those I love from the truth, and even now, when I'm almost on the cusp of getting the revenge I need, the thought of them knowing, of looking at me with sympathy and pity in their eyes makes me consider trying to forget it all once again.

But I know I can't.

The pain has only grown and festered inside me for the past ten years. I need to do something, and soon, or I'm going to end up hurting those I love more than any secrets could.

"Oh yeah?" I ask while watching her apply her makeup in the mirror.

"I don't have classes Friday and I don't think I'll be invited to my study group again. So I might head to Miami on Thursday afternoon, check out what's going on at my uncle's."

"I can blow off classes," I offer, knowing that I'm not going to let this opportunity pass me by.

"No, you don't have to do that. I'll only be gone for a night."

Pushing up from the bed, I walk up behind her and place my hands on her shoulders.

"But I want to. Maybe we could make a weekend of it. Just me and you." I hold her eyes in the mirror. Allowing her to see all the dirty, wicked thoughts that are running through my mind.

"Um..."

"We can go to the beach, swim in the ocean. Skinny dip in your uncle's pool and sunbathe naked."

"It's winter," she points out.

"And?" I ask, pushing her hair over her shoulder and kissing down her neck. "I'm sure I could keep you warm."

"You're crazy."

"Crazy for you."

Her cheeks heat at my words making my cock jerk in my pants.

"You should go or you'll be late for class."

"Macie."

"What? If you're going to miss Friday then you'll want to be there the rest of the week."

"Yeah?" I ask, excitement exploding inside me.

"Yeah. You made it sound... tolerable."

"I'm tolerable?" I scoff, faux hurt in my voice.

"What? N-no, no. I meant going to his house. I hate it there. Having you with me will make it more tolerable."

"How much do you hate it?" I ask, nipping at her earlobe.

"A lot."

"Then it's time to make new memories there. Erase some of the old ones. Maybe I could make you come in every room of the house," I suggest.

"There are a lot of rooms."

"Worried I don't have the stamina?"

"Not at all. I was just saying, it's a big place."

Don't I know it? Although big, it was never big enough to hide because that cunt always found me.

"I'm always up for a challenge." Despite the fact she's between me and the mirror, she glances down to where my crotch is.

"You mean, you're always up."

"And you think I'm the wicked one, Red." Wrapping my hand around her throat, I lift her from her seat. I push her back against the desk, my fingers squeezing in a way I know drives her wild. "Always thinking about my cock, huh, dirty girl?"

She licks her lips as if she's remembering what it was like to have it in her mouth.

"Thursday afternoon can't come soon enough," I groan, slamming my lips down on hers.

"Lee," she moans, running her hands up my chest and linking them over my shoulders.

"This weekend, Red. I'm making you mine," I growl, my cock twitching at the prospect of finally pushing inside her.

"This weekend," she repeats in my mouth.

"I need to go," I confess, dropping my head to hers.

"You do."

With one final chaste kiss to her lips, I make a show of rearranging myself, just so she knows how up for it I am and slip out of her room.

Thankfully the others are nowhere to be seen. The last thing I need is to explain to her protectors why I'm covered in someone else's blood.

By some fucking miracle, I make it all the way to my bedroom without being stopped by anyone. I'm stripping out of my clothes ready to take another shower when my cell starts ringing.

My first thought is that it's Macie. A thrill shoots through me thinking she's missing me already before I shut down those thoughts.

I'm already in too deep with her. I need to rein it in. Which is exactly why I lied to her earlier and said that I'm busy all week.

Truth is, aside from classes, training and working out with the guys, oh and of course a little torture, I've got fuck all to do. But as much as I need her to believe everything between us is real, I'm aware that I'm walking on a very thin line right now. Every second I spend with her changes things, and I can't allow that to happen.

I have one end goal here. And making her mine isn't it.

It can't be.

I'd be fooling myself to even think she'd want me after she learns the truth. When she discovers how tainted and broken I am.

"Hey," I say, pressing my cell to my ear. "Everything okay?" I ask, wondering if I'm about to hear that I killed someone last night.

"Yeah, I'm good, man. More worried about you. You sure did a number on your old man last night," Reid says and I swear I hear something akin to pride in his voice.

"Yeah well, I needed to relieve some stress. He seemed like the perfect punching bag."

"You still want him left alone?" he inquires.

When he and Devin turned up to help Kane, Bry and me the night Brett attacked Peyton, I was expecting him to question why I wanted him locked up like an animal. But to my surprise, he flashed me a smile I'm sure the devil himself would be proud of and handed me over the key.

"Yeah, just keep the cunt alive. I want him to regret every single thing he's done in his life."

"Fair enough. You need anything else, you just call, yeah?"

"You got it, man. Thanks."

He hangs up without saying another word. I barely know anything about the guy, only what little information I gleaned from Kane. At the same time, I trust the psycho with my life, or at least keeping my dirty secret.

I throw myself in the shower and attempt to get her coconut scent off me. As much as I might want to drown in her, I also need to keep a clear head for the next few days or my promise to myself to stay away from her is going to go down the drain.

22

MACIE

My week drags knowing that I'm not going to see Leon until after my morning class on Thursday.

I wanted to say no, to make him stay here and go to classes. I already know he's not exactly got the best track record for attendance and I don't want to be the one to screw things up for him by missing more. But I also saw the excitement on his face at the prospect of us getting away for the weekend. I could hardly refuse after the state I witnessed him in the night before.

It still eats at me that I don't know what happened, or whose blood he was covered in. I keep convincing myself that he'll tell me when he feels ready. But my patience is already wearing thin.

I've gone from wanting nothing to do with him to wanting to know all of his secrets. It's a weird feeling but one I'm fed up of fighting.

I stare at the clock on the wall, willing it to move faster.

"Anyone would think you want to get out of here," Nate mutters beside me.

"Is it that obvious?"

"Well, I've never seen you less than fully engaged in class, so yeah, it is."

"I'm excited," I confess. I never thought I would ever actually look forward to visiting my uncle's estate but I can't wait to make it ours this weekend.

Just the two of us...

My tummy flutters with the words he growled in our kiss on Monday morning.

'This weekend, Red. I'm making you mine.'

My thighs squeeze together at the thought of finally experiencing what it'll be like.

"You're like a lovesick puppy, Mace."

My chin drops at his words. "I didn't say I was in lo—"

"Never said you were," he interrupts, probably seeing my panic. "But you're heading in that direction."

His eyes hold mine, telling me that there's no point in arguing.

"I can't help it. When we're together it's just... I don't know. Right, I guess."

"I'm happy for you." He smiles softly at me before I look to the other side of the room again at the clock and he chuckles.

The second our professor brings our lecture to an end, I pack up my stuff and race for the door. The sound of Nate's laughter follows me, but he doesn't stop me like I expect him to.

I fly around my room once I'm back, packing everything I could possibly need for the weekend.

I might have lost my mind, but I allowed Charlie to take me shopping last night and bought new lingerie and sexy nightwear. I'm not sure I've actually got the confidence to wear it, but I shove it in my bag just in case.

From the moment we met, Leon has brought out a whole new person I didn't know was hiding within me. For all I know, I might give him a full-on fashion show of all my new outfits.

A smile tugs at my lips as I think about how he might look at me. I love it when his eyes darken with desire because of me. It's the biggest turn on that I can do that to him.

"I hope it's me that's putting that smile on your face," a deep voice rumbles from the doorway.

Spinning around, I find the man himself leaning against my doorjamb watching me.

"How long have you been standing there?" I ask, shoving the last few things into my bag.

"Long enough to see all the lace you just shoved into your bag."

My cheeks burn with embarrassment, which he must either notice or sense because he marches into the room and holds my face in his giant hands.

"Don't shy away from me, Red. I can't wait to see you in every single one of them."

"I bought them for you," I confess.

"Fuck, you're perfect."

His lips find mine before I can respond, leaving me breathless. He releases me in favor of picking up my bag and throwing it over his shoulder.

"You ready to hit the road?"

"Sure am. Let's go."

I grab my purse and cell, sliding my other hand into his before we head out.

"I bought snacks for the journey," he says, moving the bag that's on the passenger seat when we climb in.

"You've thought of everything."

"Thought of nothing but this weekend with you all week."

"Me too," I whisper.

"Ready to have some fun, Red?"

"Hell yes."

In seconds his engine revs beneath us and we peel out of the parking lot. Putting college and our lives here behind us for a few days.

I sigh in relief as I lower the window and breathe in the fresh air.

"When was the last time you went to your uncle's?" he asks after we've been driving for a few minutes.

"Uh... last summer."

He gives me a double take, his brows pulled together.

I'm about to ask what's bothering him when he speaks.

"You didn't go there for the holidays?"

Shit.

"Um... no."

I twist my fingers together, knowing that he's about to ask me what

I did do. I know that I'm not going to get away with lying to him like I did everyone else so they didn't look at me with pity in their eyes.

"But he's your only family, right? Where did you go?"

"I... um... booked a cabin in the woods and spent the entire break there," I confess quietly.

"Alone?"

"Yes."

I startle when his palms slam down on the wheel.

"Fuck. Fuck."

"It was okay. I enjoyed it."

"You shouldn't have to spend the holidays alone, Macie."

I shrug. "It is what it is. It's normal to me."

His fingers twist around the wheel. His healing knuckles turning white with the force of his grip.

"That's bullshit."

"I like my own company. What about you, big family Christmas?"

"Not last year. It was just me, Luca and Mom for most of it. Luca was in a really bad place so even when he was present in body he wasn't really there. Mom tried to make the best of it, but his mood was infectious."

"I'm sorry."

"It's all good. I've since discovered the reason for his mood was his girl and they've finally kissed and made up."

"Peyton?" I ask, although I already know the answer. Letty told me all about her when we met for lunch this week.

"Yeah. We all grew up together but she moved when we were fifteen."

"I can't wait to meet her. Letty had only good things to say about her."

He looks over at me. His eyes running over every inch of my face briefly before he turns back to the road.

"You're really just slotting right into my life, huh?"

"I... um... She invited me for lunch, I could hardly—"

"Hey, it's okay. Letty is good people. You could do a hell of a lot worse than having her as a friend." He glances over again and I can't help but feel like he's holding something back.

"But you still don't like me hanging out with her?" I assume.

"No, not at all. It's just... weird, I guess. I've never done any of this before so it's strange knowing my friends are hanging out with my girl."

"Your girl?" I ask, my heart beating wildly in my chest.

"Yeah," he agrees, reaching over and lacing our fingers together. "That okay with you?"

"Yeah," I breathe, "I think it is." I can't help but laugh at the absurdity of it all.

"What's so funny?"

"You are literally everything I said I never wanted and here I am agreeing to be your girl. It's mental."

"Sometimes what we need is exactly the opposite of what we think we want."

"See, you just get it. You get me."

"Yeah, baby. I do."

We manage to turn the conversation to less serious topics for the rest of the journey. We munch our way through the snacks that Leon brought. And after drinking an entire bottle of cola, I demand he stops at a gas station so I can pee.

He's leaning against the side of his car waiting for me when I emerge from the shop.

He's got a pair of shades on his handsome face, his hair falling over his brow. He's wearing a white shirt that's pulled tight across his wide shoulders and chiselled chest.

My mouth waters as I close the space between us.

He looks delicious. And all mine.

Some giggling to my left drags my attention away from him. I look over to find some girls—probably still in high school—drooling over him.

"Looks like you've got a fan club," I say, stepping up to him.

He widens his legs and I stand between them as he wraps his arms around my waist.

"I hadn't even noticed them. Too busy missing you."

"You're so damn smooth, Dunn."

"I try," he jokes.

"Here, I bought you a gift."

"From the gas station?"

I shrug, feeling silly for picking up the novelty item just because I thought it would make him smile.

"Yep. I always get the best gifts," I laugh. "Here." I pull the football air freshener from behind my back and hold it in front of him.

He lifts a brow. "Red, are you trying to say that my car smells?"

"W-what? N-no, I just thought it was cute."

"I'm joking. I'm joking. It is cute. Thank you."

Leaning forward, he brushes his lips against mine. It's a simple kiss yet it makes every muscle south of my waist clench in desire.

I'm not the only one who feels it either because I don't miss his cock hardening against my stomach.

"I can't wait to have you alone, Macie. I've spent all week imagining all the things I want to do to you."

"Lee," I moan, knowing that it's completely mutual.

"Get in the car, Red, before we give those kids something to really look at."

"You wouldn't dare."

"Do you really want to try me?" he asks. Lifting a brow with a wicked smirk playing on his lips.

Part of me really wants to just so I could see what he'd do. But the other part doesn't want to put on a show for those young girls.

"I think it's time to continue."

"As you wish, baby."

I place a quick kiss to his lips before dragging myself out of his hold. Slipping back into the passenger seat.

"You're a tease," he mutters, joining me in the car. Ensuring I see him shift his erection in his pants.

"I just bought you an air freshener," I say innocently.

"Yeah and it made me hard. What the fuck is wrong with me?"

"Three days without any action," I point out knowing that the last time I touched him was Monday morning.

"Oh baby, trust me. My hand has seen plenty of action."

"Well, lucky for you, you can give it the weekend off," I deadpan as I hook his new accessory over his rearview mirror.

"Red, I've got plenty of ideas for what I can do with my hands. Trust me, they don't end in my pleasure."

"Jesus," I mutter, my thighs clenching.

"You wet for me, baby?"

"That's for me to kno-o-oh, Leon," I squeal when his hand pushes under my skirt until his fingers skim the lace covering me.

"Open up for me, baby. I want to know how excited you are for the weekend."

Hesitantly, I open my legs and gasp the second he runs his knuckles over my soaked panties.

"Oh, baby. You're not making my situation any better."

"Lee, you're driving, you should be concentra— shit," I gasp as he tucks a finger beneath the lace, dipping it into my wetness.

"I'm more than capable of doing two things at once, baby." His finger pushes inside me. I'm powerless but to part my legs further and slump down in the seat. "Good girl. When you come, I want to hear my name, Red."

I nod, unable to speak as he finger fucks me faster.

"Leon," I whimper, my release coming faster than I expected.

"Yes, baby. Squeeze my fingers tight."

"Oh God."

"Come, Red. Come all over my passenger seat."

"Leon," I cry as I do exactly as I'm told. Wave after wave of mind numbing pleasure racing through me.

The second it's over, I slump back in the chair. My eyelids lower as tiredness hits me.

"Sleep, baby. I'll wake you when we're there."

I drift off before I even realize it with Leon's hot hand still wrapped around my thigh. Something about his touch relaxes me like nothing else can.

I miss the rest of the journey and the next thing I know I hear a noise. When I open my eyes we're parked out front of my uncle's huge house.

I blink a couple of times trying to push the drowsiness away before I look over at Leon.

"Are you okay?" I ask when I notice his body is locked up tight. His face in the mask I remember from the first time I saw him.

"Y-yeah. It's huge."

"That's what she said," I deadpan, hoping it'll shatter the weird tension in the car.

Leon throws his head back and laughs and I breathe a sigh of relief.

"You're something else, you know that?"

"It would be boring if I were like all the others, don't you think?"

"Damn right. Come on, then. I want the grand tour to get a grasp on how many rooms I've got to make you come in. We can already tick car off the list."

My body burns up at his words.

"You're going to be busy."

"And you're going to be exhausted. But I already know one thing," he says, looking over at me.

"Oh yeah, what's that?"

"You're never going to forget me."

"I think that's already true. I don't need a sex fest in my uncle's house to ensure you're under my skin."

His eyes bounce between mine as unreadable thoughts flicker behind his eyes.

I'm desperate to demand he tells me what he's thinking but I already know he won't. So I give him some space in the hope he figures out that he can tell me whatever it is in his own time.

Pushing my door open, I stand and stare at the house that's haunted so many of my nightmares over the years.

It's late, the sun beginning to slip behind the trees on the horizon. It makes it look like paradise. I'm sure to many it would be, however it's more like hell to me.

Night times here were always the worst. After he started drinking, that's when the real monster used to come out. That's when the vile words and the pain used to commence.

I lose myself in my less than pleasant memories of the time I spent here as a child. When Leon finally steps up behind me, wrapping his arms around my waist, I have no idea how much time has actually passed.

"I get the feeling you don't want to go inside."

"I don't have the best memories of being here," I confess. "The years after my dad died weren't good ones."

His lips press against my neck and I shudder.

"It's over now. You've got me to keep you entertained instead."

"Hmm... That sounds so much better."

Leon follows me inside. He's silent as he looks around at everything. His shoulders are still tense but his face is more relaxed. I wonder if his reaction to the place is just because he knows I don't really want to be here.

"Let's check the place out. See if we can figure out what's setting the alarm off."

"Okay," he places our bags by the stairs and follows me down the hall to the kitchen.

LEON

I've spent the last ten years hiding my feelings, masking what happened and how it... Shattered me. Ruined me. Destroyed me.

But never have I had to fight as hard to keep it all from erupting as I do walking into that cunt's house.

From the second I step through the door. The scent. The sight. Everything comes rushing back.

The pain.

The mortification.

I follow Macie from room to room looking for anything that could be triggering her security notifications.

"This place is spotless. I assume there's a housekeeper," I observe.

"Yeah, she comes in once a week. She hasn't found anything, but then she doesn't go in all the rooms. Some are... off-limits."

"Why? What is your uncle hiding?" I ask through gritted teeth knowing full well her uncle keeps more secrets than most are probably aware of.

I also know that Macie herself keeps one very big one.

"Beats me. I try not to pry for fear of what I might find. He's not exactly..." She considers her words for a moment. "Open and honest."

I want to scoff and tell her he's the biggest cunt on the planet. Somehow I manage to keep the thought inside.

She sweeps the formal dining room, the wood is all dark, the ornaments all gold, expensive and pretentious.

Richard Fletcher always did want to appear to be better than he was.

He hated being second best to Macie's dad.

I often wondered if that was what drew him to me. I was second best too.

He must have seen that from the way Brett talked about us, our future, what he wanted for Luca. All his dreams for his golden boy.

She leads me to a room which looks about as relaxing as being stuck in a hornets' nest before dipping into every room on this level of the house.

"I swear it's just a fault with the system but they're adamant it's something inside."

"Guess that means digging into your uncle's secret rooms."

She visibly shudders at my suggestion.

"He won't know. He's not here," I say confidently until a thought hits me. "He's not likely to come back... is he?"

Fear and panic like I haven't experienced since I was eleven years old rushes through me.

I have no doubt she can see it on my face but other than narrowing her eyes at me, she doesn't comment.

I need to be careful though because at some point she's going to figure it out. That's fine. I want her to know. But I want to be the one to deliver the blow, not let her put the pieces together herself.

"No, he won't be coming here."

"Where is he?" I ask lightly in the hope that she might be more willing to divulge the information now we're here.

"He's..." she hesitates, clearly wanting to follow the cunt's orders of not letting anyone find him. I can see she's torn, it twists her beautiful features. She wants to trust me, but for whatever reason she's still got loyalty to him. In the end, she plays right into my hand, proving where her trust and loyalties really lie. "He's in a care home."

"Oh," I breathe, not expecting her to say that.

"He's kept it out of the media, as I'm sure you're aware, but he's got early-onset dementia. Last summer he almost burned this place to the ground, so we found him a secure facility where he can be safe, both from himself and the media.

"I'm sure I don't need to tell you that he's got plenty of enemies. Many who would love to hear that he's now incapacitated. Weak. Something he never wanted to be."

Yeah, baby. One of those enemies is me.

"Better to be safe than sorry, huh?"

"I guess."

"You don't want him safe and well looked after?" I ask.

"He's family," she shrugs. Happy that this room is okay, she turns to leave.

"I'm sorry," I whisper behind her. "I'm prying. I'm just trying to get to know you better."

"I know, Lee. I'm the one who should be sorry. I just hate talking about my family, my past. It's painful, you know."

More than you could possibly understand.

"Where to next?" She leads me to the formal living room, which is decorated the same as the previous room. Heavy ostentatious drapes hanging around the large windows, showcasing the rolling hills in the distance. Hills that I know lead to his coaching facility. The one which holds so many traumatic memories for me.

"I'm ordering Chinese," she tells me. I stare out of the window remembering that little boy who turned up here so excited that first year.

I was going to be training with Richard Fletcher. *The* Richard Fletcher.

He may not have been his quarterback brother who Luca looked up to as a young boy, but he was still a legend in his own right. One of the best wide receivers to grace the NFL in our lifetime and he was going to teach me, *me*, everything he knew.

It was a dream come true. Or so I thought.

Turned out he saw more in me than just a future star because he singled me out from all of the boys attending that summer. He made sure I knew just how special I was.

"Is that okay?" Macie asks, reminding me that she said something a few minutes ago. I stand there with my skin itching like a million ants are crawling all over me.

"Y-yeah, that's fine. I'm starving," I lie, immediately regretting it because if I still can't stomach it when it's delivered she's going to know.

"Did you want to choose a dish or..."

"I'm easy, you pick your favorites. There isn't much I don't like."

"Okay," she breathes, looking back down at her cell to place the order.

I return to the window, battling with the demon inside me who wants to find a match and—do what the man himself failed to do last year—burn the place to the ground.

I want to see everything he's ever cared about crumble around his feet, and unfortunately for Macie, that includes her.

I jump a mile when she joins me and places her small hand on my upper arm.

"Shit, sorry. You scared me."

"Leon, are you okay? You seem... distracted. Distant. I thought you were looking forward to this, but right now you look like you want to be anywhere else in the world."

Turning to face her, I force a smile on my face and slip my arms around her waist.

"I'm sorry, baby. It seems I didn't leave my troubles behind in Maddison."

"Want to talk about it?"

I shake my head. "Just family stuff." It's not a lie. I've got my father locked in a fucking warehouse like a prisoner. And Luca knows I'm lying to him with every word that comes out of my mouth.

He's giving me time, but I know he's going to get fed up soon.

What with him, Peyton and Letty on my case, I know they're going to break me down sooner rather than later.

I can only keep all these plates spinning and lies festering for a certain amount of time. I fear the expiration date is approaching faster than I want to acknowledge.

"Okay. How about I distract you instead?" she offers.

"Now that I can get on board with. But maybe we should finish the house first, at least we know it's done then and we can finally relax."

She reluctantly nods, knowing that I'm right.

"Okay, second floor then?"

"Lead the way, Red."

She reaches up and drops a quick kiss to my lips before turning and pulling me out of the room. Allowing me to watch her ass in her tight skirt as she climbs the stairs.

We inspect each room we come across until we find the first locked door.

A shudder rips through me at the sight of it.

I don't need to ask what room it is. I already know.

I've been inside more than once. And Macie might not remember, but she's seen me inside that room as well.

I fight to keep my breathing steady as she walks past it.

"I'll need to grab the keys," she mutters, moving onto the next open room and slipping inside.

I'm still standing in the hallway when she emerges.

"All good."

"Great," I force a smile but I don't feel it.

My stomach twists painfully. Bile burning up my throat as the images of what happened to me inside that room, what Macie witnessed, play out in my mind.

The scent of his rancid breath in my face feels almost as real as it did back then. His brutal touch, barbed words, and the pain. Fuck, the pain.

My fists clench with my need to fight for that little boy. For all the others who had gone before and I'm sure the ones who followed.

The bell rings downstairs before Macie emerges and finds me on the brink of losing myself.

"I'll go," I call, grateful for the escape. Giving me the chance to breathe before I have to face her again.

I knew this would be hard. Pretending that I've never been here before. That the events that have happened under this very roof didn't change my life forever.

"Thanks, man," I say, grabbing the takeout from the delivery guy after figuring out how to open the gates for him. I suck in deep lungfuls of air while the door is open.

"This smells amazing," I say walking through to the kitchen where she's arranging plates for us on the counter.

"It's the best thing about this place."

"Well, I'm more than ready to test it out."

"The fridge is stocked, grab whatever you want to drink."

My instincts want me to reach for a bottle of Richard Fletcher's finest whisky. I can see it proudly displayed in a liquor cabinet on the other side of the room.

Later, I tell myself, instead pulling out a cooled bottle of white wine from the fridge. I quickly locate two glasses as Macie takes the food to the table that sits in front of the floor to ceiling windows that looks down toward the training facility.

"Your uncle's got some land here, huh?" I mutter, fighting like hell to keep my memories from the forefront of my mind.

"Yeah, it's insane. I haven't even seen it all. He bought it after my grandparents died. I got a percentage of the money but he got the majority, he found some loophole to stop me from getting everything my father was rightly owed."

"Asshole," I seethe.

"What goes around comes around. One day this will all be mine."

I raise a brow at her, curious as to what she means by that. She's never come across as a person who cares about money in all the time we've spent together in the past two weeks.

"You want his money?"

"Of course. It's not for the reasons you might think, though."

I narrow my eyes at her, wondering once again, what secrets of her own she's hiding.

"So enlighten me."

She smiles before putting a forkful of egg fried rice into her mouth.

"Not right now. I thought you had fun things in mind."

Despite everything—my need to run away from this place as fast as possible and forget all about what happened here—a wave of desire washes through me at the thought of making her mine here.

She might hate him, but as a kid I was under the impression that he doted on her. It's why he made her keep her distance from us, and sent her to the best school he could find. I'm looking forward to ruining his perfect little niece under his own roof.

"Yeah, baby. I do. But not until you've done what you need to do and you can relax."

She stares at me across the table, probably confused. It's not like me to wait to take what I want, but this time is different.

I need it to be perfect, and not in the way she's imagining, I'm sure.

"Okay well, let's finish this, check the rest of the house and then maybe I should show you my bedroom," she suggests, her voice is pure lust.

"You got the keys to those locked rooms?"

"Yeah, on the side in the kitchen."

I glance over wondering how I didn't see them when I got the drinks."

"Good, let's go." I throw what's left of my wine back and stand. I'm feeling too impatient to sit here stewing about everything.

"O-okay." She picks up the final prawn cracker and pops it past her red-stained lips. I watch, remembering just how those lips felt around me and I harden, ready to get this show on the road.

"Let's start with the top floor. We'll do the locked rooms last because..." A shudder rips through her making me even more curious about those rooms.

"Okay, lead the way."

I continue trailing her in and out of every room. My eyes scanning everything looking for the information I need.

"So what's your uncle's prognosis?" I ask curiously.

"I'm not sure. He's getting worse, but while his brain might be failing him, his body is still relatively young so—"

"It could be a long road?" I finish for her.

"Exactly," she says sadly. Anyone else might believe that sadness is for her uncle's short life, but I know better and I'm starting to think she hates him almost as much as I do. Which could mean...

No.

I force the thoughts away not wanting to believe they could be true.

"Grab the bags," she says, swinging open a door in the far back corner of the house. I do as I'm told and get them from where we left them at the top of the stairs and follow her into what I assume is her room.

It's not what I was expecting at all.

There are almost no signs that a little girl has ever lived here.

The decoration is almost the same as the rest of the house. There are certainly no dolls or toys, or anything from her past.

Sadness for the little girl who lost everything and found herself here makes my chest ache.

She was just as unlucky as me to end up in the middle of this.

"Final rooms then we chill," she says before I get a chance to really think about what all this means.

"Sure."

"Where are you going?" she asks when I head for the stairs. There's only one room I want to search now, one place that could give me the answers I need.

"Going to the first locked door," I say, hopefully innocently enough. We discovered another five locked doors up here, the easiest thing would be to start here, but I don't know what they are.

"Okay. Let's— Shit," she curses when her cell rings. The fact she's swearing tells me just how out of her comfort zone she really is here.

"You go, meet me down there."

"Okay."

My heart pounds harder with each step I take. By the time I can see the door in front of me, my head spins to the point I wonder if I'm about to pass out.

I never wanted to come back to this place. I was happy to banish its existence from my mind, but knowing it's possibly the only place I can find out what I need without torturing the information out of Macie. Although, now we're here, that outcome is becoming more and more appealing.

My entire body jolts in anticipation as the lock clicks open.

I'm shaking, my body freezing with fear despite the sweat that coats my body. Disgust rolls through me, threatening to bring up my Chinese all over his ridiculously thick carpet as I swing the door open.

I'm hit with a musty smell which doesn't help my stomach.

With a huge breath in through my mouth, I step inside and lift my eyes from my feet.

My breathing falters as I take in his huge carved walnut desk in the middle of the room.

My fists curl as the pain of gripping on to the edge hits me as if it's happening right now.

Images flicker through my mind, the words he said to me. The way he convinced me to come here in the promise of showing me his trophies, all the incredible things he collected during his NFL career.

I was young, naïve, I had no clue back then that he wanted something else from me. I didn't even give the fact it was only the two of us a second thought.

I was too starstruck to question anything.

I thought he saw potential in me, that he was helping prepare me for greatness, not grooming me to be his own little toy.

I heave as I step behind his desk, standing exactly where he would have been as he... As he shattered my entire life, my soul, my body.

Anger surges forward and my hands tremble as I begin ripping open the drawers of his desk, looking for anything that will point me toward that care home.

All I need is a name. An address. A clue.

He thinks he's got away with all this. That he's going to get to live out his final years in comfort, even if he doesn't remember most of his days.

He has no idea what's coming for him.

My eyes widen as I drag open the bottom drawer and a folder appears.

Acorn Lodge.

It sounds like a holiday destination. And staring at the front of the folder, it seems it's trying to look like one too.

A smile curls at my lips as I stare down at it.

"Got you, motherfucker," I mutter, slamming the drawer closed.

Falling back into his office chair, I rest forward on my elbows dropping my head into my hands as the images in my head only get clearer. The musty smell in the room gives way to one I remember almost as if it was yesterday.

His smell.

My skin prickles as the shudders racking my body only get worse.

I'm not stupid, I knew coming back here after all these years wouldn't be easy, but fuck...

I clench my fists, willing them to stop shaking. Begging my heart rate to slow before I pass out on his fucking office floor.

I bet he would have loved that...

I don't realize I've moved, that I've started pacing back and forth battling with the memories playing on loop in my mind until a shadow falls in the doorway.

My entire body recoils, my brain thinking that it's him, that he's come back for me.

"Leon, what's wrong?" Her soft voice flows through me like silk all over my rough and jagged edges.

But when I look up, I'm right back there. Just a helpless child staring into her light blue eyes begging her to help me, to stop him. To save me.

But she didn't.

My feet eat up the space between us in a flash. I'm standing before her, my fingers around her throat as I slam her up against the wall.

"Lee?" she questions, her voice strained with the tightness of my grip. "Y-you're shaking."

My chest heaves as I stare into those blue eyes. The exact ones I've dreamed about for years. Sometimes my memories morphed and she saved me but only occasionally because every other time, she left me. She turned her back, she walked away like I wasn't worth saving.

Like I was nothing.

"You have no idea, do you?" I seethe, lowering down until our noses are almost brushing. "Not a fucking clue what you've done."

"I-I-I don't know what you're talking about."

"You fucking ruined me, Macie Fletcher."

"What are you—" she squeals when I lift her from the floor and drop her onto her uncle's desk. The one he was so fond of using for activities other than working. Where he taught very different lessons from the ones needed on the field.

Pulling her sneakers off her feet, I throw them across the room, reveling in the sound of things falling from the shelves that line the walls.

She tries to scramble away, but she's too slow. I'm on her in a flash, my hands pinning her hips to the wood beneath her.

"You were right, you know." She stares at me, her breath racing past her lips, fear in her blue eyes. "We were meant to meet. I'd been looking for you for ten fucking years. Never in my wildest dreams did I think you'd just walk into my life completely innocent."

"I don't know what—"

"Yes, you do," I shout, startling her. "Yes, you fucking do."

Wrapping my hand around the neck of her shirt. I pull until the thin fabric rips from her body.

"I've waited so fucking long for this."

MACIE

"**O**h my God," I gasp as my shirt practically disintegrates around me.

I stare at Leon, my chest heaving with a weird mixture of fear and excitement racing through my veins.

His eyes are dark and wild like they were the night he turned up on my doorstep covered in blood.

Right now, he's not the Leon I know. Not the guy I've been falling for despite my better judgment. He's someone else entirely. Someone full of pain, anguish, and torment.

A memory hovers on the periphery of my mind. But like almost everything that's happened in my time under this room, I force it back down in the box I learned to lock it all in.

Forgetting has been the only way I've been able to deal with it all.

I couldn't talk. I was too terrified of what he would do. So instead, I ignored it.

I know it's not healthy, that it will continue to eat at me until my dying day but it was—it is—my only option.

Use my pain to help others. Use it to push me forward, to motivate me, to do everything I can not to allow others to be hurt in the same way.

His fingers deftly pinch the clasp of my bra between my breasts, allowing them to spill free. He doesn't even see the new white lace lingerie I bought just for him.

He's gone. Lost to whatever is controlling him right now.

"Leon, please." I've got no idea what I'm asking for. I should be begging for him to release me, to treat me like he usually does with tender touches and light kisses.

But being back here. In a place that holds so much pain. It feels right.

I want to feel everything right now. And—stupidly—I want to help him. I want to take his pain too, allow it to blend with mine.

Maybe, just maybe, it can make us stronger.

I almost laugh at my crazy thoughts.

But then his mouth closes around my nipple and everything leaves my head as a spark of pleasure so strong hits me between the legs.

"You bit me," I gasp when he pulls away. I notice the deep teeth marks on my breast.

"Yeah, and you loved it. You act all innocent, don't you, Macie? But deep down, you're just like all the others. Kinky little whore who'll do anything a football player wants of her."

"W-what, n-no? I'm not like— argh," I cry out again as he moves to the other side.

My hips lift off the desk, my panties soaked as the pain mixes with pleasure. Sending me into a head spin like I've never experienced before.

"See, Red. You love it."

His calloused hands run up my thighs, pushing my skirt up around my waist.

"You've got such a pretty pussy. It's such a shame to have to ruin it."

"Oh fuck," I cry when he rips the lace from me, drops to his knees, sucking my clit into his mouth. "Fuck, fuck." I writhe, trying to get away from his wicked mouth but needing more at the same time. "Leon," I scream when he pushes two fingers inside me. He reaches up high, finding the spot that drives me crazy.

He eats me like he's starved, like he can't get enough of me. He builds me higher and higher until I shatter, screaming his name. I twist my fingers in his hair, pulling him closer.

When he finally pulls away, his eyes are still as dark and intense as before. And his face glistens with my release.

"You shouldn't taste so sweet, Red. You should be bitter, poisonous," he spits.

My head spins from my release and I struggle to get a grasp on what he's saying to me.

What's happened to him? Where has my Leon gone?

Then all my insecurities from the last two weeks hit me all at once.

He never really wanted me, did he?

The sweet Leon I got to know, the one I fell for, he doesn't really exist.

The wicked guy from Charlie's room that night who was getting off on hitting her, making her scream, he's the real Leon. I was stupid enough to fall for it.

Tears burn my eyes as he snaps open his belt, rips his fly open and pulls out his hard cock. Violently fisting it for a few seconds as his eyes run over me.

I should get up. I should get up and run.

But what would be the point? He'd catch me.

H-he said he'd been looking for me.

Why? Why me?

What did I ever—

"Oh shit," I gasp as he rubs the head of his cock against my sensitive clit.

"I'd stay nice and relaxed if I were you," he warns.

"Leon, what are you—"

My words are cut off when his eyes connect with mine.

Tears pool in the corners of my eyes as I stare at a man I don't know. A man full of hate and need for vengeance for—

"You don't remember me, do you, Macie?" he asks coldly.

"I-I don't kn—"

"It really would have been in your favor to have looked a little harder back then. It might have prevented all of this."

"What are you—"

"Showing you how it feels."

I know what he's about to do, but still, I don't tell him no, I don't demand he stop, and I know that it's because deep down, I know. I know what he's talking about even if I refuse to accept it.

It can't be him. It just can't.

But it is.

"Leon," I cry when he lowers his cock to my entrance, pushing inside ever so slightly.

I'm so ready for him, so wet, that it slips in with little effort, my body telling him that I want him. Even if my head is all over the place as memories erupt within me faster than I can control.

I remember a scream, a shout, and the sound of flesh on flesh as two of the boys went at it on the other side of the wall.

I remember running, my lungs burning knowing that I needed to do something to stop them.

They were all older than me. Stronger than me. Even if I were on the right side of the wall, I couldn't do anything about it.

So I went to the only person I knew who could stop them from killing each other.

I went to my uncle. My guardian. The man entrusted to keep me safe after the death of both my parents.

I could barely breathe when I got to his office door.

I didn't knock like I'd been instructed to, I knew there wasn't enough time so I swung the door open and—

"Fuuuck," I cry as he thrusts inside me, filling me in one move.

The tears that were filling my eyes break free at the pain radiating through my body from his intrusion.

To my surprise, he holds still for a few seconds. Letting me believe my Leon is still in there somewhere, protecting me, looking after me. Right when I think he's going to emerge in this monster's place, he pulls almost all the way back out of me and slams back in.

My back slides across the desk with the force. His fingertips digging into my hips deep enough to leave marks, ensuring that tomorrow there will be evidence of what he did.

"Leon," I cry when he repeats the action over and over.

I have no idea when it happened but between one thrust and another, the pain melted away in favor of something else.

Pleasure.

Oh God.

This shouldn't feel this good. He shouldn't feel this good.

I reach out, my nails digging into his forearms as he holds me. My heels pressing against his ass as he thrusts into me, dragging him deeper.

"Fuck, you feel good," he says, his anger slipping away for a few seconds as he loses himself in me.

I stare up at him, begging to see those sparkling green eyes look down at me like I actually mean something to him.

But when he finally does open them, that's not what I see.

"Do you remember yet?" He grits out, his jaw popping and the muscles in his neck tightening as his release edges closer.

"Leon, I—"

I try to push up on my elbow to get to him. But he sees my intention and pins me back to the desk with his hand around my throat.

"You knew," he spits. "You knew what he was doing. To me. To others. And you did nothing. You looked into my eyes. And. You. Did. Nothing. Fuuuuck," he cries as his cock twitches violently inside me.

Unexpectedly, he reaches out and pinches my clit, that along with his pulsating cock is enough to send me crashing into my own release.

The room falls silent for long seconds as we both try to catch our breath.

"You were right, Red," he says, straightening up and slipping out of me. "I never wanted you. I just wanted to ruin you. And him."

Reaching over, he grabs a folder from the drawer and throws it down on my chest.

"And now I've got you both."

"No, Lee. Please let me—"

"No," he booms. "You should have talked ten years ago. It's too late. The damage is done."

He looks down to tuck himself away but before he does, something puts a smile on his lips.

"Fuck, no," I cry when he pushes two fingers deep inside me. I'm so sensitive I can barely stand it.

When he pulls them out, I realize what caught his attention because the red blood is obvious against his skin.

"I guess I should feel relieved he never got to you, huh?"

My chin drops when he pushes his fingers into his mouth and licks them clean.

He takes a step back before reaching for me. He drags me off the desk and I stumble into the corner of the room barely able to stand on my own two legs.

I watch in horror as he upends the desk, sending everything on top crashing to the floor.

The shelves go next before he takes a signed baseball bat that was on display and sets to work on destroying all the glass cabinets housing my uncle's trophies.

"Leon no," I cry, not giving a crap about my uncle's stuff, but knowing he's never going to be able to come back from this. "Please, Lee. Don't—"

"You don't get to tell me what to do," he bellows. "You fucking broke me, Macie. Ruined me. Left me with that monster. You. Did. Nothing. All of this. It's your fucking fault."

"No," I cry, tears cascading down my cheeks. My legs trembling as my entire body shudders.

"I never wanted you. How could I?"

With one more look up and down my body, his nose turned up as if I disgust him, he takes off, bat still in hand.

Unable to hold myself up, I slide down the wall, sobbing as the sound of him destroying everything in his wake fills my ears. I hear the front door slamming shut behind him and the house I hate, the house that keeps me awake at night, finally falls silent.

"NOOOO," I scream, my voice hoarse with emotion. "NOOOOO."

Keep reading for more Leon & Mace in The Retaliation You Deliver.

THE RETALIATION YOU DELIVER

MADDISON KINGS UNIVERSITY #7

1

LEON

Aloud bang jolts my body awake but I don't respond. I just lie there unmoving, my eyes tightly closed.

"Come on, let's go," a deep unfamiliar voice booms, echoing off the bare walls around me.

Blowing out a long breath, I remain immobile.

"Dunn," he barks. "Let's fucking go. You've got people waiting on you."

It's those words which force me to react.

My pulse increases, my heart slamming against my ribs as I crack an eye open.

The pain in my head makes me wince as the bright light assaults me.

The officer standing in the opening of the cell stares at me in impatience.

"I don't need anyone," I complain, my voice rough, my throat burning with each word.

"Well, unlucky for you, they're here."

"Fucking hell," I mutter, pushing myself up until I'm sitting on the rock hard bed in the cell I was thrown into last night.

Probably not the finest night of my life but the less I think about the events of yesterday, it's probably for the better.

"I'm free to go?" I ask, shoving my feet into my sneakers and refusing to look up at him again.

"Yeah. So long as we don't find you drunk on one of our beaches again."

"Trust me, I've got no intention of coming back to Miami ever again. Only bad shit happens here."

He's silent as I push to stand. My head spins, the pounding at my temples almost unbearable as my stomach turns over. Sucking in a deep breath, I'm willing the need to puke away, not really wanting to piss this guy off more by leaving the cell with the contents of my stomach on the floor.

I lift my arm to the frame of the opening the second it's in reaching distance to steady myself.

"Nothing less than you deserve," the officer mutters.

"Don't judge me," I snap, pissed off with his attitude. "If you'd been through what I have then you'd have reached for the bottle too." He looks back at me, a little pity edging it's way into his expression and making me instantly regret saying anything.

I sign some paperwork when we get to the desk and after a few words of warning about my behavior he allows me to leave out of the double doors.

My steps immediately falter when my eyes land on the two people who instantly stand from the chairs, the words of the officer about people being here to collect me come to the forefront of my mind.

Peyton's face is twisted in concern, whereas my brother looks murderous.

His teeth grind and his jaw pops as he stares at me. His entire body is locked up with tension that's radiating off him in waves. If it weren't for the fact we were standing in a police station, I'm sure he'd be on me, taking his frustration out on me through his fists.

The air is heavy and thick between us like you can cut it with a knife. Even when Peyton places her hand on Luca's chest and whispers something in his ear, he still doesn't relax.

"Let's go," he spits, turning his back on me and storming through the double doors.

We both watch him go as my legs finally start to work again, taking me to Peyton.

"I haven't seen him this angry in a while," she mutters sadly, staring at the door he just stormed through.

My lips part to respond but I quickly find that I have no words.

Ripping her eyes from the door, Peyton turns her silver eyes on me. "Are you okay, Lee?"

"I... uh..."

She reaches for my hand, squeezing it in support.

Pulling on my mask and finding the strength I've used to get me through the past ten years, I force a smile onto my lips.

"I'm good. I'm sorry I dragged you down here to bail me out."

"Anytime. But—" I suck in a breath, knowing what's coming next. "You're going to need to explain what's been going with you. You're not brushing this one under the rug."

"I know," I say sadly. I think I realized last night that my days of hiding my dark past are over.

Macie knows the truth now so it won't be long until everyone else does.

My chest aches as I think of her. Images of our final minutes together flicking through my mind. Regret floods me as I remember her cowering in the corner of the room as I took my frustrations out on everything inside her uncle's house. The memory of the tears tracking down her face as she watched me. The horror of our reality is so clear in her eyes.

She really had no idea. But she does now.

She knows exactly who I am. She's also discovered that everything she feared about our relationship was true. I didn't go into it for her, not in the way I made it out like I did. I just wanted revenge. I wanted her pain. I wanted to teach her a lesson so she would know the mistake she made that day.

Peyton lacing her arm through mine drags me from my nightmare and I come back to the here and now.

Together we walk out of the station, with the sun searing my eyeballs the second I step out of the building and look up.

"You okay?" Peyton asks, clearly noticing my reaction.

I grunt a response and head toward where Luca is leaning against his car with his hands curled into fists at his sides.

"Just take me to my car and I'll get out of your hair," I say, needing to get away from the both of them and their probing stares.

"Fuck off, Lee," he barks, pushing off from his car and stepping up to me.

"Can we not?" I ask, although I already know what his answer is going to be.

"No," he snaps, his palms landing solidly on my chest and making me back up.

I don't have the energy or the strength right now to fight him.

"No, we're fucking doing this. Why the fuck are we here, Lee? Why did I get a call from Mom at the break of dawn to tell me that you'd been fucking arrested and needed bailing out from jail in fucking Miami of all places."

"I'm not talking about this right now," I mutter, trying to step around him.

"You don't have a fucking choice, asshole," he seethes.

"Luca, give him a break," Peyton says softly, coming to stand beside him.

"A break? A fucking break? He's had a long enough break. He's been lying to me for years. We've bailed on classes to come and get his drunk ass. He owes us an explanation."

"I don't owe you anything."

"I need the fucking truth," he says, fisting my shirt and slamming me back against his car. "Why the fuck are you here? Who do you know in Miami?"

Our green eyes hold, both of our chests heaving. Him begging me to talk and me desperately trying to come up with a way to get out of this.

I don't see Peyton move to our sides once more, but I sure hear her words.

"It's her, isn't it? It's Macie."

Luca's brows pinch at her words.

"You came with her." Peyton says matter-of-factly.

"Why?" Luca asks, clearly assuming that his girl is right.

"We're not doing this here."

"No? Then where are we doing it?"

"Not in a fucking parking lot when I can barely see straight."

"You're not getting out of this."

"Take me to my car."

"Fuck that. You're not getting behind the wheel. You smell like a fucking brewery. Get in my car. We'll get yours brought back."

Thankfully, he takes a step back, getting out of my face.

"What about Macie?" Her name is like a gunshot through my heart and my eyes immediately find Peyton's.

"What about her?" I spit. "She's where she should be." *In hell.*

Luca lets out a sigh.

"Just get in the fucking car," he demands, ripping the back door open and all but throws me inside.

"Alright, alright. Jesus."

I climb in, and immediately rest my head back.

I'm so fucking tired.

I almost drift off instantly until there's a loud thud against the car and my eyes fly open.

"Great," I mutter to myself, finding Peyton crushed up against my window as Luca damn near attacks her mouth.

All I can hope is that she helps chill him the fuck out because I already know that I'm not going to be able to cope with the long drive back to MKU with him demanding to know everything.

I need to tell him. I know I do. But not like this. Not when he's driving and has no way to react in a manner I know he's going to.

Closing my eyes once more, I cut off my view from what's happening outside my window.

I should probably remind them that we're in a police station parking lot but I don't. Watching them both get dragged in for public indecency might be the only thing that could amuse me right at this moment.

Not long after the show they've put on, the driver's door is ripped open and Luca drops into his seat.

"What? Not gonna fuck her?"

"Shut the fuck up, asshole," he groans before Peyton joins us.

I keep my eyes closed but I feel the second she turns back to look at me, her attention makes my skin prickle with awareness.

"Just drive. I don't need your pity."

"What? That wasn't—"

"Don't justify yourself to him, P," Luca snaps.

"Fine." Rustling tells me that she spins back around before the car rumbles to life and we start to move.

"Who are you messaging?" Luca asks.

"Letty. I'm getting Macie's number."

My fists curl at my sides that Peyton feels it's necessary to check up on her.

"Leave her alone."

"I love you, Lee. You know that. But nope... that's not going to happen. I know something big has happened to find you in this position and something tells me she's hurting just as much as you are now."

That same image of her cowering flickers through my mind once more before it morphs into me being inside that room with *him*. My body being forced over that desk and just waiting for the pain.

"You know fuck all."

"Leon," Luca growls.

Ignoring both of them, I lie across the back seat of his car and beg that the car will lull me to sleep.

"No, please. No, don't," I cry as his hand grips the back of my neck, forcing my body to bend over.

"You want to be the best, boy, then you need to learn to follow instructions." His voice is deep, hoarse with his excitement. I recognize it from the previous two times.

When it's like this, just the two of us, he's like an entirely different person. One that I'm sure very few know exists.

Only, he's not a person. He's a monster. One who haunts my nightmares, constantly makes me look over my shoulder and generally fear life in a way I've never experienced before.

If I thought being the forgotten twin was bad, then this... this is insurmountable.

His hand slides down my spine causing bile to rush up my throat, burning the sensitive flesh as I fight to keep it inside.

Throwing up all over his desk won't make this stop. Nothing short of killing him, or myself, will make this stop.

"No," I cry, unable to contain it when he pushes my shorts down, exposing me to him. "No, please. I'll do anything, please."

A jolt from a touch pulls me slightly out of my nightmare before the warm hand continues to nudge against my shoulder.

"Leon, it's—"

I react without thinking, swinging my arm out to get him away from me, anything to get him the hell off me. Only when I hear a cry, it's not from an angry turned on man who I've just encouraged even more, but a soft female one that turns my blood to ice.

My eyes fly open and I find Peyton hanging between the two front seats, tears filling her eyes as she cups her mouth.

"Holy shit, fuck. I didn't mean—"

"It's okay, Lee. I know you didn't mean— Luca no," Peyton cries out and the door above my head opens and two large hands grab me.

"What the—"

"Luca," Peyton screams again but before I know what's going on, I'm thrown against the car and his fist connects with my jaw.

I don't fight back. Why would I?

I'm the one in the wrong here. I'm the one who just hit his girl, I'm the one keeping secrets, driving him crazy.

He gets two more solid hits in before Peyton manages to scramble out from the car and calm him down.

"You fucking hurt her again and I'll fucking kill you. Twin or not, you're not hurting anyone else I love. I've sat by and let you destroy everything around you for years. I've watched Mom stare at you when she knows you're not looking with tears in her eyes wishing she could somehow get to you. Whatever this bullshit is, Lee. It's over. You owe me the truth."

"I owe you fuck all," I mutter, keeping my eyes on the dirt beneath my feet.

I have no idea where we are, and when I look up, I find we're just on the side of the road.

"Let me help you." His voice changes, the anger subsiding and the caring brother I know slipping back in. "Let us help you. Whatever it is, we can handle it together."

With a nod, I step forward and pull Peyton into my arms.

"I'm sorry," I whisper in her ear as I hold her tight.

She returns my embrace and until her warmth surrounds me, I don't realize just how much I need it.

"It's okay. Just please, let us in. We're here for you. Whatever you need."

I nod against her, willing the emotion filling my eyes and clogging my throat to subside before I pull away.

"Take me home, please."

Releasing Peyton, I slip back into the car without looking at Luca.

I can't. If I see the concern that I know is written all over his face, it'll break me.

2

———

MACIE

Everything hurts when I come to, but nothing beats the pain in my chest as the images of last night play out in my mind like a movie.

I didn't manage to drag my sorry ass from the ground for hours after Leon blew through the house, taking his aggression out on everything in his path. Or, at least that was what it sounded like. I've yet to find the strength I need to go down and see the destruction left in his wake.

When I finally managed to get to my feet, the only place my shaky legs took me was up to my room and to my bed.

But my room here didn't provide the comfort I craved.

I needed safety, security, and this house has never provided me with either of those things.

I always thought of it as the house of horrors, and the events of last night only go to prove just how right I was.

Sucking in a deep breath, I force my eyes open and sit up.

They burn, the skin around them sore from all the tears I shed last night. I'm sure if I were to look in a mirror, I'd find them red and bloodshot from my lack of sleep.

Every single time I closed my eyes, I saw him. That poor little boy at the hands of my uncle. The monster.

How did I not realize it was him?

Now that I know, it's so freaking obvious.

The image of him on that desk is clearer than ever, his green terrified eyes as they locked onto mine. His full parted lips as they silently pleaded with me to help him.

The tears start all over again despite thinking I must've already run out after all the crying last night.

Silently they run down my cheeks, dropping to the sheets beneath me with quiet dull thuds.

My head spins with everything as I try to get a grasp on how I really feel.

Anger surges through my veins keeping my muscles pulled tight. Betrayal tastes bitter on my tongue.

But that's not it, because despite everything. I understand.

I get why he felt the need to do what he did, and a part of me hates myself for it because I know that I should be hating him.

He's the one who played me, who hurt me, who used me. All the things I feared he was doing right from the start.

But the broken little girl inside of me recognizes the broken little boy in him and all she wants to do is pull him into her arms and make everything better.

Damn her, naïve little child.

My muscles pull as I climb from the bed and pad toward my bathroom.

With every move, his scent hits my nose and that along with the slight ache between my legs, ensures that I never forget that last night really happened.

I brush my teeth without looking at myself, too scared to discover what kind of devastating state I'm in after he left me behind.

The second I spit the toothpaste out, I turn to the shower, strip off the shirt I slept in last night and step under the burning hot spray.

I usually can't stand it scalding, or at least I haven't for a lot of years but today, I need it.

I need the pain, I need the burn, I need to remember that out of all of this, something good has to happen.

Lifting my hand to my chest, I recall Leon throwing the welcome pack from Acorn Lodge down on me.

I knew it was what he wanted. The second I pieced it all together in my head, it was obvious that my uncle was his intended target. I guess I was just the added bonus and collateral damage to his endgame.

He must hate you, a little voice says in my head.

I fall back against the tiled wall, not even registering the cold.

How good of an actor is he to have made me believe he really wanted me? The things he said to me, the way he touched me. How could he do that when I'm sure all he wanted to do was hurt me?

For the ultimate pain.

Make me fall and then pull the rug from beneath me.

I slide down the wall and curl myself into a ball, wrapping my arms around my legs and resting my head on my knees.

I want to chastise myself for being so stupid that I fell for it. But I knew it was coming. I told myself time and time again that it—that he —was too good to be true yet I continued to see him, continued to fall, and allowed him to shatter my rules and my well constructed walls.

I made it so easy for him.

Was he laughing at me the whole time?

He told me that I was different. But really, I'm no different than all of them.

It only took him days to get into my panties. And this weekend, whether it went the way it did or not, we'd have taken that final step together, of that I have no doubt.

I'm no different to all the jersey chasers I hate, falling for the player almost without a second thought.

I have no idea how long I sit there under the stream of water, but eventually my skin is pruney and my tears have once again dried up and I know it's time to move.

I haven't fought my entire life to crumble to pieces because of a guy.

He's not just any guy though, is he?

Climbing to my feet, I go through the motions of washing up but I'm completely moving on autopilot.

It's not until I walk back into my room and the sound of my cell vibrating in my purse fills my ears that everything comes crashing down around me once more.

Sitting at my vanity table, I rummage around in my purse until I find it.

That silly little girl inside me hopes for it to be him. For him to apologize and tell me that he never really hated me, that he understands that I had to do what I did back then.

But I already know it's not.

There's no way he's going to forgive me that easily, or ever.

I left him to—

I swallow down the lump in my throat, unable to even think the words let alone acknowledge what happened to him inside that room that day.

And how many times after?

Lowering my cell, I heave at the thought of what he's been through. The abuse I helped subject him to with my inaction.

I'm out of the chair before I even register I've moved and in seconds, I'm on my knees in front of the toilet, emptying my stomach into the bowl.

Tears once again cascade down my face as I fall back on my ass and breathe in and out, counting each breath.

It's a move I haven't had to use for years in order to get control of myself and I hate that I've got to revert back to it.

Once I'm stronger, I brush my teeth once more and go back to find where I abandoned my cell.

I find it face down on the floor between the vanity and the bathroom.

Turning it over and waking it up, I find what I was expecting.

The call wasn't from Leon but an unknown number.

And there's not just one call but eight.

Curious, I open the one voicemail and put it on speaker as I press play.

"M-Macie? It's Peyton, Luca Dunn's girlfriend." My heart pounds against my rib cage as her words flow through me. "We... um... we just wanted to check that you're okay. If you could call me that would be great. Th-thanks, bye."

All the air rushes from my lungs.

Do they know?

Something tells me they don't. I have a sinking suspicion that there are only three of us who do know the truth.

Needing to at least attempt to find some strength before I return her call, I drag on a clean set of clothes and blow-dry my hair.

I tell myself that I'm not putting it off any longer. I have no idea what Peyton knows about last night, that we're even in Miami. But the fact she's even calling means she must know something.

My stomach drops into my feet as a thought hits me.

What if something happened to him? He was so angry when he left last night. He could have—

As I dial her number, the ringing is loud in the room. My pulse is thundering through my entire body as I wait for the call to connect.

If something has happened to him, I'll never be able to forgive myself for allowing him to storm out the way he did.

"Hey, can I call you back in ten?" she asks the second the call connects.

"Uh... s-sure."

She cuts me off before I get to ask if he's okay or not.

The next ten minutes are some of the longest of my life, and I've endured many painful waits in my time so it really is saying something.

The second the screen flashes with her name now that I've saved her contact, I can't answer it quick enough.

"Is he okay? I blurt out the second the call connects, needing to know that nothing serious has happened.

"Y-yeah, he is."

"Oh my God," I sigh, falling back on my bed and allowing just a little bit of relief to flow through me. "Where is he?"

"We're currently halfway between Miami and MKU. You were in Miami with him, right?" Her question confirms what I already knew. She really has no idea what's going on or what happened.

"Y-yes."

"He won't tell us anything but we got a call from their mom first thing this morning because he was sitting in jail and needed bailing out."

"What?" I screech, once again sitting up.

"He was picked up on the beach for being drunk and disorderly."

Oh Christ.

"Has he been charged?"

"No, just a slap on the wrist for acting like an idiot. Are you okay?"

"Y-yeah, I'm fine." Probably one of the biggest lies I've ever told in my life because really, I'm far from fine. I'm falling apart but no one needs to know that apart from me.

"You're lying, I can hear it in your voice."

"You don't even know me," I whisper, instantly regretting it in case she takes it the wrong way.

"We're taking him home. Someone will collect his car unless you want to..." she trails off and it's the first time I realize that I'm stuck here.

"I don't have a key."

"Give me your address, we'll make sure you have it by the end of the day."

"N-no you don't—"

"Macie," she breathes. "We might not have the slightest clue with what's going on here but we want to help. Me and you might not have met yet, but Letty has told me wonderful things and I trust her, so I trust you. Do what you need to do, drive back with his car, and let me know once you're home safe. Don't worry, we'll keep an eye on Lee."

Too choked up to say anything else, I stutter a thank you and hang up. I quickly send her a message with my current address so she can send the key before falling back onto the pillow.

Thoughts race around my head about what he did after leaving here last night that ended with him in a jail cell. I can only imagine how he must have been feeling.

I awake with a shock as the house alarm blares through the silent space around me.

Scrambling around the bed, I find my cell and open the security app, shutting the thing off.

"What the hell?" I scream as my cell pings with the automated message from the security company that I'm more than bored of seeing.

My stomach groans as I sit there, and I know my time hiding out in this cold and unfamiliar room is coming to an end. I'm going to have to go out there and see the damage he's caused and finally figure out what's setting this damn alarm off before I try to drum up the courage to get into Leon's car to head back to MKU.

The second I agreed I knew it was a mistake. Being in there is just going to remind me of him, of the short time we've spent together. It's going to smell like him for Christ's sake and I hate to admit it, but it's going to make me miss him.

I have no right to miss him.

I deserve every bit of this pain for what I did to him. But equally, he doesn't deserve to get it from me either.

Jesus. We're both as screwed up as each other.

I felt stupid when I admitted to him that I felt like we'd been brought together for a reason. Turns out I was right, but I never would have guessed the reason, or the fact that the reason we seemed to click so well probably has something to do with our mutual pain and hatred for the same man.

———

I expect the house to be trashed but I never could have prepared myself for the amount of devastation Leon left in his wake last night.

Everything on the shelving unit, from ornaments to picture frames are broken, shattered and destroyed as I make my way down two flights of stairs and toward the kitchen.

My uncle's liquor cabinet is missing its glass doors, bottles of vintage whisky are smashed all over the floor, the scent filling the entire main floor of the house.

Mary, his housekeeper, is going to love me for this.

Part of me wants to start tidying it all up, but a bigger part of me has wanted to see this place burned to the ground for years.

This house, the entire estate holds nothing but bad memories for me.

Turning my back on the mess, I make myself a coffee then head toward the other rooms we didn't check last night.

I'm half expecting to find something disturbing behind each door, but with each one I open, all I find are boxes and random crap. Thankfully, there is no twisted sex den or evidence—at least visible evidence—of the kind of stuff that twisted prick was into.

A shudder rips through me once more at the image now burned right at the forefront of my mind from his office ten years ago.

I'd banished it from my head, that and everything else that man subjected me to over the years. But it's like Leon opened Pandora's box because all the memories are just spilling out around me.

The second I push open the final door, I discover the culprit of the alarm because a panicked bird flaps around by the widow.

"How the hell did you get in here?" I mutter, walking over and pushing the windows as wide as they'll go to give the bird its freedom.

"You've got it easy," I tell him. "You can fly away and forget this place ever held you hostage. I've never been that lucky."

I stand there for a few minutes, looking out over the rolling countryside toward the outbuildings where his boys used to stay every summer.

Richard Fletcher's summer camp was notorious, and only the very best or very wealthy got a spot.

But all that money and power, all it was hiding was dirty secrets and potentially years of abuse.

Parents willingly handed their boys over to my uncle believing they'd be safe here. That he'd been vetted, not only that, but he was a celebrity. A player most parents had grown up watching, a man many of the father's looked up to.

What a joke.

The man is nothing but a child abuser.

I have many regrets. Not helping that little boy—Leon—will

always be my biggest, but coming up a close second is that I never got any evidence of what was happening here.

I was only eight at the time. I didn't really understand what was happening, what I saw that day, until a few years later, but by then, it was too late.

My uncle and I had no relationship left.

He might have been paying my tuition at school, for my holidays that ensured he never had to see me, but that was the extent of our relationship by that point. And that was more than fine by me. I'd come to terms with the fact I had no family long before he cut me off.

I always figured that I was better off alone, and that at some point, I'd get a chance to be able to make my own family.

Surely at some point I was going to find some friends who would accept me for who I was.

Turns out that was wishful thinking, because here I am, eighteen and a college freshman still without a family.

Sure, I've got my roommates but my friendship with them isn't exactly ride or die. Nathan is close, I guess. But it's still not what I imagined when I thought about finding that perfect group of friends years ago.

Now, I figure it was just a pipe dream.

Maybe I'm destined to be alone forever. Maybe God, or whoever, has a different plan for me.

3

LEON

"Do you think you should go and check on her?" I ask, realizing that Peyton has been in the diner bathroom for longer than probably necessary.

"Nah, she'll be out in a bit," Luca says confidently over his mug of coffee.

We drove for about an hour after I woke up from my nightmare. The atmosphere in the car was unbearable as we all sat there in silence, lost in our own thoughts.

I want to know what they're thinking, how they thought I ended up here, I'm pretty confident that whatever conclusions they've come up with aren't anywhere near the reality.

"So your dirty weekend didn't exactly go as planned then," Luca deadpans, changing tack from previously just asking me outright what the hell I'm playing at.

"No, not entirely," I admit, although if I'm being honest with myself, I got exactly what I came here for.

I finally got to play my hand with Macie and now I've got that cunt's location.

So why don't I feel like I've actually achieved anything?

All I feel is guilt.

Guilt and loss.

"So is she from Miami then or was it just a random getaway to keep her hidden away from me?"

"I wasn't hiding her," I mutter.

"Sure. That's why the only people who have met her are Letty and Kane. What are you so worried about? It's not like I'm going to steal her from you."

"It's complicated."

"When isn't it?"

Finally, movement over by the bathrooms catches my eye and when I look up, I find Peyton heading our way.

"Everything okay?" Luca asks her.

Peyton flashes me a look and I can't help but wonder what I'm missing here.

"Yeah. All good. I've got the address you need too."

She passes Luca her cell and he stares down at it. His brows lift momentarily.

Already bored of trying to figure out what they're talking about, I slide out from the booth.

"I'm going to take a piss."

Pushing through the bathroom door, I stop in the middle of the room and suck in a deep breath.

I thought I had everything figured out, thought I had a plan and that as I put each piece of the puzzle together, things would start to make more sense.

But now that I've got what I've been searching for, I feel even more lost than I did before.

I should be shouting for joy that I can find Richard Fletcher and finally show him just how wrong he was to mess with me all those years ago. I've got Macie exactly where I've always wanted her. Broken and regretting ever walking away that day. So why don't I feel good about any of it?

I do what I came in here to do before heading back out.

The booth the three of us were sitting in is empty, a few bills sitting on the table and when I glance out of the windows, I find Peyton and Luca standing beside his car deep in conversation; about me I'm sure.

"Let's go," I bark as I approach, making them jump apart like naughty school kids.

Yep, definitely talking about me.

"I need some fucking sleep."

They both stare at me for a beat, my eyes flicking down to the cut in Peyton's lip from when I hurt her earlier.

I really am just fucking all this right up.

The remainder of the drive back to Maddison is as silent as the journey to the diner.

Every few minutes I sense Luca looking at me in the rearview mirror.

Initially, I just glared back, not allowing him to see beneath the mask I've got firmly in place. But as the minutes and miles pass, I begin to give up caring and allowing my mask to slip.

Letting him see how fucked up and broken I am. I'm sure in the coming hours he's going to finally drag—or beat—the truth out of me.

My time for hiding is over.

My hands tremble with thoughts of how I'll say the things he thinks he wants to hear. He thinks that by learning the truth that he'll be able to help me. What he doesn't know is that I'm long past the point of help. I've been drowning in this darkness for too long to believe that one painful confession will fix the broken parts of me.

By the time we pull up outside our house, I'm more than ready to dive head first into my bed. My body aches, I stink to the point I'm surprised neither of them has complained and I'm fucking exhausted. If the events of the night before weren't enough to wipe me out then this morning surely did.

"Lee, wait," Luca calls as I all but run toward the house. I stop but I don't turn around. I've already seen enough pity in his eyes this morning to last me a lifetime. "Take your time. I'll be here when you're ready."

"I'll never be ready," I mutter.

"Well time's run out, Brother. Deal with your shit and get yourself together then we're talking."

My heart is like a runaway train in my chest knowing how that conversation is going to go, but I know I've got to finally get it over with.

————

It's almost six hours later when I finally pull the door open and step out of the safety of my room.

My hand trembles as I pull it closed behind me. I want to believe that if I'm quiet enough, I might just be able to sneak out of the house unnoticed and put this off just a little while longer. But I know it's wishful thinking because I hear them downstairs waiting for me.

I think Luca thought we were going to have this heartbreaking conversation one-on-one. In the past, that's always how I've imagined it going. But right now, on the brink of bleeding my darkness out all over him I realize that it needs to be more than just him.

"Hey, how are you doing?" Letty asks, jumping up from the couch and racing toward me. She has no idea what I'm about to confess but she knows it's huge and as she wraps her arms around me, I can't help but feel her support. She's going to be the one to help me get through this as whole as a broken me can be, and Peyton is going to be the one to support Luca.

"It's going to be okay," she whispers in my ear. "Whatever it is, you know you've got us."

I nod, unable to speak around the lump in my throat.

Taking my hand, she leads me over to the couch she was sitting on. I sit directly opposite Luca who has Peyton pinned to his side.

We stare at each other as the atmosphere in the room grows heavy.

"Lee, I know you're—"

"Macie isn't just some random girl I picked up," I blurt out, deciding to start with her; it seems like the easiest thing to talk about right now.

"I know. Peyton got her address. She's William Fletcher's kid. Richard Fletcher's niece. You went after her for a reason, didn't you?"

"I've been looking for her for a few years, yeah. But the night I found her, it was by complete accident. I was about to bang her roommate and she stormed in and..." I trail off, I'm sure they don't need the full details of that night.

Letty's hold on my hand tightens, letting me know that she's still here with me.

"Why were you looking for her?"

"She... uh... she knew something about me, was hiding information I needed."

Luca's eyes narrow. "You met her before? When we were at camp she was always hidden away like a princess locked in her ivory tower."

"She was yeah, but she saw something she was never meant to. I never spoke a word to her until a couple of weeks ago."

"I'm confused," Peyton says, her brows drawing together.

Luca quickly fills her in on who the Fletchers are before they both turn back to me.

"What did she see, Lee?"

I suck in a breath knowing that I'm not going to be able to talk around this and find a way out of it.

"R-Richard Fletcher. He wasn't... wasn't the man everyone thought he was."

Luca's eyes narrow in confusion.

"Why? What was he really like?"

"He was... he... Fuck." I drop my head into my hands. Even after all these years, I can't bring myself to say it out loud.

I thought it would go away, that I'd be able to keep it hidden forever.

I hoped I'd find him and put my demons to rest by getting my revenge. That might still happen, I guess. But not before I have to spill my guts to the very last person I ever wanted to know the truth.

"What did he do, Lee?" Letty says softly, wrapping her arm around my waist, holding my trembling body tight.

I breathe in. Then breathe out. Trying to keep myself under control. My fists clench and unclench as I try to form some words, anything to put an end to this.

"He was an abusive cunt who wasn't only interested in having boys at his home for football," I say in a rush hoping that they won't catch it and I can just leave it at that.

The second Letty's sob rips through the silence though, I know she understood every word of it.

Her other arm wraps around me as she presses her face into my shoulder, her tears soaking my shirt instantly.

I fight to stay in place and be what she needs me to be, but every muscle in my body screams to get up, to run, to try and put those few words behind me like they never left my mouth.

"No," Luca spits. "N-no. We went there every summer. You loved it there. It was... it w-was—"

I look up at him and the second my eyes connect with his watery ones he sees the truth.

"No," he sobs. "No. Please. Tell me you're lying." I hold his stare, unable to do as he requests. "Goddammit, Leon," he booms. "Tell me you're fucking lying. Tell me he didn't— FUCK," he roars, jumping up from the couch and storming out of the room.

"Lee, I'm sorry, I—" Peyton looks between me and the door Luca just stormed through.

"Go. I'll be okay."

"O-okay." She's gone in a flash leaving me alone with Letty who's still clinging to me like her life depends on it.

"I'm not going to shatter, Let. It's okay," I say, gently pulling her away from me and taking her hand in mine.

"All those times we joked about secrets, never did I think that—" She hiccups, cutting off her words.

"It's okay."

"No, Leon. It's not. It's really fucking not." Her bottom lip trembles as she speaks. "He hurt you, he r-rap—"

"Shh," I comfort her when her voice cracks on that word. "It was a long time ago."

"I don't care, Leon. He had no right to do that. You were a kid." She trembles with anger for me as she holds my gaze.

I'm so fucking relieved that they're full of fire and fight instead of pity and sympathy.

"I want to fucking kill him for you."

"Why do you think I've been looking for him, Cupcake?"

Her eyes widen.

"No. No, Lee. You can't. If you get caught then he'll completely ruin your life. Fuck, please. Don't do that."

"Jesus, Let. I'm not going to walk up to him with a gun in public and shoot him point blank for the world to see."

"O-okay, g-good," she sniffles. "So what are you going to do?"

I shrug.

"You know where he is though?"

"Thanks to Macie, yeah."

"Fucking hell. Macie. What have you done to her?"

"She's in Miami at her uncle's place."

"That wasn't what I asked."

"She knew, Letty. She stormed into his office one day and... she saw what was happening."

"Holy shit. Did she know it was you?"

"You think she would've let me anywhere near her if she knew it was me?"

"Macie is a good person, Leon. I'm sure you've figured that out over the past couple of weeks."

Have I? Or will my opinion of her always be tainted by our past?

"It doesn't matter. I needed her to help me find him, and she led me right to him."

"So that's it. Everything between you was fake, everything you said you felt for her was a lie?"

"Means to an end." I shrug. It's cold, I know it is. But it's the truth.

Macie was right. Me and her, we'd never work.

The player and the nerd. It's not exactly how things go.

I'm sure she's got a plan for her life and following me to whatever city I end up in probably isn't at the top of her to-do list once she graduates. Not that I think we'd ever have made it that far should anything have continued.

"That's bullshit, Lee, and you know it."

"Do I? She was a pawn in my game, Cupcake. Why do you think I never intended on her meeting any of you."

"Oh," she says with a laugh. "So that's why you took her to a Harris party. You thought none of us would be there."

"You weren't meant to make friends with her," I mutter.

"Well, I did. And while I might be devastated for what you've been through, Lee. While I might sit here and hold your hand and cry with you, don't think I'm not fucking furious with you for treating her like a piece of shit."

"She never helped me, Letty. She knew and she did nothing."

"She was a child. What did you really expect her to do? Her only guardian was an abusive cunt of a man. You really think she was going to go up against him?"

A shudder of fear runs down my spine again at the possibility of him hurting her.

"He never touched her."

"Oh, know that for a fact do you? Because ten minutes ago none of us had a clue he ever touched you."

"She was a virgin," I shout, my frustration getting the better of me.

"Was?" Letty questions, one brow shooting up.

"Yeah, *was*. I stole that from her just like that cunt stole everything from me."

All the blood drains from Letty's face as she stares at me. It's like suddenly she's staring into the eyes of a stranger.

Of a monster.

Of him.

"Tell me you didn't, Lee. For the love of God tell me you didn't hurt her."

A wicked smile curls up at the corner of my lips as I remember sinking into her tight pussy for the first time and how fucking good it felt.

"Oh, yeah, I hurt her. But she was fucking begging for it."

I don't see her hand coming, but I sure as fucking feel it as her palm connects with my cheek in a burning slap.

"Who even are you?" She spits, her lip curled in disgust. "I get that this is hard, Leon. I get that you're hurting. But she doesn't deserve any of this. She's good, innocent, pure, and you fucking ruined her."

"Just like he did me. Karma's a bitch."

She stares at me for a beat longer before following Luca's lead and storming from the room.

Well... that went well.

———

I sit on the couch with my head in my hands for the longest time alone in our living room.

I knew this would happen.

The second they discovered the truth, all of them have run from me.

I get it. I'm tainted. Poisoned.

With a groan, I push up from the couch knowing there's only one thing I can do right now. Only one person I can visit.

It's been days since I beat him within an inch of his life, he's long overdue for a visit from his favorite son.

The second I step into the hallway, I hear their voices from the kitchen.

Anger swirls around me that they haven't got the fucking balls to talk with me in the room but are happily gossiping about me when I'm not there.

"I'm glad I've given you all some fucking entertainment."

Three guilty faces turn my way.

"No, Lee, that's not what—"

"Do what you want. Talk away. Try to imagine what it's like. I'm going out."

Without hearing another word from them, I storm out of the house without thinking.

Once I get outside, the spot in the driveway where my car is usually parked is empty.

Fuck. My car.

Storming back into the house, I march straight up to Luca.

"Give me your keys."

"Uh... I... uh..."

"Give me your fucking keys."

"Fine," he sighs in defeat, digging his hand into his pocket before throwing them at me. "Don't fucking break her."

"Would I?" I ask, rolling my eyes. I turn my back on them, storming from the house again before Luca can remind me of what happened to his very first car.

I don't need to hear him tell me about how I wrote off his first love when I collided with a wall.

It was an accident. One he's never going to let me forget.

The second the engine rumbles to life beneath me, I feel a little more settled.

I love driving, it's one of the only ways I found I can really forget and put things behind me, well... until Macie.

Being in her company made everything go quiet.

With her miles away in Miami right now, and with the memories of what I just told everyone in that room rattling around in my head, everything is as loud as it's ever been.

And I need it gone.

I'm on the verge of getting everything I ever wanted.

Revenge on Macie and vengeance on her uncle.

Yet, I don't feel anything like the relief I expected to feel when the time finally came.

If anything, I feel more lost than ever.

I drive on autopilot as my head spins with the events of the past twenty-four hours. My grip on the wheel is tightening until my knuckles turn white and the almost healed cuts from my last visit to my father are splitting open once more.

I sit in Luca's car outside of the warehouse, which holds my prisoner and I stare at the dark building.

What happens next?

I've got to Macie. I can get to Richard. Okay, so Macie could warn the staff or even move him before I get a chance to make my move, but something tells me she won't.

Then there's Brett.

I've wanted him gone for years.

I've hated him for as long as I can remember, not only for how he cast me aside but for the incredible pressure he put on Luca, the way he ignored Shane, and how he's treated our mother.

All of us deserved better than him.

He might have provided us with money and all the opportunities we could have wanted—well, as long as they involved football—but that's not what's important.

Money doesn't buy happiness. I should know. I've been fucking miserable for as long as I can recall.

Until you were with her.

I force my thoughts down.

I've done what I needed to do. Whatever that was between Macie and I, it's over.

Dead.

Forgotten.

Okay, so maybe not forgotten.

Without meaning to, she gave me something I've never experienced from anyone else. But no matter how her acceptance of me, even the dark and ugly parts I allowed her to see, meant to me. It'll never be enough for me to get past that one small moment in time all those years ago.

She'll always be that little girl to me who left me to the slaughter.

Sucking in a steeling breath and forcing thoughts of her from my mind, I climb out of the car.

Darkness surrounds me where I'm deep in the cover of trees now that the headlights are off. It's not quite dark out yet, but it's almost there. I know that by the time I come back out, I'm not going to be able to see my hand in front of my face.

I'm halfway to the warehouse when a noise, the crack of a twig and the rustling of leaves in the undergrowth catches my attention.

I spin on the spot, my heart in my throat, as I expect to see the shadow of someone approaching.

But there's no one there.

I stand motionless in the darkness waiting to hear it again, convinced the noise was made by a person, but when nothing but the sound of the wind rustling through the leaves fills my ears, I figure that it must just be an animal.

I'm being paranoid, I know I am. My need to keep what I've done here from everyone is eating at me.

Even now that they know the truth, I'm not sure they'd understand this.

Hell, I'm not even sure if I understand this.

Confident that no one is about to jump out at me, I turn back toward the building and head inside in the hope of finding some peace while delivering some pain.

The beast inside me sings with joy and my fists curl.

Fuck, I really need this.

4

MACIE

I knew it was a bad idea the second I agreed, but nothing could have prepared me for how I'd feel when I pulled Leon's car door open and got assaulted by his scent.

Tears burn my eyes as memories of our time together flicker through my mind as I sway slightly on my feet.

But it's the lesser of two evils.

I either stay in the house that I hate or I force myself to endure his scent for the long journey back to Maddison.

Leon might have hurt me yesterday but even still, he's the lesser monster when the choice comes down to my memories of my uncle or him.

Sucking in a deep breath, I lower myself into his driver's seat, unable to stop the laugh falling from my lips when my feet are miles away from the pedals.

It takes me a few minutes but eventually I manage to figure out how to move his seat, get the engine started and the mirrors just right.

Driving his car without him, possibly without his permission, feels all kinds of wrong. But it's better than staying here or taking a bus back to campus.

Without overthinking it, I put the car into drive and press my foot on the accelerator, immediately regretting it when the car jolts forward with power that I'm not used to.

"Holy crap," I breathe, my heart thundering in my chest, my foot slamming the brake pedal through the floor. "Shit."

It takes me a few seconds to get a grip on myself, and when I'm ready to try again, I press it a little gentler. The last thing Leon needs right now is for his car to be smashed into pieces by me.

I've already done enough damage.

He might not deserve it, but I can't help feeling like the least I can do is deliver his baby back to him in one piece.

The drive back to Maddison is long, but quick and that's probably my own fault because I refuse to stop.

Once I was on the highway, all I wanted to do was to get as far away from Miami as possible, as quickly as possible.

By the time I pull up outside the address that Peyton messaged me with, it's dark and my body aches from sitting in the same position for hours. My head steadily throbs from my concentration and dehydration. But none of it was enough to make me prolong this more than necessary.

My hands tremble as I stare up at the house he lives in for the first time.

It never really occurred to me before that he'd never invited me back here. He'd told me that it was full of football players and that was enough information for me not to walk through the front door, even if I was with him.

But now, I realize just how big of a red flag that probably should've been.

I was so swept away by the whirlwind that was Leon Dunn that I never really stopped to question some of the most obvious things.

I was too lost in my own insecurities. Too distracted by him to see it.

Feeling stupid, I climb out of the car, needing to get away from the constant reminder of him.

Pulling my cell from my bag, I find Peyton's conversation and tap out a message to let her know that I'm here before taking off in the opposite direction of the house.

I have no idea if she's inside. If he's inside. But I do know that I haven't got the energy to see either of them.

Every step I take away from the house feels like I'm walking through wet cement.

My eyes burn with tears but I refuse to shed any more.

I'm back now. I'm home.

I can put the past two weeks behind me like they never happened and move on with my quiet, secluded life without any parties or hot football players to distract me from what's important.

My future.

My goals.

The walk back to my building is longer than I was expecting and by the time I step up to the front door, I can hardly keep my eyes open. So the last thing I need is to find Letty sitting against the wall waiting for me.

"There you are," Letty breathes, rushing over to me and pulling me into a hug.

I try to keep it together, I really, really do. But the second her arms engulf me, I lose every bit of control.

An ugly sob rips from my throat, my body trembling in her arms.

"I-I'm sorry," I whisper, my voice cracking with emotion.

"It's okay," she says, sounding almost as cut up as me, and when I pull back I discover that I'm not the only one with tears cascading down my cheeks. "I know, Macie. He told us."

"Shit," I breathe.

"I—we—had no idea."

"Christ." Wiping my cheeks with the backs of my hands, I look up at the dark night sky above us, focusing on the twinkling stars for a few seconds.

"I had no idea it was him," I whisper. "If I knew then—"

"Shall we go inside?" I look up at my floor, seeing the lights on in the living area.

It's Friday night, I'm sure everyone's out partying but I really don't want to walk in there and discover they're having a rare night in and have to deal with all the questions.

"Or we could go to my place," she offers. "Kane will be there but we can kick him out."

"N-no, you don't need—"

"Let me help."

Before I know what's happening, she's got her arm around my shoulders and is leading me toward her car.

The short drive to her place is in silence, although it's not an uncomfortable one.

Even with everything that's happened, I still feel that connection to Letty. And the fact he's told them and she doesn't hate me tells me that she either feels it too, or he never got to the part that involved me. I'm seriously hoping for the former.

"This place is nice," I say, looking around at their open plan apartment.

"Thanks. It's not much but it's home."

Footsteps sound off from down a short hallway before Kane's booming voice fills the space.

"I've been waiting for you, get your ass nak— oh, we have company," he says, cutting himself off the second he sees me. The moment he registers that Letty's been crying, his brows pinch, concern filling his handsome face. "What's wrong?" he asks, his voice softer than I'm sure it usually is.

"I'll tell you later. Do you mind giving us a little space?"

"You're kicking me out?"

"No, just hang in the bedroom or something," Letty suggests.

He stares at her, amusement filling his face.

"It's no fun in bed alone, Princess. You know that."

"Christ, you're insufferable. Go hang out with Devin or something."

"I'm sure I can find some trouble to get into," he says, wrapping his hand around the back of her neck and pulling her in for a kiss that's entirely too erotic considering they have company.

My cheeks heat as his tongue finds its way past her lips and I force myself to drag my eyes away from them.

Taking a few steps forward, I give them some privacy as I check out their place.

It's cute, cozy. All the things I would say are the complete opposite of Kane. It amuses me that a man like him has fluffy cushions and a fuzzy blanket over his couch.

I guess it just goes to show what the love of a good woman can achieve.

He mutters something to Letty that makes her groan before chastising him and pushing him from the apartment.

"Sorry about that, he's—"

"Completely in love with you," I finish for her. "I think it's cute."

"It is. Just... don't tell him that," she jokes. "He doesn't like that people know he has a soft side."

"I'm sure everyone knows. It's in his eyes every time he looks at you."

She laughs. "If only it was always that way," she mutters, walking into the kitchen and pulling the refrigerator open. "Wine?" she asks, holding up a bottle.

"Umm... I don't really drink."

"After the past twenty-four hours, I'm surprised you haven't turned into an alcoholic."

She's kinda got a point.

"Just a small one. I'm the world's biggest lightweight," I concede.

"I think you deserve it," she says, pouring what I definitely wouldn't describe as a small one.

"Thank you," I whisper when she passes it over.

"Come sit." She curls herself into one side of the couch while I take the other. She stares at me for a beat while I try to come up with where I should start. Thankfully, she beats me to it. "Are you okay? Did he hurt you?"

I blow out a long breath at that question as I try to figure out the answer.

Did he hurt me? Yes.

But I wanted him to. I needed him to.

"I understand why he did what he did."

"That's not what I asked, Macie," she warns.

"I know, I just..." I take a huge sip of wine as I try to get my thoughts together. "I knew it was too good to be true," I blurt out.

"I'm going to kill him for hurting you. I warned him. I fucking warned him," she seethes.

"You can't be mad at him. What he went through—"

"Still doesn't give him the right to hurt you no matter what's happened. You were a kid, Macie. He said it was ten years ago, so you were what... eight?"

I nod.

"Did you even understand the significance of what you walked in on that day?"

I shake my head because I didn't, I truly had no idea at the time. I knew it was bad. But I didn't know things like that happened, that people could be just that evil to take advantage of kids like that.

My uncle being mean to me was one thing. But one of his boys. Never in a million years would I have thought that was even possible.

"No. I had no idea how serious it was. It was only in the years that followed that I understood what I even saw."

"None of it was your fault, Macie. Leon had—has—no right to blame you for it."

"He's hurting, Let. It's festered inside him all these years, slowly eating away at him."

"You're too understanding."

"Trust me, I'm not letting him slip back into my life as if nothing happened, but I get it."

"Your uncle... he hurt you too, didn't he?" she asks, although from the concern on her face, I think she already knows the answer.

I nod. "Just not in the way he did Leon."

"It doesn't make it right, or better, or even easier to deal with."

"I guess," I mutter, not wanting to confess that over the years I've felt weirdly lucky that my uncle never touched me like he did Leon.

"Were there others?"

"I assume so, but Leon was the only one I ever saw. I was banished from that house not long after that incident."

"You never told anyone?"

I shake my head ashamed that I was never brave enough to say anything.

"Christ," she mutters, taking another giant mouthful of wine. "I knew he was hiding something awful, but I never thought it was something like this."

We fall silent, both of us sipping on our drinks lost in thought.

It doesn't take long for the alcohol to start to have an effect on me and by the time I sip the last drop into my mouth, my head is starting to spin.

Letty must sense it because she looks up at me.

"Ready to tell me what he did yet?"

"Umm..."

———

When I wake the next morning, it's with my second ever hangover.

Rolling over, I groan into my pillow as my head pounds, my brain feeling like it's suddenly too big for my head.

"Damn you, Leon Dunn," I moan.

Before I found the courage to tell Letty the truth, she refilled my glass and before I knew it everything was pouring from my lips. To my relief she never once judged me, even when I confessed to wanting Leon to do what he did, that I was more than willing to take the punishment he was dishing out.

I understood when she opened up and confessed to having similar experiences with Kane at the beginning of their relationship.

Listening to her talk about how toxic the two of them were made me feel better about what happened, about how I felt when he was so lost in his anger, his darkness. It fed something twisted inside of me that I didn't even know existed. But it seems I might not be the only one to have felt that way.

My cell pings dragging me from my hazy memories of the night before and I blindly reach out to grab it from my nightstand.

Letty: How are you feeling? ☺

"Ugh." It's the smiley face that does me in because it means that she probably feels completely fine whereas I'm once again dying.

This is all his fault. All of it.

If he never picked up Charlie that night then we might never have collided.

Is that what you'd rather have happened? To never have met him?

With another groan, I throw back the covers and make my way to the bathroom on unsteady legs.

I'm pleasantly surprised by the time I get there because I feel nowhere near as bad as the last time and when I look at myself in the mirror, I feel almost normal aside from the pounding at my temples.

But what stares back at me in my reflection, however, that is a freaking mess.

Leon Dunn, what have you done to me?

I stand there for long minutes just telling myself that I'm okay. What happened... happened. Now it's time to move on.

I know that's the truth, that he's not going to want anything to do with me now, hell, I should want even less to do with him after the way he treated me. So why does my chest ache as I consider never seeing him again?

I want to say it's fear for what he's going to do now that he's got the information he wanted. But it's not. In all honesty, I don't care what he does next. That's exactly why I've done nothing about the fact he knows of my uncle's whereabouts.

Plus, he's safe there. He pays thousands a month to ensure his privacy and safety. I highly doubt Leon's going to be able to walk straight in and act on the revenge he craves so much.

I wash up before pulling on an oversized hoodie to hide in and finally, when I can wait no longer for coffee, I slip out of my room.

Voices carry down the hall to me the second I close my door behind me and my stomach drops into my feet knowing I'm going to have to say something about why I'm here.

I should be in Miami having the time of my life with Leon. But here I am nursing a hangover and dare I say it... a broken heart.

No.

I slam that thought down the second it hits me.

He can't have broken anything that didn't belong to him.

Throwing my shoulders back, I gather some inner strength from somewhere deep inside, hell knows I know it exists after what I've been through in my life and with my head held high, I walk toward the kitchen as if this is just another Saturday morning.

"M-Macie?" Nathan stutters the second I emerge.

"Morning," I sing, wincing as my overly happy voice hits my ears.

Way to go trying to look like everything is normal. Well done, Macie.

"Uh... shouldn't you be in Miami?" he asks, his eyes following me toward the kitchen as I grab a mug.

"Yeah... change of plans."

His stare burns into my back.

"You okay, Mace?" Jace pipes up.

"Yeah, of course. Why wouldn't I be? I'd much rather be here than in Miami anyway."

I kick myself for saying too much knowing that I look like I'm making too much of an effort to convince them.

I sense Nathan step up behind me and the dread in my belly only gets worse.

He's not going to let this go. He's already warned me what he'll do if Leon hurts me.

"Macie?" he growls, and I drop my arm from where I've just started the coffee maker.

"Everything is okay, Nate. Really."

"Yeah? Then turn around and look me in the eyes as you say that."

Fine.

Spinning on my toes, I tell myself that I can easily convince him I'm fine. I've been convincing the world of something similar since the day my mom died, sending my life into what seems to be one very long roller coaster ride that I just know is going to crash at some point.

My eyes lock on his jersey-covered chest once we're face-to-face, but it takes me a couple of seconds to lift my eyes to his.

I hope like hell that by the time our gazes connect, I've found the strength I need to put his worry to bed.

I think it might be wishful thinking.

The second his concerned hazel eyes come into view, my own fills with tears and I can't help but allow my bottom lip to tremble.

"Shit, Mace."

He pulls me into his arms, holding me tight as I silently cry into his chest.

Most of it is for Leon and everything that happened, but some of the tears are just from pure frustration at how badly I'm handling all of this.

I shouldn't care.

I knew he was going to pull the rug from under my feet at some point. I should have been prepared for this.

But instead, here I am sobbing like a baby.

Maybe it would have been different if he just got bored of me. If he cheated with a jersey chaser even.

I don't think anything could have prepared me for the reality. For how painful, brutal, horrifying our truths really were.

"I-I'm o-okay," I stutter against his chest as his hands rub up and down my back.

His body tenses at my lie.

"Jace, could you—"

"Yeah, I'm heading out anyway. Shall I tell the guys you're not gonna make it?"

"Thanks, man," he says, twisting me into his side and guiding me over to the couch.

"Y-you should go. You don't have to stay and babysit me. I'm a big girl."

"It's okay," he assures. "I'd rather make sure you're okay than work out again."

"Okay," I breathe, knowing that I'm not going to win no matter how much I might protest.

He gently lowers me to the seat before returning to the kitchen for my coffee, preparing it for me, and bringing it over.

By the time he's sitting beside me on the couch, Jace has left and the dorm has fallen silent.

I've got no idea where Charlie is. Sleeping probably, I guess the question is... in whose bed?

"I need to kick his ass, don't I?"

I can't help but burst out laughing at the serious expression on Nate's face.

"No, Nate, you don't."

Leon's been through enough. I don't think having an angry basketball player on his back over this is what he really needs right now.

"Don't protect him, Macie."

"I'm not... I— It's complicated."

"I've got all day," he says, resting back, getting comfortable with the story he thinks I'm going to tell.

Shaking my head, I keep my eyes on my knees knowing that he's going to be disappointed in me for the words that are about to leave my lips.

"I knew it was all too good to be true. I saw this coming, I just didn't—"

"Macie," he growls just like I was expecting him too. "Do not put this on you. I don't want to hear that you were never good enough for him and expected to be hurt. That's not how it's meant to be."

"Maybe not, but it's the truth. Come on, Nate," I say, finally looking up at him. "He's one of MKU's kings and I'm..." I hold my hands out to my sides. "I'm just me. Shy, inexperienced geek. We were never going to work."

"That's bullshit and you know it, Mace. You're worth a million of him."

My breath catches at his words.

He might be my closest friend, but he's never said anything like that to me before.

"I mean it, Macie. He's a douchebag who can't see what's right in front of him."

He scoots a little closer and my eyes widen when he reaches out, tucking my hair behind my ear.

It's Leon's move.

My heart pounds, my eyes fluttering closed as his finger brushes the shell of my ear.

In my head, it's Leon and instinctively I lean a little closer, getting lost in the sensation and his touch.

It's not until his lips brush mine that I come crashing back to Earth with a body jolting bang.

"Holy crap," I jump up, my heart racing and my eyes wide as I stare down at Nate who's still leaning over into the space I was just in. "What the hell was that?" I ask, barely able to speak through my increased breaths.

"I can't see you sad, Mace. It kills me."

"And that was your answer?"

He shrugs, a little regret creeping into his expression.

"I'm sorry, I—" He cuts himself off, his eyes dropping from mine for a beat.

When he glances up once again, he looks back in control. Like the Nathan I'm used to.

"I'm sorry. I just wanted to wipe that look off your face. Leon is a fucking idiot for screwing this up."

I shrug. "I'm not sure there was really anything to screw up. The whole thing was..." Incredible. Mind-blowing. "A mistake."

"That doesn't mean it's not allowed to hurt, Mace."

"I know, but I'm stronger than Leon Dunn. He can kiss my ass," I say, throwing my hair over my shoulder.

"Damn right he can, but only after I've kept my promise to you."

My brows pinch as I try to think back to what he might have said to me.

"Oh, no, no, no," I chant when the penny drops. "Don't go anywhere near him. I don't want you to get hurt because of me."

He pushes to stand and comes almost toe-to-toe with me.

"No one hurts you and gets away with it, Mace."

"Please. Please don't."

"I can't promise that. Just know that what I'm capable of isn't anywhere near what he deserves."

My lips part to argue for Leon. To tell Nathan that Leon's already been to hell and back, but I soon slam them shut. That is not my story to tell. And I'll take it to the grave with me if that's what he wants.

"I don't need you to defend my honor, Nate. Leon and I are done, and I think it's probably for the best if we all just move on and forget it ever happened." I know that's what I'm going to try to do at least.

5

———

LEON

My weekend starts exactly as my week ended.

A fucking disaster.

Much like my entire life, if I'm being honest about it.

After leaving my father barely conscious, I jumped back into Luca's car and ended up at The Locker Room.

I've been here a couple of times since that night. It feels weirdly therapeutic being where my father made his final mistake.

Bry looked less than amused when he saw the state of me but after a little convincing, he ushered me to one of his darkest booths and left me with a bottle of the most expensive whisky the place has.

It wasn't a surprise to me when I found out the kinds of things that go on under the roofs of his establishments that run across the country.

It's no secret that Brett's a scumbag so it only seems fitting that in each of his favorite states he has a place where he could let his inner demon loose.

A shudder rips through me as I think about all the ways he fucked us all over, but no one as much as our mother.

Why she stayed with him for as long as she did, fuck only knows. She says it was for us. But kids do just fine with separated parents. I want to believe that there's another reason just to relieve a little guilt that it's our fault she stuck it out and got treated like shit for years.

My head steadily pounds as I lay there trying to remember how I got from the bar to here at some point in the middle of the night.

But everything is hazy. Sadly, the parts about my life I want to blur into nothingness never leave though. And I still vividly remember exactly how she felt beneath me on that desk. How fucking tight she was as I pushed inside her, how she cried my name when she came.

"Fuck," I bark, bringing my fist down on the pillow beside me but regretting it instantly when my knuckles split open, blood beginning to pool at each wound last night left behind.

But the pain of that is nothing compared to the booming voice of my brother only seconds later.

"LEON," he barks, his footsteps thundering my way before he slams his body against my door, ensuring the lock gives way and he comes flying in.

His lips part to shout some more but then he sees the blood and his expression falters.

"What do you want?"

He hesitates for a second.

"Where the fuck is my car?"

"Oooh... umm..." His expression turns murderous. "I can't remember," I confess, glad that my secret hasn't changed how big of an ass he can be.

"You fucking what?" He thunders.

"I'm sure it's fine, Bro. Chill."

"Don't you fucking tell me to—"

"Luca," Peyton shouts as he lunges toward me.

He damn near stops mid-air at the sound of her voice which amuses me greatly.

"You're so fucking whipped, Bro."

"If you've so much as scratched it, I'll fucking kill you," he seethes.

"Have at it. Doubt anyone would miss me."

His jaw ticks at my words, darkness seeping into his green eyes, which is better than pity.

"You haven't fought this hard to give up now, Lee," he warns as Peyton sucks in a breath behind him.

"No, so what am I supposed to do?" I ask, genuinely interested in where he thinks this is going to go now that my past is out in the open.

"Keep fucking fighting. Or he wins."

"He's never going to win. And even if I do drown. He's not going to be alive to see it."

Luca pales at the unspoken words in my statement.

"No, Lee. You're not putting your future at risk for that... for him."

Throwing the covers off, I push to stand, standing toe-to-toe with my brother.

"Fucking watch me. I've waited ten years for this, you can fucking forget it if you think I'm going to put it all behind me and let him live the rest of his life being worshiped by kids all around the world for his achievements in football."

"And killing him will achieve what?"

"It'll stop him," I whisper coldly before spinning on my heels and storming toward my bathroom in the hope that they'll both be gone by the time I reemerge.

I stand under the burning torrent of water, letting it wash away our father's blood that's splattered up my arms. The open wounds on my knuckles burn, but I barely acknowledge it, instead I clench and unclench my fists, needing more pain.

I've thought of a million and one ways I've wanted to end that cunt's life over the years. Each and every one of them involves me looking him dead in the eyes as the life drains out of him so he knows exactly who's done it.

I always thought it would be relatively easy. Sure, his disappearing off the face of the Earth put a wrench in the works, but I figured it would still be easy to get to him. Even if he just bought an even bigger estate and was hiding inside it; I always thought I'd have a chance to get to him somehow or someway.

But now, with him in a secure facility. I have no idea how I'm going to make that happen.

I can hardly rock up to the place and convince the staff who've never seen me before that he's my long lost uncle and get a free pass into his room.

It's obviously going to take more planning than that. It's also going to need people with skills, with the lack of morals to see something like this through.

The second I'm out of the shower, I find my cell in my pants pocket from last night and find the person I'm going to need for this.

Someone whose morals are more than just a little lacking.

———

"What the fuck?" I mutter the second I step out of the house and find my car sitting in the driveway.

I know Luc said he was going to get it delivered back but fuck, I wasn't expecting it here already.

Canceling the Uber I'd requested, I walk toward my car and pull the door open.

I should be shocked by the fact my keys are sitting right in the middle of the driver's seat for anyone to steal, but that isn't what captures my attention when I step closer.

It's the scent.

Her scent.

My car smells like fucking coconuts and innocence.

"Motherfucker."

Unable to resist, I drop down into the seat and suck in a deep breath.

It settles me in a way I don't like, it reminds me just how much easier she made everything in those couple of weeks. How being with her cleared all the poisonous and twisted thoughts in my head until all I could think about was her.

I thought it was good. But really. It's a weakness.

She's a weakness.

And one I don't need or want.

I have a game plan and I intend on following it through to the end.

So what if she didn't turn out to be the evil bitch I wanted her to be? So what if Richard isn't going to be an easy target to get to?

Nothing worth getting is ever easy. And revenge, payback for what he did to me is most definitely worth the effort.

With my endgame in mind, I start the engine and back out of the driveway. Movement in the living room window catches my eye, and when I look over, I find Luca glaring out at me.

Our eyes hold for a beat before I gun the engine and fly off down the street.

He's angry, I get it. I've been angry for ten fucking years. But taking it out on me isn't helping anyone.

I turn the volume up in the hope of drowning everything out as I make my way out of town. It helps to a point but it's never going to be what I need.

What you need is her.

Slamming my palms down on the wheel, I force that little voice of reason from my head. It might be the truth but like fuck am I going down that road when everything I've waited for is finally within reach.

I got what I needed from her. More actually.

Never in a million years did I think she'd be a virgin. That I'd be able to leave that kind of impression on her.

She'll never be able to forget me now. Ten years ago maybe. But now? Never.

I'll be a part of her for the rest of her life. Under her skin, seared into her memory until her dying day.

A wicked smile curls at my lips at just the thought.

Innocent little Macie Fletcher. Ruined by the big bad football player.

She must be fucking livid.

I punch in the address I was given into the GPS when I'm slowed down by some traffic in town before following it over the border to Harrow Creek.

I've never spent any time over here. Even after becoming friends with Letty and asking her to take me with her when we were kids because I was curious, she always refused, saying it wasn't a place she wanted me to be.

But now I've got an excuse, although I soon discover that I don't really get to see any of the delights the run-down town has to offer because when the GPS tells me that I'm almost at my destination, I haven't seen anything aside from trees and countryside which makes the place look much more peaceful than I know it is.

I don't need stories from Letty, and now Kane, to know the darkness that surrounds this place, all I need to do is turn on the TV and look at the news. There's always some kind of gang fight, drug bust or unsolved murder. The place really is the pits of hell, yet there's a huge part of me that craves to be right in the middle of it.

"Whoa," I mutter out loud after I turn left into what I thought was no more than a dirt road to discover that it opens up to a hidden set of gates. "What the hell is this place?"

As if by magic, the gates begin to open before me, revealing the rolling countryside. As I drive through, my eyes are as wide as dish plates as I take it all in, and then the most incredible building emerges in the distance.

It's huge. It's also kind of terrifying. I can't help but laugh because it suits its owner to a tee.

The dark gothic building stands out from its surroundings with the sun shining down on it today, but I can only imagine that when it's dark and we're in the middle of a storm that it just vanishes as if it never even existed.

A shudder runs down my spine as I pull to a stop out in front of the house. I know the man who lives here. I've been invited as a friend, but even still, a little unease trickles through me.

The moment I kill the engine, one of the double front doors opens and the man of the house appears.

He's smiling, and while to everyone else that might be a good thing as you're welcomed into his house, on Reid, it just makes him look even more dangerous than he usually does.

"Quite some place you've got here," I say walking up to him.

"Welcome to my manor, Lee."

Reid steps aside and allows me inside.

My eyes scan all around me looking at my surroundings as I trail behind him when he leads me down a long, wide hallway. I'm not sure what I was expecting but it's... normal.

If it weren't for the impressive security gates, the ominous building, or the man himself, I'd think this could be just your average family home.

"Drink?" he asks, gesturing for me to take a seat at one of the huge couches that are angled to look over his land through spotless floor to ceiling windows.

"Coffee would be great."

I watch him move effortlessly around his kitchen. I've only met him a couple of times but he seems different, relaxed... less, well... scary.

"You're staring," he mutters without looking up.

"S-sorry. You're just different."

"Yeah, well, there are things under this roof that do that to me."

"Things?"

He looks up at me and winks, clearly wanting to keep his secrets.

"Yep. You want cream?"

"No, thank you."

I keep my eyes on him as he walks over with two mugs in hand as I try to work him out.

I thought I was good at putting on a mask and acting in a way people expect of me, but it seems that Reid might just be the master at it.

"So what can I do for you? It's not often I get a call requesting a home visit."

"You were the one who suggested I come here."

He thinks for a moment. "That's right, I did. Clearly I wasn't thinking."

I narrow my eyes on him. I can't imagine Reid anything other than completely in control at all times.

He stares at me for a beat before I remember what I came here for.

"I need a favor," I blurt out.

"Another one?" A wicked smile tugs at his lips as a crash from somewhere inside the vast house sounds out before I hear a scream, although I've got no idea if it's in horror or from pleasure.

There's no way he doesn't hear it, but he doesn't react so I push it aside.

"Y-yeah," I stutter knowing that I'm going to owe this man big time if he's able to help me out with this.

"For your sake, I hope it's fun for me. I don't hand out favors for just anyone."

He sits back, taking his steaming mug of coffee with him and takes a sip. It has to burn but he doesn't so much as flinch as he swallows.

Sitting forward, I rest my elbows on my knees and suck in a large breath as I tell him exactly what I need from him.

"You're going to owe me, you know that right?" he mutters, looking entirely too happy about the situation.

"I figure that I already do, so adding a little more isn't a big deal," I say as if owing the devil himself isn't terrifying.

I have no idea why he agreed to help with the Brett situation but he did. He has every right to tell me no this time and show me where the door is, although from the bloodlust I recognize in his eyes, I don't think he will.

"I guess that all depends on your payment terms."

"I guess it does. But I need this man wiped off the face of the Earth for what he's done so whatever it is, will be worth it."

"Why? What did he do?"

I swallow down my apprehension before giving him the very basics.

"He used to be my football coach."

Reid's eyes hold mine, searching as if he can read the truth in their depths.

Suddenly his body tenses and the mug in his hand goes flying across the room, shattering against the wall behind my head.

My eyes widen in shock as my heart rate picks up.

His jaw ticks, the muscle down his neck pulsating.

I almost expect him to come at me, but his anger isn't directed at me.

"Consider it done," he forces out, his voice deep and raspy.

The relaxed Reid from before is gone.

"Th-thank you."

Footsteps pound down the stairs before Reid's friend from the party the other weekend appears in the doorway shirtless with his pants undone and his hair sticking up every which way.

"You alright, man?" he asks, looking between the two of us, clearly expecting us to be fighting.

"Yeah," Reid grits out. "You remember JD, right?" he asks me.

"Uh... yeah. How's it going, man?" I ask, although I don't need to. It's obvious he's good from the state of him.

More footsteps follow, only softer this time. A hand snakes around JD's side before a woman appears, clearly dressed in the shirt he's missing.

"You okay?" she asks, staring directly at Reid.

The tension in the room instantly ramps up and I can't help but feel like I might have just outstayed my welcome.

"I'll be in touch, Lee," Reid says coldly, pushing up from the couch and marching over toward the woman. "JD will see you out."

I can't rip my eyes away as he steps right up to her, threads his hand into the hair at the nape of her neck and crashes his lips down on hers.

She squeals as he lifts her. Her bare legs wrapping around his waist before he marches them both from the room.

"What did you say to him?" JD asks, amusement dancing in his eyes.

"I... uh... asked for a favor." I shrug.

A door slams and he looks over his shoulder.

"Huh. Well, are you done?" He nods to my now empty mug and I stand.

"Yeah, I got what I needed."

He leads me toward the front door and in seconds, I'm back at my car, staring up at the imposing house with way more questions about the ongoings inside that place than I did before I entered.

6

MACIE

I lay on my bed staring up at the ceiling as the sounds of the others getting ready for their night out stirs around me.

They begged for me to come but I'm not interested. I would rather be in my own room, curled up and watching Netflix.

I've easily reverted back to my old reclusive life, but I can't find it in me to care.

The Macie I was when I was with Leon wasn't the real me, I rationalize. He made me crazy, pulled me from the place I feel safe—my comfort zone. I spent so much of my life not knowing what's around the corner and where the next hit is going to come from that I'm more than happy being locked away and being completely in control.

The music from the living room is so loud that I have no idea we've got visitors until someone knocks on my door.

"Macie?" Nate shouts, and I wince.

Earlier it was hella awkward. I appreciated his concern, his need to go and hurt Leon for what he's done, but what I really didn't need was for him to step over the line like he did.

I've never felt that way about him, and I was under the impression he didn't feel that way toward me either. But now, I'm wondering if that's not the case.

I want to think that he was just feeling sorry for me, took pity on me for being screwed over by the first guy I ever let close but I'm terrified it's more than that and the friendship that I've valued since starting here is about to be destroyed because of it.

"You've got visitors."

My heart jumps into my throat as the first face that pops into my head is Leon.

I know it's stupid. There's no way he's going to seek me out after everything but my stupid, naïve little heart can't help hoping.

"Okay, hang on." I roll off my bed and pull on an oversized cardigan over my shoulders before heading to the door.

"Hey, what's— oh," I breathe when I see more people than I was expecting, only one of which I recognize, standing behind Nate.

"I hope you don't mind us gate-crashing but I had a feeling you might need some fun." Letty smiles as she steps around Nathan and invites herself into my room.

"Uh..."

"You were in bed at seven p.m. on a Saturday night, weren't you?" she asks, seeing the messy sheets.

"Um..."

"You definitely need us."

Dumping two bags onto my bed that I didn't realize she had carried in, the others step around a confused looking Nathan and they join us.

"You okay?" Nate asks, ignoring the newcomers and looking directly into my eyes.

"Y-yeah. I think I am." I have no idea what Letty is planning. But I trust her. I know she only has my best interests at heart.

He hesitates for a couple of seconds as Letty and the others pull drinks and food out of the bags they brought with them and begin making themselves at home.

"Okay, well... we're heading out in a bit."

"Have a good night." I smile at him, but it doesn't come as easy as it used to and I hate it.

I see the same hesitation on his face too.

"We're going to be okay, right?" he asks, clearly feeling as uneasy about this as I am. "Earlier, I didn't mean for it to—"

"We're fine, Nate. Promise," I say, hoping that I'm right. It would kill me to lose him because of this.

With a smile and nod, he slips from my room.

"He was hot," one of the girls says.

"Hands off, Vi. He's a freshman, you'd eat him alive."

"He looks like he's man enough."

"Ignore them," Letty says as she and the one with pink hair step up to me while the other two continue to bicker. "That's Ella," she says, pointing to the petite blonde. "And the one who wants to screw your roommate is Violet."

"And I'm Peyton. It's nice to finally meet you," Pink says, shocking the hell out of me by pulling me in for a hug. "I'm so sorry," she whispers in my ear. "If we had any clue then—"

"It's okay," I tell her.

All of this is no one's fault but my own. I knew from the first time I looked into his eyes that I was making a bad decision. If only I'd listened to myself.

"So we thought you might need a night full of distraction. We've got drinks, food, face masks, the works."

My smile almost splits my face as I look between the four of them.

"I've never had a girls' night in before."

"Well you're about to have one. Boy talk is banned, in fact, from this moment on, the male species doesn't exist."

"What the hell will we talk about? Anyway, I want to know if Leon Dunn is as good in the sack as everyo— Ow. What the hell was that for?" Violet sulks as Letty throws her cell at her. "What? I'm just curious."

"I'd love to tell you," I say, swallowing down the emotion her question drags up. "But I don't have anything to compare it to."

"He made you scream though right."

"Jesus," Peyton mutters. "You need to get laid, Vi."

"It's like you're forgetting that you got railed by a frat guy last night," Ella mutters. "And—" she adds before Violet gets a chance to argue. "I heard it all so don't even try to deny it. What was his name? Peter, Percy..." Letty, Peyton and I snort with laughter as Violet's face twists in horror.

"Perry, it was Perry. Jesus, El, I wouldn't screw a Percy, who do you think I am?"

"Desperate is what you are."

"I'm sorry," Letty says softly. "I don't know why I thought this was a good idea."

"It's perfect," I assure her, my eyes not leaving Ella and Violet. "They're a good distraction."

"They were warned not to mention his name," Peyton mutters. "Glad they listened."

"I'm going to have to get used to it. It's kind of like a rite of passage to regret your first, right?"

They both stare at me with sympathy written all over their faces making me think that I'm wrong.

"Everything will work out," Peyton assures me.

"N-no, I don't think there's a future for—"

"Like I said, things will work out."

I want to argue with her and insist that everything between Leon and I is over, but even thinking about the words makes my chest ache.

I hate him for what he did. But I also understand his motivation.

My head spins with the whole thing.

"Drinks," Ella calls, holding up a neon bottle of something I already know is going to ruin my Sunday.

"Just a small one," Letty says with a wink.

"Oh yeah, I know exactly what your small ones are like."

She snorts a laugh. "I don't do small things." She winks and my cheeks burn, the image of her and Kane that first night I met them flashing before my eyes. "I know you don't either," she whispers quietly in my ear, making my entire face heat.

"Okay, pass it over," I say, knowing that I'm going to need it.

I don't think anything of it and throw the bright green drink back in one, regretting it instantly.

"What the hell is that?" I mutter as my mouth continues to water with the sour taste while my throat burns with the strength of the alcohol.

"Sour apple. We've got raspberry, too," Violet says happily, holding up a bright pink bottle.

"This is going to hurt tomorrow."

————

Three hours, more drinks than I can count, and a face mask that has been on way too long. I've got my arms above my head dancing around my dorm room with Ella and Violet who are singing Taylor Swift at the top of their lungs.

"I can't remember the last time I had this much fun," I shout, my head spinning, the wide smile on my face making my cheeks ache as my hips move with the music.

"It was time for you to let your hair down," Letty says excitedly, coming up to dance with me.

"We should go dancing. Like, dancing, dancing," Violet suggests.

"We're having a night in, remember," Letty says, the only one that seems to have kept her head tonight.

"No, let's go dancing," I say, forgetting about everything other than how good this feels right now.

"Are you sure?" Letty asks.

"I'm finding us a party," Ella announces, grabbing her cell from the side and immediately focusing on it, or at least trying to. I can't imagine she's seeing things all that straight right now.

"I need to get changed," I blurt out, knowing that my pajamas aren't going to cut it for wherever we're going to end up.

"Let's find you something sexy," Violet says, dramatically pulling open my closet and rummaging through it.

"Ugh, Macie. You need to go shopping, girl."

"I've got something. I brought spares," Ella shouts, throwing her cell on my bed and diving for one of the bags she brought with her. "Here," she says, throwing a scrap of fabric at me.

"What the hell is this?" My face scrunches up as I wrestle with the material, trying to figure out which way up it even goes.

"It's a dress. Come on," she says, stepping up to me. "Off."

"B-but I don't—" I don't get a chance to argue because she has my top off in a heartbeat ensuring I flash them all my bare breasts.

My arms fly to cover myself up.

"Chill, girl. We've all seen a pair before. Here." She tugs the fabric over my head and down over my exposed body. "Shorts off. Sexy panties on," she demands, swatting me on the ass before turning back toward her bag for another almost nonexistent dress.

In only a little over an hour, all four of us have managed epic transformations.

Gone are the caked on face masks and in their place is flawless makeup provided by Ella and expertly styled hair courtesy of Violet.

I stand in front of my mirror with another drink in my hand and stare at the woman looking back at me.

"Hot, right?" Ella asks, coming to stand beside me.

She's gorgeous, petite, yet curvy. A classical beauty. I bet she has men following her everywhere.

"I... uh..."

"Any man would be lucky to get anywhere near you, Macie. Start embracing the fact you're a sexy woman with curves women around the world would die for."

"Are we ready?" Violet asks.

Looking over my shoulder, I find she's wearing a short skirt and crop top which shows more skin than I think I'd ever be able to, unless I was on the beach, but she looks stunning.

"Yes," Letty agrees.

"Good, I've got us a ride. Come on girls, it's time to show MKU how it's done."

My stomach knots as the sudden realization that this might have been a bad idea rolls through me.

Letty must sense my hesitation because as the other two grab their purses and head out of the door, she lingers back, catching my hand in hers.

"You're allowed to enjoy yourself, Macie. The past is in the past. You don't need to hide from him, from anyone."

Her dark eyes hold mine as emotion clogs my throat.

"I..." I swallow, not entirely sure what it is I want to say. "I think I've spent all my life hiding," I confess.

"Well then, it's time to break free of your cocoon, Macie. It's time to own the beautiful butterfly you've become."

My hands tremble at the thought of embarking on a life everyone else around campus sees as normal.

"El," she calls, startling me.

"Yo, bitch, what's up?" she shouts back from down the hall, her voice slurred.

"Whose party are we going to?"

"Basketball," is all that comes back and knowing that Nate, Jace and Charlie will be there settles something inside me.

Yeah, they'll probably be pissed that I turned them down, yet I'm willing to turn up with the girls, but I know they'll understand, and look out for me.

"Okay," I say, throwing my shoulders back in the hope I both feel and look a little more confident. "Let's do this."

Linking her arm through mine, Letty leads me from my room and then the dorm.

There's a car waiting out in the parking lot with music booming from the windows. Violet immediately heads toward the driver's side, sticks her ass out, ensuring her skirt rises just that little bit too high to be out in public as she threads her hand around the back of the guy's neck and slams her lips down on his.

"Uh... who's that?"

"I have no idea," Letty confesses. "Violet gets a little crazy when she drinks."

"You don't say," I mutter as we watch her crawl through the window so she can sit plastered to the guy's side.

"You're a whore," Ella shouts happily, making Violet flip her off before turning her attention back to the guy.

"Come on then, our carriage awaits."

The three of us slide into the back, the booming bass of the music rattles through my body as the guy flies from the parking lot.

Violet screams as he floors the gas, throwing her arms up in the air as if she's on a roller coaster.

"Is she always this..."

"Wild?" Ella finishes. "Yeah. And they think I'm the crazy one."

"Oh because you're totally sane," Letty mutters.

"You love me."

"Yeah, but you're totally crazy."

"Alright, ladies. I take payment in the form of kisses and blow jobs," the guy driving announces as the car jolts to a stop outside a massive house.

My eyes meet his in the rearview mirror and he winks, making my eyes widen in shock and my stomach to drop to my feet.

"He's kidding," Ella says. "And if he's not. Vi can make payment in full. Come on."

I slide out behind Letty, more than happy to leave Violet to do whatever she needs to do.

Without looking back for fear of what I'll see, I allow both Letty and Ella to lace their arms through mine and lead me toward the house.

There are drunk students filling the front yard. Some call out as we pass but I keep my eyes on where we're going. My legs are already unsteady, I don't need anything else distracting me.

"Ignore them. We're just here to enjoy ourselves," Letty whispers in my ear as we step into the house.

"Oh my God," I breathe. There are people everywhere but the whole place has an entirely different vibe to the Harris party that Leon took me to.

Where that was intense, this is... I don't know, chill.

Everyone is laughing, having a good time. And as we pass, no one really pays us any attention.

"Drinks, ladies, then we dance," Ella says, grabbing a couple of Solo cups and filling them with some vodka. "To girls' night," she says loudly, holding her cup up so that we can tap ours against it.

Together we down our drinks. I've had so much to drink now that I barely even feel the burn as it hits my throat.

"Right, let's do this."

As if she knows exactly where to go, Ella leads us to a room, which is full of bodies moving in time with the music that booms from the speakers someone has set up in the corners.

Anyone would think Ella owns the place as she pushes through the crowd and finds us a space in the middle.

Forgetting about where I am and the eyes that I'm sure are on me with the dress I'm wearing, I pretend that I'm back in my dorm room just with the girls and without a care in the world.

Closing my eyes, I focus on the beat, of how my body moves and the tingles running through my veins from the copious amounts of drinks I've had tonight.

It feels good. Freeing. I push every single thing about my life from my head and just enjoy it.

I have no idea how many songs pass when I sense someone step up behind me.

"Who are you and what have you done with Macie?" A familiar voice shouts in my ear.

Spinning on the spot, I find Nate smiling as he runs his eyes over me.

My initial reaction is to cover up, but the alcohol coursing through me soon reminds me that I'm not that Macie tonight. Tonight, I'm just like Letty, Ella, and Violet. I'm enjoying myself and not caring what anyone else thinks of me, what I'm wearing, how I dance or what I do.

"Hey," I say, a confident smile curling at my lips.

"Dance with me?"

I hesitate for a second and hurt covers his face.

"It's not like that, Mace. I just wanna hang out with my friend."

"O-okay," I stutter, concerned about leading him on.

He grabs my hand before I have a chance to change my mind and pulls me toward him, although not up against him and I sigh in relief.

"Relax, Mace. What I did earlier was a mistake. I'm sorry. I'm glad they managed to get you here though, you deserve this." He spins me away from his body and I squeal in excitement.

We dance like idiots together for the longest time. A wide smile plays on my lips as I just enjoy this time with my friend that I never would have had if I kept myself locked up in my bedroom.

Maybe this kind of life isn't so bad.

"Oh no. No, no, no," someone squeals behind us. "If you think you get to just turn up here and expect—"

I spin around just in time to see Ella's tiny palm connect with a guy's face.

Anger flickers through his expression as the red handprint on his cheek blooms but it's soon pushed aside for something else. Something I wouldn't have recognized if it weren't for my time with Leon.

Heat.

It surges through him like a tsunami as he steps toward Ella. His eyes wide and dark, his nostrils flared.

If I were her, I'd probably be terrified because the guy is huge, but thankfully Ella isn't me because she squares right up to him.

"Uh... who's that?" I mutter to Nate who's standing behind me, watching the show.

"That's Colt. He's the Panther's running back."

"R-running b—" I don't get to question him about it because my answer appears in front of me as Kane sweeps Letty into his arms, while Luca Dunn does the same to Peyton.

"I-I need to get out of here," I breathe, keeping my eyes on the floor, too terrified to find him and have to look into those eyes again.

"Y-yeah, okay. Let's go."

Nate laces his fingers with mine and begins pulling me through the crowd.

My skin tingles more with every step we take. And I know exactly why.

He's here.

And he's watching.

7

LEON

I was planning on going home after my visit to Harrow Creek, but when I got to the intersection on the border of Maddison, I found myself heading in the opposite direction toward Rosewood.

I parked at the very end of the beach and walked to Luca and Peyton's spot.

I figured that if it helped give him some clarity over the years, I thought it might be worth a shot for me because I really needed to clear my head.

I stare at their initials carved in the tree with my hands buried deep in my pockets, my heart like a lead weight in my chest.

What Peyton and Luca share, even with their time apart, is something most people can only dream of.

Even as kids, it was clear to see that they were destined to be together.

It was always me and Luca. He might be my twin and we might have kinda been stuck with each other but he's always been my best friend, and equally, I've always been jealous of his relationship with Peyton.

The three of us were pretty tight until… until Richard happened. Then I backed away.

I know the cracks in mine and Luca's relationship are my fault. I know I pushed him closer to Peyton because of my inability to deal with what happened, but still, I sat on the sidelines and watched them fall in love knowing that unless I found a way to deal with my shit, then I was never going to have that for myself.

I drop to the ground, pulling my knees up and wrapping my arms around my legs as I stare out at the ocean. The sun is busy making its final descent for the day, casting the water in a bright orange hue.

I sit there for the longest time, reminiscing on how different life could have been if Richard Fletcher was never a part of my life. Hell, if my own father accepted what I told him and helped me instead of brushing it under the rug in favor of helping his friend.

If just one thing happened differently, then maybe I wouldn't be here now with two men's lives hanging in the balance.

If only I would've told Mom instead. Coach maybe. Anyone other than him. Maybe it would have been dealt with years ago. Maybe Mom would have grown some balls and left that prick sooner, maybe Peyton and Luca never would have been hurt the way there were.

Maybe. Maybe. Maybe…

I blow out a long breath and all the possibilities flutter around in my head.

All of this is my fault. If I weren't so fucking scared then I might just have saved everyone a lot of pain and heartache.

Could I have saved Macie though?

I shake my head, not wanting to have her factor in all of this, but I can't help it.

Somehow in only a matter of days, she managed to achieve something that no one else ever has. Letty's got close over the years, but both of us have always known that we were always destined to be friends. But Macie managed to get herself under my skin almost from that very first moment I looked into her eyes.

I thought it was because I had been searching for her for so long. But after the two weeks we spent together and how empty I feel now after only two days without her, I'm really starting to wonder.

My fists clench as I allow myself to admit for the first time just how badly I need her, how much easier she'd make all of this right now.

"FUUUUCK," I shout into the silence around me.

This wasn't how it was meant to go. I wasn't meant to... want her.

I'm meant to hate her.

I do hate her.

But also I... Fuck, I need her.

Agonising minutes pass as I sit there convincing myself that going to her dorm is a really fucking bad idea until my cell pings in my pocket.

> Colt: Hot redhead at basketball party. Get your ass here.

In the past, that kind of a message would get him the result he's after. But the thought of being with any redhead that isn't her is suddenly less than appealing. Although, admittedly, it's probably what I need. Some nameless, faceless woman to take it all out on. From behind, she could be Macie.

My cock stirs at the thought of taking her from behind, of her full ass, the smooth, pale skin of her back and her thick red hair wrapped around my fist as I fuck her until I lose some of this fucking tension.

> Leon: She's all yours tonight, man.

I let out a sigh knowing that I made the right decision, even if my body isn't on board.

> Colt: Not tonight. I've got my eyes on a spitfire.

> Leon: Leave Ella alone.

I can't help but laugh at the way he follows her around like a puppy yet claims not to want her.

> Colt: No can do, man. You can't see what she's wearing.

He must sense that I'm about to give up and put my cell away because he starts typing again.

> Colt: I miss my wingman. Come on, bro. Come get fucked up with me.

I stare at his words, the need for the sweet oblivion that could come from meeting up with him and doing exactly as he says becomes too hard to deny.

> Leon: On my way. Get the drinks ready.

> Colt: Yes, bro!

Without looking back at my surroundings, I push through the undergrowth and back toward the parking lot.

It takes me ages to get out of town but when I finally do, I breathe a sigh of relief, my mouth watering for a taste of the strongest alcohol Colt can find me.

I'm almost in Maddison when he sends me his location and I drive straight to the house, not bothering to change. I really don't give a fuck what anyone thinks of the state of me. I'm not here for them, I'm here just to get fucking lost.

It's what I'm good at. It's what I know.

The party is in full swing as I sit behind the wheel of my car watching the students fool around in the front yard. Someone has a hold of the hose and is spraying everyone in sight.

Their shrieks and laughter filter down to me and I wonder just how it might feel, to be that carefree and enjoy yourself without the constant darkness trying to consume you whole.

When my thoughts begin to piss me off, I push the door open and climb out walking up toward the house while glaring at the guy with the hose to ensure he knows what a bad fucking idea it would be to direct it at me.

I'm halfway up the yard when the front door opens and the one person I wasn't expecting bursts out with her hand in another's.

She's drunk, that much is obvious the second my eyes take her in.

My fists curl both knowing how much she hates being out of

control but also at the fact that someone else is touching her when she's wearing...

Fuck me.

The silver dress is wrapped around her body like a second skin. It's short, almost too short, and low-cut, showing off her impressive cleavage.

My cock immediately hardens at the sight of her as images of bending her over in that dress slam into me.

No fucking way is that motherfucker getting anywhere near her.

I don't even register who he is, it could be Luc or Kane for all I know. My entire focus is on Macie as I fly toward them.

Her scream filters through my red haze as I pull my arm back but it doesn't stop me throwing my fist into the prick's face.

"Leon," she screams, her tiny hands wrapping around my upper arm in a pathetic attempt to restrain me while the guy goes stumbling back against the wall.

It's not until I've got him pinned up against the wall by his throat that I realize who he is.

Nathan.

A little bit of guilt flickers through me knowing that Macie sees him as her only friend but it's not enough to make me stop.

"Don't fucking touch her," I bark, swinging again and this time connecting with his nose with a satisfying crunch.

"Stop please, Leon. Please," she cries behind me, her voice rough with emotion and slurred with the alcohol she's consumed.

Leaning in close to Nathan, I watch as the blood pours from his nose as the front door opens behind us.

I know who it is before he even opens his mouth.

"Leon, let him go."

"If you fucking touch her again, I'll kill you. You got that, *bro*?"

"I-I," he stutters before spitting blood at my feet. "Only one of us has hurt her, *bro*, and it's not fucking me."

His palms slam down on my chest and I make it easy on him and stand back.

He might be taller than me but I've got at least twenty pounds on him and could take him to the floor in a heartbeat if I wanted to.

Macie immediately rushes toward him, concern glittering in her watery eyes.

I keep my eyes on him, and he knows it.

"I'm fine," he says, dodging her attempts to touch him.

Smart man.

"Leon, what the fuck?" Letty screeches when she finally joins the party in the front yard.

Ignoring all of them, I walk up to Macie who's still trying to help a reluctant Nathan.

"Let's go," I demand, reaching for her hand.

Her entire body tenses at my words and she jumps back, out of reach.

"Are you fucking insane?" she screams, her face hard with anger.

It's fucking hot.

"You don't get to turn up here, throw your weight around then demand I leave with you. I'm nothing to you, you've made that very clear, Leon."

"I'm not leaving here without you," I blurt out, my words shocking myself as well as her if her wide eyes are anything to go by.

"Then I guess you're not leaving."

I sense the others step up behind me, but if I think they're there to back me up, I've got another thing coming because they all sidestep me and stand with Macie.

Shaking my head, I stare the people closest to me, those I fucking love, going up against me in favor of her.

The girl who allowed me to endure the pain and torture that turned me into this monster.

"So that's it is it? You all finally get the truth and you turn your backs on me. Thanks for the support, assholes."

Marching forward, I move around Luca ready to leave but his hand grips my upper arm.

"We're not against you, Brother. We're just with her too."

"You don't even know her," I spit. "She's a traitorous bitch who doesn't deserve your loyalty." I say it loud enough so that she has no way of not hearing every venomous word as it passes my lips.

Luca releases me and I storm forward toward my car. The offer of getting fucked up with Colt long forgotten.

"Leon, wait," Macie cries and my body stops of its own accord.

My heart pounds as she walks around me. She stands before me with her shoulders squared ready to fight and a fierce determination on her face.

I'm so lost in her angry blue depths that I don't see her hand coming until pain explodes across my face and down my neck.

Pride for my girl swells within me as I stare at her shocked face.

"You hit me," I growl, taking a step toward her.

"You deserved it," she says, standing her ground.

"You're going to regret that, Red."

She screams and I throw her over my shoulder and take off toward my car.

"Leon, get the fuck back he—" Luca starts but when I spin around, I find both Peyton and Letty holding him back.

Both girls stare at me, their eyes begging for me not to hurt Macie but I also see an understanding within their gazes.

With a nod at them, I take off once more while Macie squeals and wiggles over my shoulder.

"If you don't stop that you're going to find yourself fucked on the hood of my car for everyone to watch."

"You wouldn't dare," she hisses back, the alcohol giving her confidence.

I stop the second we're in front of my car and slam her down on the hood. I quickly wrap her legs around my waist, placing my hands on either side of her head and lowering down until my nose is almost touching hers.

"Fucking try me, Red."

My entire body trembles with my restraint as she writhes against me.

"I hate you," she seethes.

"Good. The feeling is fucking mutual."

Her chest heaves as she stares up at me, her nipples hard behind the thin fabric of her dress.

"You look like a filthy slut, do you know that?"

"Fuck you, Leon. I don't give a shit what you think of me."

A smile curls at my lips.

"Keep talking dirty to me, baby. It's not going to get you out of this any quicker."

"Do your worst. I'm already as fucked up as you are. Can't ruin what's already broken, Dunn."

I shake my head, a humorless laugh falling from my lips.

"You're lying. There's plenty of you for me to shatter."

I pull her from the car, aware that we've still got an audience, and despite threatening it, there's no fucking way I'm letting anyone watch as I fuck her, not even my brother.

"Let's go." Wrapping my arm around her waist, I push her toward the door.

"I'm not going anywhere with you," she growls.

"No? I don't see you fighting or anyone coming to your rescue."

Her chin drops in realization as she looks over her shoulder at our audience.

"Traitors," she cries and I push her into the car. "Oh no. No. No. No." She tries to push past me, her balled fists raining down on my arms and shoulders and I throw her over the console and onto the passenger seat.

"Fight all you like, we both know who's going to win, Red."

"Fuck you," she hisses, going for the door but quickly finding it locked. "I'm not going anywhere with you."

"I don't think you're really in a position to make demands, baby."

I start the car and then turn to look at her, a wicked smile curling at my lips.

Her hair is a wild mess of curls around her face, her cheeks are red, both from hanging upside down I'm sure.

Her dress is all twisted ensuring she's showing off even more cleavage than she was when she first stumbled out of the house, and her dress is so high up on her hips I can see her black panties covering her pussy.

"What?" she barks, her nails digging into the sides of the seat, her chest still heaving. If she's trying to pretend I don't affect her then she's doing a really shit job.

"You've got no idea, do you?" My brows pull together as I stare at her, unable to believe she doesn't know how fucking hot she looks right now.

She's like my kryptonite.

I know I shouldn't touch her but fuck if I can help myself.

"Just drive and get this over with so I can go home."

"Careful, Red. Anyone would think you don't want to spend the night with me."

"I don't," she huffs, crossing her arms over her chest and staring out of the windshield as if I'm not even here.

A chuckle falls from my lips.

"Pretend all you like, baby. I can read you like a book."

"Oh yeah. So you know how I'm planning on killing you?" She shoots me a wicked look that only makes my cock harder.

"No. But I do know that you're wet as fuck for me right now."

She scoffs.

"You're delusional, Leon."

"Been called worse, Red."

I floor the gas, my wheels spinning as we speed away from the house.

Luca, Peyton, Kane and Letty are still standing in the front yard staring at us but I barely look at them. I don't care about their opinions. They've made enough bad decisions in the past few months that none of them can criticize me right now.

"Where are we going?" Macie demands when I fly past the turnoff toward her dorm building.

My teeth grind as her soft, slightly slurred voice flows through me.

"How much have you had to drink?"

"How is that any of your business?"

"Because you don't drink, or party, yet here you are."

"Yeah well, excuse me if I need a way to forget what happened recently," she spits.

"Try doing that for the last decade."

"You're a selfish asshole, you know that?"

"Me?" I ask, all the air rushing from my lungs in shock.

"Yes, you. You walk around going after the revenge you think you're due yet you have no idea what anyone else has been through. The only pain you know is your own. You don't stop for a second to even consider what everyone else might have been through."

"He didn't fucking ra—" I cut myself off, not even able to spit the words out in anger.

"Just take me home, Leon. I'm not having this conversation with you right now."

"I didn't have any intentions of talking, Red."

"I want to touch you less than I want to talk to you," she spits, disgust oozing from her tone.

"Not interested now you know the truth, huh?"

"W-what?" she asks, rearing back, her eyes boring holes into my profile.

"You were more than happy to touch me before."

"This has nothing to do with... with him and what he—" She swallows the words just as much as I did. "This is about me, Leon. The way you treated me."

"You were begging for it."

She shakes her head, blowing out a long breath.

"Stop the car."

"No."

"Leon, stop the fucking car," she screams like a mad woman.

"So you can run away? I don't think so."

"Leon," she growls.

"You seem to be missing something, Red." I glance over, ensuring she can see the danger and threat lurking in my eyes. "I've searched for you for ten years. You really think I'm going to let you go that easily."

"You walked away pretty quick the last time," she quips.

"Yeah, I've regretted it ever since. I should have taken you up on your offer and fucked you in every single room of that cunt's house until you didn't know your own name and couldn't feel your own body."

She gasps, but while she might think I hear her shock, I don't. All I hear is desire.

"You'd have like that, huh?"

"No, I—"

"You want my punishment. You know you were wrong. You know that you owe me. And you fucking love it."

"Shut up," she demands.

"No need to be ashamed, Red." Reaching over, I run my palm up her thigh.

Her body trembles beneath my hand making my cock ache for her.

"I'm more than happy to deliver all the punishment you deserve. I've spent ten years imagining all the things I'd do to you when I finally got my hands on you. I just never realized just how much fun it would be."

"Leon," she whimpers as my fingers get higher.

Her hands grip my arm tighter trying to force me away from her but she's nowhere near strong enough.

"Oh baby," I moan when I finally find the soaked fabric of her panties. "You remember the last time we were in a car together?"

"Leon." It's meant to be a warning, we both know that, but my name leaves her lips as barely a whisper.

"Yeah, that was hot watching you come all over my fingers. Did you think about that the whole way back to Maddison while you were trapped in here?"

"No," she cries as I apply a little more pressure, her nails digging into my skin, the pain feeding the darkness threatening to explode within me.

"I bet you squirmed all the way home remembering just how good it was."

"No, I hated you all the way home. I hated myself."

"Good. You should."

I take a sharp right without indicating, which sends her flying into the door before I slam my foot on the brake as I pull into the parking lot.

"Where—"

Her face twists up in confusion as she stares up at the hotel before her.

"Why are we here?"

"Because I want you somewhere where the others can't come rescue you."

Her breath catches at my words.

"Macie?" I ask, killing the engine and turning to look at her.

"What?" she spits.

"Do you trust me?"

Throwing her head back, she barks out a laugh as if I've just asked her the most insane question.

Reaching out, I grip her chin and pull her eyes back to mine.

"Macie?" I growl.

"No, Leon," she spits, looking at me as if I'm nothing more than a piece of shit on her shoe. "I don't trust you. I don't even know you. The person you showed me before was an act, wasn't it?"

I shrug. "I guess that's for you to decide."

Her jaw ticks under my fingers.

"Let anyone know there's an issue, and things will only get worse for you," I warn, releasing her and climbing from the car.

MACIE

My body trembles as I watch Leon climb from the driver's seat before he slams the door so hard the entire car rocks with the force.

My head spins, the alcohol from tonight making everything a little hazy. But there's one thing that is very clear to me, being alone with Leon right now is a bad idea.

His eyes are wild just like they were in my uncle's office on Thursday night.

The look terrifies me, but at the same time, he's not wrong with everything he's said about how my body reacts to his wicked taunts and dangerous threats.

It's wrong. So freaking wrong.

I never should have allowed him to put me in his car, not that I'm sure there was anything I could have done to stop him. And I know I shouldn't follow him into this hotel, but I also know that I'm going to allow it to happen. My curiosity, my desire, is too strong to walk away and not find out what he's planning.

He might think I'm scared of the darkness within him, but the reality is, I've never wanted to dive in and lose myself more in my life.

The parts of him he considers broken speak to mine and drag out the girl I've spent all these years trying to hide.

My cell vibrates in my purse as Leon begins to march around the front of the car to get me.

Quickly, I flip my purse open and pull my cell out.

> Letty: I know you probably hate me right now, but you need this. You both do. Fight like hell, girl. He deserves all your wrath and anger.

I can't help but laugh at her words. Yeah, I want to hate her, but I also trust her. Now that I know a little background on her and Kane, and how well she knows Leon, I trust her even more.

I just hope that she's right and that after tonight, things might go back to making more sense once more.

He rips my door open and stares down at me with my cell in my hand.

"You're not calling for help," he spits, yanking it from my fingers.

He stares down at the screen and laughs.

"She's right," he mutters. "I really do fucking need this. Get out."

He wraps his hand around my upper arm and drags me from the car.

"Fix your dress. You look like a cheap whore. This place only welcomes exclusive ones."

My chin drops in shock at his words.

"Then maybe you should go and find one of those."

His fingers grasp my chin once more, his grip painful as he glares down into my eyes.

"Maybe that's my plan. Maybe there's already one waiting for me and you get to watch."

All the air comes rushing from my lungs and tears burn the backs of my eyes. But it's not his words that affect me, my reaction is purely from the thought of him being with someone else. I hate it, and I hate myself for my reaction because I shouldn't care.

"We'd better hope you don't have performance issues again then, won't we?" The words slip from my mouth without instruction from my brain.

His eyes darken as his nostrils flare.

"You're playing a dangerous game, Macie."

"I'm not the weak little girl everyone thinks I am, Leon," I hiss. "Our paths might not totally align, but we've both fought our way through one way or another. It'll take more than a few harsh words from you to break me down."

"Good. I'd be bored if it were that easy."

He gives me ten seconds to right my dress seeing as I'm moments from flashing anyone who could be looking our way then he reaches out and takes my hand in his.

I fight my reaction to his simple touch, my arm burns with heat at his harsh grip.

"Don't say a word," he warns as we step into the fancy hotel.

I'm used to wealth, I've grown up having money thrown at me in the hope it'll keep me at arms length but even still my eyes widen at the luxurious red and gold decoration along with the ornately carved pillars and furniture.

Leon walks me right up to the reception desk and hands over a black and gold card.

"Good evening, Mr. Dunn. I hope you're well," the receptionist says, holding his eyes and smiling. She's probably well into her forties but still, she doesn't seem to have any problem trying her luck with him.

"I'm great, thank you, Whitney." The smile he flashes her sends a wave of jealousy through me. I haven't seen him smile since we arrived at my uncle's on Thursday and I hadn't realized until this moment how much I missed it. "We'll just need the room for the night."

"No problem. How is your father? We haven't seen him in a while."

"Oh, he's been a little under the weather."

I stare at Leon's profile as a coy smile tugs at his lips. Whitney probably misses it, but there's more to his words than he lets on. I'd put money on it.

"Okay, well you know where to go," she says, sliding the card back at him, a seductive smile on her lips. "If you need anything, you know where I am."

My free hand curls into a fist at her blatant flirting.

"Thank you, Whitney. Have a good night."

"You too." He winks at her. Actually freaking winks.

My teeth grind at both of their actions as he drags me away, but even still the hussy never so much as looks in my direction. She's too busy stripping Leon naked in her head.

The elevator doors open the second we step toward them and I gasp in shock when he pushes me inside and slams me back against the wall.

"Le—" His name is cut off when he presses his hand against my mouth, forcing me to breathe through my nose in an attempt to catch my breath.

"Jealous, baby?" His green eyes sparkle with excitement and danger as he stares me down.

I shake my head as much as his harsh grip allows.

"What would you do if I invited her up? You know she'd agree."

My teeth grind and he feels it.

"She'd be all over it. She's wanted me for a long time."

A growl rumbles up my throat before I have a chance to catch it.

His smirk turns evil as he steps into my body, pressing me against the wall.

"Innocent little Macie Fletcher," he murmurs. "If only everyone knew, huh."

His hand slips from my face and I drag in a deep breath.

"Fuck you," I seethe.

"If only they knew what a filthy little slut you really are."

"Leon," I gasp as he wraps his fingers around the fabric hiding my breasts, tugging it aside to expose me.

"Look at that," he mutters, his eyes locked on my bare boob, his finger flicking my hard nipple. "Your body defies you, Macie. It always has."

"I hate you."

"Sure. I wouldn't expect anything else. He made sure there was nothing left of me to love anyway."

I have to slam my lips shut to stop myself from telling him that that can't be true.

I refuse to believe that everything I've seen of Leon since we first met was fake. I want to believe that he never would have been able to keep up that lie as well as he did if that sweet Leon didn't really exist somewhere under all this anger.

I hold his eyes, wanting him to read my thoughts, not that I think for a second that he'd believe me even if he could.

One side of his lips curl up before he lowers his head to my chest and sucks my nipple into his mouth.

"Oh God," I gasp, my head falling back against the wall as he sucks harder, until a bolt of pain shoots down my body, zeroing in on my clit.

He laps at me, bites me, teases me until the elevator dings alerting us to our arrival.

Taking a huge step back, he runs his eyes down the length of my body, heat burning in his eyes, his cock trying to break out of his pants.

I should feel ashamed of the state of me, but staring at his reaction gives me confidence, it shows me just how much power I've still got over him even when he doesn't want me to have any.

Covering myself up, I push from the elevator wall and walk out ahead of him.

I have no clue where I'm going but I'm sure he'll soon point me in the right direction if I take the wrong turn.

His stare burns into my back as he follows me down the hall.

"Stop," he booms when I'm beside the door.

Stepping up behind me, the heat from his body damn near scalds my bare back as he taps the pad beside the door with the card.

With his arm clamped around my waist, he swings the door open and walks me inside. The feel of his hard length pressing against my ass makes my thighs clench with desire.

I shouldn't want him as fiercely as I do. Especially when he's this angry. When all he can see is his need to hurt me.

"So this is where you bring all your expensive whores to impress them?" I ask as the hallway opens up to an impressive suite with floor to ceiling windows that showcase all of Maddison County in the distance.

"I don't need to impress anyone, Macie," he says, immediately walking over to the kitchenette and pulling out a bottle of whisky from behind a glass door.

He pours himself a generous amount before knocking it back in one go.

"This is my father's place. He's the one who feels the need to impress. I, on the other hand, don't really give a fuck what people—what women—think of me."

"I guess that's good seeing as you treat them like shit."

"What do you know about how I treat women?"

"Other than from experience?" I quip.

His brow lifts and I take a step toward him, needing to show him that I'm not scared of him, no matter how much he threatens me.

Now I know the truth, I see more of him than I think he's even aware of. He's angry, sure. Who wouldn't be given the situation? But under all that pain and anger is a lost little boy who desperately needs to be told that it's going to be okay.

He might think that my uncle was the one to ruin his life, to plant the seed of darkness inside him. But he's the one who's watered it and let it grow. Allowing it to fester inside of him until it begins to seep out.

He's held on to his need for revenge for so long now that he can't see anything else.

I should know. I've lived with the guilt for as long as he's lived with the pain.

"I know you've only fucked redheads for years. And I think we're more than aware as to why, aren't we?" Reaching out, I swipe the bottle from his hand and lift it to my lips.

I regret it the second the strong alcohol hits my lips but I refuse to back down, to show an ounce of weakness in front of Leon.

He needs this. He needs me to fight. So that's what he's going to get.

I'm done letting him take the lead and following him down a track full of lies and deceit.

He's played his cards now. I know the truth. And one way or another, I'm going to make him face it.

Because if he doesn't... well, I don't think either of us really need to go there.

"I'm fucked up, what can I say?" he says with a shrug, not even bothering to deny it, which makes me weirdly happy. "None of them mattered until I found the one I wanted."

"Oh yeah? How good was I?" I force out through my burning throat.

"You have no idea how good it felt to fuck you over his desk. To take your innocence from you just like he took every bit of my childhood, of my life, away from me."

"Is that what you imagined all these years? How lucky for you that I basically fell into your lap."

He takes a step toward me, snatching the bottle back.

"Oh Red," he says after swallowing a few shots. "What I've imagined has been so much worse. Open."

Unable but to do as he demands, my lips part and I tilt my head back as he fills my mouth with whisky.

I try to swallow fast enough but he pours too much and it spills from my mouth and down onto my chest, soaking into my dress.

"Filthy little slut."

The strap around my neck tightens before the sound of ripping fabric fills the space a second before cool air breezes over my naked chest.

Finishing off the bottle, he drops it to the floor before taking a step toward me.

"I'd run now, if I were you, little Macie Fletcher."

His chest brushes my nipples and I swallow down my reaction.

"I'm not scared of you, Leon," I tell him, staring him dead in the eyes. We've both experienced the devil in our lives and he is not it.

"Silly, silly girl."

It takes a second for my brain to catch up with my body but the second my overheated skin presses against the windows, everything comes crashing back.

"Leon," I whimper, the icy cold glass almost painful against my breasts.

Squeezing my eyes closed, I try to forget that I'm standing here damn near naked for the entire town to see.

All they need to do is look up and... A shudder rips through me.

"What do you think they'll all see when they look up at you, Red?"

"P-please don't," I beg, hating that I do as I turn my head to the side.

"Do you think they see the sweet little Macie Smith that you pretend to be? Or the filthy liar that you really are?"

"L-Leon."

"I know what I see," he growls in my ear. His deep voice sending a shudder of desire through me.

It's wrong. Oh so wrong but even like this, I can't help the way he affects me.

"You. Are. A. Filthy. Liar. Macie. Fletcher." Each word punches the air and I feel them like physical blows. "And it's time everyone discovered the truth."

"And you?" I inquire, feeling brave.

"This isn't about me."

"But it is. Don't you see, my lies are intertwined with yours. You expose me, I expose you. Is that what you want? The world to know why you're so angry, why you hate yourself and everyone else so much?"

"Shut up," he booms, confirming what I already know. I just touched a sore spot.

"You've never spoken about it, have you?"

The length of his body presses against mine. His heat is almost enough to make me forget about my current position.

"Shut the fuck up."

"You've never told anyone how it made you feel to be used like that. To be abused by someone you trusted."

"Macie," my name is suddenly more like a plea for me to stop talking.

"Well, now you can. I already know your dirty little secret, so you can tell me everything. You can explain how dirty he made you feel. Hell, you can even tell me that you enjoyed it, if you wa—"

"Enough," he booms, his hand slamming down on the glass beside my head, making me flinch. "This isn't about me."

"You played me, Leon. You convinced me that I was crazy for thinking you didn't have an ulterior motive and yet you did all along. What I want to know is, were you always this much of a cunt, or did he make you this way?"

A low growl rumbles up his throat at my question, at my language as his hand lifts to the nape of my neck, crushing my cheek against the glass.

"I want you to watch them watch you. I want you to look in their eyes as they see you for what you really are."

A violent shudder rips through me at his words, but I swallow down my fear.

Those people down there are nothing. No one. They probably haven't even seen me. And even if they do. They don't know me. I could be anyone. I'm just a body. Just a woman enjoying her night.

Squaring my shoulders, I straighten my spine with my new found confidence.

Leon Dunn isn't going to break me.

I survived Richard Fletcher, I can survive Leon.

He's a pussy cat compared to the devil I was forced to live with.

His fingers brush my hip as they curl around the tiny bit of lace left covering me.

"Is this really going to make you feel better?" I ask. "Is shaming me like this really going to get you what you need? Is it the retaliation you've desired all these years?"

"I should have brought a fucking gag," he mutters as he pulls the fabric from my body. "Maybe I should use this. Shut you up with your own panties."

The image that pops into my head makes my hips roll.

"Fuck," he barks as I grind against his hard cock. "You asked for it."

A second later, the lace of my panties brushes my lips.

"Open."

I refuse, biting on the inside of my lips.

"Defiant little bi—"

"Argh," I scream when he spanks my ass so hard I feel it all the way down to my toes. "Fuck," I mutter against the lace that's suddenly stuffed in my mouth.

My hand immediately lifts to pull it out, but I don't get anywhere near it because he snags both of my wrists and pins them behind my back.

The snap of leather fills the room as he pulls his belt free.

"Oh God," I moan around the fabric

"No, baby. He's not going to help you now. You've handed yourself over to the devil. And guess what?" He pauses for a beat as if I could actually respond. "It's playtime."

He binds my hands tightly behind my back.

I tug to see if I'm able to free myself as he chuckles to himself.

"It's cute that you think I'd let you escape."

I moan in frustration bucking against his hold.

"Because if for any second you thought Thursday night was it. That I got you out of my system, you'd be very much mistaken."

"I hate you," I seethe, making him laugh harder because he knows that while my head might believe my words. My body doesn't.

My heart is pounding, my chest is heaving, and I can already feel my desire dripping down my thighs.

It's mortifying because at any moment, he's going to find out just how badly my body craves him.

It's wrong. Oh so freaking wrong.

So why does it feel so right?

I cry out once more and he brings his palm down on my ass, the force of the hit only pressing me harder against the glass.

"I bet you look beautiful from down there. All wanton, just waiting for me to touch you."

His fingers grip my hips so hard I have no doubt he'll leave marks as he pulls my lower body from the windows.

I cry out when he spanks me again.

"So pretty," he muses, rubbing the burn with his palm. "Are you wet for me, Red?"

I shake my head, not willing to submit to him despite the fact we both know I'm lying.

"Huh, that's funny, because I can smell it, baby. I can smell just how badly you need me. So fucking sweet it makes my mouth water."

He moves behind me and when I glance back, I find he's on his knees, my ass right in his face.

My hips roll, my body desperate to feel something, to have the need that's coiled tight within me snapping into a million pieces.

He can do that. I know he can. And I know he knows that I want it.

Is this all part of his game? Torture me with his barbed words, his brutal touch and leave me waiting. Begging.

No. I won't beg. And not just because I can't right now.

With one hand squeezing my ass cheek he runs a finger over my puckered hole.

"I should take this too. Take all your firsts and ruin you for anyone else."

My breath catches in my throat at his wicked words as my pussy clamps down on nothing as another wave of desire washes through me.

I don't want that.

I don't want him to take everything from me.

Do I?

He begins circling around the sensitive skin, it's an alien sensation but one that makes the need within me grow.

"I bet you'd be so tight you'd damn near strangle my cock," he mutters and I begin to wonder if he's actually talking to himself more than me.

Then suddenly, his finger is gone and I try to cry out when something much gentler presses against me.

A moan rips from my throat, muffled by my panties as he licks at me.

My legs tremble as my pussy gushes.

I scream, my fists clenching in their bindings as he pushes his tongue inside me.

So wicked. So dirty.

But I love it.

"You want it, don't you? You want to feel my cock buried so deep in your ass you have no idea where you end and I begin."

I shake my head again denying that his words are true.

He punishes me with a slap. Then another and another until I'm sure my ass has his glowing red handprint on it.

"Pretty," he murmurs, trailing his fingers up my inner thighs, collecting up my juices as he moves. "Macie, Macie, Macie. So wet for me. Such a little lying, filthy whore."

I push back, offering myself up to him, needing his tongue again, his fingers. Anything.

"Anyone would think you're enjoying this. Being on display for the entire county to watch as I eat you."

A groan rumbles up my throat, my need to demand he does just that desperate to fall from my lips.

Thankfully, in only a heartbeat, I realize that my demand is unnecessary.

I scream around my panties as he licks up the length of me.

"So fucking sweet."

My legs tremble with my need to let go as he laps at me like a man starved.

He circles my clit, bites down on my sensitive skin and plunges his tongue deep inside me.

My hips roll desperate for more as my cheek and breasts stick to the window as my body heats, sweat coating every inch of me.

I moan and mewl, itching to pull my panties from my mouth so I can really let go but no matter how much I try to spit them out, I can't.

Shifting around so his back is to the window, Leon sucks on my clit once more, but this time he slides two fingers inside me. The intrusion burns but the pain is so freaking good that I almost come the second he strokes my walls.

Dragging my eyes open. I stare down at him as his cold, evil ones glare up at me.

Everything he feels for me shines bright in the green depths. His hate, his anger, but more importantly, his desire.

He might want to punish me, but despite all the bullshit surrounding this situation, he wants me just as badly as I do him.

The broken parts of us just align.

We might be a car crash waiting to happen. But like this, right now, stripped bare with our pain bleeding from us for the other to see, we work, even if he refuses to acknowledge it.

We might have experienced different things. But we're the same. Deep down, we've got the same fractured souls. We crave the same revenge, we're desperate to deliver the same retaliation.

The only difference is that I think he's got the means in order to follow through with the thoughts that have run around my head for years.

He can put an end to the torment, the nightmares. But he's got to be able to accept the past, what's happened to him if he's ever going to find a future for himself.

A moan rips from my throat as my orgasm finally begins to crest. But just as I'm about to fall, Leon rips his fingers from my body and releases his vicious hold on my clit.

I pant, my chest heaving as I desperately try to drag in the air I need through my nose only.

Thankfully, he takes pity on me and after pushing his way up the window, he plucks the lace from my mouth and throws it to the floor.

"Oh God," I moan, sucking in huge lungfuls of air.

His hand grasps my chin, forcing my head back so I have no choice but to look into his dark green, sadistic eyes.

An evil smile curls at his lips as both them and his chin glistens with my juices.

"You're a sick bastard, Leon Dunn," I spit.

His smile widens but he doesn't say anything, instead, he shoves two fingers deep into my mouth.

"Lick them clean."

My eyes narrow on his, my hate burning through them but as much as I want to defy him, I find my tongue lapping at his digits, my own tastes exploding in my mouth as his eyes flare with desire.

I suck on them, making him groan, and just before he pulls them free, I sink my teeth down into his skin.

Immediately, the coppery taste of his blood fills my mouth.

"You fucking bitch."

"Yeah? What are you going to do about it? You're nothing but a scared little boy, Leon Dunn. A scared, broken, little boy who doesn't think he's worth anything."

His hand clamps over my mouth, stopping my wicked words. He pushes me backward and I don't fight it.

He needs to hear these things, he needs to properly deal with what happened and if that means he needs to hurt, then so be it.

I'll make it hurt because I know it's the only way to heal.

I'll also be right here to take all of it from him.

We don't stop until we're in the bathroom. He spins me, forcing me over the counter, my chest pressing against the cool marble, my nipples pebbling against the smooth surface.

His eyes hold mine in the mirror as his chest heaves.

My words hit their target, I can see the hurt in his depths and he hates me for it.

Good.

"You finished?" he asks, taking a risk I won't keep taunting him when he removes his hand from my mouth, although he doesn't move it very far because it just slips down to my throat, squeezing in warning.

"Are you?" I quip.

His jaw ticks giving me the answer I already knew.

"You want to drown in the darkness of your past?" I ask him, holding his stare. "I'm more than happy to go down with you, Lee. But it's not going to be easy. Pasts like ours are messy, painful. And until you accept what you've been through, you're never going to see the light."

I don't even realize he's pulled himself out until I feel the hard head of his cock at my entrance.

"Shit," I cry as he thrusts forward.

My feet leave the floor as my head collides with the mirror in front of me.

"What is it you're hoping to achieve here, Leon?" I force out as he pistons in and out of me in punishing strokes. "You want me to tell you that you're evil? That you're nothing? Or do you want me to tell you that you're getting your revenge by punishing me? Or..." I add, knowing this one is going to sting. "Do you want me to tell you that you're just like him, taking whatever you want, hurting whoever you want without caring about the consequences?"

"FUUUUCK," he roars, his thrusts are so hard each one hurts as he hits my cervix.

"You. Know. Nothing."

"Wrong," I spit. "I know everything. That's why you hate me. You're ashamed. You're scared. You think you're weak."

"NO," he booms, his grip on my hips painful as his cock swells, letting me know that he's about to explode. "NOOO," he cries but before he comes, he pulls out of me, lifts me from the counter and pushes me to the floor.

I land on my ass with a thud, pain shooting up my spine as he fists his cock in front of me.

I'm enthralled looking between the fierce expression on his face and the way he violently tugs at himself.

"ARGH," he cries, his entire body locking up for a beat before jets of cum shoot from his cock, covering my chest.

He stills for a moment, his hand resting on the wall above me, the room falling silent for long seconds as we both fight to catch our breaths.

I watch him from my seat at his feet, his eyes closed, his face twisted in torment, all his hate for himself, for the world, oozing from his every pore as I wait for what comes next.

My body aches, my arms and shoulders pull, and my pussy clenches around nothing as it tries to find what it needs to climax as I shiver against the cold tiles beneath me.

Any thought that this might be over is obliterated the second he opens his eyes.

They're even colder than they were before, if that's even possible.

"Look at you at my feet covered in my cum." He smiles and my stomach tumbles.

I might claim not to be scared of him, but right now he looks unhinged.

I breathe a sigh of relief when he reaches behind me and releases my arms, but it's short-lived because he only frees one hand.

He looks around the room briefly before lifting me and placing me in the shower. He lifts my arms and reloops his belt around my wrists.

"What the hell are you doing?" I scream as he connects his belt to the rail in the shower. "Leon," I cry when he takes a step back.

"Open your legs, I want to see your swollen cunt."

My breath catches in my throat.

"Who are you?" I breathe, desperate to see just a hint of the Leon I thought I knew instead of this monster I'm staring at right now.

"Just a broken little boy," he mutters, turning his back on me and storming from the bathroom without so much as a glance over his shoulder.

"LEON," I scream, harshly pulling at the railing above me in the hope I can dislodge it somehow, but it's pointless. "FUUUUUCK," I scream, kicking my legs in frustration.

9

MACIE

 My body shivers against the cold, my arms ache, my fingers feel like ice up above my head. They went numb a long time ago but I gave up fighting to release myself before that happened.

Only minutes after he left the bathroom, the main hotel room door slammed shut.

At first, I hoped he was just playing mind games with me, that he was still here and just trying to punish me, but I knew it wasn't the case because I felt his presence was gone.

My tears have long dried up, my hope vanishing with it.

He's not coming back.

I'm going to be found stuck here in the morning by some poor member of the hotel staff who's going to have to rescue me, see the state he left me in.

That bothers me less than the pity I know is going to be in their eyes as they release me.

I don't want their pity.

I knew what I was getting myself into tonight. I knew the beast I was poking with my words. I knew he was going to react badly to the truth. It's why I did it.

I wanted it all. His wrath. His pain. His punishment. I deserve every bit of it.

But more than that, he deserves to break free of the bindings that are still wrapped tightly around him since the very first time my uncle touched him. He is exactly what I said, he's a broken little boy now trapped in a man's body.

He has no idea how to move on, how to deal with the pain he's experienced. But he's going to have to face it or the darkness festering inside him will kill him, beyond what everything my uncle did to him.

And I can't allow that. I already have to live with the guilt of doing nothing that day, I can't deal with having his life on my conscience too.

I have no idea how long I sit there, wishing I had a way to reach out to someone to come and save me.

Eventually my exhaustion gets the better of me and I drift in and out of a fitful sleep with my head resting against my arm, my body covered in goose bumps and Leon's dried cum on my chest.

I want to say I regret tonight. But I think Letty might be right.

We needed this.

We both have demons from our past that need to be banished, need to be exorcized, and I think together is the only way we're going to do it.

Individually, we can easily go under, lose ourselves to the darkness just like Leon has been doing the past ten years. But together, we can find a way through it all.

The sound of a lock clicking then a door opening has me wide awake in a heartbeat. I sit up, praying that Leon is about to appear in the doorway.

Either that, or Letty. I have no idea why I consider her worthy of helping me with this but I know she won't judge the situation I've found myself in.

She gets it. More than I do, if I'm being honest.

"Leon," I cry, my voice rough from crying and exhaustion.

Whoever it is crashes around in the main suite for a few minutes, and I come to the conclusion that it must be him because if it were anyone who'd come to actually rescue me, they'd be in here the second I called out.

My heart jumps into my throat when heavy footsteps head my way. I pray for him to appear, for his eyes to have softened, for him to have found the solace he needed in letting his darkness reign.

But all of that is forgotten when he does emerge and I'm faced with reality.

"Leon," I breathe, concern for the broken man who has somehow buried his way under my skin even when I hate him rushes forward.

Silently, he walks toward the bathtub and turns the faucet on.

He doesn't say anything, he doesn't even look at me as he works, pouring a generous amount of bubble under the running water, filling the room with a floral scent replacing the lingering smell of sex and pain.

Finally, he turns to me, lifting his hand to his split lip and wiping away a trickle of blood. But as I get closer and his injuries become even more apparent, I realize a split lip is the least of his worries.

"What happened?" I ask when he moves his busted knuckles toward the belt holding me in place and releases me.

His eyes find mine for a beat, and I gasp at the pain in his dark depths.

"Leon," I say breathily as my useless arms fall to my sides. My pain is forgotten as I stare at him.

He shakes his head so slightly that if I weren't paying as much attention as I am, I'd miss it.

Reaching out, he scoops me up from my floor and holds me against his body.

His shirt is stained with blood, his face, his neck, his arms, all are covered much like the night he came to my dorm.

I thought that night was bad, but the aura he's giving off right now is downright terrifying. And the fact that he's not even speaking makes it that much worse.

Walking me over to the bath, he lowers me into the growing bubbles and hot water.

My skin burns as I sink into it but the warmth is welcome after the hours I've been trapped and freezing stuck in the same position.

Pulling my legs up to my chest, I wrap my arms around them, noticing the blood that transferred from him to me.

I have no idea who it belongs to, and if I'm being honest with myself, I don't care. There's a sick part of me that even wishes it's my uncle's.

I know Leon wanted his location for a reason. I'm not stupid, or naïve. I know that whatever he's planning isn't just a pleasant social visit to reminisce on old times. When Leon does go and visit, I have a feeling it will be the last time anyone sees him.

It should terrify me that I think he's capable of something as serious as that. But honestly, all I feel is relief.

I've wanted to stop my uncle from hurting anyone else for years. He may be incapable now seeing as fate took over and ripped away his opportunities to get close to anyone, hell, to even remember anyone. But still, he doesn't deserve to breathe the same air as us after all the destruction he's caused.

Rustling fabric behind me catches my attention, and when I look over my shoulder, I find Leon shedding his clothes, dropping them into a heap on the floor.

I gasp at the dark bruises on his ribs that match those darkening his face.

Whoever he saw tonight clearly gave as good as he got.

Without saying a word, or asking permission—not that I really expected him to—he steps into the tub behind me, quickly sinking into the water.

His muscular legs slide along the outside of mine, his simple touch making me shiver with awareness.

I sit motionless, not knowing what to do or what he needs right now.

My heart thunders in my chest as I wait for the other shoe to drop, for some spiteful words to fall from his lips.

But nothing ever comes.

When he does move, all he does is lace his arm around my waist and pull me back against his chest.

I shudder as his lips press to my shoulder and my eyes shutter at the simple move.

I shouldn't react to it, but I can't help myself.

Silently, I follow his lead and lean back against him as he reaches for the sponge and rubs some soap into it.

He starts on my arms, rubbing rhythmic circles into my skin, cleaning every inch of me. He pays extra attention to my shoulders, massaging them with the soft suds.

I moan as he presses his fingers into my aching muscles, appreciating the attention after being abandoned for hours.

Happy with one, he moves onto the next as my head falls lax and I just lay there enjoying his touch.

It's so different from how he treated me earlier tonight, it makes my head spin, but it doesn't stop me from enjoying it.

I want to think he's feeling guilty, making up for leaving me like he did, but this is Leon Dunn we're talking about, and anything could be going through his head right now.

Once he's finished washing my arms he moves on to my chest, cleaning that with the same meticulous precision he did my arms.

I try to fight my reaction but I can't hold it in when he brushes the sponge over my nipples.

His hand on my waist tightens as my gasp cuts through the air. But still, he says nothing. He just continues with the task at hand.

My head spins with confusion.

The Leon that walked out of this bathroom was so full of hate and anger, so much so he's returned covered in someone else's blood. But the Leon who's silent behind me really is lost and broken in all the ways I accused him of.

Unable to stand the silence anymore, my lips part.

"Le—"

"Don't. Please," he breathes, and I immediately slam my lips shut again.

The time to push him has gone.

Silence falls around us once more, the only thing that can be heard is his shallow breathing and the bubbles popping around us.

It's long, agonizing minutes later when he sits forward slightly and places his lips to my neck.

"Lee, I—" I gasp once more as his hand snakes down my stomach until his fingers brush my clit. "Oh God. I don't think—"

"Let me, please. I need... I need..."

"Okay."

Widening my legs, I throw one over the edge of the tub to give him better access.

His movements are slow and measured. His brutal touch and burning pain from before is gone.

His lips continue to kiss down my neck making my skin erupt in goose bumps as he plays my body to perfection.

Reaching lower, he dips two fingers inside me, his thumb pressed against my clit.

"Lee," I moan, arching my back as my long lost release begins to return.

"Need to feel you coming, baby." He bites my shoulder lightly. It's the biggest tease and the first time I really accept how much I love his brutal side because I crave the pain just as much as he does. But that's not what this is about.

His free hand lifts to my breast and he pinches and twists my nipple until I finally fall over the edge.

"Oh, shit, shit. Fuck, Leon," I cry as wave after wave of pent-up pleasure rolls through me. My nails dig into his thighs as I ride the release out, his movements don't stop until I'm wrung out.

"Oh shit," I gasp, staring at the little bloody crescents on his thighs from where my nails dug into his skin. "I'm so sor—"

"Don't," he barks and I once again slam my lips shut.

His arms wrap around my body, pinning me back against his solid chest. He's hard, his length pressed against my spine, but he does nothing about it.

I can feel his heart thundering in his chest as his panting breaths race past my ear, but still he does nothing.

Minutes tick by as I wait for him to say something, to do something, but he never does.

I desperately want to know where he went, who the blood belongs to, but until he offers up some information, I'm determined to keep my mouth shut. Both of us have already caused enough damage to each other tonight.

"It's cold," he finally says, gently pushing me forward so he can get out.

He grabs a towel and wraps it around his waist before pulling another from the shelf and holding it out for me.

Hesitantly, I stand from the tub and step into it.

He wraps me up, his eyes holding mine the second he turns me to face him.

I stare up at him, waiting for him to do something, thinking that he's going to kiss me, but he never does. Instead, he just reaches out and tucks a wet lock of hair behind my ear.

The move makes me swoon and I chastise myself for forgetting what he's done to me tonight.

Just because he's being weirdly sweet now, it doesn't erase this evening. Even if I did crave the pain, I never asked to be tied up and left for hours.

Just remembering it makes my arms ache.

Sweeping me off my feet, Leon walks us from the bathroom and straight toward the huge bed that looks out over the twinkling lights of the town before us.

He pulls the towel from me and lifts the sheets, encouraging me to get in.

I hesitate. What I really should do is leave. I should walk out when he needs me most, but one more look in his haunted green eyes and I know that I can't bring myself to do it, not yet at least.

Seeing his pain, his torment means I do as he wants and crawl under the sheets.

He sheds his own towel seconds later and I watch as he slips in beside me.

We lay on our sides staring at each other silently for the longest time.

I beg him to talk, to tell me anything that might relieve some of his burdens but he doesn't. Eventually he must get fed up with my silent pleading because he shifts us, turning me over and pulling my back against his front. He clamps his arm around my waist, holding me tightly to him.

My exhausted body sinks into the luxurious mattress beneath me and I'm almost about to drift off when he finally speaks. I have no idea if he thinks I'm already asleep but I keep still and try to keep my breathing shallow in the hope he doesn't stop.

"My dad knew," he whispers. "I told him what had happened that summer. It took every ounce of strength I possessed to confess. Richard was his friend. One of his best friends. I knew telling him, having him accept it was going to be hard. What I never expected was for him to dismiss it as if it was nothing, as if it was normal."

Tears burn my eyes for that lost little boy. For the scared little girl who wasn't able to help.

Guilt stronger than I've ever felt wraps its claws around my chest until it's almost impossible to keep my breathing steady.

"He told me that I just had to get over it. That Richard was the best teacher I'd ever get. That he'd improve my chances of the NFL more than any other. That I had to listen to every word he said to me, and follow all his instructions."

A shudder rips through my body and there's no way he doesn't feel it.

"That year was the first. The first of three. Each summer after that first one, I would beg my dad not to send me but he always refused. Told me how lucky I was to attend such a prestigious camp that boys across the country coveted. Lucky," he spits.

"The only lucky thing about that whole experience is that I somehow survived it."

His arms release me a little, his fingers starting to draw circles on my belly.

"I know you're awake, Red."

I tense but I don't respond, I'm too scared he'll stop and turn back into the vicious Leon again. I could handle that version of him earlier, but I'm too exhausted to even think about it now.

"Everything you said earlier is true. My entire teenage and adult life has been overshadowed by him, by my need to take him down. Without it, without my need to find you, to hurt you, I don't know who I am."

"He shouldn't have the power to make you forget yourself like that, Leon."

"I know. But he does."

I nod because I understand. I was that person for a lot of years as well.

"Will you tell me what you went through?" he asks, his gentle movements against my skin lulling me to sleep.

"Maybe one day," I whisper before sleep claims me and I drift off into oblivion where none of this exists.

10

LEON

The weight of his body presses against mine, pinning me to his desk and my stomach rolls knowing what comes next.

"No, please," I cry, exhausted from a full day of running plays. "I can't do this, please," I beg, but like always, it doesn't stop him.

He knows what he wants and he couldn't care less about me.

"Be a good boy, Dunn. Stay nice and still. That's it," he encourages, although I know he doesn't mean it. He might pretend that he wants me to be compliant but we both know he loves it when I fight, which is why I've given up.

I've learned that if I just comply, it's usually over faster, the pain almost bearable, the disgust that rolls through me almost ignorable. Almost.

"No," I cry as he pushes his hand into my shorts.

"You know you love it as much as I do. You can't hide it from me, boy."

The tears that started burning my eyes when he locked his gaze on me at the end of practice finally fall. Big fat tears dropping onto his desk beneath me as he takes exactly what he wants from me, leaving me a broken, hollow child with nothing but a splintered soul and a tarnished body.

I hate you, I silently sob.

"No, no, please," I cry, suddenly jolting awake and sitting upright in bed. "Fuck. Fuck," I pant, lifting my hand to chest covering my racing heart.

My stomach churns as if the events of my nightmare were real, my need to puke up my disgust for what I allowed to happen is almost too strong to ignore.

I suck in deep breaths as the sweat covering my body begins to cool, making me shiver with the memories that just seemed so vivid.

After a few seconds, my surroundings come back to me, memories of the night before, not just my nightmare slam into me and I look to the other side of the bed.

Macie.

But it's empty.

"Red?" I call, although I don't know why. Throwing the covers off, I pad around the suite naked looking for her, praying that I'm wrong about what that empty side of the bed means.

"Macie?" I ask, poking my head into the bathroom, but the only sign that she was here is my belt still hanging from the shower rail.

"Fuck. FUCK," I scream, pulling my arm back and planting my fist in the center of the mirror that's hanging over the sink. The exact one I used to stare into her eyes as I fucked her last night. "FUCK."

I stumble back, colliding with the wall, slipping down the tiles until my ass hits the floor.

What the fuck is wrong with me?

Flashbacks from the night before hit me.

Her at the window, the way she reacted to me. How vicious I was. How she called me out on my bullshit and only fueled my anger. How I left her tied up.

A sob erupts from somewhere within me as my body trembles.

She's right.

She's right about all of this. If I can't get over all of this it's going to suck me under for good.

———

The next time I come to, I'm curled up on the bathroom floor, my body aching and shivering from the cold.

I figure it's what I deserve after I left Macie in here to the same fate.

Groaning, I roll onto my back, stare up at the ceiling and wonder where the hell I go from here.

A knock sounds out around the silent suite and I push up onto my elbows, listening in the hope whoever it is goes away.

They don't.

Only seconds later the knock comes again, quickly followed by a voice I recognize.

"Leon, I know you're in there. Open the goddamn door."

"Fucking hell," I mutter, climbing to my feet and padding across the room to the pile of clothes I abandoned on the floor before our bath last night.

The memories of having her in my arms, both of us covered in bubbles and hot water comes to mind making my cock stir.

Tugging my boxers and jeans up my legs, I realize that I no longer have a shirt.

Macie.

Scrubbing my hand across my face, I push my hair back, pulling on the ends until it hurts knowing that I left her no choice but to flee in the middle of the night wearing a shirt that was covered in blood.

"Leon, I swear to God, I'll break this door down if you don't— Oh hey," she says with a fake ass smile the second I pull the door open.

"How did you know— Macie," I mutter, turning away from my know-it-all best friend and walking back into the room.

"Yeah, Macie. Did you think she just magically transported herself back home in the middle of the night?" Letty quips sarcastically.

"Did you come here for a reason, or just to piss me off?" I ask, grabbing the tablet on the coffee table and ordering myself a coffee to be brought up.

"She's okay, in case you were wondering," she says, dropping onto the couch and folding her arms across her chest.

"You made a mistake letting her come with me last night."

"Oh, I'm sorry, I didn't realize I was either of your keepers. You're both in charge of your own destiny."

"I'm destined to go to hell, Let."

She stares at me, refusing to accept my words.

"What happened to you? She might have been mad, but there's no way Macie did that," she says, nodding toward my busted face.

"I wouldn't put it past her," I mutter, walking over to the floor to ceiling window I had her pressed up against last night.

"I know you went out, that you left her…" She cuts herself off and I wonder just how honest Macie was with her about what went down here last night. "Where did you go?"

"To blow off some steam before I did something I'd regret."

"So you're telling me that you don't regret last night."

My lips part to tell her I don't. But then I picture Macie, her arms above her head, shivering cold as I returned, and guilt lashes at my insides.

"Exactly." I watch in the reflection of the glass as she pushes to stand and walks over to me. Her hand slides down my arm until she takes hold of my hand. "I get what you're doing, Leon. So does Macie. But hurting her isn't going to change the past. And in the long run, you're only hurting yourself more."

I scoff, not wanting to listen to her advice.

"You really like her, don't you?"

"No," I bark, startling her. "I fucking hate her, Letty. How can't you see that? She stood there and watched as that cunt abused me."

"She was a child," Letty shouts back, matching my volume and anger. "Have you even asked her what he did to her? You said he never sexually abused her. But do you know why she was too scared to say anything, to help you. Don't you think that knowing Macie like you do, that maybe, just maybe there was a very good reason why she couldn't help you."

"She should have run last night. Hell, she should have run the second she discovered all of this, but she didn't. She stood here last night and took whatever punishment you delivered because she felt she deserved it. She knows she was wrong, she knows she hurt you and she's willing to see this through because she wants you to punish her. But she doesn't fucking deserve it, Leon."

I stand there silently, feeling like a scolded child as she pins me with a fierce look.

"I get your need for... for this," she says gesturing around the room. "Hell knows I've been there. And hate sex, well, it doesn't really get much hotter. But you've got to talk to her. You share something that no one else can understand, not really. Did you ever consider the fact that you weren't ever meant to find her for revenge, but because she's the only one who can help heal you, help fix everything that's all fucked up in your head?"

"Letty," I sigh, hating how well she's got all this figured out.

"Leon, Macie is... She's the sweetest person. The kindest person. And despite her better judgment, she's still here. Still fighting for you."

I think of her brutal honesty last night.

"You wouldn't be saying that if you heard the things that she spat at me only hours ago."

"The truth?" Letty asks.

A knock at the door halts our conversation and I walk across the space to get the coffee I ordered.

Placing it on the coffee table, I fall down on the couch only for Letty to copy my move only two seconds later.

"What do you want, Leon? What do you really want?"

"I want it all to go away. The memories, the nightmares, the pain."

"And you think hurting her will do that?"

I shrug because I have no fucking clue what it will take to achieve the peace I need.

"I think you know exactly what you want, you're just too chickenshit to admit it. I should have taken Kane up on his offer of coming here with me to knock some sense into you," she mutters, stealing my coffee seeing as I didn't offer her one and taking a sip. "This needs some sugar. You need sweetening up."

I watch her as she drinks half the mug before finally passing it over. "Thanks," I mutter, rolling my eyes at her.

"So what happens now?"

"Continue with my bullshit life?"

"What about him? You know where he is now, you can't tell me that you're just going to ignore that."

"I'm not telling you anything."

"And Brett? We know you know where he is."

"He's gone."

"Good. He should have fucked off years ago. But that's not the point."

"What is the point exactly, Letty?"

"The point is that if you fuck this up, you're going to end up allowing them all to ruin your life as you rot away in prison for all this. Don't think I haven't worked out why you're suddenly friends with the Harrises, Lee. It's not a fucking coincidence."

"What if it is?"

"I'm not fucking stupid so don't treat me like it." She pushes to stand, running her fingers through her hair and letting out a long sigh. It's the first time I notice just how exhausted she looks.

"We're all here, Leon. We all want to help. All you've got to do is let us in."

"And if you don't like what you see?"

"Goddammit. We love you, Lee. Some fucked-up event from your past doesn't change that. It doesn't change who you are. We love you for the slightly broken, dark parts of your soul. Your past makes you you. But if you want a future, you need to embrace it, accept it for what it was and find a way to move forward."

"You've got an amazing girl out there who needs to heal just as badly. You can put your own pain aside for a bit and help her too, come out of it together, or you can both drown together. But let me tell you now, that both of you are too fucking awesome to drown.

"But that's your decision to make.

"Are you going to fight, or are you going to give up and let all of this consume you until there's nothing left?"

With that said, she turns her back on me and storms out of the suite, leaving nothing but her words hanging in the air.

"Goddammit," I boom, throwing the mug and what's left inside at the wall, watching as it shatters, much like my life.

She's only been gone a few minutes when my cell starts ringing. Pulling it from my pocket, I groan at the name staring back at me.

Swiping the screen, I put it to my ear.

"What the hell did you do to my brother?" Reid barks.

"He was helping me burn off steam."

"Jesus, how much steam did you need to get rid of? You did a fucking number on your old man too."

"Shit was fucked up."

"Yeah, I get that man. But listen, as fun as continually leaving him half-dead is, you need to put an end to it. You can't go into a new season with this hanging over you."

"That's months away."

"This isn't you, Leon."

"What the hell do you know about me?" I snap.

"Fine. Fine. But if you don't make a decision soon, I'm going to make it for you. You can't continue like this."

"What about my other issue?" I ask, knowing that Brett isn't the only life hanging on by a thread right now.

"We're on it. Working out a plan of action. I'll be in touch once we have something."

"Great."

"Leon?"

"Yeah," I mutter.

"Don't beat the crap out of my brother again. I need his ass to keep business running."

"Yeah, sure," I agree, hanging up on him before he can do it to me.

I fall back on the couch with a sigh.

I need to go back to reality and deal with all this shit. But really, I just want to let myself drown here.

―――――

"Lee," Luca's deep voice booms up the stairs seconds after I heard the doorbell ring. "You've got a visitor."

I still. She wouldn't come here. Not after she ran in the middle of the night, would she?

My chest aches as I think about finding her side of the bed empty this morning.

I needed her after that nightmare, I fucking needed her and she'd left.

"Leon," he calls again.

"Get rid of them, I'm not interested."

"That ain't gonna work, Bro," I hear the amusement in his tone and it just pisses me off.

"I'm busy jerking off," I lie, "Get rid of them."

I don't hear anything else, and I can only assume that he's done as I've said and I lift my laptop again. That is until the floorboard outside my room creaks and my door is pushed open.

"Luc, I said get rid of— oh," I breathe when my visitor appears.

One look in her eyes and she bursts into tears.

"Shit," I throw my laptop on my bed and scramble up, pulling her trembling body into my arms. "I'm so sorry, Mom."

"I-it's n-not your f-fault, Lee. I'm the one who should b-be s-sorry. I'm your mom and I didn't know," she sobs, making me hold her tighter.

Fucking Luca.

"I didn't want you to know. It's not your fault."

"But I should have known. I should have seen it, sensed it. I failed you."

"No, Mom. No. You didn't. The only person who failed me was Dad."

She pulls her head from my chest, my heart constricting at the sight of the tears streaming down her cheeks.

"H-he knew?"

I nod, not that she needs me to confirm it. She knows.

"Fucking asshole. How could he? How could he do that to you?" she seethes.

"It's okay, Mom."

"No," she snaps, ripping herself from my arms. "No it's not, Lee. He let you go there knowing that you were being... being hurt. I'll kill him. I'll fucking kill him for hurting my baby." Her body vibrates with anger as she stands in the middle of the room looking like her world is crumbling around her. "I hate him," she sobs, her voice broken and utterly defeated. "I hate him so much."

"Mom," I say softly, taking a step toward her.

She stares at my chest for a moment before her eyes roll up to meet mine.

"I'm so sorry," she sobs, throwing herself at me, breaking down in my arms.

My own eyes burn with emotion as I move us backward and sit down on the edge of my bed.

"Everything is going to be okay, Mom," I say softly. Even though everything feels anything but fine right now, I know that I need to do whatever I can to make it that way. Mom, Luca, Shane, Macie, Libby, we've all been through too much to have to keep dealing with this shit.

It's time to finally put an end to the asshole who's controlled our lives for so long.

I think about Reid's words from earlier. He's right.

Torturing Brett has been fun, freeing in a way. But I can't keep it up.

Every time I go there, every time I look into his traitorous eyes a little more of his poison trickles through my veins.

"Do you know where he is?" Mom asks.

"B-Brett?" I ask, wondering briefly if she means Richard.

"Yeah."

I shake my head, hating that our mom was subjected to his bullshit for so long.

I know she's as suspicious as Luca after what went down with Peyton and Libby but I refuse to put this weight on her shoulders as well.

"I don't."

She pulls away from me.

"Leon Dunn, if you are lying to me I'll—"

"Mom," I breathe.

"S-sorry. I just don't want you to end up in trouble because of him. He doesn't deserve any of your time or attention. He needs to rot in hell for all the shit he's pulled, all the pain he's caused."

"Couldn't agree more." And that's exactly where I'm going to send him.

"So..." Mom starts and I suck in a breath knowing that she's about to change the subject and pull the rug from beneath me once more. "Luca mentioned a girl."

Jesus.

"Of course he did," I mutter, anger swirling within me at his need to stick his nose right in the middle of my business by getting Mom involved in this.

"He said it could be serious."

Fucking hell.

I scrub my hand down my face wondering how I'm going to get out of this.

"She's Richard Fletcher's niece."

She stills in my arms.

"Oh that's a... coincidence."

"Yeah. Coincidence," I mutter.

"Leon," she warns, her eyes pinning me with a warning look that I remember all too well from my childhood.

"Probably best you don't know."

"Leon, if you've hurt—"

"Mom, can we please not? Things are... complicated."

"Yeah," she breathes. "When aren't they?" She falls silent for a moment and I allow her the time to think. All of this must have hit her like a wrecking ball after all. "Leon," she says much softer this time. "Life is too short to mess around. If you think she can make you happy, then you need to go for it. You've been through too much already to miss out on something that could give you the peace you need."

She places her hand on my bruised cheek and I lift mine to it.

"Follow your heart, Lee. Not your anger," she begs.

My lips part to respond but I find pretty quickly that I have no words for her.

"I'm going to see Kayden in a bit. I promised him I'd take him to the arcade." A smile twitches at my lips that despite our cunt of a father, that my little brother has the most incredible family around him. "You up for it?"

"Yeah, yeah I am."

"Get ready and I'll meet you downstairs."

She pushes from my bed and walks toward the door but she turns back to me before disappearing.

"I'm not going to push you to talk, Lee. But when—if—you're ready, I'm right here. Nothing you can tell me will ever change how I feel about you. Nothing you could do could change how much I love you."

"Thanks, Mom," I say, forcing the words past the lump in my throat.

"But for the love of God, you need to stop fighting. It's ruining your pretty face," she says, lightening the mood.

"What, this?" I ask, pointing to myself. "All the girls love a bad boy, didn't you know that?"

She shakes her head and laughs as she disappears from my room muttering, "It sounds like you only need to worry about one girl."

I laugh to myself for a beat, before pushing from the bed and finding a change of clothes. Mom's right, I look like hell so I need to at least try to look a little more presentable.

Music booms from one of the guys' rooms beneath ours as I make my way down the stairs to find Mom but I don't see anyone until I step into the kitchen.

Then, both Luca and Mom glance up at me from their seats on the counter with matching apprehensive expressions on their faces.

"Don't stop on my behalf."

"We weren't talking about you," Mom argues.

"Sure."

As I close the distance between us, Luca stands from his stool and walks toward me.

"I'm sorry, but I had to—"

"It's okay," I say, opening my arms and pulling him in for a hug. "I'm glad you did." He hesitates for a second before his hand lands on my back.

"Where's Peyton?" I ask, noting her absence.

"She's helping get Libby set up at the rehab facility."

"She's finally been discharged?" I ask, a genuine smile pulling at my lips.

"Yep. Fingers crossed this next stage of her recovery is as easy."

I nod at him. "You coming with us?"

"To the arcade? Hell yeah." He slaps me on the shoulder. "Come on, Bro. Let's go be normal for a change."

I walk out of the house with Luc and Mom and for the first time in a long time, a little bit of hope flutters in my belly.

Maybe there is a future for me in spite of my dark past.

MACIE

I felt guilty as hell calling Letty in the middle of the night, but there was no way I was getting into a taxi wearing only Leon's blood-stained shirt, and I also knew that I couldn't stay.

I might have drifted off to sleep quite easily but that was only because of the alcohol and the fact I was exhausted. The second I woke with a start, realization slamming into me, I knew I couldn't be there when he woke up.

By some miracle I managed to slip out of the tight hold he had on me and silently padded across the room without waking him.

I ignored my ruined dress and opted for his shirt instead. I regretted it the second I pulled it over my head and found myself surrounded by his intoxicating scent. But I knew I had no other choice.

I dialed Letty's number and prayed that she'd answer. My other option was Nate or Charlie and I really didn't want to get them involved and stuck in the middle of all of this. Nate has already had to deal with Leon's anger, that's more than enough. Letty knows though. She understands. And I knew she knew she'd pick me up looking like the car crash that I was, not judging me for a second.

There's something so refreshing about just being in her presence and I was so freaking relieved when she answered her cell on the third ring and told me that she'd be here in less than thirty minutes. I was even more relieved when she turned up alone. I trust Letty, which means I trust Kane, but equally, I didn't need him seeing me like this.

The second she pulled up in front of the hotel, I ran from the dark corner I'd hidden myself in and jumped into her car.

And as if she knew just how desperately I needed to get away, she floored the accelerator and got the hell out of there.

I had no idea if she should have been driving. She was drinking at the party and I don't know how much she actually had.

She didn't speak for the longest time, she just allowed me to drown in my own regrets after the events of the night. All she did was reach her hand over and squeeze mine tightly as she drove us across town.

When she did speak, she didn't ask what had happened, how I ended up in his bloody shirt or why I was running, she just simply asked if I wanted to go back to theirs instead of going to the dorms.

But as tempting as hiding in her apartment was, I knew it was wrong.

I told her to bring me back here, and she did. And it wasn't until we were safely inside my room after she insisted on walking me up that I broke down and told her everything.

"Kill him, Macie. Kill him," Nate shouts, dragging me back to the here and now.

I glance at the screen to see the guy he's shouting about and aim my gun in his direction.

"Shit, that was close," he breathes, continuing on with the game and ignoring the fact that I'm clearly not paying an ounce of attention to what's going on.

Glancing over at him, I wince at the state of his face. Guilt coils its way around me. It's a feeling that I'm more than used to, but not when it comes to Nate. That feeling usually only belongs to Leon.

"I'm okay, Mace. You don't need to keep looking at me like I'm about to break. It's not the first time someone's punched me, and I doubt it'll be the last."

"That's not the point," I mutter as he pauses the game so he can turn his attention solely on me. "It never should have happened in the first place."

He stares at me, one brow lifting.

"He's possessive for someone who claims he doesn't want you, don't you think?"

"He doesn't want me. It's—"

"Complicated. I know, you've said. A few times, actually."

I hold his eyes, begging him not to ask me what happened last night again.

I might have been forthcoming with the information with Letty, but Nathan doesn't need details of what happened. He wouldn't understand, of that I'm sure.

Nathan is so sweet, gentle, caring. That hearing how Leon treated me—despite the fact I would argue that I wanted it—would horrify him, I'm sure.

No, what happened last night is better kept quiet. My memories need to stay locked up in that little box where I've pushed everything I don't want to deal with for years now. I'm well practiced at it. If I don't, I fear I might start thinking about doing something crazy. Like turning up at his front door and demanding he do it again.

I slam the door shut on that line of thought before it runs away with me.

"I think I'm done with this," I say, putting the controller down on Nate's bed and standing from where we were sitting side by side resting back against his headboard. "I need some fresh air."

"Want company?" he asks, following my move and dropping the controller as he kicks his legs off the bed.

"No, I'm okay. I'm just going to walk around for a bit, then I've got assignments to do."

"You could have the night off, you know."

"Like I did last night?" I regret the question the second it falls from my mouth because I know it'll only make him more suspicious. "I won't be long."

I walk out of his room without looking back because I just know the pity I'll see that's going to be written all over his face.

I grab my purse and jacket and slip out of the dorm. Jogging down the stairs, I take a left and head across campus. I breathe in the early evening air, hoping it'll help settle me in the way this place has since I first arrived.

This place felt like home until I drove back into town on Friday. Now it just feels like everywhere else I've been. A place where I merely survive.

I don't realize how far I've walked until I approach the entrance for the park where I come every Monday night.

There's hardly anyone around as I walk through the gates and make my way to my bench.

Lowering myself down, I suck in what I hope is a calming breath. But it doesn't help. This place is as tainted by him as everywhere else.

For just those few short days, he became such a huge part of my life that now it feels like he's left a huge gaping hole with his absence.

I hate it.

He shouldn't have been able to worm his way in that easily.

I've spent my life building up my walls, refusing to let anyone close to me and somehow he managed to obliterate them without me even knowing.

I sit there for the longest time looking out over the town laid out before me as the sun sinks behind the horizon and lights begin to illuminate the darkness.

I'm so lost in my own head that I startle when my cell pings in my purse.

"Please don't be the freaking security alarm again," I mutter to myself, opening the zipper and reaching inside. The last thing I need is to go back to that house any time soon. It was already full of bad memories, and now Leon's only made them worse.

Knowing that was him that day makes me feel physically sick.

I never once forgot what I did that day—or what I didn't do—and I often wondered what happened to him. That is until the awful possibilities of how he might have dealt with what my uncle did, used to hit me and I would shove it all back in the box.

I never expected that little boy to remember me, to actively look for me all these years later.

I certainly never expected to fall for him.

I drop my head, holding my cell in my hand as pain engulfs me, wrapping around my chest until I find it hard to suck in my next breath.

Needing a distraction, I turn my cell over and stare down at the screen but that distraction I crave never comes because the name staring back at me makes my heart jump into my chest.

Leon.

My hand trembles as I stare down at it, wishing I could read whatever he has to say without it showing that I've read it.

I sit there for long minutes telling myself that I don't care what he's said. That I'm just going to delete it and never know.

After all, he probably hates me for leaving like I did last night. From how tightly he was holding me, I got the impression he didn't want me going anywhere.

In the end though, my curiosity gets the better of me and I swipe the screen, tapping on the app and opening his message.

> Leon: The windows are privacy glass. No one but me saw you last night.

All the air rushes from my lungs as I stare down at his words.

The memory of being pressed up against the windows as he whispered all those wicked things in my ear about others being able to see me hits me and my skin heats.

I didn't want to like the idea of being on show for everyone, but some dark and twisted part of me loved it. Loved showing the world that I was finally being punished for what I did. That karma was showing her hand and delivering me the retaliation I deserved.

I squirm on the bench remembering his hands on my body, the way he teased, licked and bit me.

Dammit.

No, damn him.

I hate him. But... but I can't deny that I want him. That his dark and cracked parts don't align perfectly with mine.

I want to help him, I want to show him that it's possible to put my uncle behind him and live a life that's not full of hate and anger but I'm not sure he'll ever let himself do that.

Maybe once he's got his revenge, a little voice in my head says as trepidation for what he's planning races through me.

He knows where my uncle is now. What's his next move? How is he going to get to him, if that's what he's even intending? That place is secured like Fort Knox. He's not just going to be able to walk in, dish out whatever punishment he deems worthy and walk out again.

I startle when my screen lights up once more.

> Leon: I'm sorry.

Pain pierces my chest as I stare at those two words.

Two words I never thought I'd hear—or see—from him.

The urge to reply is so strong it almost gets the better of me. But only seconds later, I realize I don't have to.

> Leon: You look beautiful in the moonlight.

My heart jumps into my throat.

Is he here?

Is he watching me?

No, he can't be. Why would he randomly end up in this park? This is my park.

I lower my cell, staring at the path before me for a few seconds before I risk looking up.

My breath catches when I look at the entrance and find a dark figure in the shadows.

His ominous presence might terrify some people. Hell, being out in the light he should terrify me, especially now I know what he's capable of but that's far from the case because even at this distance, the chemistry that I'm becoming used to crackles between us as the tether I always feel between us pulls tighter.

But I can't. I know I can't.

Standing, I keep my eyes on him for a beat so he knows I've seen him then I lift my cell and tap out a very simple and to the point reply.

> Macie: I'm sorry too.

Then I turn and leave the park in the opposite direction. Tears fall from my eyes with every step I take, but I know it's the right thing to do.

Last night was... intense, incredible, so many things, and it would be so easy to fall into the abyss with Leon and drown with him.

But I haven't fought my entire life to drown in someone else's darkness.

It's late by the time I get back to my dorm, much later than I was intending and thankfully, my tears have long dried up. All I can hope for is that I look stronger than I feel so I don't invite even more questions and concern from Nathan when I step inside.

"Jesus, Macie. I've been so worried about you."

"I'm sorry, I lost track of time," I lie, cringing as the words pass my lips.

"I've been calling but your cell is off."

"Yeah, I forgot to charge it last night. I'm gonna..." I point down the hall toward my room.

"You're okay though, right?"

"Yeah, Nate. I'm good. It'll take more than Leon Dunn to bring me down."

He smiles at me, but it doesn't meet his eyes. He knows I'm lying but for whatever reason he decides not to call me out on it and lets it go. For now at least.

———

To my surprise, I never heard another word from Leon that night. Part of me expected him to turn up at my dorm to try to talk to me. It was obvious he wanted to, but there was no sign of him, and the others never said that he tried.

I should feel relieved that he's decided to leave me alone, but I'm not. Mostly, I'm concerned. The Leon I experienced on Saturday night wasn't in a good place and I have no idea where he's gone from there.

I left after he gave me what I'd asked of him and started to open up. In hindsight, maybe leaving wasn't the best thing. Maybe I should have stayed and pushed harder.

All these questions and what-ifs run around my head on repeat for the next three days.

Letty checks in on me every day but she wisely steers clear of talking about Leon when I make a point of not asking how he is. Yesterday, we had lunch together, Peyton too, who was happily telling me about her sister's recovery from an overdose. It's good to hear something positive for a change and I pray that her sister continues to fight her demons. They talk about Kane and Luca, but still, skirt around the topic of Leon and what has happened between us.

It's both a relief and torture at the same time.

Talking about it makes it all feel so real, but at the same time, ignoring it makes me start to believe none of it really happened, that the connection we shared even briefly wasn't there. He might have been playing me all that time, but you can't fake that kind of chemistry. I might not have a lot of experience with such things, but of that I'm sure.

I didn't need Saturday night to confirm that, but it sure solidified the fact.

I don't receive any more messages from him. Yet multiple times a day I stare at my cell wishing there was something, anything to let me know that he's okay.

I watch the clock as it ticks around to the end of my study session on Wednesday night. I never rejoined the one I walked out on that night with Leon, but thankfully another group allowed me to join them. I can't help wondering if they're regretting it already because it's not like I've contributed much tonight. In fact, much like the last session I attended, I have no idea what they're even talking about.

Movement at the end of the aisle of books beside us catches my eye. I have no idea why, but my skin prickles like I'm being watched.

My heart jumps into my throat thinking that it could be him, that he could be here waiting for me.

Butterflies explode in my belly.

It's wrong, so wrong but I can't help craving his dirty words and brutal touch.

"Okay so, I think we should call it a night, I'm starving," the guy who seems to be in charge of this little group says. I've been paying so little attention that I don't even know any of their names.

A round of agreement sounds out as everyone starts packing up, but I don't move. I'm frozen to the spot thinking that he's standing in the shadows watching me like the other night in the park.

When I look over again, I don't find anyone and I tell myself that I'm being stupid and letting my imagination run wild.

He's not here. He's not interested. He got what he wanted from me and he's moved on.

The realization sends pain shooting through my chest, but the sooner I accept it, the better it will be in the long run.

Everyone says their goodbyes and disappears toward the exit while I slowly begin to pack my stuff away.

I force myself to keep my eyes on my things and not look back, but that becomes impossible when a shadow falls over me and a familiar scent fills my nose.

It was him.

He was watching you.

My breath catches in my throat as I wait to see what he's going to do. What he's going to say.

"Macie?" he breathes, forcing all the air from my lungs in a rush.

My spine straightens yet my body still refuses to turn to look at him because I know that the second I look into his eyes, everything might come crashing down around me.

I might be worried about him. I might be missing him, craving him. But it still doesn't erase our past, his actions, his lies.

"What do you want, Leon?" I snap, my voice coming out colder than I was expecting.

"I just... I just want to talk, Macie." His rough voice hits me where I'm sure he intended it to.

Is this genuine or is he just playing me all over again?

I hate to doubt his intentions. But it's his own fault.

He should expect it after he shattered my trust by proving all my insecurities right.

He never was with me because he wanted to be. It was all a game. A game to get exactly what he wanted, consequences be damned. Just like every other football player I've ever met. My own father couldn't get his own way, so he took the easy way out after Mom died and left me alone to deal with both their deaths. My uncle, well, he did anything in his power to make sure his life was as perfect as he wanted it to be. And then there's Leon. Is he really any better than them?

Sucking in a deep breath, I throw my shoulders back and turn around, immediately finding his eyes.

"You want to talk?" I ask, holding my voice steady. "What exactly do you want to talk about?" Fear flickers across his features as if I'm about to stand here and announce to the entire library that he was abused by my uncle. "How you played me?" I forge on, not allowing his feelings to dampen down my anger. "How you tied me up in a bathroom Saturday night and left me? For hours," I hiss.

"Macie, please."

"Why should I?" I scoff, turning my back on him once again and stuffing my books into my bag.

"Because you're right. Everything you said on Saturday. You're right."

"I don't trust a word that comes out of your mouth anymore, Leon. You got what you wanted. You stole my first time from me, you've got my uncle's location. What more do you need?"

"You," he states as his warm fingers wrap around my upper arm and spins me back to him.

He takes a step forward until the heat of his body seeps into me.

I stare up into his dark green eyes. But unlike all the other times they've been this color, it's been with anger. Right now, it's pure emotion.

He makes it sound so simple. Just pushes aside everything we've been through as if it never happened.

"Leon, it's not that eas—"

"Nothing worth fighting for is easy."

"You're not playing fair," I whisper.

"I thought you already realized that I don't play by the rules, Red." He smirks, and part of me wants to smile too. But then I remember just how true those words are.

"You should go," I say, pulling my bag up higher on my shoulder.

"Not without you. I've spent all week planning what I want to say to you. I can't wait any longer."

"You don't owe me anything."

His hand slides down my arm until his fingers tease mine but he never completely captures them.

"I do. I owe you the truth. I owe you all the things I've never been brave enough to say."

I shake my head, refusing to accept his words.

"Everything you went through... it's almost as much my fault as it was his. You owe me nothing. What you did last week. I understand. It hurts. But I get it. I know why you went after me. If the roles were reversed, maybe I would've done the same. I condemned you to that hell. I deserve everything you can throw at me."

"No," he states much more firmly than I was expecting. "But I don't want to do this here. Please, just give me an hour. If after that hour, if how you feel still stands, then I'll let you walk away as if none of this ever happened."

I gasp, dragging my bottom lip into my mouth as I gaze up at him.

Does he really mean that?

"I do."

I startle when I realize that I must have asked that out loud.

"One hour. You have one hour to say what you need to say and then you take me home. No games."

"No games," he agrees.

With a slight nod, I pull my fingers away from him, taking off across the library following the journey of the others I was here with tonight but knowing that he's hot on my heels.

Nothing is said as he steps up beside me as we walk toward the parking lot until we approach his car.

He opens the passenger door for me but I hesitate before dropping into the seat, questioning my sanity for agreeing to this.

"I'm not playing you, Macie."

"Yeah, I've heard that before."

He reaches out and tucks a lock of my hair behind my ear. My entire body tenses at the move but my skin burns as his finger brushes me.

"I'll never lie to you again. Anything you want to know, I'll tell you."

"Anything?" I ask, praying that he's being honest with me because if I even consider trusting him with this and he ruins it again, it's going to break me.

"Anything."

"Fine. Your one hour starts now."

Ripping my eyes away from his, I drop into the seat and fasten my seat belt.

"Thank you," he breathes, closing the door behind me and jogging around the hood to join me.

12

LEON

All week I've fought my need to see her. I've tracked her cell around campus, my muscles twitching to walk out of my own classes so I could go and join hers, wait for her when she was finished, or just pull out the seat beside her in the coffee shop and just be with her.

But I didn't.

I stayed strong and gave her the space she needs after she walked away from me on Sunday night.

Watching her turn her back on me after I followed her there was brutal, but no less than I deserve.

But tonight when I saw that she was in the library again, probably suffering through another dull as fuck study session when she could be doing something much more fun, my restraint snapped.

I've spent all week drowning in my misery, trying to come up with how I can bring all of this to an end that doesn't involve ruining my life in the process.

Everyone around me is right. It's time to properly start dealing with all this shit and look forward, not back like I've done for the past decade.

Richard Fletcher has taken enough from me. My innocence, my

childhood, I refuse to let him have my future or any more of my happiness.

He shouldn't hold that power over me.

I breathe out a calming breath as I wrap my fingers around the door handle and pull it open, knowing that I'm about to get assaulted by her coconut scent and lose myself entirely to her presence.

She's addictive.

She's also mine, she just might not realize it yet.

She sits in silence, twisting her hands in her lap as I start the car and back out of the space.

A million and one questions dance on the tip of my tongue but I swallow them all down, not wanting to bombard her when she's clearly already questioning her sanity by allowing this to happen.

The second I'm off campus, I floor the gas, speeding us toward a place I know that we can be alone to talk.

She's given me an hour and like fuck am I wasting any of that time by driving like an old woman across town.

A little whimper rumbles up her throat as I take a corner a little too fast and I can't help but smile. My innocent little Macie loves the thrill of a fast ride, even if she won't admit it.

Images from Saturday night come back to me and my cock swells in my pants as I think about her hot little body pressed up against the hotel window.

The Macie I met that first night when I was with Charlie who looked like a rabbit caught in headlights never would have stood there like that thinking that everyone below could see her beautiful naked body.

But my Macie isn't the shy one everyone else sees. She sheds her pretense, that mask that everyone sees when she's with me and I get to experience the woman she's forced into hiding all these years.

What I want to know is why. Why does she feel the need to hide the incredible woman that she is and what she really wants?

I mean, I know the answer.

It's him.

The same cunt who ruined my life.

But we both know what he did to me. What he took from me.

What I want to know is how he crushed her soul, her spirit because I already know it was in a different way to me.

I'm glad it was different. I'm glad he never touched her like that. But I know that there are plenty of other things that could have hurt her just as badly.

"Leon?" she questions when I turn into the overgrown dirt road I brought her down the night we had our first date. Only this time when the trees open up before us, there is no canopy or twinkling fairy lights. It's just the two of us tonight. Two broken souls that have dark secrets that the rest of the world have no right knowing. "You're not playing fair," she whispers breathily.

"I wanted us to be alone."

"There are a million places that could happen. Why bring me back here?"

"Because it holds good memories, and I think we're going to need them around us for what we need to talk about."

"Why?" she asks, still refusing to look at me.

"Because I want to know everything. I want to understand. I want to take your pain away."

"You can't, just like no one can take yours."

She pushes the door open and climbs out before I get a chance to say anything.

I stay in my seat and watch as she walks toward the lake's edge.

She kicks her shoes off and steps into the water.

I give her ten seconds more before I push the door open and join her.

Coming to stand beside her, I leave a couple of inches between us despite the fact I'm damn near dying being this close and not touching her.

Swallowing around the giant lump in my throat, I clench my fists and start talking.

"I thought he saw something special in me. I knew I was better than most of the boys at camp thanks to our father's endless training and insistence that we be the best. I thought that was why he invited me to his office the first time to see his trophies, to experience what a successful career in the NFL really looked like.

"Of course, I'd lived every day of my life listening to my father talk about it, but hearing stories from someone else about how it's the best job in the world was addictive. I ate up every single word he said.

"I might have been forced into football but it was still my life. The sport ran through my veins from the day I was born. It still does. It's just tainted with pain now."

"Leon, you don't—"

"No, Macie, I do. It's time I let some of this out."

Toeing off my shoes, I move a little deeper into the water, not caring about the fact it's going to start soaking up my pants. All I care about right now is Macie and finding a way out of this black hole I've been living in for so long.

"I thought he genuinely cared, that he just wanted me to succeed because I was his friend's son. I was so wrong. And I trusted him way too easily."

"We were out training one day and I pulled my hamstring. It wasn't bad, not really but it meant I had to sit out the afternoon which pissed me off.

"Richard told me that he wanted me to get it checked out and to head up to his office once the others all headed back to their rooms to shower and get ready for dinner.

"Well," I say with a shudder. "Safe to say he never actually checked my leg, and when I finally left that room, my hamstring wasn't the only reason why I was limping."

A sob rips from her throat, her hand covering her mouth, and I know that if I were to actually look over, I'd find tears glistening in the moonlight on her cheeks.

"I was so ashamed of what I let him do," I continue. "All the others, Luca included, were in the cafeteria having dinner by the time I got back but I walked straight past them and threw myself into bed.

"I had every intention of pretending I was asleep by the time they all reappeared but I don't actually remember them coming back. I think I cried myself to sleep. My body allowing me the reprieve from the memories and the pain that ripped through my body."

"Jesus, Leon. I'm so—"

"Don't," I snap. "Don't tell me you're sorry. That's not why I'm telling you. I don't want your pity. I don't even want your guilt. Not anymore," I confess.

"But I could have stopped it."

"No, baby," I say softly. "You couldn't."

"But I could have told—"

"He got away with it for years, Red. The confession of one eight-year-old girl wasn't going to stop him. He was *the* Richard Fletcher. He was loved in every state, he was hero-worshiped for his abilities on the field. No one would have ever believed you over him."

"But I could have got evidence or something."

Unable to stop myself, I finally reach out and tangle our fingers together.

I half expect her to pull away but she doesn't and I like to think she can sense just how much I need this right now. That she knows how much she settles everything inside me just by being here.

"His actions aren't on you, Red. None of that was your fault."

"Not what you said before," she mutters, anger filling her tone.

"I've said a lot of things before. Many that haven't been true."

A sad laugh rips from her lips as she thinks back to all the lies I've told her in the past few weeks, I'm sure that's what she's thinking.

"I hate him so much. It has eaten away at me for ten fucking years, Macie. I had to direct it somewhere or it would have destroyed me."

"So you thought you'd destroy me instead?"

"I never thought I'd ever find you. I'd made you out to be this evil, sadistic bitch in my head. I'd imagined all the ways I could punish you for that day and as the weeks and years passed it morphed into an obsession. All I could think about was getting my hands on the both of you, how badly I could make it hurt. How I could ruin your lives like you both did mine."

"And now?" she asks simply.

"Now there's only one of you that I want to hurt. Actually, no. That's not true. I don't want to hurt him. I just want to end him."

"There's not much of him left," she says quietly. "He's not the person you remember any more. He's... That man who hurt you, he died years long before he ended up in that place."

"If that's your way of trying to tell me not to go after him, then I've got to tell you, baby, that it's not possible. I might know that I was wrong about you. But him? Never."

"I'm not stopping you from doing anything."

Finally, she turns her head and looks at me.

Her blue eyes are dark, full of anger, hate and unshed tears making my breath catch in my throat.

"W-what are you saying?"

"Did you know that I was the one who found my dad?" she asks, her voice suddenly hollow, completely void of emotion.

"N-no."

"I was only in kindergarten. So young and innocent. Yeah, I'd experienced death. Losing my mom was brutal, but I didn't understand it. I just knew that she was gone and never coming back. I knew that Dad was broken because of it.

"I remember sitting at the top of the stairs at night listening to him cry, shouting, breaking things, in his attempt to deal with his loss.

"I thought it would get better. That's what everyone was telling me. That the pain would lessen and life would continue, albeit differently.

"But Dad wasn't getting any better. He was drinking heavily, although of course I didn't know that at the time. All I knew was that he wasn't the man I knew. When he spoke to me he sounded different, when he held me, he wasn't as soft."

I flinch at her words and she notices.

"He never hurt me. But he was drowning and thought by holding me tighter, he might just stay afloat.

"But then I came home that day with my nanny. She went to the kitchen because she promised me that we could make cookies and I ran upstairs to change and wash my hands.

"I knew something was wrong the second I got to the top of the stairs. I don't know how, I just sensed it.

"Dad's bedroom door was always closed. He barely went in the room after Mom died, it was too painful for him. But that afternoon, it was wide open.

"Without thinking, I walked inside, calling out for him. There was no response."

My heart thunders in my chest, my hands trembling because I

know what's coming next. I know how he died, I just had no idea she was the one to discover the truth.

No child. Hell, no adult, should be subjected to what she found that day.

"It was the puddle on the bathroom floor that made me walk in that direction. Only, what I thought was water, I soon discovered was something else."

She's so strong as she recalls those events. Her voice is solid, unwavering as if she's talking about someone else, or even a movie she's watched.

An overwhelming sense of pride for her washes through me.

I have no idea how she's done it. How she's survived and can stand here now bleeding out her reality as if it doesn't hurt like hell, because I know it does.

She's just fucking stronger than anyone I've ever met before, and that's really saying something because I'm surrounded by some fucking fierce people.

A crack of thunder in the distance startles both of us, and when I drag my eyes from Macie's I find the stars that were twinkling above us are quickly being swallowed by angry storm clouds.

It seems eerily fitting.

"He was lying on the floor, curled up in the fetal position, a blade still in one hand and a photograph of the three of us when I was a baby in the other." Finally, her voice cracks with emotion as she recalls the scene.

I take a step toward her as her first tear falls but she holds her hand up, stopping me from doing what I so desperately need to and pull her body into mine.

"I remember screaming. I remember my nanny's feet thundering up the stairs but then it all gets hazy. I have vague images of paramedics, police, and other people I didn't recognize. I remember my nanny holding me, her tears dropping into my hair, her body trembling. But I didn't remember crying myself.

"The one thing I do remember as vividly as if it happened this morning was the look on my uncle's face as he walked toward me hours later.

"We were still at the house. It was the last place I wanted to be but it wasn't like I had much choice. I had no family aside from him.

"I have no idea what he was in the middle of, but it was abundantly clear the second he looked at me that he wasn't happy about being dragged away from it.

"I never liked him. He was cold, unwelcoming. Nothing like he was portrayed in the media. But even my dad used to say good things about him so I wanted to believe it was all in my head. That really, he was just as nice as my dad. They were brothers after all.

"I have no idea if it was just me he hated, or all kids. I could only assume that seeing as he ran a summer camp for gifted boys that it was just me.

"He gathered up the bags that my nanny had packed for me and all but pushed me out of the house. Although, looking back, I'm sure it didn't look as bad as it felt, social services never would have let me leave with him, or at least I like to think that would've been the case.

"The second he got into the car with me, he demanded that I keep my mouth shut and do my best to make myself invisible.

"I remember trying to curl myself up so deep into the seat, trying to hide, hoping that it might just swallow me whole and that I could go and be with my parents."

"Fucking hell, Macie," I say, my own voice sounding much more effected by her story than hers.

I close the space between us once more, and this time she allows it.

Wrapping my arms around her, I discover that she's not dealing with this as well as she appears because her entire body is trembling violently.

Another clap of thunder echoes around us, but she doesn't even try to move, just stands there trembling as I hold her.

"Everyone told me that losing a parent as a young child was probably the worst thing I'll ever experience," she whispers so quietly I probably wouldn't hear it if she wasn't pressed against me. "But clearly, they were wrong, because losing two and being committed to life with your neglectful and abusive uncle was the worst thing that any child could experience."

My arms tighten around her as I drop my nose to her hair,

breathing her in and hoping that she can find some strength from me. Not that I have much of it left. I can barely keep myself standing most days, I have no idea how I'm meant to hold her up too. But I'll do everything I can to make it fucking happen because she deserves it.

"My room at his house," she says. "It was nothing more than a prison when I was forced to be there. He would ignore me for days on end, leaving the door locked forcing me to stay inside. There were so many days when the only thing that passed my lips was water from the faucet in my bathroom.

"The day he swung my door open and demanded I pack a bag because I was leaving was one of the best days of my life.

"School was hell, I hated it. I never fitted in. But I didn't care, because for the first time someone actually cared about me again.

"Okay, so it wasn't the same because it was their job. But it didn't matter to me. I was just grateful to be fed every day and to be treated like a person, not an unwanted pet."

I suck in a shaky breath wondering for the first time if I actually got the better end of the deal with Richard. At least I was only subjected to him for a few weeks of the year and I was forgotten when he was done with me, able to continue with my life. But Macie... What she had to live through...

"I went back there for the first few summers before he figured out he could dump me at some camp wherever he could find one. I have no idea why he didn't think of it sooner seeing as he ran a camp of his own but I never questioned his decisions because I knew it would only result in pain."

"Did he hit you?" I ask, not really knowing if I want the answer.

"A few times. But he preferred his torture to come in the form of things that left no physical evidence.

"I spent hours trying to find a way to break out of my room so that I could sneak down to the kitchen for food when I knew he was out with you all. It worked after a while, I managed to pick the lock and I would take whatever I thought he wouldn't notice and stash it under my bed.

"But the day I found you, I'd heard some of the boys fighting. It was brutal and I couldn't sit there listening to them without doing something.

"I knew he was in the house, so I risked leaving my room to get help before they hurt each other. In hindsight, maybe I should have left them to it."

"No," I state firmly. "I might never have seen you then."

She fights her way out of my arms and stares up at me as the first flash of lightning lights up our dark surroundings.

"You wouldn't have hated me for ten years."

"I wouldn't have you in front of me right now then."

Her expression softens as more tears fill her eyes.

"Lee, don't do that," she warns.

"Do what? Tell the truth?"

"I have no idea what the truth is."

"This," I say, sliding my hand around the nape of her neck and threading my fingers through her hair. "This is the truth."

I brush my lips over hers gently, half expecting her to slap me for making a move but instead, she just remains motionless in my hold.

Lightning flashes again as I pull her lip into my mouth, encouraging her to join in.

The sound of giant raindrops hitting the ground around me mixes with the rumbling thunder in the distance and the blood rushing past my ears with my racing pulse.

"Red," I growl, needing her to do something, even if it is to pull away.

Pressing my hand against the small of her back, I press her soft body against my hard one and she gasps feeling my length against her belly.

"Only you, Red. Only for you."

Her lips part hesitantly, but the second my tongue brushes hers she dives into the kiss. Our tongues duel, our teeth clash as our hands roam, trying to pull the other closer.

The rain hits us, but neither of us even try to move, more than happy to drown in this than our usual darkness.

13

MACIE

The rain soaks through my shirt and begins running in rivulets down my skin. I can't find it in myself to care as Leon's tongue strokes mine and his hands slide down my back until he squeezes my ass.

I moan into the kiss as the move presses us tighter together, the unmistakable hardness of his length presses against my stomach.

Opening up and telling him what I've been through was hard. I've never spoken those words out loud before, but I knew I needed to. Much like him, my past has been poisoning me slowly for years.

The reason I hide in the shadows, too afraid to poke my head above the parapet and really embrace who I really am, how I really want to live all stems from those years being forced to live under my uncle's roof and being utterly terrified to do the wrong thing.

I know that one day he would take things too far, I just never thought it would involve someone other than me.

My feet leave the ground as the rain continues to lash at us, cooling my quickly heating skin as Leon walks us somewhere.

I'm so lost to him, in the relief from the memories of my past that I don't even care where we're going.

Right now, I'd let him walk me right in the pits of hell if it meant he never lets me go.

I can barely remember a time where I felt safe, but being in his arms right now, it reminds me that I did once have this feeling. I was too young to appreciate it, to acknowledge it until it was gone.

But I feel it right now.

No matter how much our pasts want to drag us under, I know that while I'm in his arms that I'll never go under.

It's scary. Terrifying. Especially because the rational side of my brain knows that I shouldn't trust a single word that comes out of his mouth.

I panic when he bends and begins lowering me down. I dig my nails into his shoulders, making him growl but the second my back connects with the hood of his car, I relax slightly. Well that is until he drags me down so my pussy rubs against his length.

"Oh God," I moan into our kiss as the rain pounds down around us.

"I need you, Macie. I need you so fucking bad," he moans against my lips. His hands skate up my stomach, squeezing my breasts until it just starts to hurt.

My back arches off his car, offering myself up to him when he releases me in favor of the buttons running down the front of my shirt.

He drags the fabric open the second he's undone the last button and immediately goes for the clasp on my bra.

"Leon," I moan as the cold rain splashes on my burning skin, tickling as it runs off me.

Dragging his lips from my neck and down my chest, he captures one of my nipples, lapping at the rain water and searing my sensitive skin with the heat of his tongue.

My back arches once more as my fingers thread through his soaked hair holding him against me as I shamelessly roll my hips against him.

"You're the only thing that makes it go away, Red. You're the only one I can be myself with. You're the only one who understands," he says, pained and unfiltered emotion in his voice as he kisses down my stomach, leaving my bare breasts open to the elements once more.

Sliding his hands up my thighs, he pushes my skirt around my waist a second before the most incredible sound falls from his lips.

A laugh. A full on belly laugh.

For a second, it feels so good to hear it that I forget about my current predicament.

In a rush, I push up on my elbows to find what's amused him so much to see him staring at my panties with a wide smile on his face.

"Oh shit," I hiss, remembering what I mindlessly dragged up my legs this morning.

My cheeks heat as I watch him stare at me. Water drips from his hair and face, his sodden shirt sticking to every sculpted line and indent of his body.

"You've got no idea what you do to me, do you?" His eyes roam up my body, finally meeting mine and I gasp at the desire staring back at me.

I hold his gaze, biting down on my bottom lips as I silently beg for him to do something.

My chest heaves, the thunder continues to rumble in the distance as he stands motionless just staring at me.

"Little innocent Macie Fletcher and her white cotton panties laid out on the hood of my car dripping wet and desperate for my cock. Who would've thought it?"

The excited twinkle in his eyes makes my heart happy.

Remembering his words from not so long ago, I echo them.

"You're the only one I can be me with. The only one I don't need to hide from."

"Oh, baby. You don't need to hide who you are from anyone. You're fucking incredible."

Without saying another word, he presses his palms to the inside of my thighs, opening me up as wide as I'll go as he drops to his knees before me.

"And you taste like fucking heaven and I'm starving."

In the blink of an eye, he's got my panties pulled aside and he licks up the length of my pussy, making me cry out in the silent night around us.

My thighs clamp around his head as the intense sensation consumes me, making me try to fight him off.

"Macie, Macie, Macie," he chants. "Be a good girl and let me eat you, baby."

My legs are forced wide again as he sucks on my clit before dropping lower and spearing his tongue inside me.

I cry out into the night as the feeling of him between my thighs and the cold rain pounding down on my skin becomes too much.

"Leon."

My grip in his hair must become painful as I drag him closer, but he never complains, only growls against me, sending bolts of pleasure shooting around my body.

Focusing on my clit, he teases my entrance, making my pussy greedily try to suck him inside.

"Please, Leon. Please," I beg, digging my heels into his back in my need to get him closer.

"Filthy girl," he mutters against me, finally giving me what I need and pushing two fingers inside me, immediately curling them so he hits the spot that makes me cry out and for my release to come surging forward.

"Leon," I scream, my back lifting from his car as my orgasm slams into me.

His tongue doesn't stop its assault on my pussy as I ride out my high, my heated skin erupting in goose bumps as the cool breeze whips past me.

"I'm addicted, baby," he says, pulling his face from between my thighs, wiping his mouth with the back of his hand.

"More," I breathe, making him laugh, but I'm not about to sit up and demand he takes me home, not when I can see his cock trying to bust out of his pants.

A wicked smile curls at his lips as he shakes his head at me.

"You've fucking ruined me, Red. Fucking. Ruined. Me."

Without taking his eyes from mine, he stands, rips his fly open and pushes his pants down over his ass, freeing his length.

"Leon," I whimper, dropping my eyes down his wet body to where he's fisting himself. "I need—"

"I know what you need, Red," he assures, allowing me to slide down the hood of his car until he lifts the bottom half of my body with one firm hand on my ass.

My thighs clench with desire when he rubs the head of his cock through my wetness.

"So wet for me, Red. Have you been thinking about this since Saturday night?"

"Leon," I warn, urging him to hurry up. I need to feel him inside me. I need to feel the burn of him stretching me open.

"You loved it, didn't you, you filthy slut?"

"Oh God," I moan, heat surging to my core at his words.

"Yeah, you fucking did. You feel that?" he asks, pushing ever so slightly inside me, letting me feel just how slick I am for him. "You feel how wet you are?"

"Yes. Lee, please. I need yo— argh," I cry when he slams inside me.

My body stills as his intrusion burns but that pain is soon forgotten when he pulls out torturously slow hitting every single nerve as he moves.

"Holy shi—" My words end in a gasp as he reaches up and twists my nipple. "Oh shit, Lee."

His hips work faster, pistoning in and out of me with such force, I slide up and down the hood of his car.

Rain continues to drench both of us, the sound of it hitting his car and our surroundings, the only thing that can be heard over our increased breaths as we both race toward our climaxes.

"Macie. Fuck. You're perfect. Fucking perfect," he grits out, his body pulled tight with his movements, his muscles rippling under the soaked fabric of his shirt.

He looks delicious and the words he just said to me are on the tip of my tongue, because despite all the parts of him that he hates, his past that he feels has ruined him, to me, he is perfect.

He sees me in a way no other person ever has. He knows who I really am and embraces it.

I always thought we met for a reason, I just never could have predicted that it would be our pain, our pasts, that would eventually entwine us together forever.

Because even if this doesn't work out. Even if I can't find it in me to trust him again, I already know that our connection will never fade.

It was born out of something bigger than either of us.

Out of darkness. Out of pain. Out of desperation. And I'm pretty sure our souls will always seek each other out because of it.

With all the unknowns circling around us, one thing I know for sure is that I'll always dance with him in the rain.

He stills, his eyes holding mine as an intensity I'm becoming used to flashes through them.

"Is that a promise?"

"Is w-what a p-promise?" I stutter, hoping like hell I didn't just say that out loud.

His hand slides up my slick skin until his fingers circle my throat. His possessive hold sends a wave of heat through me as his thumb gently strokes my pulse point.

"I'll always dance in the rain with you, too."

I gasp, hearing confirmation that I did indeed say that thought out loud.

"I-I-I don't—"

"No," he states. "No more. Don't ruin it. Not yet."

As he says those words, a little defeat creeps into his expression, as if he already knows that I'm not just going to accept him back into my life like I think he was hoping for.

It would be so easy to push everything that happened aside and to move forward together with this crazy thing between us, but I can't. I need to be stronger than that. I haven't fought all my life to just give up and fall into the arms of a man who's hurt me.

I can't.

I won't.

His hips roll once more, immediately reigniting my approaching release.

Reaching up, I wrap my hand around the back of his neck and drag his lips down to mine.

I need him. All of him.

His tongue licks into my mouth as his hips pick up speed once more.

"Come for me, baby. Come all over my cock. Show me how much you love it."

His growled dirty words finally tip me over the edge and I cry out into the night as my body clamps down on him, wave after wave of intense pleasure making my muscles weak and making lights spark behind my eyes.

"Macie. Fuck. Fuck," he grunts, his movements becoming erratic as he also finds his release.

His fingers dig into my ass as his cock jerks inside me, filling me.

Folding his body over mine, he tucks his face into the crook of my neck and sucks in a shuddering breath.

Long silent seconds pass as we just hold each other, both of us coming down from the epic high of being together as the rain begins to slow around us.

A shiver works its way down my body and he holds me tighter, seemingly not ready to let me go quite yet.

When he finally speaks, it forces a messy ball of emotion so huge into my throat that I have no chance of responding.

"Th-that was a goodbye, wasn't it?"

My eyes burn with tears and I just manage to catch the sob that wants to erupt from my throat.

"I-I think... Please can you take me home?" I whisper.

Pain lashes at my chest knowing that I just hurt him. But it's the right thing to do.

Whatever this was tonight... it wasn't the start of something, I know that for sure.

After a beat, he lifts his weight from me and unwraps my legs from around his waist.

Without looking at me, he turns away to give me some privacy and takes a few steps away.

His shoulders are pulled tight with tension.

I desperately want to help, but I can't.

I need to stay strong and think of myself, not him and his pain.

Sliding from the hood of the car, I right my underwear, feeling the evidence of what just happened between us slipping from my body, before starting to button up my shirt.

His loud roar stops me, my fingers stilling in front of me, my eyes flying to where he's standing in front of the tree with his fist implanted in the trunk.

Oh God.

"L-Leon?" I breathe, not even sure if I say it loud enough for him to hear me.

"Don't. Just... don't." He spins away from the trunk, picks up our wet discarded shoes and marches toward his car, shaking his bloody fist out as he moves. "Get in. We need to get out of here."

"O-okay," I whisper, rushing to finish my shirt and to race around to the passenger door.

The tension that radiates from him when I slam the door behind me is almost unbearable.

My fists curl on my lap, my nails digging into my palms until I swear I start to draw blood.

I want to reach for him, to tell him that everything will work out, that it will be okay, but I can't.

The drive back through town is as silent as the one we made earlier, but it's far less comfortable with Leon's anger rolling off him in waves.

"Th-thank you," I stutter when he pulls up outside my building and kills the engine. "I... um... guess I'll see— What are you doing?" I ask when he pushes the door open and moves to climb out.

"Walking you to your door," he states as if it's the most obvious thing in the world.

"It's okay, you don't—" The determined look in his eyes when he turns to me cuts off my argument.

I stare at him for a beat, appreciating how he looks with his still damp hair falling into his eyes, the heavy layer of stubble on his chin and his shirt still clinging to his muscles. He looks hot, there's no other way to put it and it makes the ache in my chest that I'm desperately trying to ignore even more painful.

He waits for me to step beside him, then he presses his burning hand to my lower back and guides me toward the door.

I bite back my argument knowing that saying goodbye to him is only going to be harder with him insisting on being a gentleman.

I come to a stop just before the front door to the building knowing that I'm not going to be able to let him come inside.

"Well... um... thanks, I guess."

A sad laugh rips from his throat at my words and his hand lifts to rub the back of his neck.

"Yeah, you're welcome," he mutters, his eyes dark and full of regrets.

"I'll see you arou—" I don't get to finish my sentence because the door behind me crashes against the wall and I'm pushed aside as someone comes rushing out.

It takes me a second to register what's happening as Nate flies toward Leon.

"Nate, no," I cry, but it's too late.

He pulls his arm back a beat before his fist collides with Leon's cheek with a chilling crunch.

Almost as oblivious as me, Leon stumbles back with the force of Nate's punch, tripping over a bump in the sidewalk beneath his feet and falling to his ass with a thud.

"Holy fuck," Nate breathes, staring down at Leon with wide eyes as he shakes his fist out. "I... shit, I didn't mean to."

"It's fine," Leon grunts, climbing to his feet as his cheek glows red from where Nate hit him. "It's the least of what I deserve."

"What have you done to her?" Nate demands barely glancing in my direction.

If I didn't already know that I look like a mess then that just confirmed it.

"He didn't do anything. We got caught in a rainstorm," I answer before Leon gets a chance to say anything, which makes Nate's eyes finally turn to me.

He looks over every inch of me before his shoulders relax a little when he must realize that I'm telling him the truth.

"You need to leave her the fuck alone," Nate barks.

"I know," Leon mutters, his eyes holding mine captive.

I swallow nervously, my fists curling once more to stop me from reaching out to him.

"I'll see you around, Red."

My eyes bore into his back as he turns and walks away from us, begging him to turn around, to sweep me into his arms and to say fuck it, taking me inside to continue what we started out by the lake.

But he never does.

The second he disappears from my sight, the sobs I've been holding finally bubbles up and I fall into Nate's chest.

"Macie," he breathes, his arms wrapping around me as I cry. "Come on. Let's go inside."

He ushers me up to our dorm, and by the time we're standing outside my room, I feel a little stronger.

"I'm okay," I say, finally pulling away from him. "I'll be okay."

"I can hang out if you need company."

"I appreciate that, I really do, but I need to be alone. And I really need to shower."

"Are you sure he didn't hurt you?"

"No, Nate, he didn't. I think I might have been the one to cause the most pain tonight."

"Okay. Well, if you need me, I'll be in my room."

"Thank you. You're a good friend." I pull him in for a hug, hoping that he knows how much I really do appreciate him.

"I hate seeing you hurting," he breathes in my ear. "You deserve more."

I'm hit with a wave of guilt so strong that it almost brings me to my knees.

"Mace?"

"Actually, can you come in for a moment?"

"S-sure."

I push my door open and hold it open for him to join me.

"Is everything—"

"I need to tell you something." Walking over to my nightstand, I pick up the photo of my parents.

I've always put it away or hidden it when I know anyone's going to be in here, but since Leon, I've been way more forgetful than I usually would be.

"O-okay," he says, standing in the middle of the room looking confused.

"I haven't been completely honest with you."

His eyes narrow as I step toward him and hold out the photo of my parents.

"My name isn't Macie Smith, Nate. It's Macie—"

"Fletcher. I know."

My chin drops as I stare at him looking down at my parents.

"I saw this the week you moved in, Mace."

"Oh," I breathe, feeling totally deflated.

"I don't care what your surname is, or who you're related to. If it makes you happy to distance yourself from them for whatever reason, then that's up to you.

"I want to be friends with you, Mace. Not for your name, or for your connections."

"Well, that's good because I don't have any connections. If you know them, then you know some of the story."

"Yeah. I'm sorry."

I shrug. "It is what it is. I'm sorry I never told you."

"It's really okay. But there's more to this than just your name, isn't there?"

"Yeah," I whisper, taking the photo back and staring down at my parents' smiling faces.

My chest still aches from talking about my dad earlier, and seeing him happy before Mom died doesn't make any of it any easier to take.

"But a lot of that isn't my story to tell."

"It's Leon's."

"Our pasts are intertwined in ways I never could have imagined."

"Is that why he sought you out?"

I nod, not wanting to lie to him.

"Yeah, although finding me while he was... entertaining Charlie was just luck. He had no idea I was here."

He nods, accepting my words before his eyes capture mine, a seriousness I don't like flickering through his.

"You really like him, don't you?"

"We're a disaster, Nate."

"That wasn't what I asked." He lifts a brow, trying to make a point.

"It doesn't matter how I feel. We've both got too much baggage to make anything work."

"Do you really believe that? Don't you think that all of it might be easier to carry if you both share the load?"

My chin drops in shock that he's suddenly encouraging this.

"I thought you hated him."

"I hate how he's treated you. But none of that seems to have stopped you from wanting him, and I trust you, Mace. If you see good in him that we can't, then I'll take your word for it."

"Is that why you hit him, because you trust me?" I ask.

"No, I did that because he deserved it. Although, I wasn't expecting to actually do it."

I can't help but laugh at the horrified look on his face as he recalls what happened outside.

"Hurt like a motherfucker," he admits lifting his hand to inspect his knuckles.

"My hero," I joke.

"I'm glad you're okay, Mace. And whatever you do with all this, I've got your back, okay?"

"Thank you," I breathe, that damn lump back in my throat.

"I'll leave you to get cleaned up. You look like you've been dragged through a hedge."

"You really know how to make a girl feel good about herself."

"I was trying to be polite and not tell you that you looked like you'd been fucked six ways from Sunday."

My cheeks bloom at his words.

"You better have got yours, Mace. That's all I'm gonna say."

He walks to the door as a smile curls at my lips as the memory of being on the hood of Leon's car assaults me.

"Yeah, I did."

He groans as if he's in pain before disappearing from my room and leaving me alone to try to process the events of the night.

14

MACIE

"Macie?" Nate's voice booms through our dorm, the urgency in his tone makes me drop my pen and climb from the bed.

I went to classes yesterday morning, but I struggled to focus. My mind kept drifting back to last Thursday and the events that followed my morning classes. The second I could escape the auditorium, I ran back here—via the coffee shop for cake—and I've hid ever since.

I've tried to make progress on all my assignments, but my mind keeps drifting to Leon, wondering what he did after he left here Wednesday night, if he got himself into another fight, if he's okay.

He looked and sounded so broken when I told him to bring me home that I can't shift the dread that's sitting heavy in my stomach.

"Mace?" Nate booms again, making me move a little quicker thinking something is wrong.

"What is it?" I ask, racing around the corner to where he's sitting at the dining table with his tablet.

"Have you seen the news?"

"Uh... no. Why?"

"Look."

He spins his tablet around and I take a few steps closer so I can read it.

"Football legend Brett Dunn was found dead in a hotel room. Holy shit," I gasp.

"Have you spoken to Leon?" Nate asks as I lower myself to the chair beside him so I can read more.

"N-no, nothing since Wednesday night. Shit, he died on Wednesday night." I lean forward, scanning the words quickly. "Found in a hotel room. Suspected overdose. Jesus."

"I can't believe I'm about to say this, but maybe you should check on him and see if he's okay."

I stare at the image of Brett from his heyday the press have posted alongside the breaking news.

"Leon hated his dad," I mutter, wondering how he's taken the news.

"He's still his dad."

"Crap." I sink back into the chair, torn about what to do.

The sensible part of my brain tells me to push it aside, let him deal with it however he needs to and to not get involved. But a bigger part, a much louder part wants to go to him. For some reason that part seems to think that he's going to need to hear that it's okay not to mourn a man who helped condemn him to hell despite everyone expecting him to be devastated.

"What are you thinking?" Nate asks.

"I..."

"Go to him, Mace. Something tells me he'll want to see you."

Nate's cell rings, and I nod at him to answer it. He pulls it from his pocket and stands, lifting it to his ear as he walks toward his room.

Pulling his tablet closer once more, I properly read through the details again.

"Shit," I hiss.

I'm still sitting there debating what to do when Nate returns.

"Everything okay?" I ask as he goes to grab a bottle of water.

"Yeah. Why are you still here? Follow your gut, Mace."

I nod, pushing the chair back knowing what I need to do.

I brush my hair and throw it up into a messy bun before switching my pajamas for a MKU hoodie and pair of jeans. I don't bother with any makeup. If I am brave enough to knock on the door of his house, I'm not sure anyone will care about how I look.

Nate smiles at me as I make my way back through the living area. Charlie has appeared and is talking his ear off about something.

"Hey, Mace. How's it going?" she asks, pausing whatever she was saying.

"Uh... yeah. Great," I mutter, tugging the main door open before she gets to question the fact things clearly aren't great at all.

The drive to Leon's house is quick. Quicker than I was hoping because as I pull up on the street out front, my hands tremble.

What if he doesn't want you here? A little voice asks as I stare up at the impressive building.

I already know what angry Leon is like. Add grief to that and I could be about to walk into something terrifying, assuming he doesn't slam the door in my face the second he lays eyes on me.

After how things ended on Wednesday night, I wouldn't blame him if he did that.

Knowing that I can't sit out here like a creep all day, I suck in some courage and push my door open.

His car is sitting in the driveway along with Luca's so I can only assume he's here.

My entire body trembles by the time I step up to the front door and press my finger to the doorbell.

I'm more than aware that he never wanted me here before. He never even tried to invite me into his home. I don't know why I think he's going to want me here now.

But it's too late because I can already hear heavy footsteps heading my way.

I have to fight with myself not to turn on my heels and run like a bat out of hell.

Sucking in a breath, I wait for the door to open. It seems to take forever for someone to appear on the other side.

The second it opens enough to reveal an arm, I know it's not Leon's. His tattoos are different.

"Hey, sweetheart. How can I help you?" A huge dark-haired guy I recognize purrs at me as his eyes take a leisurely trip around my body.

"I-I-I'm looking for Leon," I stutter like an idiot.

"Should have guessed. You're a redhead."

"Yeah. His type, right?" I mutter.

"Yeah, you're right up his alley. He could really make use of you right now, Red." He winks and my stomach turns over at his use of the nickname Leon calls me. It sounds all kinds of wrong on this guy's lips.

"He's up in his room. Feel free to go and surprise him anyway you see fit." He stands aside and I hesitantly take a step into the house. The scent of my childhood hits my nose and I almost turn and run once more. The whole place smells like boy and football. It's a scent I used to find comforting, until my life turned to shit. Then it became the scent of horrors.

I'm almost at the stairs when he speaks again. I have no idea where I'm going but I figure it's a good start.

"His room is the far door on the top floor. But if he's busy, you're more than welcome in mine."

I don't justify his comment with a response, instead I just take off up the stairs.

"Name's Colt by the way."

Colt.

He's the one who's got a thing going on with Ella.

I'm sure she'd be thrilled to hear him suggesting I visit his room.

Shaking it off, I focus on the task at hand and climb the stairs until I'm on the top floor.

I pass the first door and head straight to the one at the end like Colt said.

Sucking in a breath, I lift my hand and knock.

Nothing.

"L-Leon?"

Nothing.

Not willing to come this far and get nowhere, I try my luck and twist the door handle.

It lowers, the latch releasing and the door swinging open.

"Leon?" I call, although I already know he's not here. I can feel it.

Unable to stop myself from learning more about the man who's thrust his way into my life, I take a step forward and into his space.

I know I shouldn't but my need to know more is too much to deny.

The second his scent engulfs me, I instantly feel more settled. It's a feeling that I try to not think about too much because it's terrifying that one person—when he's not even here—can affect me so much.

His room is tidier than I thought it would be.

Football trophies line shelves, clothes cover a chair and spill from drawers but the floor is mostly clear. There's a desk with his laptop and books scattered over the top, and messed up black sheets cover his bed.

I walk around, taking everything in, and embarrassingly lifting a shirt from his chair and bringing it to my nose.

Where are you, and how are you coping right now?

With his shirt still in my hand, I walk over to the window and stare out at the backyard.

They've got an impressive pool, bar area and more loungers and chairs than I'm sure are needed.

I bet they throw some killer parties here.

I'm still standing there staring out of the window, completely lost in my own head minutes later when a shiver suddenly runs down my spine seconds before a door slams and locks behind me.

I damn near jump out of my skin, spinning around to find a sweaty and very angry looking Leon glaring at me. His chest is heaving, his shirt is sticking to his skin much like the other night, but today it's sweat that makes it cling. His fists curl at his sides as his eyes darken the longer our contact holds.

"I'm... I'm sorry, Colt said you were..." I trial off when he reaches behind his head and drags his shirt up his sculpted torso, revealing the hard planes of his stomach and deep V which disappears into his sweats.

But it's what I find below his waist that makes my breath catch in my throat.

He's hard.

Really freaking hard.

My heart picks up speed as my stomach flips in anticipation as he takes another step toward me.

"You should probably leave," he warns.

Another step.

His scent fills my nose as his heat begins to seep into me, making me burn for him.

"What if I don't want to?" I ask, forcing my voice to sound stronger than I feel.

"You'll probably regret it."

My chest heaves as my eyes hold his, trying to appear that I'm not freaking the hell out right now.

"Wouldn't be the first time."

He reaches out, and with a touch more gentle than what he seems capable of right now, he tucks a loose strand of hair behind my ear.

"Why are you here, Red?"

"I-I... um... I wanted to check on you."

His eyes drop to mine, taking in the length of my body. It's a move that seems fairly pointless seeing as I'm wearing a baggy hoodie.

"You saw the news?" he asks me coldly.

"Y-yeah. Are you..." His eyes find mine once again and my words get stuck in my throat. "Are you okay?" I squeak out.

"I don't know what I am right now, Red." He takes the final step toward me, forcing me to take one back and bump up against the window.

His hands grab the back of my thighs and he lifts me until I'm balanced on the window sill, my legs around his waist, his cock pressed against my core.

"But I know what I need."

"Oh yeah?"

"Yeah." Releasing my thigh, one of his hands wrap around my throat, making me swallow nervously. "I need to get out of my own head. I need to hurt someone."

I swallow again, holding his stares, hoping that he can read in them that I'm not scared of him.

"And I need you."

His lips slam down on mine in a punishing kiss. Our teeth collide as his tongue twists with mine, his hands slipping under the fabric of my hoodie and roughly grabbing my breasts.

"Leon," I moan into his kiss.

"You made a mistake coming after me today, Red."

I shake my head as he plunges his tongue back into my mouth.

"No," I mumble into his kiss. "I'm exactly where I need to be right now."

"Fuck," he barks, ripping his lips from mine and dragging my hoodie up my body before throwing it over his shoulder. His lips go to my neck, kissing, sucking and biting down toward my collarbone as he tucks his fingers under the bralette I'm wearing, making quick work of getting that on the floor as well.

He presses me back against the window, the cold glass biting into my skin but I barely pay it any mind as his hands cup my aching breasts, his fingers pinching my nipples and sending bolts of electricity straight between my thighs.

"Oh God."

"This isn't privacy glass," he growls against my neck. "If there's anyone down there, they can definitely see you."

"I don't care," I moan, my head falling back against the window with a bang when he grazes his lips across the sensitive skin of my breast, his rough scruff scratching me, making it that much more intense. "T-take what you neeeed," I moan as his lips wrap around my nipple.

He sucks until it hurts before switching to the other side. My fingers twist in his hair, tugging until I know it stings, but I also know that he craves the pain as much as I do.

"I came for you. I came to help. Use me. Take me. Hurt me."

"Fuck, Red. You've got no idea what you're asking for."

"I don't care, Leon. I want to be here. I want to be what you need."

He stands once more, his lips crashing against mine as he lifts me into his body and carries me across the room.

I land on his bed with a thud and he immediately goes to my jeans, undoing them and dragging them down my legs, my panties—white cotton again—quickly follows.

Pressing his palms to my inner thighs, he opens me wide and he drops to his knees.

He runs his nose up the length of me, breathing me in. My cheeks heat knowing what he's doing but the second his tongue flicks my clit,

I forget all about being embarrassed by my body and just focus on what he's doing.

"Leon," I cry when he sucks me into his mouth.

"Yes, baby. Let the entire house know you're mine."

My fingers twist in his hair, my nails scratching at his scalp as he continues to eat me like a starved man.

He laps up all my juices, plunging his tongue inside of me and driving me wild until I'm right on the edge of my release.

But he knows every time I'm almost there because he slows down, changes his angle, his technique, ensuring my release ebbs away making me cry out in frustration.

"You're an asshole," I scream when he does it once again, the grip I had on my orgasm slipping once more.

"That's not news to me, Red," he mutters against my thigh before biting so hard on my sensitive skin that I'm convinced he's broken the skin.

He sucks on the skin, lapping at the sting with his tongue making me writhe and my pussy clench on nothing but air with my need for him.

The second he lifts from my leg and looks up at me, I discover I was right because he's got a little blood on the corner of his lips.

"Y-you bit me," I gasp, reaching down to wipe the red stain away.

"Yeah. That means you're mine now. I own you, Macie. I have since the moment I looked into your eyes a decade ago."

My breath catches in my throat as he stares deep into my eyes.

There's such a huge part of me that begs for me to push my concerns aside and dive head first into whatever this crazy thing with him is, but the sensible side, that's controlled my life for over a decade, just won't let go.

She craves safety, security. She needs to know we're not going to drown. While my wild side wants to swim in Leon's darkness despite the fact we might just go down together.

But isn't going under together better than surviving alone?

Pushing my knees to my chest, he crawls on the bed.

"So fucking beautiful, laid out there waiting to be filled with my cock, Red."

My cheeks burn at his dirty words but I can't deny the heat that pools in my core.

I keep my legs up as he releases them in favor of pushing his sweats down and releasing his cock. It springs free, brushing against my core and making me shudder with need.

"Leon," I moan as he takes himself in one hand and teases me.

"Tell me what you want, Red."

"You, Lee. I want you."

He drops his cock down to my entrance, pushing in ever so slightly but nowhere near enough.

"Not good enough. Tell me exactly what you want. I want to hear the words fall from your innocent—" He runs a finger along my bottom lip. "Sweet lips."

His eyes hold mine, his damn near black with desire and fire burning behind them.

"I want you to f-fuck me," I say as confidently as possible.

"More," he demands.

"I-I—" I swallow down my nerves as I stare into his eyes. I came here because I knew he'd need me. Now I need to follow through and give him what he needs. "I want to feel you inside me. I want to feel your cock so deep inside me I can barely stand it. I want you to fuck me until you get out of your own head and I want to watch as you lose control."

"Fuck, baby." He folds over me, crushing my legs between us as his cock finally pushes inside me.

My body tenses but it's nowhere near as uncomfortable as the past couple of times, it's like my body knows his now and is ready for whatever he's got for me.

His hands cradle my face in an uncharacteristically tender move for the mood he's in before his lips crash down on mine once more, his tongue forcing its way inside to find mine.

"How did you know?" he mumbles into our kiss.

My brows pinch. "I-I saw the new—"

"No. You came here. To me. How'd you know?"

"Because I know you, Leon." I mimic his move, cupping his cheek in my palm as he lifts up to release my legs, allowing them to wrap around his body, bringing us closer.

"You deserve so much more than what I can give you right now."

"I don't care about what I deserve. I want to be what you need. I meant what I said. Take whatever you want. I'm here. I'm... I'm yours."

"Fuck," he groans, finally rolling his hips, dragging his cock out of me and hitting all my nerves on the way.

I tremble in his arms as his tongue licks into my mouth with slow, measured strokes.

He moves slowly for long minutes but with each one, I feel his restraint lessen.

"Let go, Lee. I won't break."

Pushing up on his palms, he stares down into my eyes. I see the second he loses his fight. Something flashes behind his eyes and before I can blink, his hand is around my throat as he pulls out of me only for his hips to piston forward, filling me to the hilt.

If it weren't for his hold on my throat, I swear I'd fly into the headboard with the strength behind his thrust.

"Leon," I cry when he pounds into me over and over. The tip of his cock hitting my cervix causing a new bite of pain but it's well overpowered by the pleasure of his cock dragging against my sensitive walls.

"Yes. Red. Fuck," he barks as his movements become erratic and his grip on my throat tightens.

But right before I'm about to fall, once again, he stops me.

"Not yet, Red. Not until I'm ready."

His hand releases me and I suck in a deep breath but the relief is only brief because his harsh grip digs into my hips and I'm flipped over.

With his hand on the nape of my neck, he presses my face into his pillow as he drags my ass in the air.

"Fucking perfect," he growls before his palm connects with my ass and I jolt forward.

Pain blooms on my cheek, but he brushes his fingers over it soothing the pain as he pushes back inside me.

If it's possible, it seems like he gets even deeper.

"Oh shit," I gasp when his finger brushes over my darkest place causing a shudder to run down my spine.

"One day, Macie. One day I'm going to own you completely."

His finger drops lower, dipping inside me alongside his cock, collecting up my juices before he brings it back to my puckered hole, pushing a little inside.

"Oh, oh, oh," I chant as the alien feeling assaults me.

"Fuck that's tight," he groans as he pushes a little farther inside as he hips continue their punishing rhythm.

Unable to help myself, I push back, needing more, desperate for him to let me fall.

"You really are a kinky little bitch aren't you, Macie Fletcher? You love the idea of me being balls deep in your ass, don't you?"

"Leon," I cry, his words mixing with what his cock and finger are doing to me and making me race toward my release.

This time when it begins to crest, he doesn't stop or change anything; he just lifts me and chases the pleasure I'm so desperate for.

My entire body begins to tremble seconds before I shatter, lights flashing behind my eyes before everything goes black.

I'm consumed by the earth shattering release he finally drags out of my body.

When I come back to myself, he's roaring out his own release, his cock twitching violently inside me, his finger now even deeper in my ass.

Aftershocks rock my body before I'm thrown head first into a second release that I don't see coming.

"Macie," he growls, his hips circling as he drags every last ounce of pleasure out of me.

I expect him to collapse on me, or even to fall to the bed beside me, but he does neither of those things. Instead, he wraps his arms around my waist and lifts me from the bed.

15

LEON

I manage to lose my sweats as I walk us into my bathroom, so by the time I step into the shower stall with her still wrapped around me like a spider monkey, we're both naked.

I twist the dial before slamming her back against the wall, she cries out as the cold assaults her from all angles.

"And to think, I was expecting you to cuddle," she moans as I drop my face into the crook of her neck, sucking on her soft, coconut-scented skin.

"Not yet, Red," I growl out against her. "I need to get you clean so I can dirty you up all over again."

The truth of it is, I've been running all morning and I fucking stink.

"Did it work?" she asks, making me pause as I nip at her collarbone.

"Did what work?"

"Did you manage to outrun your demons?"

Pulling away from her body, I look up into her eyes.

They're still blown with desire, her cheeks pink from her release. There's a faint red mark around her throat from my tight grip as I fucked her and teeth marks from where I've bitten her. She's never looked more beautiful.

"Not possible, baby."

"I'm sorry about—"

I slam my lips down on hers to cut off what's going to fall from her mouth next.

"Don't," I growl into our kiss, my grip on her ass tightening as the water finally warms around us.

She nods, her tongue joining mine as I push it past her lips.

Threading her fingers into my wet hair, she scratches at my scalp making a growl rumble up my throat and my already hard cock to twitch in need.

Kissing across her jaw, I brush my lips over the shell of her ear.

"Are you sore?" I ask. "And don't lie to me because you think it's what I want to hear."

"A little," she confesses. "But not enough to stop you."

Releasing her ass, I wrap my fingers around her throat once more, pressing my fingertips into the red patches from before, hoping to make them brighter so every motherfucker will know that she's owned.

"You fuck up my head, Macie Fletcher," I admit, staring into her eyes as her chest heaves and her pulse thunders against my harsh grip. "But fuck. I don't want it to stop."

Releasing her throat, I lower my hand to my length and find her entrance before dropping her down on it.

Her muscles ripple around me as she hisses at the intrusion telling me that she was lying earlier. There's a part of me that cares, that wants to pull out and take care of her. But there's a bigger part that fucking loves that I'm the one causing her pain, knowing that for the coming hours, days even, she's not going to be able to forget me because every time she moves, she'll remember this. Remember me.

"Macie," I groan, stilling inside her body once I'm fully seated.

"Don't stop," she breathes. "I need—"

"This?" I ask, pulling almost all the way out before surging back inside her tight, hot body.

"Yes," she cries.

"Might want to hold on, baby. This is going to be fast."

Her hands wrap around my shoulders, her nails digging in causing a bite of pain that I feel all the way down to my cock.

"You're coming twice before I fill your pussy with cum again, Red," I warn her.

She nods as her tits bounce from the force of my thrust.

"Leon," she cries as my fingers find her clit, pinching until it must hurt and sending her crashing into her first release.

My teeth grind as I fight to stave off my own, knowing that I need to watch her fall again before I allow myself to drown in her.

"One," I say. "Ready for one more?"

"Oh God," she whimpers. Her eyelids starting to drop with her exhaustion, her arms now hanging limply over my shoulder.

"Don't pass out on me yet," I chuckle, grinding my hips, ensuring I hit that spot deep inside her which I know will wake her up.

"Lee," she moans softly, her head falling back against the wall.

I up the pressure on her clit as I thrust inside her at the speed I know she loves.

"Come on, baby. Come for me," I demand. "Show me how much you like being impaled on my cock, taking everything I have for you."

Her muscles tighten around me, making my teeth grind once more as I fight not to blow my load too soon.

She whimpers, her body tensing once more as her release begins to approach.

"Such a filthy little whore, Macie. And all fucking mine."

She moans, her head shaking from side to side as she tries to absorb both the sensations of my touch and my dirty words.

"Who owns you, Macie? Who owns this pussy? This body?"

"Y-you," she stutters, her body beginning to tremble with her need to let go.

"Who? Say it. Say my name."

"You, Leon. You fucking own me," she cries, falling head first into another orgasm, squeezing me so tight that I have no choice but to follow her over the edge.

Leaning forward, I press her against the tiles, holding her tight as I fight to catch my breath.

"Oh my God," she breathes against my throat, making me shiver.

"Yeah. I needed that," I chuckle, high on endorphins only she's able to provide me with.

I give myself a few more seconds before I pull away, letting her legs drop from my waist so she can stand.

"I'm not sure I can."

"I won't let you fall, baby."

She gasps, her eyes finding mine as I say those words. Words I hadn't accepted were true until they just passed my lips.

"Lee?" she breathes.

But unable to deal with the weight of those words, of what I'm beginning to realize I feel for her, I press my fingers against her lips.

"Not now."

She nods and I slip my hand away, reaching for the shower gel so I can clean us both up.

My body aches as I wrap her up in a huge towel and sweep her into my arms to carry her back to my bed.

I lay her down on the bed and climb in beside her, pulling her into my body.

"So I do get cuddles then?" she asks, making me smile.

"I've never cuddled a girl I'm fucking before," I confess. The only other girl I've ever cuddled with was Letty, and that was entirely different to this right now.

"Oh, I'm just a girl you're fucking. Remind me why I came here again."

Rolling over and pinning her side to the bed, I brush my lips over hers, too addicted to her taste not to.

"You came to check on me."

"Because I'm an idiot."

"Not an idiot. Somehow you knew just what I needed and you turned up like a fucking miracle."

Her eyes hold mine, the intensity that's been in them since I first found her here lessening and my heart constricts knowing what's coming next.

"A-are you okay? Finding out about... that must have been a shock." Empathy oozes from her. She's lost both of her parents after all, she has firsthand experience with how I should be feeling right now.

Unfortunately for her, I haven't exactly reacted to the news like a normal person.

A laugh tumbles from my lips making her rear back and look at me with her brows pinched.

"A shock. Yeah, you could call it that," I mutter.

The last time I saw my cunt of a father, he was tied up where I left him in that warehouse with his life hanging in the balance from the beating I gave him.

"What's so funny?" she asks, not judging me at all for my reaction, instead, reaching for me and cupping my cheek in her tiny palm.

My lips part, all the truths ready to tumble out, but I manage to catch them before they spill out around me.

"What is it? You can trust me, you know? Whatever it is."

Can I? Can I lay here with her in my arms and tell her everything I've done, everything I planned to do without her freaking out?

Sucking in a breath, I start at the beginning to see how it goes. But I can't deny my need to finally let out what happened with my father is becoming more and more impossible to deny. And for some fucked up reason, I want to trust her with it because I think there's a slim chance that she won't be totally horrified by it.

"My little brother," I start, holding her eyes so she can see just how hard it is to talk about all of this. "His mom is... his mom is Peyton's sister."

"P-Peyton's sis— and your... dad?"

I nod, letting her connect the dots.

"And he's five, right? How old is she?"

"Twenty-three."

"Holy shit," she gasps.

"Luca and Peyton have been the world's most perfect couple since they first looked each other in the eyes in kindergarten. It turns out that dear old dad decided that she was going to be a threat to his golden child's football success so in his fucked-up mind, he went after Libby thinking it would end their relationship."

"Jesus Christ. But she was a child."

"Seventeen. She was pretty wild, had daddy issues, so when he told her all the things she was desperate to hear, she was putty in his hands.

"Well, he got her pregnant. Libby told her mom, Peyton overheard what Brett had done and told Luca." Macie's eyes are wide as saucers as she soaks up every one of my words. "He refused to believe our father would groom his girlfriend's sister and turned his back on Peyton. Their mom made them leave town not long after everything went down and we all lost touch. We had no idea there was a baby, Dad had no idea there was a baby, or at least we didn't think he did."

"How did you find all this out? When did Peyton come back?"

"Libby lost control after Kayden was born, she turned to drugs and after a while she just left."

"Oh God."

"Peyton and her mom raised Libby's son. But then Peyton's mom and Kayden were in a car accident, her mom didn't make it and Kayden was seriously injured."

Macie's eyes fill with tears.

"Peyton moved them back here to be with their aunt. She enrolled at MKU where she and Luca collided again."

"I bet that went well," she mutters.

"Well, put it this way, I had to rescue her after he abducted her and locked her up in the Kappa's pool house."

Her eyes widen in shock before her brow lifts.

"What?" I ask.

"Abduction and locking up. You two have a lot in common, huh?"

"Well, we are twins," I say with a shrug and a wicked smile.

"I guess so.

"So your dad groomed Peyton's sister and had a baby with her. Libby turned to drugs, and now he's dead in a hotel room. I feel like I'm missing something."

"Peyton got a job at a bar downtown. The Locker Room," I say, studying her reaction to see if she'd heard of it. When there's no sign of recognition, I continue. "It's an exclusive sports bar. Only members are allowed inside, it's seedy, it's got waitresses that twilight as... hookers," I confess.

"Peyton?" Macie gasps in horror.

"Oh no, she never did any of that. Probably one of the only girls in there with some integrity. But she needed money to pay her mom and Kayden's medical bills. And it's the best paying place in town. It's also owned by m—"

"By your dad," she finishes for me, clearly guessing where this is going. "Did Peyton know?"

"No, but he did. Of course. Manipulative cunt. He attacked her along with his manager. They were going to rape her until Luca stopped them."

"Holy shit. Your dad sounds like a fucking asshole."

"He's a fucking cunt, Mace. I can't even begin to express how much I hate him."

"What happened?"

"Luc knocked him out, and by the time I got there, he was still out cold. He also called Kane to come and help, and he and Bry, the bartender, also called Reid."

"R-Reid Harris?"

"Yeah. You want someone wiped off the face of the Earth, then Reid is a pretty good place to start."

"He's scary," she confesses with a shudder.

"If you're on the wrong side of him, yeah. But he's a good guy deep down."

"If you say so."

I hesitate continuing with my tale because it's the next bit that is really going to test just how badly she wants to be here. How much she really wants to associate herself with me.

I know telling her is a risk. But who else can I tell who would understand?

Luc might hate our father, but I don't think he'd get it, my need to torture him like I did. I can't tell my mom, she'd probably have me committed after everything, and that just leaves Macie.

"What is it, Leon?"

"Are you sure you want to hear the rest?"

"If you want to tell me, yes. If you don't, I understand."

"You already know the darkest parts of me. You've already seen it. I might as well give you all of it."

"What did you do, Leon?"

"Reid was going to kill him. The second he learned that our dad laid a finger on Peyton, and what he did to Libby, he was after blood. He looked at me like I'd lost my mind when I told him no."

"You let him go?" Macie asks innocently.

"Hell no," I laugh. "I asked them to put him somewhere. Somewhere no one would find him, but that I only had access to."

"O-okay."

"They locked him up in this warehouse over the border into Harrow Creek. Tied him up, treated him like the piece of shit he is."

She nods, concern flickering through her eyes. But she hasn't attempted to run yet so I take that as a good sign.

Sucking in a deep breath, I prepare to spill the rest.

"I used to visit him often. Let him know exactly what I thought of him. The night I turned up at your dorm. The blood... it was his."

"Holy shit, Lee."

"Taking it out on him, it felt like some kind of cleansing. Knowing he was hurting, knowing I could cause him pain much like he'd caused me, Luc, Shane, Kayden, Libby, our mom. Everyone I love has had their lives touched by that cunt at least once. He's hurt all of them."

My entire body trembles with anger as I think about my motives.

"I just... I can't even describe it. Even now. I know it was wrong. But I had to do something. He groomed Libby. He did the same thing that Richard did to me. He was just as bad. He saw what it did to me, yet he did the same damn thing. He cheated on Mom time and time again, making her feel worthless. The pressure he's put on Luc." My fists curl as red hot fury races through my veins as I think of all the ways he's wronged those I love.

Macie slides closer, the heat of her towel-covered body seeping into mine.

Her hand slides from my cheek to grip on to the back of my neck, pressing her brow against mine.

"I'm here," she whispers. "It's okay."

"No one knew he was there aside from the Harrises. Reid and Devin were taking care of him. Making sure he didn't die before I was ready for him to."

"But the news said—"

"I know. I-I don't know how. No one knew, Mace."

"Someone must have. Maybe it was Reid or Devin."

"Reid's assured me they didn't kill him."

"The report said he died of an overdose in a hotel room. How'd he get from a warehouse to a hotel?"

"I don't know, Red. I don't fucking know what's going on," I confess, my voice hollow.

I wanted to be the one to end him. I wanted to make the final play after he'd controlled all our lives. But someone has taken that from me.

Part of me wonders if I never would have been able to do it and that's why I've been putting off making that final move, content with keeping him on the edge of death.

Her lips part before she sucks the bottom one into her mouth, sinking her teeth into it. My cock twitches at the move wishing I could do the same.

I remain still as she thinks. My heart pounds knowing that at any second she could push away from me, telling me that I'm a twisted, sick cunt just like my father and run as far away as she can get.

I can't believe my luck when she does speak and something unexpected falls from her lips.

"Can you be tied to this? Are you at risk?"

"I-I don't know. I mean, the police haven't turned up yet. The press is saying it was an overdose. He was found in the hotel room I took you to with a whore. Both of them OD'd."

A shudder rips through her.

"W-where we were?"

"Yeah. Don't worry, I won't take you back."

"Someone will have seen him," she whispers.

"Apparently not. There's no witness of him arriving. It's his personal suite, no one else—aside from us—stays there. He will have slipped in the back door unnoticed."

"But how?"

"I have no idea. I didn't exactly leave him able to move the last time I saw him."

"The night we were at the hotel?"

"Yes, but it wasn't his blood that night. When I got there, Devin was there. He saw something in me, my need to fight, to exorcize some demons and he helped."

"For complete psychos, they sound like half decent friends."

"They're loyal to the core. Just don't cross them."

"I think it was them. They took this one and saved you from having to do it."

I stare into her kind, innocent eyes. Hating that I'm burdening her with this bullshit.

"They might have been involved, but there's more to it. If they wanted to kill him, put an end to it, they'd have put a bullet through his skull and buried him where he'd never be found."

She shudders.

"They're Hawks, baby. That's a normal day for them."

"You're right. Something doesn't add up. Someone knew."

I think back to that night when I thought someone was watching me in the shadows when I went to visit him.

Was it someone? Were my instincts right? But who?

"And he's got enough enemies by the sound of it."

"If they knew, it meant they followed me. It means they knew something was going on."

"So, it was Luc?"

"I don't know, Red. It doesn't seem like his style."

"Libby? They OD'd. She'd be able to get her hands on drugs."

"She's in a rehab facility."

"They can leave though, right?"

"I have no idea. I'm not even sure where the place is."

Silence falls around us as we both lose ourselves in our thoughts.

"Does it even matter?" she finally asks. "He's gone. He's out of your life. Isn't that the most important thing here?"

"Yeah, I guess."

"But you wanted to be the one to do it?"

"I'm not even sure I did. I've kept him alive for weeks. If I really wanted to do it, I would've done it by now."

"So... this was all part of your plan. Revenge on your dad, me and Richard."

"Yeah," I say, tightening my arm around her waist and crushing her body against mine. "But it seems to have been a little derailed."

"I don't know," she says with a shrug. "You fucked me over. Your dad has gone. All that's left is my uncle."

Dipping my head to kiss her jaw, I whisper. "Can I fuck you over again?"

"Again?" she asks, her brow lifting in shock.

Trailing a finger over her collarbone and down to the swell of her breast. I tuck my digit under the fabric of the towel, and pull it free, exposing her to me.

"Always."

Her eyes drop from mine to the obvious tent in my towel.

Pressing her palm to my shoulder, I allow her to push me onto my back as she crawls down the bed, pulling the towel from waist, exposing my cock.

Staring down at it, she licks her lips, and I groan.

"Red?"

Taking her time, her eyes roll up to meet mine.

"You should probably be running after what I just told you," I breathe.

"I know. But I'm not going to."

Dipping her head, she keeps her eyes on mine as she runs her tongue up the length of my cock. It jerks violently at her delicate touch and I fist the sheets to stop me from reaching for her and taking over her movements.

16

MACIE

What the hell am I doing?

With my eyes locked on Leon's dark hungry ones, I run the tip of my tongue up the length of him, letting his taste fill my mouth and his scent invade my senses.

He's just confessed to having his father locked up in some warehouse like some freaking animal and torturing him to get his anger from his childhood out and here I am about to suck his cock into my mouth.

I should be running.

Fast.

He might be quick to warn me about the Harrises being dangerous, but has he looked in a mirror? He was going to kill his own father.

But knowing all that. Listening to him confess his darkest parts, I still can't find it in myself to leave.

I'm also not scared of him. Not even in the slightest.

"Macie," he groans, his fingers twisting in the sheets as I lick the head of his cock, teasing the slit, lapping at his precum.

My heart thunders in my chest, images from what he described running at a million miles a minute in my head.

I think of him that night he turned up at my dorm covered in blood and lost to his darkness.

He was with his own father.

A shudder rips through me.

If I had known then what I know now, I would've... done nothing differently.

He needed me that night. He needs me right now. And there's nowhere else I'd rather be in the world.

Pushing everything aside, I focus on right now.

Reaching out, I wrap my fingers around the base of his length, and suck the head into my mouth, licking at it like it's a popsicle.

"Fuck. Fuck. Macie," he growls as I sink down on him until he hits the back of my throat. Then I lift off again, repeating it, running my tongue around him until he's trembling beneath me.

"Mmm," I hum as I move letting the vibrations flow through him.

"Shit. Red. So fucking good."

Unable to hold back, his hand finally releases the sheet in favor of my hair as his hips begin to lift from the bed.

"You gonna let me come in your hot little mouth, baby?"

I nod around him, upping my suction knowing that he's close.

"Fuck, yeah. Filthy slut. Fuuuuck," he groans as his orgasm slams into him. His cock jerks in my mouth, his salty cum hitting the back of my throat.

His eyes slam shut but I keep mine firmly on him as he rides out the pleasure.

In that moment, I feel like the most powerful woman in the world bringing this dark, slightly broken man to his knees.

"Fuck, that was good."

His hands grip me under my arms and he hauls me up his body, slamming his lips on mine and plunging his tongue into my mouth not caring about the fact he can probably taste himself on me.

"Why are you still here?" he asks when he finally releases my mouth.

I stare down into his confused eyes as he gazes up at me.

"Did you think you'd scare me off with what you've done?"

"Y-yeah. It would scare most people."

"It's a good thing that I'm not like most people then, isn't it?" A smirk twitches at his lips. "It's fucked up, Lee. I'm not going to pretend it isn't. But our lives haven't exactly been a bed of roses. I get your need for revenge, to hurt those who hurt you and those you love. I can't deny that I haven't had similar feelings about the man who hurt someone I care about."

His breath catches the second he realizes that I'm talking about him.

Reaching up, he tucks a lock of my hair behind my ear and I lean into his warmth.

"Tell me more, Red. What would you do to him?"

I shrug, not really having any specific ideas like I'm sure he does.

"I just want to make it end. I want you to feel safe. I want you to be able to put it behind you. To be able to have a future that's not tainted by him."

"Trust me, baby. I want that too."

Feeling his length once again hard beneath my core, I roll my hips and his eyes shutter.

"Should I be worried about the amount of blood you send down there?" I ask with a smirk.

He laughs and I can't help joining him, feeling utterly ridiculous, well that is until he reaches for himself and thrusts up inside me.

"I could say the same thing about how you're always wet for me, Red."

"Have you seen yourself?" I ask sitting up and running my fingers down his chest and over his abs as I sink even deeper onto his cock.

It feels incredible but I don't move, instead just allowing my body to get used to it as the burn fades.

"Leon?" I ask, looking him dead in the eyes.

"Yeah, baby?"

"Whatever you want to do to him, I want you to do it." His lips part in shock. "If you need my help, you've got it. I'll do whatever I can to make all this right for you. But I have one condition."

"O-okay," he breathes.

"Nothing happens to you. I don't want you to do anything that's going to damage your future in any way. I don't... I don't want—" I look away from him, the weight of what I want to say pressing down on my shoulders.

Reaching out, he tucks his fingers under my chin and forces me to look back at him.

"What, baby? What don't you want?"

"I don't—" A sob rips from my throat. "I don't want to lose you," I confess.

His eyes shutter, emotion filling them as his Adam's apple bobs as he swallows.

"Macie," he breathes, rolling us so I end up pinned beneath him, his forearms caging my head in. "I'm not going anywhere. You're not going to lose me."

"G-good. Because I kind of like you."

"Oh yeah?" he asks, a smile twitching at his lips. "I thought you hated me."

"I should. But I don't. I can't."

"I know the feeling, but I can't either, baby."

His lips find mine once more before his hips roll, making me gasp.

"Let me show you how you deserve to be treated."

And that's the last time his lips leave mine until we're both fighting for breath after finding our simultaneous releases. But this time there's nothing hurried, no hate, no anger... just want, need, hunger and dare I say it... love.

———

We're still laying in his bed, our limbs entwined a long time later when my stomach growls. No words have been said between us, but we don't need them.

Everything we needed to say has been said either via words or with our actions.

"Hungry?" he asks, pulling his head from the crook of my neck where he'd been resting.

"What gave me away?" I ask with a laugh as my stomach growls again.

"Come on," he says, untangling himself from me and rolling off the bed. "I'm taking you out for food."

My eyes leisurely run down the length of his naked body, lingering a little too long on his hard length that I'd been feeling pressed against my thigh for a while. He really is insatiable.

"Baby, looking at me like that isn't going to get you food faster."

"I know. I just... do you know how hot you are?"

He bursts out laughing.

"I'm glad you think so. At the beginning there for a bit, I didn't think you'd noticed." He winks and I throw a pillow at him.

"Arrogant jerk."

"You love it," he jokes, throwing it back at me then spinning on his heels and walking toward his dresser, his fine ass on full display.

"Yeah," I mutter, my eyes locked on his peachy behind. "I kinda do."

He shoots me a look over his shoulder and laughs.

"I'd get up while you can, Red," he warns, stepping into a clean pair of boxers and pulling them up his legs.

I slide to the side of his bed, my muscles pulling and aching in the most delicious way as I push to stand and search for my discarded clothing.

Once I'm dressed and have attempted to put myself back together, I walk over to the door where Leon's loitering.

"Ready?" I ask him, pushing my hair back from my face.

"Yeah," he says, but he doesn't make a move.

"Is everything okay?" I ask when he just continues to stare at me with an intensity that I'm beginning to get used to.

"Th-thank you. I'm sure coming here was probably the last thing you wanted to do after everything. But... thank you."

"I told you, I wouldn't be anywhere else." Reaching up on my toes, I brush my lips over his.

"Let's see if we can get out of here without you being stolen from me by one of my teammates."

"Colt's already tried," I confess and his steps falter.

"Colt's just asking for a beating."

"Leave him alone. He knew I was yours the second he saw the color of my hair," I deadpan.

"Fuck. I'm sorry."

"Don't be. The past is in the past right? We look forward."

"Fuck, baby. That sounds so fucking good."

Leon has his arm slung over my shoulder and we're almost out of the house without bumping into anyone when the front door opens and three people step inside.

Luca's eyes widen, Peyton smiles, and an older woman, who I can only assume is their mom, her eyes almost pop out of her head at the sight of me tucked into Leon's side.

"Macie," she breathes, a smile curling at her lips as she takes a step forward. "It's so nice to meet you."

"Uh... hi," I squeak, suddenly overcome with nerves.

I've never experienced anything close to meeting the parents before, I have no idea how I'm meant to react.

"I-I'm sorry for your loss," I say with a wince.

"Aw, sweetie, thank you but I think we can all agree that none of us are sorry."

Leon snorts as he tries to contain his laugh.

"Yeah, I guess. Still, it must have been a shock."

"We've been out making arrangements for the funeral," Luca says, making it sound about as appealing as picking up dog poop. "I think we can safely say that keeping it small is going to be out of the question."

"I guess that's what happens when most of the country has no idea what a cunt he was."

Their mom gasps in shock at Leon's harsh words but none of them argue.

"Just one final thing we need to toe the line for. Once it's done, we can finally break free,"

"Bring it on," Luca says, pulling Peyton into his arms and dropping a kiss to the top of her head.

"How's Shane?"

"About as good as you two," their mom mutters. "I'm sorry you had such a shitty father," she whispers, now looking a little emotional.

"We're just heading out for food. You hanging around for a bit?" Leon asks his mom.

"Just going to have coffee then I'm going to babysit Nadine so Shane and Chelsea can have a night off."

"Okay, we'll see you soon then. Call me if you need anything."

"You can run as fast as you want, Lee. I will get to know your girl sooner or later." She winks at him and he groans as he ushers me out of the door.

"It was nice to meet you Mrs.—" I hesitate because I have a feeling she won't want to be called Mrs. Dunn.

"It's Maddie, sweetie. Have a good day, both of you."

With his hand on the small of my back, Leon pushes me from the house.

"I'm sorry."

"What for? She seems nice."

"She is, she's just a little overexcited about you."

"She knows about me?" I ask. I saw the shock on Maddie's face, but something tells me it wasn't shock because she didn't know I existed.

"I told her about you," he confesses, pulling his passenger door open for me. "She knows who you are, your... connections."

"Oh?" I breathe, surprised he told her that much.

"I didn't give her details, but she's not stupid. She knows I was up to something when we first met."

"You mean, she doesn't think the sun shines out of your ass and that you treat women with the respect they deserve?" I ask, quirking a brow at him.

"Oh she knows there's no sunshine here, baby. I've been only dark clouds for years."

Despite being more than capable of doing it myself, Leon grabs the seat belt and reaches over me to strap me in.

"And as for treating you right. How many orgasms did you have upstairs?"

"I'm not sure that's something a mom would deem her son worthy of any woman."

"Well she should because I think I treated you damn well. Play your cards right and it might not even be the end for the day."

"Is that right?" I ask, unsure if my body will be able to take any more. My lady parts are beyond sore right now, although that doesn't seem to stop them clenching at his low whispered promise.

"We'll see. I might not be able to get it up after all that earlier."

Reaching out, I cup him over his jeans.

"Yeah, that seems like a real issue," I mutter, squeezing him until his eyelids lower and a low growl rumbles from deep in his throat.

"Careful, Red. You really wouldn't want my mom to watch me rail you on the hood of my car only minutes after meeting you."

"You wouldn't?" Although my stomach flips because I know full well that he probably would.

"You really want to try me?"

Thankfully, my stomach chooses that moment to grumble once again, and with a laugh, Leon ducks out of the car and closes the door behind him.

"Anyone would think you'd worked up an appetite," he says with a smirk, starting the ignition and backing out of the driveway.

"Yeah, something like that."

"Did I completely ruin your plans for the day?" he asks, thankfully changing the topic of conversation.

"Yep," I state. "I have a date."

His grip on the wheel tightens. "I'm sorry, you what?"

"Have a date?"

"With who?" His question comes out all low and growly.

Chuckling to myself, I stare out of the window at the frat houses as we pass.

"My law textbook. No need to go all caveman on me."

"Well, I'm sorry for ruining those riveting plans."

"Prior to you, I never had any riveting plans."

"Even hanging out with Nate?" he asks.

I smile to myself, knowing that he probably thinks he slipped that question in all smoothly.

"We either hang out working or shooting people."

"Shooting people?"

"Yeah, I'm pretty hot with a gun, don't you know?"

"You're talking about Xbox, right?"

"Can you really see me at a shooting range?"

"No," he says, glancing over at me with heat in his eyes, "But I'd like to. You looking all badass with a gun is certainly something I can get on board with."

"I've never held one. You?"

"Yeah, once or twice. Dad used to take us. You might be surprised to hear that he wanted us to be the best at that too."

"Surprised you never turned it on him."

"Trust me, Red. The temptation was real."

"Where are we going?" I ask when he heads to the other side of town.

"Wait and see." He turns to me and winks before taking a left that leads toward the community center I spend my Monday nights at.

He pulls up just down the road from where he was parked that first night he found me here and kills the engine.

"Here?"

"Yeah. Come on."

I climb out of the car and he scowls down at me when he meets me.

"I was going to get that."

"Who knew Leon Dunn could be such a gentleman."

"Absolutely no one. It's even a shock to me."

Closing my door for me, seeing as I screwed up the chance for him opening it for me, he slides his hand into mine, twisting our fingers together before pulling me in the opposite direction of the community center.

A smile twitches at my lips, my mouth watering and my stomach growling when I realize where he's taking me.

Paulo looks up the second the bell above the door rings with our arrival.

"Miss Macie, what are you doing here on a Saturday afternoon?"

"Hey Paulo," I say with a wide, genuine smile as we walk up to the counter still hand in hand. "How are you?"

"All the better for seeing you. And you brought the football star back too."

"How could I refuse another of Maddison's best subs?"

Paulo's cheeks redden at the compliment. Who knew my football star could even charm old men?

"Two meatball subs, please," Leon says, making butterflies take flight in my belly.

"It would be my pleasure." Paulo turns to make our order while Leon tugs me into his side, pressing his nose into my hair and breathing me in.

"Did you just sniff me?"

"I did, baby. Problem?"

"You're ruining your rep, you know that, right? Being seen in public with me more than once, making it look like I'm your girlfriend."

His breath catches in his throat at my words.

"You are."

"I am what?" I ask, too lost in his sparkling green eyes to remember what I just said.

Dropping his lips to my ear, he whispers. "My girlfriend."

I rear back in shock. "I am?"

"Don't you want to be?"

"I... um... uh... I didn't realize we were... that you..."

Taking both of my hands in his, he turns me to face him.

The group of kids sitting at the window don't pay us any mind as my heart rate picks up and butterflies take flight in my belly.

"Macie," he says, his voice strong and confident. "Will you... be mine?"

I stare at him, not believing that this is really happening. That Leon Dunn. The Panthers #14. MKU's star wide receiver is standing in a sandwich shop asking me to be his.

Despite everything I've always told myself, despite everything we've been through, all my doubts and fears melt away as I stare into his eyes.

Everything he's told me, his darkest secrets, the parts of himself he never wanted to expose. All of it tells me that right now, the Leon I'm looking at, the one whose both been so wicked with me and also so tender is the real him.

Yes, I've still got so much to learn about him. But he has a lot to learn about me too. Our pasts might be messy, but together, I have faith that we can carve out a much cleaner, healthier future.

I know we've still got issues to deal with, because even if he told me to forget about his revenge mission on my uncle now, I don't think I'd let him because if I'm being honest with myself, I want it as much as he does. It's time Richard Fletcher paid for what he did to us, what he did to the others that we don't know about.

"I-I..." His brows pinch as I hesitate, and although it might be evil, that one little pause, the slight fear that trickles into his features tells me everything I need to know. "I will."

Before I know what's happening, he's got his arm behind my back and he's dipping me movie-style in front of the sandwich counter.

I have no idea if anyone notices us because the only person I focus on is him and the wide smile on his face.

"Macie Fletcher. *My* Macie Fletcher."

"Leon," I breathe.

"You've turned my world upside down, baby, and I never want it to stop."

Before I can respond, he presses his lips to mine in the sweetest, most intense kiss. It's innocent... mostly, but I feel it all the way down to my toes.

I'm smiling when he rights me once more, immediately pulling me back into his side as if it's where I belong.

"Two meatball subs for the lovebirds," Paulo says. "And two cookies, on the house for my favorite customer." He gives me a wink.

"Looks like I've got some competition," Leon jokes.

"If I were forty years younger, young man, you might have a problem."

We all laugh as we pay. It's just another reminder of why I love it here so much.

Leon takes our food in one hand and wraps his other arm around my waist, leading me from the shop and toward the park.

"Back to where it all started, huh?" I ask as we lower ourselves to the same bench.

"If we wanted to go right back, we'd need to be in Charlie's room."

"Yeah, or we could forget about that and just imagine it all started here."

"I couldn't believe it that night when I turned around and saw you standing there. Ten years I'd been looking for you. I'd searched social media regularly. Googled you, Richard, anyone who might be connected to you. I never found anything."

"Exactly how I wanted it. After Dad died, the media were horrible. Keeping me from that was probably the only good thing Richard ever did for me.

"I know the main reason Dad did what he did was because of losing Mom. But the press played a part. They were always there, wanting to know what was happening. He never had a chance to grieve properly and because of that we paid the ultimate price."

"I'm so sorry you lost them both like that."

Even after all these years, I don't have a suitable response when someone says something like that. So instead of saying anything, I reach out, take my sandwich and begin unwrapping it.

"They'd be so proud of you, you know that, right?"

I shrug, not wanting to hear it. Both of my parents were outgoing people. They loved life until too much of it was ripped away from them. I often feel like I would have been the ultimate let down.

"I haven't exactly done anything," I mutter.

"You survived, Macie. Do you have any idea how fucking strong you are? The fact you're still putting one foot in front of the other is a miracle in itself."

"It's just life, Lee. What else can we do?"

He stares at me and I hear his unspoken words about taking the easy way out like my dad did and I hang my head.

No matter how hard shit gets, I'll never do that. I might not have many people in my life, but I refuse to ever put anyone through what I went through when I was barely old enough to understand why my dad did what he did.

"I'm in awe of you."

"Stop it," I say, shaking my head, unable to accept his words. "You of all people can't say things like that to me. Not after what you've been through."

"I thought all my Christmases had come at once when I found you standing in Charlie's room," he says, going back to our earlier topic. "I thought you were a figment of my imagination. I've never felt anger and relief quite like that ever."

"I was mostly terrified. No one had ever held me by the throat before."

He laughs as he takes a bite of his sandwich and I forget about what we were talking about as I watch him lick some sauce from his lip and chew.

Why is that so hot?

Eating shouldn't be so freaking hot.

"You loved it, though, didn't you?" he asks, looking over at me and catching me staring.

"I was mostly just confused."

"Sure," he breathes, his voice all deep and rough. "You knew what you were walking into that night, didn't you, Red?"

My cheeks heat because I really should have, but I was genuinely just concerned for Charlie.

I shake my head. "N-no. And what I walked into, I never could have imagined."

"Me either. All my dreams came true in a hot little package."

"Stop," I whisper, my cheeks burning.

Reaching over, he takes my free hand. "I mean it. I thought I was meant to find you to take my pain out on you. I never realized that I needed to find you so that you could save me."

"I haven't saved you, Lee. All that's on you. I've just... understood."

"You more than understand, Mace."

"Yeah," I agree sadly. "Pain is certainly easier to take when it can be shared."

"Who knew?" he jokes.

"Not me. I've spent my life trying to stay away from people," I mutter, thinking of all the friendships and relationships I probably could've formed if I weren't too terrified of losing someone else. Of being used by someone else.

"How's that working out for you?"

"You've ruined it. I'm still utterly terrified though," I confess.

"I know. But I promise, I'm not going to hurt you. I'm not gonna leave you. I'm not your dad, and I'm certainly not your uncle."

"You're not your dad either," I add, sensing that he needs to hear it.

He's quiet for a moment, his jaw ticking as he thinks.

"I like to think that I've experienced all of the things a parent or guardian shouldn't be, and I hope that one day I get the chance to show how it can be done right."

"You want kids, Lee?" I ask.

"Yeah, I guess. One day. You?"

"Honestly, I've never really thought about it. I've spent all my life thinking about how to make life better for kids who've been hurt like us. I never really stopped to think about the chance of having my own. Kinda hard when I went out of my way to be alone."

"You want to help kids?" he asks, something like pride sparkling in his eyes.

"Why do you think I'm sticking around for Richard's money? I certainly don't want it for me. It's nothing more than blood money as far as I'm concerned."

Leon's brows pinch so I continue.

"I want to set up a foundation, a charity of some sort to help abused kids see their potential and make something of their lives. His money is going to make it happen. Attempt to right some wrongs."

"That sounds incredible."

"We'll see right. He's been withholding my inheritance from my parents and grandparents. Plus his own fortune. It should give the foundation a real kickstart. Just need him to—"

"Die," he finishes for me.

"Yeah."

Silence falls around us as I'm sure we both start planning just how that can happen discreetly. I never thought I'd ever seriously consider his demise, but also I can't deny that the time has come. And after all, we're probably doing him a favor. He's only going to rot in that place as his brain completely leaves him. It's probably what he deserves, to be honest. But knowing he's no longer breathing the same air as Leon, that he can never hurt him again means more to me. Finally giving him some peace is everything to me after the years he's suffered at the hands of that monster.

"I also planned something else," I confess quietly.

"Oh yeah?"

"I was..." I hesitate because I have no idea how he's going to take this. "I was going to expose him. Find others who might've been abused by him."

"Shit," he hisses, scrubbing his hand down his face.

"I don't have to," I say in a rush knowing that he's not going to want to be involved in such a scandal. "I know that it'll be hard to—"

"No," he states confidently. "You should. We should."

"Really?"

"Everyone should know what a scumbag he is—my father too. Parents across the country trust these men to look after their children and they're abusing that trust. If what we've been through can help others, then we should."

"Yeah?" I ask, hope blooming in my chest.

Twisting his fingers with mine, he lifts my knuckles to his lips.

"Some good shit has got to come out of all this, don't you think?"

I nod, hope for our futures multiplying within me faster than I can control.

"Can you hear that?"

I focus, straining to her what he clearly can.

It's faint, but I hear it. "Music?"

"Yeah. Shall we go and check it out?"

"Sure."

Leon's sandwich is long gone and after quickly eating the last of mine, he takes the bag with the cookies for later and gathers me up into his side.

The sun has set and the evening chill is descending, but tucked against his warm body, I don't even feel it.

Contentment like I've never experienced before washes through me.

For the first time in my life, I feel like I actually belong, that I'm actually where I'm meant to be.

I thought I felt it when I arrived here, but now being here with

Leon I realize that that was only the beginning of finding my home. He's the final part.

We walk down the path until a crowd of people in the distance emerges before us.

There's a grandstand that I've only ever seen deserted nestled in the trees, but tonight, it's not empty because there's a live band under the cover playing away for a crowd of people who are all sitting around on blankets having a picnic while they enjoy the music.

"Wow," I breathe.

Leon brings us to a stop a little before the edge of the people and pulls me in front of him, the hard length of his body pressing against my back as his arms wrap around my waist and his chin rests on the top of my head.

I sigh, happiness making my lips curl into a smile as we just stand and absorb the evening.

I have no idea how much time passes, I'm too lost in the music and the feeling of him holding me closer but after a while, he pulls away a little, his lips brushing my ear.

"Dance with me," he breathes.

There are a few couples off to the side of the stage who are dancing but we're nowhere near them.

I stand still, shocked by his request.

"What's wrong, Red? Think I'm going to be a better dancer than you," he jokes.

"I've got the rhythm of a baby giraffe so it's highly likely."

Laughing, he spins me around and presses our bodies together as his hands land on my lower back, ensuring there's not an inch of space between us.

Pressing my cheeks against his chest, I breathe him in and just move with his body.

Emotion clogs my throat and my eyes burn with tears as the significance of the moment hits me out of nowhere.

I learned years ago to lock up how I really feel. Showing it was a weakness. I wasn't living with Richard for long before I discovered this fact.

He didn't understand that I needed to cry for my loss, for the fact my life had been turned upside down, and he really didn't get that how he treated me made me want to cry most of the time.

I contained my tears to my room after only weeks of being there, but after a while, I even trained myself to keep them in while I was securely behind that door.

I sniffle, unable to stop myself and Leon stills, looking down at me.

"What's wrong?"

I shake my head, laughing at myself.

"Nothing. I'm happy."

The most incredible smile curls at his lips, as his eyes soften, the concern leaving them.

"Yeah?"

"Yeah. Thank you," I whisper.

"I don't deserve your thanks, Macie. I should be the one saying that to you every minute of the day."

I shake my head. "You think I saved you, you've got no idea what you've done for me. You've brought me to life, Lee."

"I'm glad I could help, baby. You just needed someone to be a little crazy with."

"You're most definitely crazy."

"You wouldn't have me any other way," he laughs.

"Everyone is going to think I'm crazy for this."

"Fuck everyone else, Mace. They haven't lived our lives. They don't know what it was like. They can fuck off with their opinions and judgment. The only person's opinion I care about is the one in my arms right now.

"I want you to be happy, Macie. I want you to keep discovering the incredible person you've kept hidden inside, and I want to be right there with you as you experience all the pleasures in life."

"Always about sex," I mutter lightly.

"Hey, I could've been talking about ice cream."

"Were you?" I ask, quirking a brow at him.

"Well, no but I could have been."

"Sure." Looping my arms around his neck, I stretch up on my toes and press a kiss to his jaw. "Thank you for this."

"This was luck. I was just craving one of Paulo's sandwiches."

As I continue looking at him, thinking about our new reality, a thought hits me.

"What is it, Red?"

"I-I'm dating a football player."

He throws his head back and laughs at my realization.

"You're doing more than dating him, baby. You're his. For good. No take backs."

"That's good because I don't want any."

"Come on, I've had enough of sharing you with others."

"Greedy," I mutter as he releases me.

"Baby, you've got no idea."

We walk back to Leon's car hand in hand, both of us smiling like idiots.

"My place or yours."

"Uh..." I think for a moment, although there really is only one answer. "Yours."

"You sure? It's full of sweaty, rude football players."

"I'm sure I can handle it. I've tamed the worst of them."

"Whipped and proud, baby."

"Wanna stop at yours and pick up some stuff?"

"Yeah, sounds good. Just... just promise me something."

"Shoot."

"If Nate is there, please don't hit him."

"You've got my word. But in my defense, he wants something that belongs to me."

"He doesn't. And even if he did, you don't need to worry, I've only got eyes for one guy, and he's not a basketball player."

"Fair enough. Can you do something for me then?" I look at him, waiting for him to make whatever weird demand he's thinking about. "Don't ever wear his jersey again. The only guy's name and number you'll have on your back from now on is mine, Red."

"Big words for someone who hasn't given me his jersey yet."

"Gonna be like that is it?"

"Sure is, Dunn. You wanna own it, you gotta put your name on it."

"Fair enough."

17

LEON

"Y**ou've got thirty minutes to pack your shit," I tell Macie the second I pull up in the parking lot behind her building.

"You're not coming up?" she asks, her brows pinching in concern.

"No. I've got something I need to do. I won't be long though."

"You haven't changed your mind already, have you?" It's meant to be a joke, but I hear the insecurity in her voice.

Reaching out, I wrap my hand around the back of her neck.

"About you? Never, baby." I brush my lips over hers. My need to deepen the kiss and take exactly what I need is almost all-consuming, but I somehow manage to pull back. "You trust me?"

She hesitates for a second and my stomach sinks even after everything I've told her, all the darkest secrets that I've confided in her that she still doesn't.

"Yeah," she finally says. "I do."

"Thirty minutes," I repeat, kissing the tip of her nose and waiting for her to get out.

The second she closed the door, I hit the gas and peel out of the parking lot.

I've just given myself one serious time limit to get what I need done.

———

I'm late getting back and I fucking hate myself for it.

I fly into the parking lot already planning my groveling speech to get back on her good side.

Thankfully, the second I spot movement over by the building, everything in me relaxes as she stands from the wall she was sitting against.

"I'm so sorry," I say, rushing over to her. "I got held up."

She stares at me, her face impassive but I can tell from the set of her shoulders that she's annoyed.

"It's okay," she says, pushing from the wall and moving to walk around me.

"No, it's not. But I couldn't find what I wanted. They'd moved it."

Her eyes narrow on me and despite telling myself that I'd wait until we were back in my room, I pull one of her gifts from my pocket.

"What's this?" she asks, looking down at the box in my hand.

"Open it. Find out."

Placing her overnight bag against the wall, she hesitantly takes it from me.

"It's not a bomb, Mace."

"I-I know. It's just... no one's ever..." She trails off but she doesn't need to say the words for me to know what was coming next.

"I thought as much. That's why I wanted to get you something."

Her eyes are full of unshed tears when she looks up at me.

"Who are you and what have you done with my wicked Leon?" she jokes, trying to push aside the magnitude of the moment.

"He's still here, baby. Unlike most people, you just get both sides."

Heat colors her cheeks and spreads down to her chest.

Nudging her hand, I encourage her to open it.

It's not much really, just something I saw when I was out one day that made me think of her. The way she's acting, anyone would think there's an engagement ring inside or something crazy.

"I like both sides of you. They're both equally as terrifying," she confesses as she swallows her nerves and pulls the lid of the box off.

"Lee," she breathes, her voice cracking with emotion as she pulls the chain from its cushion, studying the two charms that hang from it.

"I thought that maybe we could add to it. Make some memories together."

She stares at it for long seconds, her expression unreadable as my heart beats so fast waiting for her reaction I start to get a little light-headed.

Her finger runs over the book charm and then the football, sucking her bottom lip into her mouth as she thinks.

"D-do you like it?" I ask, unable to cope with the silence any longer.

"I-I... I love it," she cries, closing her fingers around the piece of jewelry and jumping into my arms.

I grunt as we collide and I wrap my arms around her, holding her tight.

"Thank you. I love it," she whispers in my ear. "Will you take me home now?"

Home.

Fuck. That word sounds so good falling from her lips.

"Hell yes I can."

With her still in my arms, I reach out for her bag and carry them over to the car.

"There's something else too," I confess, reaching into what I left on the passenger seat.

Pulling the fabric from the bag, I turn back to her and hold it up for her to see.

"Looks like it's official."

Before she has a chance to argue, I tug the jersey over her head forcing it over the top of her hoodie. She helps me out by pushing her arms into the holes.

"Turn around." She does as she's told and I push her up against the car, making her gasp as I stare at my name and number on her.

Threading my fingers into her hair, I twist, forcing her to look back at me.

"I'm going to fuck you wearing that," I warn her.

"Wouldn't want it any other way, Dunn." She winks and I slam my lips down on hers for a searing kiss. "Not in the parking lot though, hey?" she asks with a laugh when I eventually release her.

"Okay, maybe not this time. But I would."

"Oh, don't I know it." She grinds her ass back into my crotch, making me groan.

Standing back a little, I allow her to turn back around.

"Put this on for me?" She holds her wrist out and then passes me the bracelet.

"I take back what I said earlier. I'm going to fuck you with my number on your back and our future around your wrist."

I snap the clasp into place and damn near push her into the car, my desperation getting the better of me.

The short journey back to the house is tense as I white knuckle the wheel and keep my eyes firmly looking out the windshield.

I know that if I so much as look over at her, then all bets are going to be off and I'm going to end up pulling over and making her ride me right here in my goddamn car.

"Relax," she says, her voice soft as her tiny palm lands on my thigh.

My muscles bunch at her warmth, my cock straining against my zipper.

"Macie," I warn, my voice low and dangerous.

"Oh, there he is," she says, amusement in her tone.

"There's who?" I ask, confused.

"My wicked Leon."

"I hope you know you're about three seconds away from sucking me off right here."

Her gasp of shock tells me that she had no idea.

Risking a glance over at her, I find her full pink lips parted and her cheeks flushed with desire.

"You would too, wouldn't you, my filthy little Macie?"

"I-I... um..." Her hand answers for me as it slides up my thigh, cupping me through the denim of my jeans.

"Fuck," I bark, my grip on the wheel turning painful as she flicks the button and lowers the zipper.

"Do me a favor, yeah?" she asks, her voice all sweet and innocent, the complete opposite of her actions as she shimmies my jeans over my hips when I lift up, allowing my aching cock to spring free.

"Sure," I force out, desperately trying to look where I'm going and not down at the way she's staring at me.

"Don't kill us. I've got plans."

"O-okay, yeah. I'll... do my beeeeest," I moan as she licks the precum gathered at the tip of my cock.

"Macie, I need— fuuuuck."

Twisting on her seat, she lowers herself right onto my cock, taking me all the way to the back of her throat.

"Holy shit," I gasp, trying to focus as she pulls off, licking up the length of me before taking me back into her hot mouth.

"Fuck, you're good at this."

The frat houses are a blur as I pass them, my need to get onto the driveway and stop the car is the only thing I can think about, aside from what's happening down below.

"Oh God. Oh God."

Slamming my foot on the brake, the car screeches to a halt only millimeters behind Luca's.

We're at the side of the house and thankfully, there are no windows beside us, but that doesn't mean we can't be seen.

Releasing the wheel, I twist my fingers into her hair instead, helping her movements.

"That's it, baby. Suck my cock like a good little girl."

My hips roll, my need to buck up into her is almost too much to deny, but then she exposes her teeth and drags them up my length and I explode.

"Shit. Fuck. Macie, baby. Fuck."

She doesn't stop until she's swallowed every single drop of me. The second she begins to move, I drag her up by her hair and slam her lips down on mine.

"That was the hottest fucking thing that's ever happened to me."

I kiss her, plunging my tongue deep into her mouth tasting my own saltiness on hers. It only gets me hotter for more.

I'm on the verge of lifting her onto my lap when there's a loud knocking at the trunk before the car starts rocking.

"When the car's a rockin'..." someone calls, forcing us both into action.

"Oh my God," Macie gasps, frantically pushing her hair out of her face and wiping at her mouth. As if there's a chance of her still having spunk there after that kiss.

"It's okay. The guys have seen much worse."

"I don't care. The only one I want watching me giving you head is you."

"I'm sure they didn't see anything."

"You'd better be right," she mutters, gathering up her bags.

"Come on. I can think straight now you've taken the edge off."

"Oh great, I'm glad you're feeling better," she deadpans.

"Come on, I'll think of a way to make it up to you."

Taking her bags, I throw them over my shoulder before wrapping my arm around her waist and pulling her into my side.

"Just so you know," I whisper, dropping my lips to her ear. "That was the best head of my life."

"Lee," she moans, embarrassment coming off her in waves.

Pushing through the front door, we're greeted by silence. Perfect.

Steering her into the kitchen to grab drinks, I'm not expecting to find two smiling faces looking back at us.

"Oh... hey," I say to Luca and Peyton.

"Good night?" Luc asks, a wide smirk on his face as Peyton smacks him upside the head.

Macie groans, planting her face in my chest.

"He's just jealous, baby," I whisper.

"That doesn't make it any better," she mumbles back.

"Whoa, look at that," Luca says, climbing off his stool and stepping toward me.

"What?" I ask reluctantly.

"You're smiling."

"Fuck off. I smile. Often."

"Yeah. Fake ones. That one right there." He nods toward my face. "Is fucking real."

"Right, well... How's Mom?" I ask swiftly, turning the conversation away from me.

"She's good. Relieved."

"I know the fucking feeling."

"Same. Still surprised he was shooting that shit into his veins."

"Nothing surprises me when it comes to our sperm donor," I mutter, pulling the refrigerator door open and grabbing a couple of sodas.

"I guess. It just doesn't seem like him. He was such a control freak."

Peyton walks over and laces her arm through Luc's, resting her head on his shoulder. For the first time since they got back together, I'm not floored by a wave of jealousy. For once, I'm truly happy for them. Reaching for Macie, I tug her closer, dropping a kiss to the top of her head.

"Maybe the whore did it," Peyton adds.

"Seems fairly pointless seeing as she died right alongside him."

"Bad trip?" Macie asks.

"Yeah, maybe. Does it even really matter?" Luca asks. "He's gone. No longer able to terrorize any of us."

"Yeah, I guess," I mutter, but not meaning it.

Luca doesn't know what I know. He has no idea that there's something very questionable going on with our father's mysterious death.

Not wanting to stand around here discussing him, I look down at Macie.

"Ready?"

She smiles up at me, making all kinds of images spin around in my head.

"Yep."

I'm leading her out of the kitchen when Peyton's cell rings.

"Lib, how are you doing?" she asks, excitement filling her voice.

"How's she doing?" I whisper, turning back to Luc.

"Yeah, really good. Already got the staff wrapped around her little finger apparently."

"Oh?" I ask, wondering what the hell she could get rehab staff and therapists doing for her.

"Don't ask." He shakes his head.

"She always was good at causing trouble," I say with a laugh, leading Macie from the room and toward the stairs.

"Whoa, he let you back for another visit?" Colt says as he and another guy I recognize walk around the corner.

"Yeah. She's going to be here a lot," I stare. "Get used to it or get out."

"Oh, getting pussy whipped makes Leon grumpy," Colt sings. "Anyone would think you didn't just get—"

I have him backed up against the wall before he's realized I've moved. "Finish that sentence and I'll end your season before it's even begun," I growl in his face.

"Bro, chill. I'm only yanking your chain."

A low growl rumbles up my throat.

"You so much as look at her the wrong way and I'll get you fucking benched, asshole."

"Dude, you know redheads aren't my thing," he argues.

"It's just spitfire blondes, right?" Macie adds making me smirk and ensuring all the fight leaves me.

She steps up to me and runs her hand across my stomach, causing my muscles to bunch and for me to take a step back.

"You're lucky she's here," I tell him, continuing to step back.

He laughs at me, running his hand through his hair. "I can take you any day, Dunn, and you know it."

"Not worth it," Macie breathes, and I can't help but agree with her. "Work up a sweat with me instead."

"Now that sounds like an offer I can't refuse."

Without sparing him another glance, I press my hand into the small of Macie's back and guide her up the stairs before me, my eyes locked on her ass in her skinny jeans as she moves.

"I'm going for a piss," I tell her, moving toward my bathroom. "When I get back, I want you in my bed in nothing but my jersey."

Her chin drops at my demand but it doesn't stop her from toeing off her shoes and lifting both my jersey and her hoodie up her stomach.

I bolt for the bathroom before I forget my need and focus on her instead.

———

"This is nice," Macie says, digging her spoon back into the tub of ice cream that I stole from Peyton knowing that it would make her smile.

"It is. I never thought I could have so much fun in bed with a girl without being inside her."

"You're a dog," she chastises, swatting my bare stomach.

"I'm your dog," I say, snatching her wrist and pushing her hand down under the covers and into my boxers.

We haven't fooled around other than a bit of making out when I first found her in my bed having done exactly what I ordered.

That doesn't mean I'm not beyond ready to sink back inside her, but I'm aware that she's probably sore from me taking her earlier, and I don't want to break her, not any more at least. Now, I fully intend on keeping and making her happy.

Her delicate fingers wrap around my steel length as she continues pretending like she's watching the movie that's playing on the TV.

I haven't focused on a second of it, preferring to watch her and all her little reactions to whatever has been happening, committing them to memory and finally allowing myself to accept that she's it for me.

I might've gone after Macie with the need to ruin her, but in the end, it seems that she was the one who ruined me, because I already know that I'm never going to be the same ever again.

She's taken my darkness and wrapped it in her sweetness, her acceptance, her understanding.

My anger and hate might still be within me, it probably always will be to a point, but she makes it bearable. No, it's more than that. She makes it almost forgettable. Especially when she's beside me, touching me... loving me.

Love.

I let that one word repeat over and over in my mind as she slowly works me.

Is that what this is? Is this what it feels like?

I've always wondered. As I watched Luca and Peyton fall in love as kids, and then Letty and Kane recently.

Is that what they feel? This contentment, happiness, the constant burning need to claim her, mark her, make her mine.

Suddenly, everything I watched Letty go through, and Luca and Peyton over the years, it all makes sense.

It's why Macie is laying here with me right now.

It's why she's forgiven me. Why she hasn't judged me.

"I love you," I whisper so quietly that there's no chance of her hearing me.

Or so I think.

It takes a second but she drags her eyes from the TV and looks up at me.

"Sorry, did you say something?"

"Y-yeah... uh..." I panic. Not because I don't know how I feel, but because I'm not sure I'm ready to actually tell her yet.

If she doesn't feel the same and looks at me with pity and horror, I'm not sure I'd be able to deal with it.

So instead, I let my fear control me.

"Th-thank you."

"Thank you? For..." Her movements get a little more forceful. "For jacking you off?" she asks with the cutest expression on her face.

"No, baby. Just for being you. For being here. For believing in me."

"I didn't have a choice, Lee. There isn't anywhere else in the world I'd rather be."

Pulling her hand from my underwear, I press it to the mattress above her head and roll over her.

"Yeah?" I ask, brushing my nose against hers.

"Yeah." This time when she speaks her voice comes out all breathy and needy. Climbing between her legs, I roll my hips, letting her feel what she does to me. "Lee," she moans.

"You do this to me, Macie. Only you."

I capture her lips in a searing kiss, hoping that I can show her how I feel without having to confess those words quite yet.

We make out until neither of us can keep going and we pass out tangled in each other's arms.

When I come to once more, she's still pressed tightly against my body, her legs threaded through mine.

Assuming it's her heat that's woken me, I snuggle back in, pulling her tight. I'm just about to drift off again when a buzzing starts up.

Glancing over at my nightstand, I see my cell with the screen dark.

"Macie," I whisper, not really wanting to wake her but knowing that her cell hardly ever rings so it might be important. "Macie, your cell."

"Huh?" she asks groggily, opening her eyes to find me in the darkness.

"Your cell is ringing."

"What time is it?"

"No idea. Late."

"Shit. Okay."

Throwing back the covers, she untangles herself from me and pads over to her purse.

She's still wearing nothing but my jersey and the sight of her curvy legs poking out from the bottom make my cock wake up instantly.

"Who is it?" I ask when the light from her screen illuminates her in the dark room.

"Unknown. They've called five times in thirty minutes." Dread settles in my belly the second she says that. Nothing good comes from that many midnight phone calls.

She stares at it for another second before the buzzing starts again.

"Answer it," I say when she looks like she's going to ignore it.

"H-hello?" she asks after lifting it to her ear.

Her brows pinch as she listens to whoever's on the other end before her eyes lock with mine, something flashing in her eyes that I can't decipher in the darkness.

"Yeah. Okay. Yeah. As soon as we can. Yep. Thank you. Goodbye."

"What the—"

"Richard had a heart attack."

My chin drops at her words.

"He's in the hospital, but it doesn't look good. He's unconscious, on a ventilator."

"Shit."

She glances at the screen briefly before setting it on my nightstand and crawling back into bed with me.

"Is he going to—"

"She suggested I get there as quickly as possible if I wanted to see him."

"Shit," I repeat.

Reaching for my hand, she lifts it to her lips.

"It's going to be over, Lee. Our pasts can die with him and we haven't even had to do anything."

My lips part to say something but I can't find any words.

Relief and regret slam into me all at once.

I can't deny that I'm glad he could have already taken his last breath. But equally, I wanted to be there when he took it. I wanted to look into his cold, evil eyes so he knew who was responsible for his last moments.

Maybe it was a bit of a pipe dream. A fantasy.

I've never had any kind of clue how I could have made it happen. It's why I needed Reid. He's got the kind of contacts I would need.

"Are you okay?" she asks, cupping my cheek and bringing me back to the here and now.

"Y-yeah. I'm good," I tell her honestly.

"I'm going to have to go to Miami," she says sadly. "There are going to be things I'm going to have to take care of."

"Y-yeah, of course." Sitting up against the headboard, now fully awake, I pull her into my side, dropping my nose to her hair and breathing her in.

"It's going to be over," I whisper against her.

"It is."

18

MACIE

Silence falls around us as we both get lost in our own thoughts. Memories of my childhood with that evil man flicker through my mind but they quickly merge into the image of him now, weak, frail and in a hospital bed.

I don't even feel guilty for feeling glad he's in that position.

"I'm coming with you," Leon states suddenly, the determination in his voice startling me.

"N-no, you don't have t—"

"I'm coming. I'm not letting you do that alone."

"Lee—"

"I want to be by your side, Macie. Nothing you can say will deter me."

"Don't you have breakfast with Kayden tomorrow morning," I point out, remembering him saying that it was usually a weekly thing.

"Shit. I can't let him down. We didn't do it last week. But… fuck."

Throwing my leg over his waist, I hold his cheeks in my hands and stare into his eyes.

"We'll go after your breakfast. It's not like he's going anywhere," I deadpan.

Reaching up, his giant hands cover mine.

"You're coming too. I want you to meet Kayden."

My stomach flips at the thought of meeting more of his family. Although I quickly figure that meeting a five-year-old can't be half as terrifying as meeting his mother.

"O-okay."

Leaning forward, he brushes his lips over mine. I want to say no, to pull away knowing that my breath is less than fresh but the second we connect, I'm powerless but to move into his body and return the kiss.

"What time is it?"

"Almost four-thirty,"

"Hmm..." He nuzzles my neck. "What can we do with all this extra time we have?"

"Sleep?" I suggest, much to his amusement.

"Not what I had in mind, Red."

His hand slips under my shirt—his jersey—and finds my bare breasts.

"Lee." I moan when he squeezes them before rolling my nipples between his fingers.

"Now that's more like it."

He licks a trail up my neck and to my ear.

"We've got things to celebrate, after all."

It's wrong. So freaking wrong. But at the same time, totally right.

"I guess we have."

"Leon, are you ready?" Luca shouts two minutes before we're due to leave to pick up Kayden for breakfast.

"Yeah, don't get your panties in a twist."

"I swear to God, if we're late to get him because you're getting la—"

I pull the door open, smiling brightly at Leon's twin brother.

"We're ready." I push the door open wider so he can see Leon tugging on his sneakers. "See."

"You coming too?"

"Yeah. I-if that's okay?" I stutter, suddenly realizing that anyone other than Leon might not actually want me there.

He looks from me to Lee and back again. Whatever he sees on his brother's face softens his expression and he nods.

"Of course. It looks like you're one of us now."

My chin drops, not quite expecting to be accepted so easily.

"Don't look so shocked. Not all the rumors are true," he jokes.

"I-I haven't heard any—"

"He's winding you up, Red. Just ignore him. If you can deal with my rep, then his is nothing."

"Knowing how bad yours is, Dunn, that doesn't reassure me."

"Oh, ouch," Luca says with a laugh. "I think you're going to fit right in here, *Red*."

A growl rumbles from behind me, seconds before arms wrap around my waist.

"Do you mind not flirting with my girl? You've got one of your own to torment."

"I'm just being friendly. Jesus. Possessive much."

Leon scoffs at his comment but I don't ask. The last thing I want is to get in the middle of the brothers' pissing match.

We find Peyton waiting for us in the kitchen before the four of us jump into Luca's car and head across town.

The conversation is light but the reality of what the rest of our day holds forces me to blurt it out.

"My uncle is in the hospital. I don't think he's going to make it."

Leon's hand tenses in mine. It's almost as if my words are a reminder, but I know him better than that now. There's no way he's forgotten my middle of the night phone call and what it means for him —for us.

"I... um..." Peyton stutters clearly not really knowing how to approach that news.

Luca on the other hand makes his feelings known immediately. "Good. Couldn't have happened to a nicer person," he deadpans. "I hope it hurt like hell."

Leon chuckles beside me.

"We're heading out there after breakfast."

Luca glances back at his brother in the rearview mirror, concern evident in his eyes.

"You sure that's a good idea?" he asks, clearly remembering what happened the last time we were in Miami.

"Yeah. Macie needs to be there, which means I'll be there." Warmth spreads through my chest at his words. "We're not staying at the house," he states.

"We're not?"

"Nope. I've booked us a place to stay," he confesses.

"When did you do that?"

"While you were in the shower?"

I shake my head at him knowing that he only left me alone in there for about four minutes tops.

"H-how?"

"Don't worry about it. Just know I've organized something good."

He lifts my hand to his lips and kisses my knuckles.

Feeling the heat of Luca's stare in the mirror once more, I glance over at him.

"She looks good on you, Bro. Hold her fucking tight."

My heart slams against my ribs. Knowing I've got Luca's approval means more to me than it should. But a lifetime of never fitting in or belonging anywhere does that to a person.

"I fully intend to, Bro." Tugging on my arm, he pulls me closer and drops a kiss to my temple before whispering, "You're mine," so that only I can hear.

It's only seconds later when Luca brings the car to a stop. I look out at the house before us to see the front door open and a little boy comes speeding out on a pair of crutches, a wide beaming smile spread across his face, quickly followed by an exasperated but happy woman.

Both Leon and Luca step out of the car to meet their brother, but I don't move. I can't, I'm transfixed watching as they greet him.

"They're incredible with him," Peyton muses, startling me.

I'd forgotten she was still in the car with me.

"He looks so happy."

"He literally thinks they hung the moon. Like, they are the two coolest guys in the world."

"Ugh, he hasn't told them that, has he?" I joke, knowing full well that both of their egos are already big enough.

"He doesn't need to with that look on his face."

"That's one lucky little boy right there." I don't really mean to say it aloud, but I can't deny it's true.

"For a while I thought he'd been handed a shit deal with Mom and everything." She doesn't go into detail, obviously not knowing how much I know about the situation. "But, yeah, things have turned out good."

"Families don't need to be conventional to work," I say, as if I'm a freaking expert on the matter.

I've barely ever had a family let alone a working one.

"I know. And with Brett gone, this family is only going to get stronger."

Ripping her eyes away from the guys as they joke around with Kayden, she glances back at me.

"You're a part of it now, Macie, whether you like it or not. Leon has never let anyone in. Letty got somewhere close, but you... you're it for him." A lump crawls up my throat at her words. "I know it hasn't been the most romantic of starts for the two of you, but I'm pretty sure that what lies ahead is going to be so much more..."

"Satisfying," I offer before I realize what I've said. My face burns with embarrassment while Peyton laughs.

"Oh yeah. I'm sure there'll be plenty of that."

"He's like a completely different person now the weight has been lifted."

"Leon's been through some dark shit. I know you don't need to hear me say it, you're more than aware. I think more so than any of us." Her eyes hold mine in the mirror. "You know everything, don't you?"

I swallow nervously as I think about everything he confessed to me.

"All the things he's refused to tell the rest of us."

"I-I... um... I don't know what—"

"I guess it doesn't really matter anymore. It's over now. We can put it all behind us and just focus on the future." I narrow my eyes at her, my curiosity getting the best of me.

Does she know more than she's letting on? Should she be the one Leon needs to talk to?

"Yeah, I guess so."

Our conversation is cut off when the doors open and a smiling face greets me.

"Hi," I say, giving Kayden a little wave. "I'm Macie."

"I know. You're Leon's girlfriend."

"I... uh... yeah, I guess I am," I mutter, more so to myself than to him as I let the words settle in my head.

Leon Dunn's girlfriend.

How the hell did my life end up here?

"It's so nice to meet you," I say as he climbs in with the help of Leon who slips into the car behind him, pinning Kayden between us.

"You too. You're pretty. I like your hair."

Luca barks out a laugh from the driver's seat. "Oh yeah, he's a Dunn," he jokes.

"Thank you, Kayden. That's really sweet of you."

"Hey, lil' bro," Leon says. "My girl, remember. No stealing a brother's girl."

"I got it, Bro. She's a little too old for me anyway."

All four of us laugh as Luca pulls away from the house, leaving Peyton's aunt watching with a smile on her face.

"So... tell me about where we're going." I already know, Leon's told me everything but Kayden is so excited that I'm more than willing to listen to it again.

"This diner with the best pancakes in the state. Isn't that right, Luc?"

"Sure is, lil' man."

"I bet you can't eat more than me though."

"Is that a challenge?" I ask lightly.

"Yep. I haven't lost yet," he states proudly.

"Wow, you've beaten your big brothers."

"Sure have. They like to pretend they're all big and strong but really, they're a couple of kids."

"Couldn't have said it better myself, K," Peyton jokes, earning herself a scowl from Luca.

I sit back as the conversation flows around me, unable to wipe the smile off my face thinking about what I said to Peyton only moments ago about family.

All my life I've craved this. This connection, this family bond. The thing that's been missing for as long as I can remember. And now I've found it. I never, ever want to let it go.

Leon's knuckles brush my shoulder while Kayden talks at a mile a minute about something that happened at kindergarten this week.

"You okay?" he whispers.

Holding his eyes, I smile.

"Never better." It's not entirely true. The thought of having to go to Miami and deal with whatever Richard is going to throw at us fills me with dread but knowing Leon is going to be right by my side makes it feel that much more bearable.

———

Breakfast with Kayden is everything I hoped it would be and more. Seeing a softer side to both Leon and Luca as they chatted with their little brother was everything I didn't know I needed to experience.

I feel honored to have been able to experience it because I know from being on the outside that the rest of the world doesn't get to see this.

All they get from press coverage is that the Dunn twins are focused, determined, and just like their father.

The reality couldn't be any farther from the truth.

The Dunn twins are nothing like their father. I might never have met the man, but I know it for a fact just from what little I know of him. I also know that without him in their lives, they're only going to become even more incredible and go on to achieve so much more than he ever did.

A cell ringing at the table halts our conversation and Luca reaches into his pocket.

"It's Mom," he says, looking at Lee. "I'd better take it."

"Say hi for me."

Luca slips out of the booth as Kayden, Leon and I continue coloring while Peyton watches us with a smile from across the table.

"How long do you think you're going to be gone for?" Peyton asks.

I let out a sigh. "No idea. I guess it depends on how stubborn he wants to be. Knowing him, he'll end up in a coma for six months just to torture us."

"I really hope it— Is everything okay?" Peyton says when Luca steps back to the table with an unreadable expression on his face.

"Um... yeah. I just... Here," he says, passing her some money, "can you take Kayden over to the candy machine, get him something for later."

"Yesss," he hisses, missing the fact that it's all a ploy to get rid of him for a few minutes.

"Everything okay?" Peyton asks, sliding from the booth and wrapping her hand around Luca's forearm.

"Yeah, I just need to talk to Lee. I'll fill you in later."

"Okay." She pecks him on the cheek and takes Kayden's hand once Leon lets him out.

"What's going on?"

"You seen the news?"

"No."

"Apparently there's a new story about da— Brett. A drug dealer has been found beaten to death. They think it was Brett."

"What?" Leon barks, his hand searching for mine under the table. "That's insane. He wouldn't beat up a dealer."

"It would explain his injuries though."

"Yeah but..."

"They're doing toxicology tests, they think Brett's been using for a while. Makes sense seeing as he fucked off after he tried to..." Luca trails off, not able to vocalize what their father tried to do to Peyton.

"You trying to tell me he suddenly grew a conscience?"

"I dunno. Not sure I know anything anymore."

"Does it really matter?" I ask, trying to help Leon out. "The dealer was clearly a scumbag. Your father was an asshole. They're both gone. Probably better for the world that way."

"Yeah, I totally agree. It's just odd." Luca agrees.

"Macie's got a point. We should just be relieved. Who cares what happened? We'll probably never know the truth," Leon says.

A weird silence falls over our table as Leon holds my hand tighter. I know he wants to know the truth. He wants to know who discovered what he was up to and decided to get him out of having to do something drastic. I know he's grateful to whoever it was but still, he's not going to let it go easily.

"Everything okay?" Peyton asks when she rejoins us.

"Yeah, everything is great. We should probably get going, though. These two have a long day ahead of them."

Kayden's little face drops with disappointment.

"Sorry, lil' man. We'll be back here again next week though."

He perks up a little. But for a five-year-old a week feels like a year.

"And you've got your candy," I say brightly. "What did you pick?"

He holds up a bag of twizzlers and smiles.

"Ah, good choice. They're my favorite too."

He beams up at me as Leon and Luca slide from the bench.

Leon waits for me as the others go on ahead.

"Everything's going to be okay," I assure him, running my hand up his chest. "Whoever this was clearly had a plan."

"I know. I just... I want to know who knows."

"I know, so do I. But you might have to settle for never knowing and just being grateful."

"It wasn't Luca, I know that for a fact."

"Come on," I say, pulling on his arm. "I want to see what surprise you have for me."

He steps up behind me, holding me close as we walk out of the diner.

"Oh, baby. You have no idea."

"Put her down," Luca calls the second we emerge from the diner with Leon's lips attached to my neck.

"Ew," Kayden complains.

"Get used to it, kid. It won't be long until you realize that girls really don't smell all that bad."

"Yes they do," he states, giving out a little huff and folding his arms over his chest while Peyton puts his crutches in the trunk.

"Oh, do they?" she calls, jokingly.

"Well not you, obviously. Or Macie. Or Letty."

"That's good to know, lil' man," I say, using the twins' nickname for him as I scrub his hair. "Feel free to think girls smell as long as you want to," I assure him, helping him up into the car.

"You're coming again next week, right?" he asks me, his face lighting up at the prospect.

"Oh, I'm not su—"

"She'll be here," Leon says from behind me, making the most of me being half bent into the car and groping my ass.

"That sounds like a yes," I joke. The reality is that now that I've spent the morning with this little family, I don't want to be anywhere else on a Sunday morning ever again.

Climbing in behind him, Leon closes the door and jogs around to the other side.

19

LEON

Reaching over, I rest my hand on Macie's thigh and smile.

"It's going to be okay," I say softly.

"I know. I just want it all over," she whispers sadly, keeping her eyes staring out of the window.

"Me too."

"I feel like we've been given this new start, but someone has hit pause before we can even begin."

"This is our new start, baby. It's just a little bump in the road."

She blows out a frustrated breath. But while she's dreading this, I can't help the excitement that flows through my veins. Not only am I about to see the man who's ruined my entire life on his deathbed, but I've got the most incredible place waiting for the two of us once we do what we need to do.

I drive us directly to the hospital Richard is at, and no sooner have I parked my car are we heading inside to find out how long we're going to have to wait to put him and all the nightmares he's given the pair of us over the years behind us.

"Hi," Macie says when the nurse at the station of the ward we've been directed to looks up as we approach. "I'm Richard Fletcher's niece. I was called this morning about him being here."

"Ah, yes." The older, kind looking woman glances down at something on her desk. "Macie, right? You're his next of kin."

I see a shudder run through her at the sound of those words.

"Yes," Macie forces out.

"Okay. Let me just grab one of his nurses who can update you on his condition. If you'd like to wait just through there." She points toward a door that has a sign saying Family Room on the front of it.

Macie nods and turns on her heels.

I take a seat on the small couch while Macie paces back and forth, her need to get out of here palpable.

"They need to hurry up."

"Give them a break. I'm sure they're busy."

"I know. I just... ugh. I hate this. I don't even want to be here," she hisses.

Pushing up from the couch, I walk up to her and stop her movements with my hands on her shoulders.

"I know, baby. But once this is done. It's over and we can move on with our lives. You'll never have to see him again."

She blows out a shaky breath, her body trembling beneath my hold.

"Come here." I pull her into my arms and hold her tight.

"I'm so sorry," a flustered nurse says, rushing into the room and rubbing the back of her hand across her forehead. "We're rushed off our feet today."

"It's okay," Macie says, pulling away from me.

We both sit on the couch and listen to the nurse basically explain that the only thing keeping Richard alive right now is the ventilator he's hooked up to.

Macie's hand trembles in mine as she listens to the news and her eyes fill with tears that I'm sure the nurse believes are through sadness at her impending loss. I, however, know differently.

"We wanted to wait until you got here so you could say your goodbyes."

Macie sniffles, her free hand lifting to wipe away a tear.

"Could I go and do that now? I'd rather not allow him to suffer any longer than necessary."

The nurse's face softens in sympathy. "I can assure you, your uncle is in no pain."

"Okay. Th-that's good."

Is it? I think as I pull Macie into my side and drop a kiss to her head.

"There's a nurse in with him who can answer any more questions that you might have. But if you're happy, I can let her know your decision and she can turn off his machines with you there."

Macie nods. "Y-yes. I think that's for the best."

The nurse nods and stands, instructing us to follow her.

It's only a short walk to a private room with the blinds pulled closed.

"This is Macie, his niece," the nurse says, opening the door and letting us inside.

My eyes immediately fall on the man lying under the white sheets in the middle of the room. It's been years since I saw him in person, but the second I see his face, even if it is gaunt and his skin is almost translucent in color, a wave of fear and disgust rolls through me.

Standing there in that doorway, I'm just an eleven-year-old boy once again scared of what is going to happen to him next. Terrified of the pain he knows is coming his way.

"Leon," Macie whispers, her hand landing on my cheek. "You don't have to do this."

Swallowing down my fear and throwing my shoulders back, I remind myself that I'm no longer that little boy and that Richard is no longer a threat to me. He's no longer a threat to anyone lying there being kept alive by nothing more than a fancy machine.

"I'm good."

"You sure?"

"Promise, baby." I kiss her brow and walk a little farther into the room.

My eyes catch on the nurse standing at his bedside with a clipboard in her hands. I'm hit with a sense of familiarity but I can't quite put my finger on where I know her from.

"I'll leave you with Cindy," the first nurse says before slipping out of the room and closing the door behind us.

Cindy holds my eyes, clearly she recognizes me too.

I feel Macie's attention as she looks between the two of us, and I'm about to break the connection when Cindy smiles.

"Ready to do this?" she asks.

"Uh…"

"Who are you?"

"Mr. Fletcher's nurse," she says innocently. Too innocently.

My brows pinch as I stare at her, racking my brain to figure out who she is.

"Leon, would you like to do the honors?"

"Okay, what the hell is going on?" Macie spits.

Cindy smiles. "This is what you wanted, isn't it?"

"Um…"

Suddenly, a memory hits me and a smile curls at my lips.

Sneaky fucking bastards.

"It's okay, Mace. She's on our side."

Stepping up to Macie, I wrap my arm around her shoulder.

"Ready for our new start?"

"Uh…y-yeah," she breathes, but I know her hesitation isn't because she doesn't want it, but because she's just hella confused right now.

I'd explain but I'm not sure now is the time or the place. *Cindy* is already risking enough by doing what she's doing.

I'm going to owe those motherfuckers big for this.

"What do we need to do?"

"Flick this switch and then play the part." She winks and my stomach flips with excitement.

I'm actually getting to do this. I'm going to be able to stand here and watch the man who terrorized my entire teenage and adult life drift off into nothing.

"I always vowed I'd get to you eventually," I tell him, pressing my finger to the switch Cindy points out. "Yes?" I ask Macie, making sure she's okay with me being the one to do this.

"Yes. Make it happen."

The click of the switch pierces the air around us a second before all the beeping and whirring comes to a stop and silence surrounds us.

"Congratulations, Leon. Retaliation has been delivered."

I blow out a long breath, staring at the man before me as the tension that's been pulling my shoulders tight since I was a child finally starts to abate.

He's gone. He's actually gone.

"I'll leave you to say your final goodbyes. If you need me, you know where I'll be."

With a wicked smile, Cindy slips from the room.

Shaking my head, I look up at Macie who's still looking utterly bewildered by the entire situation.

"Say your farewell, baby. It's over."

"Do you know what? I've got nothing to say. Even goodbye seems too good for him."

Her face is cold, emotionless as she stares down at the man who was trusted to bring her up after she lost her entire world. My heart aches for her, for the little girl who suffered as much, if not more so, than I did.

Richard was a part of my life for a few summers. He was in hers for much longer, controlling hers, for years.

"I think we're done here," she says after a couple of seconds. "Let's go."

"With pleasure, Red."

———

It's almost twenty minutes later when we finally manage to get out of the hospital after Macie gets caught by the nurse at reception to sign some paperwork.

She's silent as we ride the elevator down to the ground floor and then we walk out of the building hand in hand.

We haven't taken five steps away from the doors when she turns to me.

"Okay, what the hell was that?"

"That, baby, was retaliation." Something catches my eye over her shoulder and I spin her around with my hands on her hips. "Hawks style."

She gasps as her eyes land on the two people leaning against the hood of a Dodge Charger.

"Reid," she whispers, her body trembling once more as realization hits. "Did you know?" she asks as the four of us share a knowing look across the parking lot.

Alana now looks much more recognizable without the brown wig she was wearing and the nurse uniform gone.

"No. I had no idea."

"Right," she breathes. For a second I think she doesn't believe me, but as she rests back into my body, I realize that she's just trying to figure it all out. "We should go and—" But even as she suggests it, Reid and Alana push away from the car and with a nod in our direction, they climb in and vanish from our sight.

"Come on, baby. Let's go find your surprise," I whisper in her ear, making her shudder for entirely different reasons this time.

"Okay," she breathes, leaning her head back on my shoulder and allowing me to capture her lips.

20

MACIE

My head is spinning as we pull away from the hospital.

I have so many questions running around that I don't even know where to start.

Fiddling with the hem of my shirt, I stare out the window watching the clear blue water of the ocean in the distance.

As a kid, I always wanted to live right on the beach. But being in Miami with Richard ruined all those dreams as being anywhere near the ocean just reminds me of him.

Breathing in the fresh scent, I rest my head back and close my eyes for a beat.

Today has been... a lot to take in.

Leon reaches over and takes my hand in his, but he doesn't say anything. I'm not sure if that's because he knows I just need silence right now, or if he's too up in his own head, but whatever it is, I'm grateful.

I don't realize that I drift off until I hear the low rumbles of Leon's deep voice a beat before his lips brush my cheek.

"Baby, we're here."

My eyes flicker open as my body wakes from its sleep and I find his eyes before anything else.

"Hey," he says with a smile, reaching out to tuck a lock of hair behind my ear.

Memories from the day hit me. "It's over, isn't it? He's gone."

The widest smile I've ever seen pulls at Leon's lips and my heart flips at the sight.

"It is, baby. It's just me and you now."

"Wow," I breathe. "That sounds so good."

"Me, you, and this place." Leon gestures out of the window and I gasp.

"Oh my God."

"It's ours for five days."

I stare at the modern angular building before us. It doesn't look like all that much from the road, but something tells me that the other side is going to be a whole other story because I can tell from here that it looks right out over the ocean.

"Really?"

"Really, baby. Wanna go check it out?"

"Hell yes," I say, jumping into action and racing from the car, much to Leon's amusement.

He catches up with me and throws his arm around my shoulders as we walk toward the front door and he finds the key hidden in a little security box.

He turns to me with the key dangling from his finger and his eyes dancing with excitement.

My breath catches in my throat at the happiness bleeding from him.

"Fuck," he suddenly barks, startling me. "Fuck." All the air rushes from my lungs as my back hits the wall beside the door. "I love you," he blurts out before slamming his lips down on mine in a bruising kiss.

His hands are everywhere as if he can't figure out which part of me he wants to touch first as his tongue twists with mine and our teeth clash with the ferocity of the kiss.

Not content with only pressing me into the wall, he reaches down and lifts me, wrapping my legs around his waist and grinding his hips, showing me just how much he needs me.

"Leon," I moan, my head falling back when he starts kissing down my neck.

"Need. Inside. Now," he growls between kisses.

I have no idea if he means me or the beach house but I also don't care.

I soon get my answer when he pulls me from the wall and walks with me to the front door which he damn near throws open as he marches inside.

"Oh wow, it's beautiful," I breathe, getting the very briefest of glances at the mostly white modern interior.

The second he leans over, I forget all about looking around and instead cling onto his shoulders and stare into his heated eyes.

"Lee?"

"I need you, Macie. I need you so fucking bad."

My back connects with the stairs, which thankfully are covered in a thick, soft carpet a second before his fingers flick the button on my jeans and he impatiently tugs them down my legs, throwing them off.

My panties go next, but he's even more impatient and instead of removing them, just rips them clean from my body.

"Oh God," I moan as the cool air surrounds my heated, sensitive skin.

Wrapping his hands around the back of my thighs, spreading them, he pushes me up the stairs a little, dropping to his knees on a step a few lower down.

"So fucking beautiful," he murmurs before surging forward and sucking my clit into his mouth.

"Oh shit," I cry, my back arching against the stairs as the sensation overwhelms me. "Oh fuck."

My fingers twist in his hair but I have no clue if I want to drag him closer or push him away.

It's too much, so intense, yet so freaking good.

"Come on my face, baby," he growls against me, his deep voice vibrating through my body, making my release surge forward faster.

Pushing two fingers into me, he curls them, hitting that incredible spot that he's found. In only a few more licks, I'm falling over the edge, crying out his name as my thighs clamp around his head.

I'm still blissed out on the high when he pulls away from me, but aftershocks still making their way through my body mean I barely notice. That all changes though when he pushes the head of his cock against my entrance.

"Ready to go again?" he asks, a wicked smirk on his lips while my release still glistens on his stubbled chin.

"Give me your worst, Dunn. You know I can take it."

"Fuuuuck," he groans, pushing forward and filling me to the hilt.

My back aches against the stairs as he drags me down, forcing himself even deeper into my body before he really starts to fuck me.

"I promise I'll give you slow and sweet later. Right now, I just need—"

"Fuck me, Leon. Take me exactly as you need to."

"Fuck, you're perfect. Fucking perfect."

He thrusts into me like a man possessed and I lap up every moment of it, clawing at his back as my next release makes itself known.

"Macie, Macie, Macie," he whispers in my ear as his body begins to tremble with his restraint. The muscles in his strong arms pulled tight on either side of my head. "Me and you, baby. It's just me and you."

With one final powerful thrust, I fall, my release slamming into me almost out of nowhere as his cock swells inside me. His body stills before he throws his head back and roars out his release.

His cock jerks inside me, filling me, for long seconds as we both begin to come down from our high.

"Fuck," he breathes, dropping his brow to my shoulders and dragging in deep, heaving breaths.

Running my nails down his sweaty back, he shudders and I feel him smile.

"I can't get enough of you, Red."

Lifting his head, he looks down at me, allowing me to see the honesty that's oozing from his eyes.

"Leon, I—"

"No," he says, pressing his fingers to my lips. "Don't say it because I did. I just... I couldn't keep it in any longer."

My heart aches for this incredibly sweet, yet broken man.

"Oh, Lee," I breathe, cupping his cheek. "You're scared I don't feel it too, right?"

He swallows, his Adam's apple bobs with the move. It's the only response I need to know I'm right.

"I'm falling right alongside you," I whisper. "It's just me and you, baby."

His fear begins to edge away at my words and a smile twitches at the corner of his lips.

"Yeah?"

"Yeah."

I shift, my body aching from the position I'm in and his eyes widen in horror.

"Shit. That must hurt. I'm sorry, I—"

"Don't apologize for that."

"I know but it was—"

"Hot," I answer for him.

His signature cocky smirk plays on his lips as he stares down at me with my legs spread and my clothes all over the place.

"Yeah, you could say that again," he mutters.

Reaching behind him, he drags his shirt over his head, allowing me to watch as his muscles ripple.

Lowering the fabric, he uses it to clean me up before lacing his arm beneath me and hauling me up as if I weigh nothing more than a feather.

When I'm on my feet once more, I get my first proper look at our surroundings.

"Lee, this place is insane."

I've been in some fancy places over the years, but this is just incredible. On paper I'd say it would probably be cold with all its harsh angles and stark white surfaces, but the reality is the complete opposite.

Walking forward, I close the space between me and the floor to ceiling windows that showcase the glittering ocean in the distance.

"I didn't have much choice at such a last minute booking but I think I might have lucked out."

"Lucked out? Are you kidding?" I laugh watching as a runner makes his way along the otherwise deserted beach below.

"All ours for five days," he whispers, stepping up behind me and wrapping his arms around my waist, placing his chin on my shoulder.

"You know, I might just change my opinion on Miami."

"Yeah, I was thinking the same."

Spinning in his arms, I stare up into his eyes. The anger, the confusion, the pain from before is hardly recognizable any more.

The loss of his father, and now Richard, has helped him push some of that behind him. I'm not naïve enough to think that he's not always going to be somehow affected by the past, but I can already see how much easier it is for him to deal with knowing that they're gone and are no longer able to hurt him or those he loves.

No words are said between us for the longest time as we just stare at each other. The events of the past few weeks running around our head.

I never would've thought after that first night when I barged my way into Charlie's room that I'd blink and end up here with my heart feeling fuller than I ever can remember and a wide, genuine smile on my face.

Sliding my hands up his chest, I cup his jaw, loving the feeling of the rough stubble against my soft skin.

"I love you, Leon Dunn." He gasps but I'm not finished. "I love the scared little boy you think is weak, I love the broken man who you think is unworthy. I love the talented football player who can take life by the balls, and I love the sweet guy that I know you only let me see."

"Mac—"

Pressing my thumbs to his lips, I shake my head.

"You've shown me what life can really be like. You've dragged me out of the shadows I was hiding in and proved that all the things I was scared of aren't all that scary at all.

"I love you, Leon, and I can't wait to turn our lives around and make a future with you."

"Macie," he whispers, his voice cracking with emotion as his eyes fill with tears. "I love you. I love you so much. You were right. We were meant to be. We were meant to find this. We were meant to find peace and happiness together."

A sob erupts from my throat but he doesn't let me cry, instead he takes my face in a tender hold and brushes his lips against mine before showing me that he can do soft and gentle lovemaking just as well as he can do hot and fast hate fucks.

EPILOGUE

Macie

Six months later...

The noise of the crowd around me rattles my bones as I watch Leon and the rest of the Panthers run out onto the field. He might be surrounded by the entire team, but he is the only one I see. Even with his helmet on, I can picture the fierce, determined set of his face, his dark eyes as he focuses on the first game of the season and how he, Luca and Kane are going to ensure they start off on a win.

My hands clap together until the skin begins to burn and I shout at the top of my lungs, cheering the man on as he scans the crowd looking for me.

It's the first football game I've ever attended. Or at least one I can remember, I know I went to Dad's as a baby but I was too young.

I know the second he finds me because a strong bolt of electricity shoots through me.

Pausing my clapping, I press my fingers to my lips and blow him a kiss, wishing him good luck.

"Girl, you have him so whipped, it's almost painful to watch," Ella says from behind me, clearly watching the two of us.

"Yeah," I breathe, although she's got no chance of hearing it.

Peyton and Letty stand on either side of me, both clapping and screaming for their guys. Beside Peyton is Kayden who's literally bouncing in his seat with excitement as he watches his two most favorite people in the world on the field before us. Next to him is Libby.

Feeling my stare, she glances over and smiles.

After spending sixty days in the rehab facility, she's managed to restart her life and was able to begin being a mother to her little boy.

She's made it look so easy, but I'm not naïve enough to believe that's the reality. I can only imagine how hard it's been for her. But thanks to Leon, Luca and Maddie, she's now got a purpose.

Understandably, Libby refused to accept any of the money Brett Dunn left behind after his fateful night with the hooker. But after a lot of discussion and back and forth, she finally agreed to accept a job as a manager of The Locker Room.

At first, I thought it was crazy allowing an ex-addict to run a bar. But I'm happy to say that I was wrong because it seems that Libby had really found her feet.

The bar is no longer a seedy sports bar but a sophisticated—as sophisticated as it can get—gentleman's club. Libby takes pride in the fact that she's helping women who are at their lowest and supporting them in turning their lives around. She works with the counselors and therapists she met while she was in the facility and is really making a difference.

She's working with Maddie to make the same change in a couple of the other locations that Brett had spread over the country.

By some small miracle, both Brett and Richard's deaths and the weeks that followed went very smoothly, seeing as both were suspicious as hell. It seemed that everyone else believed that Brett Dunn had finally caved to the pressures of celebrity life and dived headfirst into smack and pussy. And as for Richard, once Leon and I embarked on our mission to destroy his memory and football legacy with the truth, everyone was more than glad the man was no longer able to taunt the young lives he was once entrusted with.

Leon was terrified to release his story, but after only hours of us putting it out into the media, more stories started coming, until almost every day another young man would come forward to tell his story.

It was shocking, but incredible that these men are able to finally put their terrifying past behind them knowing that they're not alone in what they suffered.

Now, my dream of being able to help kids who sadly will still be forced to suffer something similar is closer than ever.

I've got the money, and we're busy getting all our plans together for when I graduate.

Thoughts of the future are equally as exciting as they are terrifying.

This year is Leon's last at MKU, he'll enter the draft in the spring and head off to better things. I know that won't be the end of us, we're barely at the beginning, but I can't imagine being here without him. A huge part of me wonders if I won't, if the second he signs for a team, if I'll decide to follow him and transfer wherever he goes.

I came here to be closer to Mom, to live her legacy, but what I've found is so much better than trying to recreate the past, I've found a future that I never could have imagined.

Leon is everything I said I never wanted but everything I never knew I needed, and I never even want to consider my life without him.

I meant every word of what I said to him that day in the Miami beach house. I love every side of him. Sometimes I even miss the dark side which seems to come out less and less these days. Having that inside version of Leon is thrilling in ways I never knew existed, and sometimes it's exactly what I need.

"Right," a deep voice booms from behind us, dragging me from my thoughts. "Let's get this party started.

Turning around, I find Devin with his arms out wide and an even bigger smirk on his face.

Behind him are his brothers, and right at the back are Reid, Alana, JD and Mav.

"Oh God, here we go," Letty mutters loud enough to ensure he hears.

"Pipe down, Mrs. Legend. I know you really love me. Don't try to deny it."

Letty rolls her eyes and shakes her head. Her and Kane aren't married and don't plan to be for quite a while but even still Devin insists on calling her by his last name, mostly just to piss her off. Letty has told me before that things between her and Devin haven't always been smooth sailing and while she might be more than happy to put it all behind them, he makes it his mission to ensure she remembers the beef they had.

"Guys," she says, ignoring him. "This is Libby, Peyton's sister."

"Oh, hey," Ezra mutters, barely sparing her a glance in favor of a girl in the row in front of him.

Ellis is slightly more polite before Devin finally drags his attention back to us from a couple of the jersey chasers who are loitering around.

The second Devin and Libby's eyes connect I swear to God I feel the sparks of electricity shoot straight down my spine.

"You two know each other." It's not a question. It doesn't need to be, the answer is obvious.

Devin pulls his mask back into place. His easy, cocky smirk returning as he walks over to Libby and throws his arm around her shoulders.

"Oh, we go way back. Right, Lib? Got into all kinds of shit together."

I glance at Libby to find her face pale and her eyes wide.

"Put her down, Dev," Reid instructs, walking up to us. "Macie, how's it going?" he asks when his eyes find me.

"It's good, thank you."

"Our boys ready to kill it down there?" he asks our group, but while he might distract most of us, my eyes are still darting between Devin and Libby.

The dealer and the ex-addict. If that doesn't have disaster written all over it, I don't know what does.

I have no idea how long I watch the two of them try to ignore each other while clearly being painfully aware of the other's presence but eventually it's Reid who once again distracts me.

"He looks like he's ready to take on the world," he says, forcing my eyes back to the field where Leon's standing with Kane.

"He is... thanks to you."

"Nah," he mutters. "I might have helped get rid of the trash, but I'm pretty sure that's everything to do with you."

It turned out that Reid had orchestrated the entire situation around Richard's demise, along with Ellis and Alana without Leon knowing. Neither of us know why he went to such effort to wipe him off the face of the Earth, but I do know that both of us will be forever grateful.

With him gone, it's like I can breathe a little easier.

His estate has been sold, everything he owned is gone, and his fortune is now sitting untouched in a high interest account, growing for when I'm ready to hit go on my foundation in a few years.

"They're going to kill it this year," I say as they get ready to start.

"With you three behind them, they haven't really got a choice."

"What's the deal with Devin and Libby?" I ask, although I regret it the second the question falls from my lips because Reid might be a lot of things but I don't get the impression he's a gossip.

"Probably best you don't ask." The crowd around us roars as the game begins so I don't entirely catch his next words, but I swear to God it sounds something like, "You should probably be thanking them too."

The excitement from the game stops me asking what he meant by that, or even if that's what he said, but I can't deny that it gets my head spinning.

I alternate between watching the game—which the Panthers win by a mile—and keeping an eye on Libby and Devin.

They ended up at either end of our group but that doesn't mean I miss either of them looking at the other, both of them sitting tight with tension pulling their bodies.

Leaning into Peyton, I whisper. "What's the deal with Libby and Devin?"

Her jaw ticks at my question, telling me that I'm not the only one who's noticed.

"I have no idea," she grinds out. "But she needs to stay the hell away from the likes of him."

———

Letty, Peyton and I are practically bouncing on the balls of our feet as we wait, surrounded by a massive crowd of fans, for our guys to exit the locker room.

When they do, I wince with the volume of the cheer that erupts around me. It's infectious and I find myself shouting along with them as some of the team come out, although it takes a few more minutes before the three we're waiting on emerge dressed in smart suits and wearing matching accomplished smiles.

"I don't think I'll ever get used to seeing the three of them this happy," Letty says before bolting toward Kane and jumping into his arms.

Two seconds later, Luca finds Peyton in the crowd and also takes off, leaving me alone and wondering where Leon went.

My eyes scan the crowd but I come up empty.

He was just right there, where can he have—

A warm, rough pair of hands cover my eyes from behind as a hard body presses against my back.

"My lucky charm," he breathes in my ear before allowing me to turn and catching me when I jump into his arms.

"You killed it out there. I'm so proud of you," I manage to get out before his lips crash down on mine.

"I love you," he breathes against my lips. "And I loved knowing you were watching me."

"I wouldn't be anywhere else," I confess. I'm already dreading the upcoming away games that are going to be too far away for me to go to. I can already see myself glued to my laptop as I watch him.

For someone who never wanted anything to do with football, one game into the season and I'm a freaking addict. Although, I'm not sure if I'm more addicted to the game or just one certain player.

Releasing me, he drops one more kiss to the tip of my nose.

"Are you ready to celebrate?" I ask, knowing that they've all planned a massive first game of the season party at Colt and the guys' new house.

It was only a few weeks after we buried both Brett and Richard that Leon and Luca sat both Peyton and I down and told us that they were kicking the rest of the guys out of the house and wanted the two of us to move in with them.

Just like the rest of my relationship with Leon, I jumped in with two feet immediately, more than happy not to have to leave him a few nights a week to sleep alone in my old dorm room. Peyton took a little more convincing because she didn't want to leave Kayden.

For a few weeks she continued to go back and forth but eventually she realized that there was only one place she really wanted to be.

They've moved down to the first floor while we've kept the top.

It works perfectly for now, although I can't help but wonder what happens after they graduate and where that'll leave me, but I'm trying to push all of that down because all I really want to do is focus on the here and now.

"I can't fucking wait."

Taking my hand, he mostly ignores the crowd who are calling his name.

He signs a couple of jerseys that are thrust at him while I stand watching in disbelief that the man who's refusing to release my hand belongs to me.

All these people here might want a little piece of him, but I know without doubt that I'm the only person who really knows him.

After a few minutes we finally break free from the crowd and head toward his car.

"Would you be mad if we didn't party tonight?" he asks once everything gets a little quieter.

"Of course not. I'm happy to do whatever you want to."

Pushing me back against his car, he runs his nose along the line of my jaw.

"You're wearing my jersey, there's only one thing I want to do."

"Winning turn you on, Dunn?" I ask with a smirk.

"No, baby. That's all you," he admits, grinding his hardness against my belly. "I've got a surprise for you."

"Oh?"

He reaches behind him and pulls a set of keys from his pocket.

"What's that?"

"Down for a trip to Miami?"

"That for the beach house?" I ask, excitement building in my belly.

We've been back to that place no less than four times since our first visit the day we officially restarted our lives, and I still can't get enough.

"It's no longer *the* beach house, Red."

My heart thunders against my ribs as my mind races at a mile a minute.

He leans in, whispering in my ear.

"Now, it's our beach house."

"You didn't?" I gasp in shock.

"I did. So now, no matter where life takes us, how hard things get. We can always go back to where it all began and remember that it's just you and me, baby."

"You and me, baby," I repeat, pulling him tighter into my body and brushing my lips against his. "Forever."

Keep reading for Leon and Macie's Bonus Epilogue!

Want more Reid? Reid Harris is coming for you this fall...
Add Book One of the Harrow Creek Hawks to your TBR now!

ACKNOWLEDGMENTS

I can't believe we're here already. This year, and this series, has just passed by way too fast.

But did I save the best until last?

Leon was... he was special. I knew his story was going to be dark, brutal, shocking. But I was so excited to dive into it. I felt like I'd been waiting years.

I'm not going to lie, I was worried about that cliffhanger. Even I sat there slack jawed wondering what I'd just written. But, as always, I let my characters lead, and that was what they were telling me. So I just went with it.

I'm so relieved most of you still love him!

This series has been so memorable for me. Kane helped me hit the top 100 for the first time, and I've met so many incredible new readers and authors because of it.

So the most important thing to say at this point, is THANK YOU. Thank you for taking a chance on me, Letty and Kane, and thank you for still being here now at the end.

The end... it sounds so final. But while this series might be done. That doesn't mean we're not going to see any of these guys again.

Anyone interested in a little more Reid, maybe?! I know I am. He is too, he's busting to get out of my head.

All I'm going to say is... 2022. Watch this space. You may already have some noticed some hints of where it might be going...

But in the mean time, I'm going to give you some delicious British boys in my Knight's Ridge Empire series. If you've read Rosewood High, then you'll already know, and hopefully love, Stella. Well, let me just say, you've seen nothing yet!

Go grab the prequel, Wicked Summer Knight (it's free) and dive into the dark and twisted world of Knight's Ridge.

Until next time,

Tracy xo

BONUS EPILOGUE

LEON & MACE EXTENDED EPILOGUE

MACIE

Three years later

The huge room is buzzing with excitement as all the graduating students get ready to don their caps and gowns. Their smiles are wide and their sense of achievement and pride is palpable.

This is what we've all been working toward for years. It's what all the stress and late nights have been about.

Yet, as I look around at them all chatting and laughing, I don't experience any of that joy.

Almost all of these graduating students will have loving family out in the stands waiting for them, buzzing to celebrate this epic success with them.

I don't.

Lifting my gown, I find my cell tucked in my dress pocket and wake it up.

Opening up my chat with Leon, I read his last message again, hoping I imagined the words.

Your King: My flight is delayed. I don't know if I'm going to make it. I'm so fucking sorry, Macie.

My heart sinks all over again.

There's only one person I want out in those stands watching as I receive my degree, but despite everything he's rescheduled to be here, he's not going to make it.

My nose tickles with emotion and my eyes burn with tears as I stare at the exit.

The temptation to rip all this off and march out is strong.

The only thing that keeps me here is how much I know I'd regret it.

I don't need anyone here. I'm more than capable of giving myself a pat on the back. Hell, before Leon crashed into my life, it was all I could do. I guess, I just thought I wouldn't have to again.

I let out a sigh and roll my shoulders back.

It's fine. Everything is fine.

Leon will get here as soon as he can, and I've got no doubt he'll do everything he can to make up for missing it.

He was pissed that he was called last minute to a 'can't miss this meeting' with his agent in New York.

I wasn't naïve going into this life with Leon. I might have been too young to really understand what Mom and Dad's lives were like before they died, but I remember enough to know that Dad was gone a lot and it was just Mom and me.

It's one of the reasons I was adamant to stay at Maddison Kings to do my degree. I knew once Leon left for Chicago that he'd be unbelievably busy. I figured that we could both travel whenever he had some downtime and we wouldn't really miss out on each other that much.

I stood by that for my junior year, his rookie year with the Chiefs.

Yes, I still had my friends. Nathan and I were still close. And Jace and Charlie were still a part of my life.

But they weren't my family.

I made it a few weeks into the first semester of senior year before I started looking into transferring my credits to the closest college to the apartment Leon was renting.

Yes, we'd spent most of the off-season together here in Maddison. But his life was in Chicago. And while I loved Maddison, the connection to my mother's legacy, home is where the heart is. And my heart left for Chicago way too often.

So I followed him, moved myself into his apartment and finished the rest of college here where we could almost always fall asleep in the same bed and wake up together the next morning.

It wasn't until a few days in to living with him properly again that I realized just how miserable I'd become in Maddison.

Without Ella's and Peyton's encouragement, I found myself retreating to old habits fast. I still had Letty and Violet, but they were busy with their lives. I spent my evenings and weekends in the apartment working, desperately trying to get as many credits as I could to potentially graduate early and shift my ass to Chicago.

Turning up here and unpacking my things beside Leon's turned me back into the fun-loving girl he was in love with, and it was everything.

He was everything.

Opening my camera, I snap a graduation selfie and send it over.

> Macie: All gowned and ready to go.

I stare at the screen, waiting for it to show as delivered. But it never does.

That one single tick gives me a little hope, although I fear it'll be pointless.

Even if he has taken off, the chances of him getting here before they get to my name is slim.

I send the same photo to our girls' group chat and then force myself to put it back in my pocket and not obsess over the notification icon.

The crackle of speakers in the distance floats through the air as the ceremony gets underway and the excitement ramps up a little.

The event organizers run around like blue-ass flies getting

everyone into order and I silently do as I'm told as the room empties out.

I've met plenty of people here, there are a few I regularly have coffee with after class. But I'm not really sure I'd call any of them friends. The connection and relationships I have with them is nowhere near what I found with Letty, Peyton, Ella, and Violet.

I smile at a few people and make bullshit small talk, but mostly, I just count the seconds, hoping that this can be over and that I can go home to wait for Leon.

There will be no celebration if he's not with me.

With a heavy sigh, I listen as the person calling names gets closer to mine.

Admittedly, a little excitement flutters in my belly as I think about walking across that stage and accepting my diploma. I'm finally finishing this part of my life and will be able to fully invest in the foundation I've been dreaming of for so long.

Peyton and Letty have made a solid start since they graduated last year, but I'm desperate to join the team and really get my claws into it.

When it's almost my turn, I lose my fight with checking my cell and dig it back out.

My heart somersaults at the sight of a message from Leon.

Please have landed. Please have landed.

I don't realize I'm holding my breath until it all comes out in a rush when I read his words.

> Your King: You look beautiful. I can't wait to see you. x

> Macie: I love you. x

> Your King: I love you too. You're going to kill it today. x

I smile sadly before I'm forced to close it down and tuck it away when my name is called.

I follow instructions and before I know it, I'm standing at the edge of the stage waiting for my turn.

I did it. I actually did it.

My heart races, and my hands tremble as the weight of the moment washes over me.

The person in front of me is called, and as I step forward, I risk looking up at the crowd of proud families that fill the stands waiting to spot their loved one up on the stage.

My stomach knots as I realize just how many people are about to watch me.

I scan the crowd for a few seconds before I swear my heart stops beating.

All the air rushes out of my lungs as I find my man sitting front and center with his eyes locked on me and a wide smile playing on his face.

'You,' I mouth in total disbelief.

My cell vibrates in my pocket, and in a rush, I pull it out because I know it's him.

> Your King: You're even more beautiful in person. Surprise.

Laughter erupts as the person directing graduates up onto the stage begins shouting at me.

"Sorry, sorry," I mutter, trying to put my cell away and not trip over my own feet at the same time.

Those little butterfly flutters of excitement from before are like birds flapping wildly as I step up onto the stage.

His attention burns into my side as I move—hopefully elegantly—across the stage.

The second my name rings out through the speakers, someone hollers loudly.

With a smile so wide it actually hurts, I accept my diploma before turning to Leon.

'Thank you.'

'I love you.'

By the time I step off the stage, I have tears streaming down my face with happiness. I should follow the others to a seat, but I'm buzzing. There's no way I can sit still. So the second I spot an opportunity to escape, I do.

I spill out of a fire exit, still looking like a maniac with tears dripping from my chin.

But I soon discover that I'm not the only one who has the plan to escape because the second I turn the next corner, I spot Leon leaving the building.

"Lee," I cry, taking off running at full speed.

The second I'm close, I jump, trusting that he'll always catch me.

2

———

LEON

I knew it was a risk. I knew I'd upset her when I told her I wasn't going to make it. I just had to hope the benefits would outweigh my little white lie.

But I wanted to do something special for my girl.

Today is a fucking big day and I want her to celebrate everything she's managed to achieve, everything she's overcome. Today marks the start of our next chapter and I am so fucking ready to make it happen.

The second she spotted me in the crowd and her face lit up like she just discovered it was Christmas morning, I knew I'd already been forgiven.

Thank fuck.

The knot that was twisting up my stomach unraveled and my tight fists uncurled.

The past three years with Macie have been more than I ever could have imagined. Even when we were apart, she was still the biggest most important thing in my life. Even above football.

There was no way on Earth I was missing today. I didn't care what I had to cancel, I was going to be in the crowd and I was going to clap and shout louder than anyone else.

My girl deserves it. She might think it's all no big deal, but she's been through so much to get here and it needs celebrating.

I want her to know how incredible she is, and how proud of her I am.

Today was always going to be hard on her. She might look like she's dealt with losing her parents, I mean, she has as much as anyone can. But I know that days like this where everyone is surrounded by their family are hard.

I want to be everything she needs, but there will always be a part of her heart that remains empty no matter how hard I try.

The second I spot her diverting from the crowd, I jump from my seat and practically shove everyone else sitting in this row out of the way in my need to get to her.

By the time I'm at the aisle that leads toward the exit, I'm practically running.

More than a few heads turn my way. Many eyes widen as they recognize me, but a few don't. Not that I'm hanging around for chitchat or to sign anything. I've got something more important to do.

A rush of warm air surrounds me as I throw the door open and run out.

I scan the area, trying to figure out where she's going to come from.

Then movement to my left catches my eye and I freeze.

Fuck. She looks incredible in her cap and gown. Her red hair curled and tumbling around her shoulders.

"Red," I breathe as she takes off running in my direction.

Fuck knows how the hat stays on, but it does and only a heartbeat later, she's jumping from the ground and straight into my arms.

All the air rushes from my lungs as we collide.

I wrap my arms around her as she clings to me.

"You're here," she sobs before slamming her lips down on mine.

The salty taste of her tears floods my mouth as our tongues tangle.

I have no idea if anyone else is out here, I only had eyes for my girl when I emerged, but I kiss her as if we're alone. My hands slide to her ass as I move us to the side of the building and press her against the brick wall.

"Leon," she moans when I make my way across her jaw and down her neck.

"I wouldn't have been anywhere else in the world today," I confess, remembering she said something.

"B-but... New York?" she asks as I suck on the sensitive skin beneath her ear.

"I didn't go. It was a cover," I confess. "I was setting up a surprise for you."

"Oh," she gasps, her hand slipping beneath my shirt, the heat of her skin burning me from the inside out.

"We need to get out of here before I do something I shouldn't."

"You're Leon Dunn. You could talk yourself out of anything in this state," Macie all but moans as she rolls her hips against my hard length.

"Not sure that's true, Red. Come on," I say, dragging her from the wall and reluctantly placing her on her feet.

Taking her hand, I tug her toward the lot I left my car in.

"Wait," she cries.

"You need to say goodbye to people?" I ask, studying her.

"No. I need to take this back or I'll be charged."

"Fuck it. Worth every penny. You look hot as fuck right now."

"You're kidding? I've got a table on my head."

I can't help but chuckle, remembering when I said those exact words when I graduated two years ago.

"The sooner we get to the car, the sooner I can prove it to you."

Her eyes darken with need before she quickly starts moving again.

The second we're in the car, I start the engine and take off. My need for my girl is too strong to waste any time.

"Don't take it off," I bark as she reaches up to take her cap off.

"Uh..." She hesitates but thankfully lowers her hands again.

"Where are we going?"

"It's a surprise," I tease, shooting her a wink.

She wants to argue, to demand I tell her what's happening but she wisely keeps her mouth closed.

I'm not going to be able to keep everything under wraps that much longer, but I'm determined to make the most of the time I have.

Macie chats excitedly as I drive toward a spot I wasn't planning on making, but the moment I saw her, I knew we needed a few moments alone before we embark on the rest of our celebration.

"Leon?" she questions as I pull off the main road and down a very bumpy and overgrown lane.

"Trust me?"

"Always, but— oh wow," she breathes as an uninterrupted view of the city emerges before us. "It's beautiful."

Pulling the car to a stop, I kill the engine and look at the most beautiful thing in the world."

"Yeah, Red. You are."

It takes her a second, her attention on the view before my words register, and when they do her cheeks blaze as red as her hair.

Sliding my seat back, I reach for her.

"Leon," she shrieks as I effortlessly lift her over the center console and straight onto my lap.

"Sorry for lying to you, Red. I just wanted to make this day everything you deserve."

"I think you're forgiven," she gasps as I rock her over the bulge in my pants.

"I've got so much planned for you. We don't have much time but I need you, Red. I need you right now."

Wrapping the length of her hair around my fist, I drag her head back and lick up her throat.

"Get my cock out, baby."

Without wasting a second, her knuckles brush the skin above my waistband making my dick jerk.

While she works on my fly, I slide my hands up her thighs, discovering the little black lace dress she's wearing beneath her gown.

"Love this," I groan, watching the fabric bunch around her waist, showing off her panties which is just as sexy as her dress.

Dipping my fingers between her thighs, I find the fabric soaked with her arousal.

"Feels like I'm not the only one who's feeling a little needy."

"Please," she whimpers as I tease her through the damp fabric.

Unable to make her wait, and aware we're against the clock, I tug her panties aside and plunge two fingers deep inside her as she slowly strokes me.

"Fuck, I love you, Red. I'm so fucking proud of you."

"Leon," she begs, her pussy clamping down on my digits.

"Yeah. Fuck, yeah," I say in a rush, ripping my fingers free and lining myself up at her entrance.

"Yes," she hisses as I push the tip in. "More. Please."

Gripping her hips, I drag her down, impaling her on my dick and making her cry out in pleasure.

"Fuck me, Leon."

We might be alone in this little secluded spot, but that solitude isn't guaranteed. Someone could turn up next to us to enjoy the view at any moment. The thought of getting caught only gets both of us hotter and in only minutes, our movements are frantic as we both race toward our releases.

"Oh my God," Macie cries as her orgasm approaches. "Yes. Yes. Leon. Yessssss."

The second her pussy pulsates, it drags my release out of me.

"Fucking love you, Macie," I bellow as I spill my seed inside her.

"Love you too," she pants.

She collapses on me, her cap finally falling off. I let it go this time and throw it into the back seat.

"I like your idea of celebrating," she whispers sleepily.

"This wasn't part of the plan. We actually should be heading toward the airport."

"You weren't planning on hanging around at the college long, huh?"

"Nope. Didn't think you'd be too bothered."

"If the other option was to be with you then absolutely not."

"You're everything," I confess.

"So are you."

"And as much as I love sitting still inside you, we've got places to be."

She chuckles against me. Her pussy clenches and my semi begins to get ideas.

"Off you get before I can't stop."

"Boo," she pouts, making me second-guess my decision.

I glance at the clock to see if we have time.

We left campus long before I was expecting to, but this little pit stop was a little out of the way.

We could probably do it but—

"Miss you already," I say sadly as Macie awkwardly climbs back to her seat.

"I'm sure we'll find some time to pick up where we left off," she says with a naughty glint in her eyes.

"I can guarantee it, Red."

Tucking myself away, I put my seat back into the right place before starting the engine and heading back the way we came with the airport in my sights.

"Where are we going?" Macie asks as she sheds her gown while I lift our packed cases from the trunk.

"Where do you want to go?" I ask.

"Silly question. There's only ever one place I want to go."

I smile knowing full well we're heading there.

Our beach house in Miami is our haven. Whenever life gets a little too much it's the place we always head to get some alone time.

It's our happy place, and exactly where I want to be right now with my girl.

"I guess we should go and find out then."

"Well, I'm assuming we're not going far or for too long looking at the size of those cases," she quips, taking in our hand luggage.

With a case each, hand in hand we walk through the departures door to go and find our gate.

"I hope I always feel this excited to be heading home."

A wide smile spreads across my lips as she gazes up at the screen showing the upcoming departures, focusing on the flight to Miami.

Chicago might be our home. It's where our apartment is, where I work. But the beach house is where our hearts really are.

It's the place I see little redheaded children running around, where I see the two of us growing old together. Where I want to have huge family Christmases with those we love and celebrate all the big things that happen in our lives.

"Me too, Red," I say before pressing a kiss to her temple and tugging her toward the counter so we can board.

3

MACIE

The moment our beach house comes into view, every single part of me relaxes.

I love this place so much. Already, it holds so many memories for us. And it's a place I hope to make so many more in the coming years.

We spent the whole drive here chatting. Leon filled me in on the video meeting he had with his agent when he refused point blank to get on a plane and explained his new endorsement offer.

The happiness on his face every time he talks about any part of his job makes me sing with joy.

He's so incredible. I mean, he was when I first met him, but he was still so stuck in the past, haunted by everything he'd endured as a kid that it clouded the amazing man who was mostly hidden beneath.

But watching him deal with everything properly and heal from the past to allow this caring, thoughtful, supportive, funny man out has been such a privilege to see.

Soon after moving to Chicago, I found a new youth center to work in, and whenever he's available when I'm on shift, he'll come and join me.

Watching him with those boys... I swear my ovaries explode every single time. I'm not ready for kids and all that grown-up stuff, but it gets me excited for when the time is right.

And when it is, I know without a doubt that our kids will have the most incredibly loving and supportive dad.

"Welcome home, Red."

"I didn't think it was possible to love a house this much," I muse as he kills the engine and pushes the door open.

"It's you. I will love anywhere we go as long as you're there."

"I agree. You're my home, but this place just hits differently."

"It does."

Silently we make our way inside while butterflies riot in my stomach.

"This was the best surprise," I tell him honestly as I slide my hands up his chest before resting them over his shoulders.

"It's barely the start of it," he confesses resting his brow against mine.

"Oh?" I ask, but I never get a response because Leon's lips find mine in an all-consuming kiss.

"Let's go clean up," he mutters into my mouth.

"Something tells me you want to get me dirtier before any cleaning happens," I tease as he hoists me up his body and begins effortlessly carrying me up the stairs.

"Busted," he laughs. "Car sex was great, but I need more. I need to peel this sexy dress from your body and take my time with you."

"You won't hear any arguments from me," I confess as I kiss down his throat, loving the way his pulse thunders against my lips.

In only minutes, he's marching us into our bedroom and kicking the door closed behind us.

The curtains are closed, blocking the bright sun and leaving the room cast in a romantic hue.

He lowers me onto the bed before climbing between my thighs.

"Do you have any idea how fucking proud I was watching you up on that stage," he whispers as he kisses down my throat and tucks his fingers under the lace at my shoulders.

The front of this dress might look demure, but that all ends when I turn around because it's completely open, exposing my spine almost all the way to my ass crack.

Without any effort, he drags the fabric down my arms, slowly exposing my pale skin to him.

His lips follow the fabric, kissing and nipping over my collarbone and down to the fullness of my breasts.

"Leon," I cry when he wraps his lips around one of my nipples, sucking it deep into his mouth.

My hips writhe, desperate to find some friction as he teases me, switching from side to side, driving me crazy.

My fingers twist in his hair, pulling until it must hurt but he doesn't comment or move things along.

"Please. More. I need—"

"I know what you need, Red. And I'll get there when I'm ready," he states, mirth dancing in his dark green eyes.

He continues tormenting me, licking, sucking, and biting until I'm begging for mercy. I'm so close, so freaking close but I need more.

Just that little bit more.

It feels like it's been forever, but realistically, it's probably only a few minutes when he drops lower. He continues dragging my dress down and over my ass, leaving me in my tiny panties and my heels.

"Beautiful," Leon breathes, lifting my leg in the air and pressing his lips to the inside of my ankle.

His kiss burns all the way down to my clit.

My chin drops ready to beg some more but he begins moving.

With his eyes locked on mine, he kisses lower and lower until he's on his front and licking across my inner thigh,

"LEON," I scream when he sucks on me over the soaked fabric of my panties.

"Delicious," he murmurs.

"Naked," I gasp when he continues. "Get naked."

Chuckling at my needy demands, he sits up a little and drags his shirt over his head, exposing his incredibly toned body.

My mouth waters for a taste of him, but I don't get a chance to focus on that thought because he's back and dragging my panties down my legs.

"Mine," he states. "This pussy is mine."

"Then you'd better make use of it," I demand, shamelessly arching my back.

A deep growl rumbles in his chest as he presses his giant hands against my inner thighs and spreads me wide open for him.

"Oh fuck yes," I cry when he licks from my entrance to my clit before zeroing in on it and sucking hard enough to make me scream.

He works me right to the edge over and over, withholding my release until I'm sure I'm going to combust from the pent-up energy fizzing through my veins.

"Leon, please," I beg.

"As much as I love you coming over my face, that isn't what's happening right now," he confesses, standing to his feet at the end of the bed, my juices glistening on his lips as he rips his fly open.

My mouth runs dry when he shoves both his pants and boxers down his legs, letting his hard dick spring free.

If I weren't so desperate for the release he's withholding from me, I'd get to my knees and return the favor. But right now, I can barely think straight let alone torture myself any longer.

And thankfully, he's on the same page too because no sooner has the fabric left his body is he back on his knees between my thighs.

"Yes," I breathe when he rubs the head of his dick through my folds, teasing me by pushing just the tip inside. "Killing me," I moan, digging my heels into his ass and making him laugh.

"I fucking love it when you get all needy."

I glare at him, silently demanding for him to give me what I need.

I'm about to shout at him, to point out that he's already lied to me today, withholding pleasure isn't going to help me forgive him but then he jerks his hips, and his cock slides inside me.

Fireworks shoot off around my body as we connect.

With his hand planted on either side of my head, he dips low and steals my lips, his tongue moving at the same pace as his dick.

I ride that delicious edge of pleasure for a few minutes as he holds back from giving me what I need, but the second I drag my nails across his shoulders, slicing into his skin with my claws that his resolve finally cracks.

"YES," I scream as he ups his pace, thrusting into me with abandon.

Our kiss turns filthy as we both take what we need and in seconds, I'm shattering beneath him as he finally lets me fall.

"Fuck, Macie. Fuck. FUCK," he bellows before his entire body stills and he spills his load inside me.

The second he's spent, his big ass body collapses on top of my tiny one, crushing me into our mattress.

I fucking love it.

Long blissful minutes pass as we both lie there, soaking each other up.

My eyelids get heavy despite the nap I had on the flight but just before I drift off into oblivion, Leon moves.

"No time for sleeping, Red. We've got plans."

"Oh yeah?"

He rolls off the bed and stretches his glorious body. My eyes dart everywhere as his muscles ripple and pop.

"Yeah, and I like where your thoughts are going. Shower?" He reaches his hand out and the second I slide mine into it, he drags me from the bed.

———

"I've laid out something for you to wear," Leon says, poking his head into the bathroom where I'm straightening my hair.

"Are we going out, do I need to put makeup on?" I ask.

"Just a little," he says before ducking out of the room before I get a chance to ask any more questions. "And don't look out of the curtains."

His parting words echo in the silence around me, and the urge to run straight to the window to see what I shouldn't be seeing is almost too much.

But I lock it down. I trust Leon with every fiber of my being. If he doesn't want me to look. I won't.

Excitement riots inside me as I make quick work of finishing my hair and applying some makeup.

The second I leave the bathroom, my eyes lock on the closed curtains.

The blinds behind them haven't been lowered so there's enough light in the room not to have to put the light on.

Every single muscle in my body burns with the need to walk over.

But I won't.

I can't.

With a sigh, I focus on the bed.

"Oh wow," I breathe, finding a stunning floral multicolored maxi dress waiting for me with a cute pair of flip-flops to finish it off.

"Boy, did good," I whisper, unwrapping my towel before finding some panties and pulling the dress on.

The halter-neck means the back is as open as the dress I wore for the ceremony earlier. The light sheer fabric falls in a pool at my feet and has a high split up my left leg.

It's truly stunning.

Once I'm dressed, I stand in front of the full-length mirror and take a few seconds to soak up the moment before I go in search of my man and discover what he's done.

Music gets louder as I descend the stairs but the hallway and living space is empty.

"Lee?" I call, but only silence greets me.

I search the kitchen and dining room before returning to the living space, ready to pull the curtains back to discover what he's done.

But I don't get that far because the second I step back into the living area, he's there, standing in the middle of the room with his hands in his pockets looking... dare I say it, nervous.

"Hey, you okay?"

"You look..." He swallows roughly. "Fuck. That dress is..."

I can't help but laugh at his inability to finish a sentence. It must be good.

"Yeah?" I ask.

"Yeah." He scrubs his hand across his face as if he can't believe what he's seeing. "Ready for your surprise?"

"I'm not sure. Your nervousness is making me nervous," I confess.

"Sorry, I just... I don't know how you're going to take it and—"

"Maybe you should show me and I'll let you know what I think," I suggest.

"Yeah, okay."

He takes my hand and leads me over to what is a wall full of windows when the blinds aren't down.

I already know the doors are open, the music is coming from out there and I can hear the waves crashing in the distance.

"Ready?" he asks, squeezing my hand before he presses the button to raise the blinds.

I try to keep it together, but I'd be lying if I said my body wasn't trembling with nerves.

At first, I see nothing but our table and chairs and a firepit, the flames licking high up into the sky. It's nothing unusual. But then movement beyond our deck catches my eye.

"Oh my God," I breathe as his surprise reveals itself.

4

LEON

I'm not sure I've ever been as fucking terrified as I am the moment I lift the blinds and wait for her to see what I've done.

My heart pounds and my hands tremble.

If I've fucked this up and she hates it, I'll never forgive myself.

I've been planning it for months, trying to get all the moving parts to work. It's been a fucking challenge, but I've done it. And I want her to love it.

The second she notices that our backyard isn't as normal as it seems, her body stills and her grip on my hand tightens.

"Oh my God," she breathes, lifting her free hand to cover her mouth. "Leon," she squeals before taking off.

She darts across the deck and gets swallowed up in the arms of our friends.

Letty, Peyton, Violet, and Charlie wrap their arms around her. While Luca, Leon, Kane, Nathan, Jace, Tristan and Knox watch with smiles on their faces.

Walking out, I join my brother and our friends. The deck is covered in flickering candles and twinkling fairy lights but with the sun still high in the sky, the effect isn't as good as it will be later. There's a huge, congratulations graduate banner attached to the house and champagne on ice, ready to celebrate.

Laughter fills the air before Macie turns to me with the widest smile I think I've ever seen on her face.

Abandoning the girls, she bounces over to me.

"I can't believe you did this. It's incredible," she squeals.

"Thank fuck for that. I was terrified you'd want it to be just us."

"I mean, I wouldn't have been disappointed but this is awesome. Where's Ella?" she asks, mentioning the missing member of our group.

"She couldn't make it," I explain.

"Damn, she's going to miss a great night."

"I'm sure," I tell her, wrapping my hands around her waist and dragging her into my body. "I'm so proud of you, Red. You deserve to celebrate everything you've achieved with those who love you."

"I love you," she says, gazing up at me with so much love in her eyes it makes it hard to breathe.

How did I find this? An incredible woman who loves me in spite of the darkness that lingers inside me, in spite of everything I endured as a teenager.

"There's one more thing," I confess, pushing my hand into my pocket and wrapping my fingers around the small item hiding inside.

No one knows I'm about to do this. I invited our friends for a celebratory barbecue for Macie. I didn't mention a word of my real intentions.

Pulling my hand free, I take a step back from Macie and lower myself to one knee.

"Oh my God," she gasps, quickly alerting the others who do the exact same. In fact, I'm pretty sure they suck all the fucking air out of the sky because I can no longer drag in the breaths I need.

"Macie," I start as the stares of everyone behind her burn into me, but the second I look up into her eyes, they all float away. "Since the second I laid eyes you, nothing in my life has been the same. You saw something inside me that no one else ever has and thankfully, it never scared you off. You've given me more than I could ever have asked for over the last three years, and I never want it to stop.

"I want you right by my side through every step of my life. I want you in the stands cheering for me as I support you in every dream you have.

"Macie Fletcher. Red. Will you do me the honor of being my wife?"

Tears flood her cheeks and her hand in mind trembles violently.

"Leon," she sobs in disbelief.

Although, I can't lie, the fact she doesn't immediately say yes freaks me the fuck out.

I hold the ring I spent longer than I want to confess to choosing. I couldn't find anything worthy of her. They were all too generic, too boring.

But the second I laid eyes on the solitaire cut diamond surrounded by bright red rubies, I knew it was the one.

It was different. It was red. It was us.

"Will you marry me, Macie?" I ask again when she still doesn't answer.

"Oh my God," she gasps, reality slamming into her. "Yes. Yes, of course I will," she cries, her voice rough with emotion.

Holding her hand out between us, she lets me slide the ring up her finger but at no point does she look at it, her gaze is locked on mine.

"I love you, Macie. I promise to be the best man I can be for you every day."

"Oh, Lee," she sighs, tugging on my arm to get me to stand. "You already are. I love you so much."

"I love you too. Happy graduation, baby."

The pop of cork sounds from somewhere behind me but I pay it no attention as I wrap my hand around the back of my girl's neck and draw her closer.

"Mrs. Macie Dunn. Has a nice ring to it, don't you think?"

"I can't wait, Lee. I—"

I don't give her a chance to finish whatever that thought was, I claim her lips in an all-consuming kiss as our friends and family cheer loudly behind us.

After years of searching for my mystery redhead, this is exactly how it was meant to be. The two of us against the world. Forever.

Loving Maddison Kings University and want to continue?
Download your copy of THE SECRETS YOU KEEP NOW and
discover Violet's story.

Or...

Are you ready for a new series?

You can grab the **FREE** prequel,
WICKED SUMMER KNIGHT NOW.

Book #1, WICKED KNIGHT is OUT NOW!
The series is a dark mafia high school bully romance and is a spin-off
of both my Rosewood High and Rebel Ink series.

THORN
SNEAK PEEK

CHAPTER ONE
Amalie

"I think you'll really enjoy your time here," Principal Hartmann says. He tries to sound cheerful about it, but he's got sympathy oozing from his wrinkled, tired eyes.

This shouldn't have been part of my life. I should be in London starting university, yet here I am at the beginning of what is apparently my junior year at an American high school I have no idea about aside from its name and the fact my mum attended many years ago. A lump climbs up my throat as thoughts of my parents hit me without warning.

"I know things are going to be different and you might feel that you're going backward, but I can assure you it's the right thing to do. It will give you the time you need to... adjust and to put some serious thought into what you want to do once you graduate."

Time to adjust. I'm not sure any amount of time will be enough to learn to live without my parents and being shipped across the Pacific to start a new life in America.

"I'm sure it'll be great." Plastering a fake smile on my face, I take the timetable from the principal's hand and stare down at it. The butterflies that were already fluttering around in my stomach erupt to the point I might just throw up over his chipped Formica desk.

Math, English lit, biology, gym, my hands tremble until I see something that instantly relaxes me, *art and film studies.* At least I got my own way with something.

"I've arranged for someone to show you around. Chelsea is the captain of the cheer squad, what she doesn't know about the school isn't worth knowing. If you need anything, Amalie, my door is always open."

Nodding at him, I rise from my chair just as a soft knock sounds out and a cheery brunette bounces into the room. My knowledge of American high schools comes courtesy of the hours of films I used to spend my evenings watching, and she fits the stereotype of captain to a tee.

"You wanted something, Mr. Hartmann?" she sings so sweetly it makes even my teeth shiver.

"Chelsea, this is Amalie. It's her first day starting junior year. I trust you'll be able to show her around. Here's a copy of her schedule."

"Consider it done, sir."

"I assured Amalie that she's in safe hands."

I want to say it's my imagination but when she turns her big chocolate eyes on me, the light in them diminishes a little.

"Lead the way." My voice is lacking any kind of enthusiasm and from the narrowing of her eyes, I don't think she misses it.

I follow her out of the room with a little less bounce in my step. Once we're in the hallway, she turns her eyes on me. She's really quite pretty with thick brown hair, large eyes, and full lips. She's shorter than me, but then at five foot eight, you'll be hard pushed to find many other teenage girls who can look me in the eye.

Tilting her head so she can look at me, I fight my smile. "Let's make this quick. It's my first day of senior year and I've got shit to be doing."

Spinning on her heels, she takes off and I rush to catch up with her. "Cafeteria, library." She points then looks down at her copy of my timetable. "Looks like your locker is down there." She waves her hand down a hallway full of students who are all staring our way, before gesturing in the general direction of my different subjects.

"Okay, that should do it. Have a great day." Her smile is faker than mine's been all morning, which really is saying something. She goes to walk away, but at the last minute turns back to me. "Oh, I forgot. That over there." I follow her finger as she points to a large group of people outside the open double doors sitting around a bunch of tables. "That's *my* group. I should probably warn you now that you won't fit in there."

I hear her warning loud and clear, but it didn't really need saying. I've no intention of befriending the cheerleaders, that kind of thing's not really my scene. I'm much happier hiding behind my camera and slinking into the background.

Chelsea flounces off and I can't help my eyes from following her out toward *her* group. I can see from here that it consists of her squad and the football team. I can also see the longing in other student's eyes as they walk past them. They either want to be them or want to be part of their stupid little gang.

Jesus, this place is even more stereotypical than I was expecting.

Unfortunately, my first class of the day is in the direction Chelsea just went. I pull my bag up higher on my shoulder and hold the couple of books I have tighter to my chest as I walk out of the doors.

I've not taken two steps out of the building when my skin tingles with awareness. I tell myself to keep my head down. I've no interest in being their entertainment but my eyes defy me, and I find myself looking up as Chelsea points at me and laughs. I knew my sudden arrival in the town wasn't a secret. My mum's legacy is still strong, so when they heard the news, I'm sure it was hot gossip.

Heat spreads from my cheeks and down my neck. I go to look away when a pair of blue eyes catch my attention. While everyone else's look intrigued, like they've got a new pet to play with, his are haunted and angry. Our stare holds, his eyes narrow as if he's trying to warn me of something before he menacingly shakes his head.

Confused by his actions, I manage to rip my eyes from his and turn toward where I think I should be going.

I only manage three steps at the most before I crash into something—or somebody.

"Shit, I'm sorry. Are you okay?" a deep voice asks. When I look into the kind green eyes of the guy in front of me, I almost sigh with relief. I was starting to wonder if I'd find anyone who wasn't just going to glare at me. I know I'm the new girl but shit. They must experience new kids on a weekly basis, I can't be that unusual.

"I'm fine, thank you."

"You're the new British girl. Emily, right?"

"It's Amalie, and yeah... that's me."

"I'm so sorry about your parents. Mom said she was friends with yours." Tears burn my eyes. Today is hard enough without the constant reminder of everything I've lost. "Shit, I'm sorry. I shouldn't have—"

"It's fine," I lie.

"What's your first class?"

Handing over my timetable, he quickly runs his eyes over it. "English lit, I'm heading that way. Can I walk you?"

"Yes." His smile grows at my eagerness and for the first time today my returning one is almost sincere.

"I'm Shane, by the way." I look over and smile at him, thankfully the hallway is too noisy for us to continue any kind of conversation.

He seems like a sweet guy but my head's spinning and just the thought of trying to hold a serious conversation right now is exhausting.

Student's stares follow my every move. My skin prickles as more and more notice me as I walk beside Shane. Some give me smiles but most just nod in my direction, pointing me out to their friends. Some are just downright rude and physically point at me like I'm some fucking zoo animal awoken from its slumber.

In reality, I'm just an eighteen-year-old girl who's starting somewhere new, and desperate to blend into the crowd. I know that with who I am—or more who my parents were—that it's not going to be all that easy, but I'd at least like a chance to try to be normal. Although I fear I might have lost that the day I lost my parents.

"This is you." Shane's voice breaks through my thoughts and when

I drag my head up from avoiding everyone else around me, I see he's holding the door open.

Thankfully the classroom's only half full, but still, every single set of eyes turn to me.

Ignoring their attention, I keep my head down and find an empty desk toward the back of the room.

Once I'm settled, I risk looking up. My breath catches when I find Shane still standing in the doorway, forcing the students entering to squeeze past him. He nods his head. I know it's his way of asking if I'm okay. Forcing a smile onto my lips, I nod in return and after a few seconds, he turns to leave.

THORN and the rest of the ROSEWOOD series are now LIVE.

DOWNLOAD TO CONTINUE READING

ABOUT THE AUTHOR

Tracy Lorraine is a *USA Today* and *Wall Street Journal* bestselling new adult and contemporary romance author. Tracy has recently turned thirty and lives in a cute Cotswold village in England with her husband, baby girl and lovable but slightly crazy dog. Having always been a bookaholic with her head stuck in her Kindle, Tracy decided to try her hand at a story idea she dreamt up and hasn't looked back since.

Be the first to find out about new releases and offers. Sign up to my newsletter here.

If you want to know what I'm up to and see teasers and snippets of what I'm working on, then you need to be in my Facebook group. Join Tracy's Angels here.

Keep up to date with Tracy's books at
www.tracylorraine.com

ALSO BY TRACY LORRAINE

Rosewood High Series

Thorn #1

Paine #2

Savage #3

Fierce #4

Hunter #5

Faze (#6 Prequel)

Fury #6

Legend #7

Maddison Kings University Series

T.M.Y.M: Prequel

TRYS #1

TDYW #2

TBYS #3

TVYC #4

TDYD #5

TDYR #6

TRYD #7

Knight's Ridge Empire Series

Wicked Summer Knight: Prequel (Stella & Seb)

Wicked Knight #1 (Stella & Seb)

Wicked Princess #2 (Stella & Seb)

Wicked Empire #3 (Stella & Seb)

Deviant Knight #4 (Emmie & Theo)

Deviant Princess #5 (Emmie & Theo

Deviant Reign #6 (Emmie & Theo)

One Reckless Knight (Jodie & Toby)

Reckless Knight #7 (Jodie & Toby)

Reckless Princess #8 (Jodie & Toby)

Reckless Dynasty #9 (Jodie & Toby)

Dark Halloween Knight (Calli & Batman)

Dark Knight #10 (Calli & Batman)

Dark Princess #11 (Calli & Batman)

Dark Legacy #12 (Calli & Batman)

Corrupt Valentine Knight (Nico & Siren)

Corrupt Knight #13 (Nico & Siren)

Corrupt Princess #14 (Nico & Siren)

Corrupt Union #15 (Nico & Siren)

Sinful Wild Knight (Alex & Vixen)

Sinful Stolen Knight: Prequel (Alex & Vixen)

Sinful Knight #16 (Alex & Vixen)

Sinful Princess #17 (Alex & Vixen)

Sinful Kingdom #18 (Alex & Vixen)

Knight's Ridge Destiny: Epilogue

Ruined Series

Ruined Plans #1

Ruined by Lies #2

Ruined Promises #3

Never Forget Series

Never Forget Him #1

Never Forget Us #2

Everywhere & Nowhere #3

Chasing Series

Chasing Logan

<u>**The Cocktail Girls**</u>

<u>His Manhattan</u>

Her Kensington

www.ingramcontent.com/pod-product-compliance
Lightning Source LLC
Chambersburg PA
CBHW030142200726
48285CB00004BC/1262